# SILENT DESTINY

*To Richard*

*Best wishes*

*J.R. Whittle*

## J. ROBERT WHITTLE
### AND JOYCE SANDILANDS

# By J. Robert Whittle and Joyce Sandilands

Single Novels
Silent Destiny (2014)
Whispers Across Time (IPPY Gold Medal 2008)
Race For A Treasure (2008)
Yesterdays (2010)
A Debt to Pay (ebook, 2011)

## *The Lizzie Series by J. Robert Whittle*
Lizzie: Lethal Innocence – Canadian Bestseller
Lizzie Lethal Innocence - *Audio Book (CD, MP3)*
*Narrated by J. Robert Whittle*
Lizzie's Secret Angels
Streets of Hope
Lizzie's Legacy

## *Victoria Chronicles by J. Robert Whittle*
Bound by Loyalty* - Canadian Bestseller
Loyalty's Reward* - Canadian Bestseller
Loyalty's Haven* (IPPY Gold Medal 2007)
* Paperback and Hardcover Editions

Laughing Through Life: Tales of a Yorkshireman (CD)
Autobiographical vignettes of Robert's life
*Narrated by J. Robert Whittle*

## *Moonbeam Series*
Leprechaun Magic
by J Robert Whittle and Joyce Sandilands
Leprechaun Magic - *Audio Book (CD)*
*Narrated by Joyce Sandilands*

3 On A Moonbeam
by Joyce Sandilands
3 On A Moonbeam - *Audio Book (CD)*
*Narrated by Joyce Sandilands*

# SILENT DESTINY

## J. ROBERT WHITTLE
### AND JOYCE SANDILANDS

Publisher's note: This book is a work of fiction. To enhance the story, real places have sometimes been used, although they are fictionalized. Characters are in no way intended to represent any person living or dead.

**To purchase any of the authors' books -**
Contact:
J. Robert Whittle / Joyce Sandilands
Whitlands Publishing Ltd.
Victoria, BC Canada
Tel: 250-477-0192
www.jrobertwhittle.com
jsandilands@gmail.com

Cover photo © Eric Said Photography, Stirling, Scotland
Cover layout by Jim Bisakowski, BookDesign.ca
Back cover photo of authors by Ocean Photography

Library and Archives Canada Cataloguing in Publication

Whittle, J. Robert (John Robert), 1933-, author
    Silent destiny / J. Robert Whittle and Joyce Sandilands.

Issued in print and electronic formats.
ISBN 978-0-9869408-5-9 (pbk.).--ISBN 978-0-9869408-6-6 (ebook)


I. Sandilands, Joyce, 1945-, author II. Title.


PS8595.H4985S55 2014      C813'.54     C2014-905285-5
                        C2014-905286-3

*To all our Scottish Kith and Kin*
*(This expression dates from 1300s)*
*Thank you Dad for introducing me posthumously*
*into your loving and unique Sandilands Family,*
*so full of fascinating and wonderful Scottish history.*
*Who knew the places this would lead us!*

# ACKNOWLEDGEMENTS

Scotland ... why would Robert choose this as the location for one of his novels? Well, first you have to understand his love of history and, then remember, that although he has lived in Canada since the late 1960s, his first love is still Britain. In 1987, he discovered that the history of his wife, Joyce, contained some fascinating historical ties to Scotland, a country so close to his home of Yorkshire, England, yet he knew virtually nothing about it. Learning that Joyce's paternal history and the beginnings of her surname went back to the early 14th century, soon after the execution of William Wallace, you can see how Robert's interest in Wallace may have begun. We had already pieced my history together and found out that some of the Sandilands' men of this era were knights of the crusades, one being the Preceptor of the Order of Knights Hospitaller at Torphichen, Scotland (1550). Originating as the Order of St. John of Jerusalem (c1048), by 1877 the original Order had become the St. John Ambulance Society in British Commonwealth countries.

So, unknown to this wife, Robert was apparently planning to write a novel featuring some of the most confusing, important and horrific times in Scottish history but, of course, he had to add his Whittlesque twist, setting it in modern times and ... well, the rest is for you to discover!

We want to thank those who helped Joyce during the editing process: Wendy Dyer, a fan who became our friend and agreed to read the first chapters and was eager for more; Mary Sandilands Strathie of Darnick, Scotland for her advice on modern Scotland, and reading a proof copy; Eric Said of Stirling, Scotland for firstly putting his wonderful Scottish photos on Facebook so I could find them, and then for providing us with his outstanding photo of the modern Stirling Bridge and the National Wallace Monument; and Marc Sandilands Stewart for his positive and humourous comments ... annoyed I couldn't send more chapters after he read the first half, that was most encouraging! These people and the countless others who continued to support us at the markets, on the street and via our Facebook pages, helped motivate Joyce through the long editing process. Your support and friendship is invaluable.

Amazingly and thankfully, our original team was still available as we began our 17th year ... Gerhard Aichelberger to advise us on printing needs, Jim Bisakowski for his graphic skills and Deborah Wright-Hatch with proofing advice. Thanks again team! There is one other person on our team that I must especially thank ... our Office Assistant, Tara

Poilievre. Despite her one-day-a-week schedule with us, for this book, she somehow found time to read as I worked, helping me keep the multitude of characters and events in perspective. She's been my memory, my sounding board, and my friend. I truly mean it when I say, Tara is responsible for preserving my mental health and, at my age, this is the highest compliment I can give!

*Silent Destiny* is a work of fiction, but we have endeavoured to weave in as much history as possible to both enhance Robert's tale and to provide the necessary realism to William Wallace's remarkable story. I was surprised and thrilled when I discovered he had included some of my own Scottish history, giving me an extra challenge. I truly hope that you, our readers, especially those unfamiliar with historical novels, will find this Scottish history so fascinating you will be drawn to other historical novels, especially those of Scotland. Every reader should love history; it makes the most remarkable stories ... we know, because books changed our lives and millions of readers are as grateful as we are!

On a more personal note, Robert and I are both still writing and working on books with no plan to stop. Our website, blog and Facebook pages continue as lifelines to our readers so please keep in touch. We have plans, but they are executed more slowly now! We will also try to keep all of our books in stock after we downsize in 2016, but they will continue to be available as eBooks.

Keep reading and liking our website and Facebook pages, and thank you for telling your friends how much you enjoy our books! Our Audio CDs of *Lizzie* and *Laughing Through Life* sold out in 2014 and we are now considering internet options. Order any of our books via our website and our main Facebook page (links below) or as ebooks. Local customers: we've added a "Pick Up in Victoria option" or phone us.

Thank you for your patience, support and love, you're the best!

With fondest regards,
*Robert and Joyce*

J. Robert Whittle and Joyce Sandilands-Whittle
November 2014
250-477-0192 PT (Victoria, BC Canada)
jsandilands@gmail.com
www.jrobertwhittle.com
www.facebook.com/jrobertwhittleauthor

# LIST OF CHARACTERS – in order of appearance or mention

Emma Walters – Professor of English Literature, UVic
Adam Gilbert Stuart – Traymore Estate Solicitor
Angus Trevelion Walters – former Lord Traymore
Sir Alexander 'Alex' Wallace – Lord Traymore's bailiff
William Wallace – Scotland's famous patriot (C1270-1305)
Mary (Walters) Wallace – wife of William Wallace
Flora Wallace – William and Mary's daughter (b. 1295)
David Wallace – William and Mary's first son (b. 1296)
Malcolm Wallace – William and Mary's second son (b. 1298)
Duncan Walters – Mary's brother
Matron Ruth Oxley – Misty House, *School for the Blind*
Tom and Charlie – Misty House carpenters
Jessie – Misty House dog trainer
Douglas Glencannon – distillery manager
Duffy (band member) – psychic
Dr. John A. Dunstan – director at National Archives
Alfred Holt – manager, *Highland Tartan Factory*
Helen – seamstress at Tartan Factory
Abe – Dorik Island water taxi driver
Neville MacLeod –Traymore House butler
Jayne and Sarah – Traymore House maids
Jennie MacKray – Emma's cousin (Walters)
Bruce MacKray – descendant of Malcolm Wallace
George Albert MacDuff – descendant of David Wallace
Professor Alfreda MacDuff – wife of George, Professor of History
Brother Ebert – librarian at monastery
Moira Johnson – owner of *Tartan Tea Shop*
Joe Thornton –Moira's grandfather, retired sexton
Monsignor Jason Sharp – cleric
Mitch Pooley – local poacher and busybody
Rodric Brodie – Land Use Department, Renfrewshire
Thomas Campbell – county water engineer
William 'Bill' Mackie – police sergeant
Jim Falconer – police constable
Jack Cameron – publican and former builder

# LIST OF CHARACTERS cont'd

Anne Dunstan – John Dunstan's sister
Frank 'Tex' Costello – handwriting expert
James MacDonald – police commissioner
Duncan Bruce – postal worker
Doctor Greare – Stirling Hospital
Nurse Brown – Stirling Hospital
Professor Barton – Police lecturer
Sgt. Roy McLean – Emma's driving instructor
Dougal Graham – bomb expert with Royal Army
Dr. Hazel Zicowski – Australian Scientist
Dr. Eric Morse – co-worker with Dr. Zicowski
Judge Moulder – Inquiry Chairman
Bishop Watson – Inquiry Member

# SILENT

# DESTINY

# INDEX

# Chapter 1 – Monday, November 6<sup>th</sup> 2006 – Emma's News

A cold wind blew fiercely across the Victoria waterfront as the shrill ring of her phone dragged Emma from a sound sleep. Professor Emma Walters muttered a strong profanity as she brushed her brown hair away from her face and reached for the phone.

"Yes?" she said, in the exasperated tone she liked to use on students who asked stupid questions.

"This is Meredith, Meredith and Stuart, barristers and solicitors, calling from Edinburgh, Scotland. Is this Miss Emma Walters?"

"It is."

"Would you hold the line for a moment please?" The female voice, with a soft Scottish brogue was courteous, although the name of the firm was lost in translation. She heard a click and the silence told her she was now on hold.

*Scotland? Lawyers?* Emma's mind awoke instantly and kicked into gear. "What the devil could they want with me at six o'clock on a Monday morning?" she mumbled.

A powerful, cultured voice with a strong Scottish accent broke the silence. "Good Morning, Miss Walters, my name is Gilbert Stuart. I am a solicitor with the firm of Meredith, Meredith and Stuart in Edinburgh, Scotland. No doubt you're wondering why Scotland is calling you … I see it's a sunny day in Victoria this morning."

"Never mind the weather! I'm still in bed as is the sun! What the hell do you want at 6 a.m.?"

"I'm sorry, Miss Walters, but the time zones did not leave us much choice for when to contact you. It was of the utmost importance that we communicate with you as soon as possible and …."

Raising her head, she missed the next bit as she tried to read the caller ID, but it merely said, *Out of Area.*

The voice continued, "… inform you that you are the only living relative of Mr. Angus Trevelion Walters of Edinburgh."

"Well, I'm awfully glad you told me," she snapped, "or I would never have known! Who was he and how am I related to him?"

"Please, Miss Walters bear with me for a moment. You are also the sole beneficiary of his estate here in Scotland."

Emma pulled herself to a sitting position and shook her head to make sure she was awake. "Are you kidding? Is this some student prank, because if I find out it is, I will have you beheaded!"

"I assure you, Miss Walters that I am the solicitor for the Walters' estate and my office is here in Edinburgh ...."

"You really *are* calling from Scotland?", she interrupted, realizing she was beginning to believe this man and his ludicrous claim.

"Yes, we are. We are sending you a package which will introduce you to the details of your inheritance and our responsibility to the estate. I must emphasize that you should act upon this matter immediately as we are under a crucial deadline by the courts. I would expect you should receive this package on Wednesday. It will include some basic information of the estate and copies of any documents we are able to release to you. May I confirm your contact information please?"

She realized she would be at home on Wednesday, but something, a brief thought, was warning her and she interrupted him. "Mr. Stuart, I trust you won't object if I return your call ... to ease my mind that this is legitimate? What is your phone number please?"

"By all means, Miss Walters." He gave her the number and hung up.

Realizing she needed a prefix for calling the UK, she went to her laptop, located it easily, and then did another search for the solicitor's office. Finding their website, she confirmed their contact number and dialed. She was happy to recognize first the receptionist's voice and then Mr. Stuart's.

"Aye, Miss Walters, let me read your mailing address back to you and you can tell me if what we have is correct." When they finished, he continued, "Assuming you wish to accept your inheritance, it is urgent that you come immediately to Edinburgh to complete the paperwork. Time is of the essence and we hope to see you in our office early next week. If you would send us an email with the date of your arrival and your flight information, we will make hotel arrangements and have someone meet you at the airport. We look forward to meeting you early next week."

"Mr. ...," she started to say, but the connection had ended. "Why does he always say 'we?'"

Wide awake now, she hurried to the bathroom, splashed cold water on her face and then peered at her image in the mirror. "Me, the sole beneficiary of a Scottish estate? Surely I'm dreaming!" She went over to the window and pulled the curtain back to see darkness. "How the devil could he know it was sunny, it's not even up yet? Did he actually check the weather before he called? This is all quite absurd!"

She paced the floor in her pajamas, staring out at the lighted harbour from her 8th storey window. *Who was it who had died?* She tried to remember the lawyer's words, but could only remember one name, Angus, and that wouldn't be of much help. She had classes at ten and two today and still a little more preparation to do for them. Sitting at her dining room table amidst a host of books and lesson papers, she began to type notes, trying to put the phone call out of her mind.

Tormented by confusing thoughts during classes, she was so glad to be home on Wednesday. She had not been sleeping very well. She couldn't keep still and did some cleaning while she waited for the courier. She ran to the phone at 10:35 when the intercom rang. The indescript male voice said he had an envelope for Miss Emma Walters and would need a signature.

"I'll be right down," she replied, already opening her apartment door.

Restraining herself from tearing open the rather thin envelope until she was back in her apartment, she pulled the tab the second she shut the door. Going to her favourite chair, she emptied the envelope and spread the papers out in front of her on the coffee table. *The way Mr. Stuart talked, I thought there would be a lot more reading material than this!* She picked up the covering letter and began to read.

With the cold, precise words of a legal document, it detailed her connection to Angus Trevelion Walters. As the accompanying one-page family tree showed, he was definitely a Scottish cousin. *Too bad you didn't live long enough to see this dad; you could have told me more about my Scottish family and had the title to yourself!* A lump in her throat told her not to think about past sadness and she continued reading. It told her that the Scottish Court had issued a Notice of Presumption. After seven years spent searching for Lord Traymore, no one could offer any explanation for where he had gone. He had simply disappeared off the face of the earth. Mr. Stuart's law firm petitioned the court to enable him to continue representing the client he had served for many years. Once that appointment was complete, they had contacted Emma.

Devouring too many cups of coffee, Emma sat fascinated as she read and re-read the papers. Mr. Stuart really hadn't given her very much information, so she found herself wanting to know more. She thought about googling the names, but decided not to add any more complications until she was near to the answers. She was to receive an old Scottish title which included a manor house situated on a private island. But it didn't end there. There was a second manor house. She began reading aloud in her excitement and disbelief ... "plus all the lands, possessions and pertinent business interests related to those properties." The letter even hinted that there was more to this estate than mentioned. She stopped and sat back in her chair, realizing she was sitting with her mouth open and tears were streaming down her face.

"Holy hell dad, what a surprise you would have gotten! I could have been the daughter of a lord, but instead ...!" She started to laugh and then she couldn't hold back the emotion. Forcing herself to continue reading, the paper said that time was of the essence, just as Mr. Stuart had stressed. She had to appear in person before the Scottish court before the 24th of November or everything would revert to the crown. *Well, we would not want that to happen would we ... or would we!* "I definitely need to learn more about this inheritance before I make a decision."

Going to find something to eat, she weighed her options. At 36 years of age and single, she was feeling quite ready for a bit of adventure to put some sparkle into her dull routine. She had simply not expected it to arrive in a courier envelope and demand such instant action.

Returning to the living room with her snack, she re-read the letter and noticed the last paragraph. It reiterated that once she had made her flight arrangements, she should send the information to them by email. Emma reminded herself that there were only two weeks left before she could claim her inheritance. "There is no time to waste!"

Phoning her travel agent, she booked her flight to Edinburgh for Saturday afternoon. She was not used to making instant or impulsive decisions, and she would have startled her friends and co-workers had they known of her plans. She also called the university, reaching a voice mail to which she explained she had been called out-of-town on urgent family business. She guessed she would not return to work for at least three months. The die was cast. She wrote a note to her landlord, including her email, and slipped it under his door as she went to collect her suitcases from the storage locker.

The next morning, she had some toast slathered with a liberal amount of peanut butter and was still eating it as she left the apartment. She found herself humming a tune as she took the elevator down to the underground parking. She usually walked briskly into the city, but today her plans required a car. Going first to the travel agent at Hillside Mall, she picked up her tickets, insurance and some brochures on Scotland. She was already daydreaming of her good fortune as she turned towards her favourite store a few doors away.

Wanting to look the part of a titled person, the thought passed through her head that she would soon be shopping for clothes in the Walters' tartan. She went straight over to the clerk and explained where she was going and that she was in a hurry. Not even considering the cost, which was totally out of character for her penny-pinching nature, she listened intently to the clerk's helpful comments.

Within the hour, she felt quite giddy as she paid for her new wardrobe. Next, she went to a shoe store where she found some expensive, but comfortable, walking shoes and a low-heeled pair of black leather pumps that would do for just about any occasion. Paying for the purchases with her debit card reminded her she needed to go to the bank.

There was an unusual spring in her step as she returned to the car and drove to UVIC to check her desk and pick up some of her personal things. A strange, unfamiliar feeling of elation passed through her body and, easily finding a parking spot, she was even more pleased. As it was before her class, she hoped she wouldn't meet anyone who had already been told of her unexpected time off. Finishing quickly, she returned to her car, arms loaded with sweaters and a jacket. She frowned as she looked at her older model Ford and visions of new cars passed through her brain. She giggled as she checked her list and headed back towards town.

Thinking back on past trips she had planned, other than a conference, she'd always wanted to go somewhere exciting and exotic … making plans on paper and tracing routes on maps, but always with the same result. Finding the slightest excuse to capitulate, she would cancel and go nowhere. But this time was different. She had no choice and no time to think that cobweb-style logic she always used. This opportunity offered a chance for her to spread her wings. *I wonder if I'll find Scottish men more appealing?* she thought, giggling again.

An hour later, after finishing the last two items on her list … purchasing her bus ticket for tomorrow's 11a.m. ferry, and going to the bank, she suddenly realized she had better get home to pack and send Mr. Stuart an email. It was finally beginning to sink in that she was actually leaving the city tomorrow for possibly three months, the longest period she had ever been away from home. With no family or close friends she needed to inform, she experienced a sudden wave of panic. *Calm down! I can buy anything I forget and I'll have my laptop so I can send emails once I know what to tell them … or then again, perhaps I won't!* It was almost too simple. *Really, who would honestly care if I never came back?*

Sleep didn't come easily that night as a jumble of thoughts rushed through her mind. Getting up earlier than her alarm, she showered and crossed off the last items on her list. An hour later, she flipped the catch on her carry-on and took it to the front door to join her large suitcase. She slowly looked around the apartment trying to think of anything she might have forgotten. At 9:10 a.m., she opened the door and wheeled her suitcases into the hallway, locking the door. Taking a deep breath, she took the elevator to the front door to wait for the taxi she had called the night before.

Arriving at the bus depot, she tagged her bags and took them to the loading area. Standing near the front of the bus lineup, she boarded as her luggage was being loaded into the hold. She had a brief moment of trepidation as the bus driver negotiated his monster vehicle out of the bus station and into city traffic. Fifteen minutes later, they were out on the highway and heading for the ferry dock at Swartz Bay. It was now pouring rain and she put her head back to relax, so glad she had decided to travel by ferry to the mainland. As the bus drove onto the ferry and parked, Emma decided to wait until the bus emptied. She leisurely followed the crowd up the stairs, avoiding the rush to the cafeteria, telling herself she would have a snack and coffee a bit later. Socializing with strangers wasn't one of her strong points, never feeling the need for frivolous conversation. Her mind had always been directed at the practical realities of life, so finding a comfortable window seat, she opened her laptop and typed *Scotland* into the search box. The Gulf Islands slipped by the windows as the large ferry negotiated its way past their rocky coastlines; she was surprised to see some images appear on her laptop that told her it wasn't all that different in Scotland.

An hour later, she was finishing a sandwich and coffee in the cafeteria when the loudspeaker gave instructions for bus passengers to return to their buses. Settled in her seat back on the bus, she waited for the ferry to dock, briefly closing her eyes when it shuddered as it eased into its berth before coming to a stop. She sighed as they emerged up the ramp onto land again for the drive to the airport where she knew she could catch a shuttle bus to her hotel.

Passengers swarmed around the bus driver when he opened the luggage compartment, everyone hurrying to claim their baggage first. Professor Walters had other plans though and standing back and aloof from the milling throng of travellers, she waited until her bags were alone on the sidewalk. Smiling, she went to take possession and heard the driver's murmured comment.

"Thank goodness everyone is not in a hurry!"

While she was waiting, she had noticed a hotel shuttle van parked nearby and now went over to ask if they stopped at her hotel.

"Yes ma'am, we'll be leaving in 12 minutes," the friendly driver replied, looking at her itinerary.

Booked into the hotel for one night, once she arrived in her room, Emma called the hotel spa to confirm her appointment and book a massage. At least she would leave for Scotland relaxed and with her nails looking their best. An hour later, she went upstairs to the spa, thoroughly enjoying her two-and-a-half hours of pampering before returning to the room eager to dress for dinner. She dearly wanted to look her best tonight, playing the part even though no one would know her secret. Later, dressed in new clothes, hairdo perfect, pretty nails and make-up applied to perfection … she was ready to show herself to the world.

As she walked into the hotel restaurant, she sensed that every eye turned to watch her. Waving at the maitre d' to get his attention, Emma snobbishly followed him to a table where she allowed him to hold her chair as she sat down. All this attention was contributing to her growing feeling of power, and then, glancing down at the menu a frown rippled across her brow. The meals were expensive and this clawed at her conservative nature. Suppressing her negative thoughts, she made an effort to relax. As she ate, she had become aware that a gentleman across the room was trying very hard to capture her attention.

Ignoring his overtures, Emma signed the restaurant bill and left, walking slowly through the foyer and out into the coolness of a West Coast autumn evening. Standing for a moment after crossing the parking area, she stole a glance behind her and noticed the man had followed her outside. Smiling to herself, she crossed the street to a bar with a small blinking neon sign. At the door, she saw the reflection of the man following her and allowed the burly, uniformed doorman to let her enter. He offered to check her coat but she declined. Making her way to the bar, she returned the barman's greeting and glanced down to see if the barstools were fixed to the floor. Smiling confidently, she slid her tall, slim frame onto the stool and crossed her legs.

"I noticed you were alone," a voice drawled at her elbow a few minutes later. "What are you drinking, sweetheart?"

Smiling to herself, Emma ignored him and ordered. When the barman brought her drink, she paid for it immediately with cash and gave the stranger beside her a cultivated, frosty stare. Taking a sip, Professor Walters watched, out of the corner of her eye, as the man fumbled around to find his money, finally standing up to search his pockets. Casually sipping on her drink, she hooked her foot onto his stool, slowly easing it away from the bar. When she heard the crash accompanied by a loud curse, she smirked, finished her drink and slipped away, giggling all the way back to her hotel room.

In the morning, she took her time, not having to check in at the airport until noon. She extravagantly ordered room service then checked out at 11 o'clock and caught the shuttle. Once checked in and relieved of her cumbersome luggage, she went to find a restaurant and killed her last hour by window shopping on her way to the departure lounge. On boarding, Emma was thankful the two seats beside her were taken by a quiet, older couple. Her window seat afforded a great view of the take-off and glimpses of BC's wonderful snow-capped mountains, before clouds made visibility impossible. Having left this early, she hoped to see the sunrise before landing in London. Served a light meal which she could barely eat, she watched a movie she had already seen and went into a sound sleep. The next thing she knew, she was being eased awake by a gentle hand on her shoulder and a flight attendant offering her a choice of breakfast meals. She pushed up the window shade and swore under her breath when the sun blinded her.

As she walked to the washroom awhile later, the captain announced they would be landing in an hour and suggested they reset their watches to Sunday, November 12th at 6:35 a.m. For the first time, she began to wonder what she was going to do upon arrival. The lawyer had said that someone would meet her and she hoped this was true as she didn't even know the name of her hotel. *I suppose I'd better get used to calling him a solicitor!*

Time went quickly and soon the captain's voice came over the speaker system again. He announced they would be landing at Heathrow in 20 minutes and gave the local weather report as foggy and wet, "... not at all unusual for a London morning this time of year!" he scoffed. She took her make-up bag out of her handbag and buckled her seatbelt again. Looking outside, she alternatively strained to see through the clouds as they descended, and refreshed her make-up. She was most eager to get her first glimpse of Great Britain.

As the plane came out of the clouds, she caught her breath at the spectacle of green fields, church spires and then the sight of unending housing developments that zipped by the window as they landed. Seconds later, Heathrow Airport filled her view and they were soon taxiing towards the terminal. After retrieving her luggage, she passed through customs with a minimum of fuss. Two hours later, she was back in the air and on her way to Edinburgh International.

"I'm actually here," she whispered, scanning the countryside before clouds again obscured her view. "My adventure has begun!"

Dragging her luggage off the carousel for the second time within three hours, she looked around for the exit sign and remembered she was being met. *By whom?* she wondered, looking around.

"Could I offer you some assistance, young lady?" The pleasant-sounding male voice that interrupted her thoughts had a thick Scottish accent. The tall man belonging to the voice, was not only bearded and good looking, but obviously a Scot. He was wearing a red tartan kilt complete with sporran, knee-high socks and shoes that had a decorative buckle. She couldn't contain her smile as the thought went through her mind that he was probably not much older than herself. His eyes were sparkling with what she could only describe as pure joy and she was instantly intrigued. In turn, her expression told him his mission was at least partly accomplished!

"I don't make it my usual practice to accept assistance from strangers, Mr. ...?" she said slowly, taking the time to study the man's face as she waited for his reply. Then remembering his other comment, she quickly added, "And I am most certainly not a young lady, sir!"

Having now heard her accent, Alexander Wallace was quite positive this was the woman he was seeking. "Aye, but if you are Professor Walters from Canada, ye may rest assured I am noo a stranger!"

Emma could have sworn the twinkle returned and she couldn't help but smile back. "Ah, well yes, I am Professor Walters but you have not told me who you are, sir?"

"I am very pleased to meet you at last, Professor Walters. My name is Alex Wallace. Graham Stuart asked if I would meet you and escort you to your hotel," he replied, taking the handle of her largest suitcase.

"Why didn't you say that at first, Mr. Wallace?" Inwardly she was sighing with relief but preferred that he not notice. She couldn't understand why he would be so happy ... and those twinkling eyes were beginning to unnerve her. She was not about to let him get off so easily. "I am greatly relieved to see you, but I can't say I approve of your manner of meeting guests, Mr. Wallace!"

"Please forgive any inefficiency, Professor Walters. As you will come to realize, this situation is most unique and has been quite problematic. As your assistant, I am now totally at your service and I trust I will be able to make up for any lack of good judgement! Welcome to Scotland," he added, reaching out to shake her hand.

"My assistant ... well, Mr. Stuart should have contacted me with an update, but I grant that could have been difficult with time differences and I did leave quickly," she murmured. As their hands met briefly, she felt an odd, prickly sensation touch the back of her neck. She shivered, and then realizing he was already heading towards the exit with her suitcase, so she hurried after him.

Explaining that he would return in a few minutes with the car, he left her with the luggage on the sidewalk at the arrivals exit. As she watched him stride away, she giggled at the way his kilt swung from side to side, conjuring up some rumours about kilts she had heard, and then his tall frame went out of sight. She suddenly realized she had accepted a ride from a total stranger, but he had given her all the correct information and she wasn't worried in the least. It was only a few minutes before a large, very shiny black car pulled up to the curb. She saw a parking attendant coming quickly towards her as her kilted chauffeur stepped out of the car.

"Och, go ahead and get in the car!" he called. "I'll put your cases in the boot."

Expecting a confrontation with the parking attendant, Emma hurriedly obeyed. "Was that man a problem?" she asked as her driver got in and pulled out into the traffic.

"Not in the least, I have my own way of dealing with little annoyances. He was just looking for a tip!"

"You mentioned that Mr. Stuart called you," said Emma.

"Yes, you see, Miss Walters, I come with your endowment. We're going to see a great deal of each other for the next two weeks ... at least." He glanced over at her but she hadn't noticed his hesitation.

"Mr. Stuart did not say who would be meeting me; are you the bailiff or ...?"

Ignoring her question, he concentrated on the road, exiting the airport area and pulling onto the busy motorway.

"Where is this hotel Mr. Stuart booked for me?" she asked, taking note of the scenery and buildings for the first time.

"Actually, I made your reservation ... it's at the *Courtyard Inn* near downtown Edinburgh. I believe you'll find it quite satisfactory. It also has a nice restaurant, a dining room and a bar. I imagine you might like to sample their food rather soon?"

"And I imagine you know my room number as well!" she quipped.

"Suite 401 is on the top floor having a perfect outlook for viewing beautiful Edinburgh sunrises."

"Well, that will be one experience I shall be missing I'm sure!"

"Oh, I would take a look if I were you. Sunrise presently is at about 7:40 a.m. and it's well worth the effort, as is sunset!"

Conversation stopped as traffic increased and the quiet, warm car had almost lulled Emma to sleep when a screaming ambulance followed by two wailing police cars revived her.

"There must be an accident," her driver commented, paying sharp attention to the traffic. "The hospital is over that way," he added, gesturing vaguely.

In a few minutes, they were in the centre of the city dealing with early afternoon traffic. Alex slowed to turn into an entryway between buildings and Emma received the sensation of driving over cobblestones. They went under an archway, and then pulled up to a quaint, yet regal-looking entrance under a small porte-cochère that displayed the name *Courtyard Inn*. Looking around at the large, four-storey building, she knew instantly that Alex had chosen the right place for her. The hotel porter greeted them as he opened Emma's door; Alex got out and stretched giving instructions to the porter to take her suitcases to the reception area.

"Take yer time," her kilted chauffeur commented with a grin, "you've all the time in the world now, Miss Walters, yer home!"

"Are you staying to have a meal with me, Mr. Wallace?" she asked coyly. "I am beginning to feel rather hungry and somewhat tired."

"Och aye, I'd be right pleased to accept your invitation! Did you manage to get some sleep during your flight?"

"I did, but it's not the same as being in your own bed!"

Accompanying her to the reception desk, Alex made sure her reservation was in order before she checked in. He told her a porter would take her upstairs to her room and there was no need to hurry; he would meet her in the *Hunting Bar* when she was ready, pointing to a nearby doorway. Emma nodded as the lift doors closed behind her.

The thistle-patterned, heavy-pile carpet caressed her feet as she followed the porter to the end of the wide corridor and found the door labelled *401*. Entering, she was instantly aware that this was no ordinary hotel room and the fleeting thought passed through her mind of the cost of such luxury. It was a suite and looked very much like her apartment back home, even having a small kitchen. Almost without a brogue, the porter explained some of the amenities, dimming light switches, hair drier, bathroom taps and shower head peculiarities, room service and the phones. She was most pleased when he called her attention to the view of Edinburgh Castle from her bedroom window.

He pulled back the living room curtain and she got her first view of Edinburgh's interesting skyline, outlined against a blue sky with only a few clouds in sight. The porter broke into her thoughts when he told her of their new, unique window system which opened and closed at the touch of a hidden button. She noted that everything was of the highest quality, almost bordering on luxury. It was a wonderful mixture of old and modern that blended perfectly, one complementing the other. *I suppose I'll be paying for this myself if I accept the inheritance!* she thought, now even more eager to learn the details of her legacy.

Quickly opening her suitcases after the porter had gone, she tried to brush the wrinkles out of her clothes and remembered the clerk had told her to hang them as soon as possible. She opened the curtains and was shocked to see the castle just across the street, but pulling herself away from the amazing view, she completed her task utilizing the spacious wardrobe and drawers in the walk-in closet.

Sitting on the bed for a moment to collect her thoughts, she looked all around her at the beautiful dark panelling and matching frame of her four-poster bed. An ensuite bathroom with shower and jetted tub made her wish she had some time to spare but she went over to the window, sinking into the soft, thick carpet in her stockinged feet. This view was quite different from the other side of the building and it struck her that she was in the end suite, no doubt larger than the rest. The view was delightful looking out across rooftops to large lighted bridge and she wondered what water that would be. *I can already see that my laptop is going to come in handy!* Her stomach rumbled reminding her to hurry. She quickly selected her grey pantsuit, switched to a small handbag, refreshed her make-up and left the room.

Silently, the lift moved almost imperceptibly downward and as the doors opened the concierge moved quickly to intercept her, "Sir Alex is waiting in the Hunting Room, marm."

*Sir Alex*! Emma repeated silently, raising her eyebrows.

Smiling as she approached, Alex rose as the concierge held her chair until she was seated. "My word, you certainly look the part," he murmured, patting her hand.

"So, it's Sir Alex is it, Mr. Wallace? I think you do have a little explaining to do!" Accompanying her statement with a well-practiced, frosty stare, Professor Walters waited for an answer. She suppressed a giggle when Alex laughed and asked what she wanted to drink.

"I'm surprised you don't already know!" she hissed.

Shaking his head, Alex shot his hand up to call a waiter. "Bring the lady a Seven Up and Rye and make sure it's Canadian Club. I'll have a glass of Highland Dew."

After about ten minutes of small talk, a smile slowly crossed the Canadian's face and now, more than ever, she had questions that wanted answers. "Who the devil are you, Sir Alex Wallace?" she asked coldly, as the waiter returned with their drinks.

"All in good time, lass, first we'll order our meal and then I'll answer all your questions."

"Please do, I'm quite famished."

"It must be our clean Scottish air ... and you have had a long trip. I would suggest having an early dinner now rather than later?"

"You are so right, what did you have in mind?"

"They cook a mouth-watering roast beef and Yorkshire pudding here, if that suits you, Miss Walters?" Watching her nod, he motioned to the hovering waitress. "Roast beef, medium, for both of us," Alex told her, looking over at Emma who nodded. "One moment!" he declared. "Would you like to eat here, Miss Walters, or go through to the Canterbury Dining Room?"

"The dining room would be nice," she said tiredly, stifling a yawn.

Obligingly, the waitress picked up their drinks and led the way to a room across the hall ... large and sumptuously decorated with only a few patrons at this time of the afternoon. Snow white linens, sparkling silverware and crystal goblets graced each table while chandeliers hung majestically overhead.

"My goodness," Emma exclaimed as he held her chair, "this is very grand, so like our Empress Hotel."

"Would you believe we're sitting in the old coaching stables?" he commented, chuckling.

"Don't start sidetracking me, Sir Alex, I want those explanations!" While she waited for him to sit down, she took a sip of her drink and then sat back and frowned at him across the table.

Sir Alex slowly settled into his chair, his eyes never wavering from this barely known woman seated across the table ... in all probability, his new boss within less than two weeks. Taking a good-sized sip of his drink, he rubbed vigorously at his beard.

"We studied you for a long time, Miss Walters. Trevelion knew he was going to die more than a year before he disappeared. He also knew, by that time, that you were his rightful heir, but it took us a long time to discover enough about you to actually locate you."

"You've been spying on me!" she declared fearfully.

"Stop!" he demanded. "Rest assured we never meant to harm you in any way. We simply needed to know if you were the right person."

Conversation ceased as the waitress served their meal shortly after and asked if they would like some wine. Alex looked over at Emma.

"I think not. I'll save it for when I can enjoy it better!" she decided.

Alex thanked the waitress and she left.

Picking delicately at the large meal, Emma was soon lost in satisfying her hunger. Her thoughts were spinning as she tried to form questions to ask Alex, but everything was getting confused in her brain. Tiredness began to take over as her appetite was satisfied. Alex suggested she should try not to go to bed too early and offered to take her for a short drive around the city.

She accepted and went upstairs to get her coat. Once out in the crisp, fresh air, she realized she was feeling much better. Returning to the hotel later, Alex told her about the plans for the next morning.

"We have an appointment at the solictor's office at 10 o'clock," he informed her as he started the car. "I will be here for breakfast at 8:30 if you would like to join me. We can walk … it's not far, but do wear comfortable shoes. I'll leave a wake up call for you at the desk. "

It was almost 9 p.m. when she returned to her suite. Drawn to the living-room window, she caught her breath as she realized why Alex had chosen this room. The spectacle of buildings and lights seen from both this room and her bedroom was truly remarkable to say the least. Pressing the button the porter had shown her, she eased the window open a few inches. Feeling the chilling breeze, she also noticed the quietness as the lights seemed to twinkle under their blanket of darkness. She closed the window and pulled the heavy curtains. *The end of Day One in Scotland; what a remarkable city this Edinburgh! I can't wait to see more!*

## Chapter 2 – Monday 13<sup>th</sup> – The Legacy

Waking the next morning to the persistent ringing of the phone, she longed to remain in the warm comfortable bed, but now half-awake, she answered and heard the hotel receptionist's voice.

"This is your wake up call. It's 7:30," she said softly.

*The day I get my answers!* she thought, swinging her legs over the edge of the bed and sitting up, yawning.

"Did I order a wake up call?" she mumbled, trying to remember the last thing Alex had said to her last night. *Oh cripes, he said he would meet me at 8:30!*

At 8:25 she walked into the dining room and found him at the table reading his newspaper.

"May I join you, sir?" she asked, motioning him to remain seated as she pulled out her own chair. "Please relax, I'm not an invalid although being waited on is certainly a lovely luxury and I assure you I will get used to it!" She put her coat and handbag on the extra chair and sat down across from him. "If I'm going to call you Alex, you must call me Emma! I'm very glad you didn't trust me to wake up this morning!"

"Good morning, Emma," he replied cheerfully, folding his newspaper. "I trust you are at least partially refreshed from the jetlag and time change? May I suggest you try a bowl of real Scottish oatmeal?"

"No, you may not and … what do you have in that cup that smells so good?"

"Highland Coffee, marm, it has a shot of Highland Dew. Here, have a taste. It's a popular combination!"

Emma accepted and a little smile appeared. "I can see why. This could become my new Scottish habit, if I'm not prudent. For today, I believe it will be perfect with two pieces of whole wheat toast!"

Alex motioned to the waitress and repeated the order. When her coffee arrived, Alex raised his cup in a toast.

"To a day Emma Walters will never forget!"

Sniffing her cup of coffee as he watched, she then brought it to her lips. "Now that's what I call a morning coffee!" she exclaimed. Shortly afterwards their toast arrived and they ate in relative silence.

As they were finishing, he commented, "I see you've brought your coat and are wearing walking shoes, excellent!"

"Are you going to the appointment with me?"

"Aye, ye'd soon be lost without me, and besides, I wouldn't want to leave you alone with any solicitor!"

The wind whipped at their coats when they stepped out of the hotel and turned north to walk along George Street. Glancing around at the magnificent stone buildings, Emma was easily reminded she was walking through much older history than was familiar to her.

Alex stopped at a massive oak door a few blocks away on St. Andrew Street and she was glad to escape the wind. Inside the main door, a receptionist watched their progress towards her desk.

"Good morning, Sir Alex, and … Miss Walters, I presume," she purred. "Mr. Gilbert is ready for you; I believe you know your way."

With Alex leading, they walked to the end of the wide hallway where he stopped to hang their coats in a closet. Proceeding to a partially open door, he tapped and pushed it open, motioning for Emma to go ahead of him. There, behind a large oak desk, sat a man of about 60 years, who could have stepped straight out of a Dickens' novel. Beaming, he rose and came over to greet them. Emma stared in disbelief as the round-faced solicitor approached, his mutton-chop whiskers wobbling and a bow-tie jiggling as his Adam's apple popped up and down. Containing herself with difficulty, the Canadian stifled a giggle and shook his limp hand. She sat down in the chair he indicated, directly opposite him, and Alex sat beside her.

Mr. Stuart's secretary, whom Alex called Kelly, entered and asked if they would like a drink. Emma, politely but aloofly, requested black tea and the men asked for coffee. The secretary returned with their drinks and took her position nearby, notepad ready.

All of a sudden, the man behind the desk was all business.

"Miss Walters, my name is Adam Gilbert Stuart," he stated loudly, his eyebrows twitching vigorously. "I am the legal representative and advisor to the late Sir Angus Trevelion Walters. We are here to inform you of details of your inheritance with an aim to swiftly wind up Mr. Walters' will and estate."

Opening a bulging folder in front of him, he selected a few pages off the top of the pile and spread them out in front of him.

"Excuse me, Mr. Stuart," Emma interrupted softly, "could you speak a little quieter please? I'm beginning to get a headache."

"Yes, of course," Gilbert Stuart replied in a much deflated tone. "I trust that you have read the material which we couriered to you in Canada. If so, we won't have to review it again ... unless you have a question, of course. In which case, please do not hesitate to interrupt." Emma nodded and he handed both she and Alex a single page of typed notes in point form. "Miss Walters, you are the legal heir to the Walters' Estate, but there are some *Conditions* you must agree to meet first, namely ...." He paused to take a sip of coffee, cleared his throat, and began to read.

1. *Sir Alexander Wallace shall remain as your bailiff for the remainder of his or your lifetime;*
2. *No part of the estate may be sold or disposed of in any way during your lifetime;*
3. *All enterprises in operation on the date of acceptance of your inheritance shall continue;*
4. *You shall be in residence in the United Kingdom not less than 175 days in any calendar year;*

Emma was now totally alert as she read along, carefully absorbing the meaning behind each word of these thought-provoking clauses.

5. *At all times you will be required to wear an item of jewellry displaying the Walters' coat of arms;* and
6. *You will agree to diligently continue the search for the missing Scottish relics.*

"Continue the search for relics? What on earth does that mean? This whole thing sounds like you are trying to make me a prisoner here!" Emma said angrily. "This is not an inheritance; it's a life sentence!" She began to stand.

"Steady lass," Alex murmured, placing his hand gently on her arm. "We can discuss these terms clause by clause if it would make you feel more comfortable."

"I'm concerned about Clause Two ... how can it be assumed there will not be some situation arise that would be cause to close one of the enterprises? Perhaps it is no longer lucrative. What do I do then?"

Alex and Mr. Stuart exchanged glances and the solicitor sat back in his chair and removed his glasses. Alex turned to Emma. "If there is an emergency or any unusual situation arises, there is a clause which comes into force whereby you can request a meeting of the Board."

"Hm, The Board, eh! Who sits on this board?" She was frowning.

"It's made up of five people including you, myself, a financial advisor, and two other people you will meet very soon!" Alex explained. He went on to clarify further details until Emma was satisfied enough with the *Conditions* to sit back in her chair.

"I would like to see this clause regarding the Board's duties, and secondly, I want to see the properties and these enterprises that you are both being so secretive about! Why did you not send this information with your initial package so I had time to peruse the details and have my questions prepared?"

"The documents were and still are in the production phase, Miss Walters, as you can imagine ...." Mr. Stuart was about to list off his excuses when Emma stopped him.

"Don't give me your drivel, Mr. Stuart; when will these papers be ready for me?" Turning to Alex, she added. "How much time do we need so you can show me these properties, Sir Alex? I understood there were two properties plus possible business interests associated with each; is this correct?" she looked from one man to the other.

Mr. Stuart rifled through his files and selected several, two of them a substantial size, and slid them across the desk to her.

She laid them out in two rows so each file was easily accessible. "There are five items here, how can that be?"

"There are actually three manors, Emma," Alex explained. "Two of them have important tenants who run the enterprises of that property. The third was Trev's residence and there is also a distillery and a wool factory. I intend to give you a tour of each of these properties in the next week. I prefer not to give you too many details in advance and, in that way, add to your enjoyment through the element of surprise!"

She looked at him sharply. "You are deciding to let me experience some joy by keeping them secret? Do you think I am a child who needs some excitement in her life? This is a business arrangement not child's play, and it affects my life, the rest of my life, sir ... and it apparently affects yours as well!" Turning to Gilbert Stuart, she frowned. "When will I be able to see the rest of this paperwork, Mr. Stuart? Could it not be sent to me by email? Is that so difficult in today's world?"

"I ... I ... this is most unusual," Mr. Stuart stammered, shaking his head and peering over his glasses at her. "We will do our best but I can promise the papers will be ready for you by Friday." He stopped and peered at her. "Would you refute your claim, Miss Walters?"

"I won't know that until I see the properties and your paperwork sir. In the meantime, I am neither refuting nor refusing my claim. I simply need time to study these *Conditions* and the estate in general, before I make an informed decision." Emma was on her feet now, glaring at the solicitor as she picked up the page of *Conditions*. "May I take this copy with me?" she demanded. "I believe I still have almost two weeks to make my decision.

"Y-yes, you may," he said meekly, "b-but allow me to correct you. We have exactly nine business days to sign and register these documents or you will lose it all!" As he spoke, he rose from his chair, drooling a little into his whiskers. He pulled open a desk drawer and, with obvious frustration, took out a clean white handkerchief and wiped his chin and forehead, sighing loudly.

Assessing the situation, Alex suggested he and Emma return to Mr. Stuart's office on Friday the 17th at 10 a.m. The solicitor regained his composure, agreed to Alex's suggestion and then hesitated, looking like he might apologise for not taking the time to familiarize Emma with the unusual *Conditions* of the estate. However, he merely instructed Kelly to set up a new appointment and then hurriedly left the room.

They were hardly outside when Emma began to vent her anger. "That's not an inheritance," she declared loudly as the rain began to run down her face, "it's a prison sentence with you as my jailer. Oh, you have a lot to answer for, Sir Alex!" Then she stormed off.

"Stop!" the strong, harsh tone of Alex's voice brought Emma to a halt, tossing her head defiantly as she turned to face him.

"First of all you're going the wrong way, and secondly you'll be making a terrible mistake if you refuse your inheritance ... and I'm not your jailer! I'm your protector! What the devil did you think a historical inheritance would be ... a pile of money and an apartment in Spain?"

A wisp of a smile touched the Canadian's face and they stood in the Edinburgh rain glaring at each other as raindrops ran off their noses. "You have four days to convince me to stay, Sir Alex. If the situation wasn't so serious, I would think it was funny, lead on MacDuff!"

Cocking an amused eyebrow at Emma's attempt at Shakespearian sarcasm, he reminded himself he had better get used to this feisty woman if they were going to survive together! He hooked her arm through his and they quickly covered the short distance back to the hotel.

"If I only have four days to convince you, we need to begin immediately ... this afternoon," he stated seriously as they walked inside. "Firstly, you'll require some dry comfortable clothes and a new paint job! I'll expect you back here in 15 minutes!" He turned abruptly and walked off.

Refraining from commenting, she got in the lift and when the door closed, she couldn't resist a word under her breath as she repeated his comment about her face. Thirty minutes later, she returned to the foyer and went to find him in the bar. She came up behind him as he stood talking to another man.

"Would you like a drink, Miss Wright?" he asked, moving a step backward to allow her to join them.

"I would like a Highland Coffee, like I had this morning."

"You heard the lady," Alex growled at the hovering waiter. "Now, let me introduce you to Freddy Roland, he breeds fine cattle and sheep in the Highlands Northwest of Stirling."

Shaking hands and exchanging pleasantries, Emma commented, "Are you from England, Mr. Roland? Your accent is different."

"No, no lass, 'am pure Scot, not like this Welsh emigrant!"

The men roared with laughter, obviously at some private joke. As the laughter subsided, Alex completed his introduction.

"Freddy my lad, Miss Walters is the new Lady Traymore, or will be very soon."

"You're the person who has inherited Traymore from Trev? So you get Dorik Island, Misty House and ...?" he said, before being quickly interrupted by Alex when he cleared his throat loudly, giving Freddy a stern look.

"Don't spoil it all for the lady, Freddy," he snapped.

Freddy took the hint and quietly excused himself saying he had to attend to some business. Alex then took her over to a corner table.

"I had forgotten," she whispered. "I will inherit an island, won't I?"

"You would have already ....," he grunted.

She sighed in annoyance. "All right, Alex, I get the point! Starting right now, I need some more answers or I am not going anywhere. Who are you and why do you need to stay with my inheritance?" A waiter went by and she caught his attention. "Are you ready for lunch or will we be stopping somewhere on the way?" she asked.

"Your decision," he quipped and she ordered a blueberry muffin and a coffee refill.

"Now I'm ready for that explanation, Sir Alex."

Alex looked at her seriously but a smile slightly curled one side of his mouth. "I am a direct descendant of William Wallace, Emma, and both our families are very proud of their Scottish heritage ... a history that goes back well before the first days of the Scottish Wars of Independence in the late 13$^{th}$ century. This is where we'll begin and I'll try to be brief; you'll find you have much to catch up on to appreciate your legacy!

"Sir William Wallace, the great patriot and rebel who became a knight, was executed by the English, but as a very young man back when freedom was thought of as something different than we perceive it today, he was taught the importance of living in a free country ruled only by Scots. When King Alexander III died without an heir, England's King Edward I sought to control Scotland. Wallace, however, was ready to fight for his principles and a movement began ... very quietly at first, in response to Edward's increasing military stance in his country. This became known as the Wars of Scottish Independence. Wallace began with small skirmishes as he sought to acquire the support of fellow Scots and, some years later, he and another young Scotsman, Andrew Moray, defeated the English at the Battle of Stirling Bridge." Knowing Emma was going to hear this story again very soon, he shortened his tale even more. "As a result, they were made Guardians of Scotland but Moray, who had been gravely injured in battle, died some weeks later. His wife was carrying a son whom she named Andrew. This son would later become Guardian of Scotland and become the 2$^{nd}$ husband to Robert I's daughter, Christina. Now there's a lady you should research, Emma! Sorry, I digress.

"Wallace was made a knight but the English were now relentless in their search to find him. It was August 1305 when Wallace was finally caught and executed. His wife, Mary Walters, had bore him three children, but sadly, she was also murdered by the English shortly after her husband's death. The orphaned children, Flora, David and Malcolm, had been secreted away to Mary's family for their protection. Her brother, Sir Duncan Walters and his house were instrumental in that regard."

Emma sighed deeply, but did not interrupt.

"When the Traymore title was introduced into the Walters' Family some years later, an important, joint decission was made between the two families. The grateful relationship of these families had become so historically beneficial since William's and Mary's executions, it was decided to make it official. Essentially it was determined that the holder of the Baronetcy title granted to one of William Wallace's grandsons, would in perpetuity, as long as the lines continued, of course, become the protector of Lord Traymore, of the Walters' line!"

"Whew, so you have to protect me for the rest of my life?" she whispered.

"For the rest of *my* life, but only if …!" he teased and they laughed.

"What about *my* title? Where did that come from and how is it possible for a female to inherit?" Emma asked.

"The Lord Traymore title was initiated by Robert I soon after gaining the throne. Pertaining to a female heir … many years ago, when it appeared there was no male to inherit, the family sought permission to change the lineage to include females."

"How lucky for me; so I'm not the first female?"

"Yes, actually you will be; that Lord lived somewhat longer and sired a male just in time. This line produced Trevelion, but unfortunately he could never bring himself to marry and later regretted it deeply. The title reverted to your father's line and the frantic search to find you began!"

Alex sat back in his chair to watch her reaction. Delving into her handbag, Emma brought out a pen and the page of *Conditions*. She silently read the words and made a small mark in front of Clause Number One. Without glancing up, she proceeded to the next clause and followed the same procedure, this time without making a mark. She looked up, as she reached for her drink, and caught Alex smiling at her.

"You think this is funny?" she asked softly.

"Does that little mark mean you've accepted the first *Condition*?"

"Yes it does, my family has accepted this condition for over 700 years, so who am I to argue with tradition? I can also understand not allowing the estate to be broken up, so I agree with that clause too," she replied, putting her mark in front of the second clause.

She continued to read but Alex broke into her thoughts. "You can do this while we're travelling, you know."

"Travelling where?" she asked.

"We'll see Misty House, the distillery and the wool factory today."

"That's only one of the manors, I assume?" she stated. "There are three manor houses."

"That's what you'll see today and it will be plenty!" he said coyly.

"All right, I suppose you're trying to be constructive and helpful, although I don't understand your secrecy. Let's get on with it!"

"I'll meet you outside in five minutes," he replied and left the table. Finishing her coffee without rushing, she put her paper back into her handbag, slipped on her coat and went out to the foyer. Within minutes the sleek black car purred to a stop under the porte-cochère and Alex came round to open her door.

"Is this your car?" she asked.

"No, it's one of yours, or it could be."

"I know," Emma sighed, "those damn papers! Where are we off to?"

"First, we're going to Misty House; it's about 60 minutes northwest."

As they drove, Emma took a great interest in her surroundings. Once outside of Edinburgh, she tried to get her bearings as houses gave way to fields, farms and sheep. An hour later, Alex turned off the motorway and onto a series of country roads. At this point, he surprised her by beginning to speak about Misty House, but she soon discovered he was still holding back information and her frustration grew evident.

"Now brace yourself, Miss Walters. I think you're going to be quite surprised by what you will discover here. I don't want you to ask any questions yet, just observe. It's a fascinating place!" he chuckled.

It wasn't long before he slowed down and turned into a long driveway that led through a lovely wooded area with fenced grasslands. They finally arrived at a large, old, stone manor house with many outbuildings.

Dying to question him, she remembered his instructions and held back her curiosity.

"Patience," he whispered, ringing the bell.

A pleasant-looking woman Emma estimated to be in her mid-50s opened the door. "Sir Alex," she said in a gently accented voice, "have you brought us a visitor today?"

"Yes, I have and she's a very special visitor, Miss Oxley. I'd like you to meet Professor Emma Walters. We're going to wander around for a little while, if that meets with your approval. We'll join you for tea a bit later."

"I shall be in my office when you're ready," she replied.

Alex pointed to a large, two-storey building and they went toward it. A sign announced it was the *Studio* and he opened a door into a large open area that appeared to be a carpenter's workshop laid out with separate areas for other projects. Two men were busy working with equipment but they called to Alex.

"Miss Walters, I'd like you to meet Tom and Charlie," he said when the men came over. "What are you working on, Tom?"

"This is a roundabout for children; it plays a tune as it moves so the kids know when it's safe to climb on board. Look at Charlie's project. He's trying to work out a system for cupboard doors and drawers that let you know when they're open. It's driving him mad!" The carpenter laughed.

Emma looked around the room which seemed to be a pretty typical woodworker's workplace with tools and lumber everywhere. *I wonder what this fascinating place is?* Forcing herself to be patient, she let her eyes flit about the room until she noticed a collection of what appeared to be some short, white, walking sticks. Puzzled, she remembered the carpenter had mentioned children ... *whose children?*

Leaving by a different door, they went into another large building that had been transformed into a children's playground. In one area, sand covered the floor and bales of hay formed an inner wall.

"A merry-go-round, how wonderful!" Emma murmured, walking towards it and giving it a little push. It immediately began playing music and she quickly stopped it, turning to her companion. "The ... what did Tom call this?" she asked.

"A roundabout. It's lovely, isn't it?"

The same happened when she tried the seesaw and set a giant ball moving. She glanced at Alex who merely grinned at her confusion and motioned her to follow him towards another door. They were almost there, when the door flew open and an attractive young woman dressed in riding gear appeared.

"Oh, hello, Sir Alex! I heard the playground music and wondered who was in here. Have you come to see the pups?"

"Jessie, this is Miss Walters. I'm just showing her around. You were next on our list; I wasn't aware we had new pups."

As they followed Jessie outside, Emma noticed a little sign on the door with rows of embossed dots in a pattern and instantly recognized it as braille. She noticed another one on the other side of the door as it closed. They went along a covered passageway to another building and soon the sound of yelping puppies was heard. Emma had noticed Alex's use of the word 'we' and she eagerly followed them into another room which seemed full of dogs, all housed in clean, roomy pens. Some of them now began to bark making the noise almost unbearable and she put her hands over her ears, but not before she noticed the braille signs on each cage.

"The pups are in the last pen!" Jessie yelled.

Emma's animal-loving instinct came rushing to the surface, forgetting the noise when she saw the tiny, suckling animals. For a moment she also forgot her cynical approach to her inheritance. *What is this place?*

Alex called to her from the doorway, interrupting her thoughts. "Come, Miss Walters, it's time we went to have tea with Miss Oxley. Thank you, Jessie."

"Alex, you have to tell me ... what is this place?" she demanded, pulling on his arm as they went in the back door of the manor. Receiving no reply, she added, "Is this some devious plan to get me to sign those documents?"

"No comment, to the former and, yes to the latter. When you hear Miss Oxley's explanation, you will be wiser and exceedingly pleased!"

"That is quite true, Miss Walters!" said a woman's voice behind the door, as it opened, and Miss Oxley herself greeted them. Emma gasped when she saw the magnificent foyer of the grand old house. A wide, curved stairway rose up to a second floor, although rather oddly, the carved stairposts supported two hand rails, the lower one being smaller. *Of course, they're for small hands ... blind children visit here!*

Alex interrupted her thoughts calling her attention to the many large paintings of kilted Scottish gentlemen wearing an array of tartans, which lined the foyer and stairway walls. She was so intent on seeing everything she suddenly felt dizzy and grabbed Alex's arm.

"What does this place have to do with children and why are there braille signs all over the place?" she asked, almost in a whisper.

"I'm going to let Miss Oxley explain, but why don't we start with tea first," Alex suggested as they entered the office and sat down. "Later, you may ask all your questions, Miss Walters."

"Oh, Sir Alex!" Miss Oxley chastised as she set out the tea tray. "Why so formal? Miss Walters, I'm Matron Ruth Oxley. It's a pleasure to welcome you to Misty House. Where are you from?"

"I'm very pleased to meet you, Matron Oxley; I'm from Victoria on the West Coast of Canada."

"Emma is the heir to the Walters' estate, Ruth. I'm afraid I've been giving her a rough time. Trev left her everything, but she hasn't seen 'everything' yet and I haven't told her a lot either!"

Ruth Oxley's eyes focused on Emma as she lowered her cup thoughtfully onto its saucer and looked kindly at the Canadian. Clapping her hands together joyously, she proclaimed, "Lovely! I do hope you enjoy your title and all it encompasses, as much as Trevelion did, dear. We miss him so very much."

"Miss Oxley, is this man always as infuriating as he is today? I only arrived yesterday and he can't seem to give me a straight answer! Now may I ask some questions?" she hissed at her grinning bailiff, who nodded. She finally let out her breath in an exasperated motion. "Will you please tell me, Miss Oxley, what is Misty House?"

"Please, call me Ruth. Misty House began many centuries ago as an experimental school for blind children and this is how we have evolved!"

Emma gasped, hardly able to contain her joy. "Of course, that's why you have two banister rails and music in the playground toys!"

"And the dogs ...," Ruth added eagerly, "every child leaves here with a guide dog of their own. The children are upstairs in class at present, but perhaps next visit you will get to meet them."

Emotion was obvious on Emma's face as she asked hesitantly, "This is one of my enterprises, but how do I finance it?"

"You don't unless you sign that paper," Alex informed her. "It's time we got on our way."

Frustrated with Alex and rather surprised to have the visit end so hastily, she shook hands with Ruth and they returned to the car. She was so deep in thought, she was barely aware of Alex until he turned on the engine and spoke to her.

"It's a nice short drive, so I suggest you just sit back and enjoy the view." Seemingly doing as he suggested, she didn't explain that her silence was because she was annoyed with him. He didn't speak again until they were nearing Stirling. "We'll stop at Bannochburn."

Ten minutes later, they pulled into a car park and, braving a cold wind, followed the signs to an impressive statue of a mounted knight in battle armour seated high on his horse. The figure of *The Bruce* gazed forever over the Bannockburn battleground where, as Alex explained, the Scots thankfully defeated the English. As she stood silently admiring the large statue, Alex brought himself stiffly to attention, his coat flapping in the wind as he saluted Scotland's greatest warrior king.

"Scotland is exceedingly grateful and proud of her heroes," he said, taking her arm and hurrying her along the pathway that led to a huge circular monument commemorating the historically important battle. As they walked, he talked about the history behind the famous battle.

"Many believe Wallace was from Lanarkshire and schooled at Paisley Abbey. He was probably born in Ayreshire though, as some of the mysteries about his life have been solved through the centuries. We now know his family had lands there."

"You've just brought back a long-forgotten memory of my father talking to us about Scotland. I'm sure dad was born in Lanarkshire." Shivering noticeably, she added, "I'm cold and now I'm also hungry. Is there a nice warm pub or restaurant nearby?"

They were on the outskirts of the town of Bannochburn and as Alex drove around a corner, he turned into the parking lot of a small hotel. Gathering her coat about her, they hurried to the entrance. A rush of warm air greeted them as Alex led her through the entryway, acknowledging the landlord's friendly greeting.

"Are you here for lunch, Sir Alex?"

"Aye Toby, is there a fire in the snug?"

"Aye, enough ter warm yer bones; ah'll be with you in a jiffy."

They found a table near the open fire and Emma went straight to the fireplace, warming her hands and then turning her back to the flames and lifting her coat a bit.

Two couples eating lunch nearby smiled when Alex laughed, causing Emma to blush and go to sit down.

"The last time I saw someone do that was my grandmother 30 years ago, although she was wearing a long dress and she hiked her skirt up a wee bit too high!"

"Behave yourself, you're embarrassing me!"

Leaving Bannochburn, Alex decided to treat Emma to a tourist view of Stirling Castle. He drove north on the Bannochburn Road then cut over towards the castle via the B8051. As they drove through Stirling … she suddenly saw it!

"Alex! Stop! What is that remarkable castle on the hill?"

"That's Stirling. Quite a sight, isn't it?" he grinned.

"It's amazing how the land is so flat and then suddenly … is it built on an extinct volcano like Edinburgh Castle?" She craned her neck to look at it until they had passed by and reached their exit.

"Now we're going to the Highlands," he announced, taking the A84 exit and entering a maze of roads. She watched fascinated as the traffic flowed around several roundabouts, a phenomenum she was still not used to in Victoria. She heard Alex chuckle at her reaction, and then they were on a less-busy motorway driving through farmlands.

"To answer your question, Stirling Castle is also built on an extinct volcano but it is also believed that glacial action played a hand in it. It's called a *crag and tail formation* and there are quite a few around Scotland. Edinburgh Castle is another. At Stirling, the castle sits 250 feet above the houses but it appears to be much higher. We'll come back another day but you could also look it up on your computer. Meanwhile, why don't I tell you about the Wallace history pertaining to Stirling? You can't see the modern stone bridge from here, but in 1297, the famous Battle of Stirling Bridge took place near the castle. At that time, it was a much narrower wooden bridge that spanned the River Forth and Wallace's unusual tactics paid off!"

For the next 15 minutes, he proudly told her the story of the famous battle for which his martyred ancestor was held in such high esteem by the Scots and hated so fervently by the English. She was so entranced she barely noticed that there were now some low green hills appearing in the distance. The only sign of human activity besides cars on the road was at the farmhouses they passed. A signpost announced that Doune and Callander were ahead and Alex told her they were going to Callander.

The number of trees, Alex called them woods, had increased now and houses became more plentiful as they entered Doune and crossed the River Teith. He pointed up the river and told her Doune Castle was on the next bend, but there were too many trees to get a good look. The road skirted the main housing areas and, within minutes, they were back on a country road with sheep grazing on either side. To the east were the green hills and to the northwest, the Highlands were already displaying their winter bleakness as they prepared for the snows.

Callander was a lovely, spread out town with such green hedges it made Emma smile, thinking of home. Turning onto a narrow road, she saw smoke rising in the distance and then the shape of a large building about two kilometers away. Stopping at a high, chain link fence, Alex climbed out and unlocked the gate. He opened it partway, ran back, jumped in the car and drove through, then repeated the exercise, glancing furtively about as he returned to the car. Emma watched with an amused expression, then laughed when he rejoined her and slammed the door, breathing heavily.

"Is someone chasing you?" she asked, but the words were hardly out of her mouth when she heard a thunderous, but vaguely familiar sound, and turned to gawk out the window. Hundreds of squawking geese, looking amazingly like Canada Geese, were hurtling themselves towards, but not touching the car.

Emma screamed, covering her eyes. "Are they Canada Geese?"

"We're at the distillery, Emma. The geese are their alarm system. Stop worrying, we're quite safe. They are Greylag geese and some say they get too friendly with their Canadian counterparts when they visit!" They were now driving along a rough track with their geese escort.

"My students will never believe this!" she cried, covering her ears.

A few minutes later she could see several of the distillery's buildings and was relieved when Alex stopped in front of what appeared to be a tall chain-link cage. When workmen opened the gate, Alex drove through and they closed it quickly behind them. She breathed a sigh of relief as they went around the first building and the noise dissipated. Her attention was drawn to a building on the right where large open doors revealed rows and rows of barrels stacked in orderly lines. Two large chimneys belched smoke into the overcast sky as a number of men moved around the area. Alex parked in front of a stone building and they got out.

"No need to ask what this place is," he chuckled, making an exaggerated effort to smell the air. "I love coming here!"

Emma gasped as the much colder wind now whipped around them, tugging at their coats before they dashed inside.

"Hello, Sir Alex!" a very definite Scottish brogue boomed through the building as a red-bearded giant of a man strode energetically towards them, his hand outstretched. After shaking hands vigorously with Alex he turned to Emma and, with twinkling eyes, commented, "And who might this fair lass be?"

"Hello, I'm Professor Emma Walters from Victoria, Canada," she replied, "and if you think I'm a fair lass, sir, you need your eyes tested!"

The men laughed, but Alex took over. "Let me introduce you to Douglas Glencannon. He's our manager here and, as might be expected, his nickname is Red! Miss Walters arrived from Canada yesterday, Douglas. She's the heir to the Walters' estate. We're doing a tour today to ah … let her get a feel for it, you might say! How about showing us the tasting room?" he asked a bit too eagerly.

Emma frowned, but then a smile tugged at the corners of her mouth as Red shook her hand and welcomed her more graciously. Having already learned how much Alex liked his nip of whisky, she could certainly understand his love of this place. They followed Red along a gleaming walkway of freshly polished floor between rows and rows of barrels and entered a brightly lit room where it was difficult not to notice the definite aroma of whisky in the air. Two white-coated men were deep in noisy discussion, each holding a glass of amber liquid.

"Mr. Glencannon, would you settle this argument for us?" one of the men asked eagerly, ignoring the visitors.

"Maybe we could let our visitors help us decide," Douglas suggested.

Three small wine glasses were produced and each one was filled with a small amount of amber liquid; then three more glasses were added and the same man poured similar quantities from an unlabelled bottle of clear liquid. Each pair of drinks was set on a small tray and offered to the three of them.

"Is this a tasting?" she asked nervously.

"Not really," one of the white-coated men replied, "just an opinion. Tell us which one you think is smoother."

The men took a taste of the first glass, swishing it around their mouths and then swallowing it. Emma followed suit. Next, they took a drink of the other glass that had no colour to it, also swishing it around their mouths and swallowing.

*This is water*, she thought, then remembering an earlier wine tasting added, *Ah, to cleanse my palate!*

They repeated this ritual three times and Alex finished first.

"The first one," he declared, holding his glass out for another serving. Emma noted that his small glass was refilled without question.

"Second one," Douglas murmured after a long deliberation.

"I think the first one," Emma said hesitantly, looking a little bewildered and quietly adding, "but I'm not a connoisseur!"

The men thanked them profusely and Douglas led them towards an outside door saying it was time Emma had a tour of her ancient distillery. She soon learned how interesting a distillery could be.

"I see you've been working on the old building," Alex exclaimed, pointing to some scaffolding across the lane.

"Yes, we decided to fix it up, so I told the masons to clean it out and start the work. You wouldn't believe what we found in the cellar system!" Hardly waiting for an answer, he continued on excitedly. "We found over 100 barrels of old whisky in a hidden tunnel. We also found what I believe to be someone's claymore which is over in the office waiting to go to the museum. They'll clean and evaluate it."

"Och, that could be a worthy find, Red. We would like to see it … and where is this whisky noo?" Alex's voice had turned dramatically emotional when he spoke of the sword, but he laughed when asking about the liquor.

"We've left most of it in the tunnel. We're waiting for the builders to make the area safe before we disturb it any further."

"You left it down in the tunnel?" Alex asked with raised eyebrows. Emma tried to stifle a giggle at Douglas' embarrassment.

"Not exactly sir, we used four barrels for the test and moved them very carefully into the basement area."

"To taste it, you say Douglas?" Alex asked eagerly.

Emma giggled as Alex teased the big man into making excuses. Finally, her bailiff turned to her and winked mischievously. "Maybe we could overlook it if we were allowed to taste a wee dram, don't you think that's fair, Miss Walters?"

Smiling, Emma nodded and Douglas led the way back to the office block. He showed them into a comfortable sitting room and left them.

"I have a question," she said suddenly. "Alex, what is a claymore?"

"Och, I've forgotten how much education you truly need. It's a wonderful piece of history, Emma," he replied with a faraway look in his eyes. "It could also be a clue."

"You're being evasive!" she chided.

"A claymore is a very large Scottish broadsword believed to have been used in battle by some of our strongest ancient warriors. It was a fearsome weapon in the hands of an expert. William Wallace's claymore has never been found, but many experts believe such a sword never even existed 700 years ago!"

The door opened and Douglas returned, holding it open for another man who carried a very long, narrow package. He carefully set the package on the coffee table in front of them and left. Grinning, Douglas extracted an unlabelled bottle from his pocket. It was clearly only a quarter full of amber liquid.

"Here's yer taster," he announced, adding two glasses from another pocket and pouring a small amount of the liquor into each.

Alex first sniffed deeply and then held the glass up to the light for a moment. He smiled and tasted the liquor and Emma saw his eyes sparkle before he drained the glass. He motioned Emma to follow suit.

The Canadian shook her head, pushing the glass towards Alex.

"You will enjoy my share far more than I, Sir Alex!" she sighed.

Alex smiled before gratefully draining the second glass.

"An opinion, Sir Alex?" Douglas asked.

"Exquisite nectar, laddie, it touches the palate like mist o' the glen!" He theatrically closed his eyes and took a quick deep breath before turning his attention on the package. Leaning closer, he just stared at it without speaking. Finally he asked, "I assume this is a blanket of yours? Has anyone seen the sword, Douglas?"

"No, I'm only surmising it's a sword from the weight and feel of it. I thought it best to wait for you," Douglas explained.

"Then I assume it's a wee bit of wishful thinking that has you hoping it to be a claymore!" Alex smiled ruefully and Red nodded sheepishly.

Running his hand lightly across the fabric, Alex experienced a brief moment of apprehension as he began to unfold the blanket. Underneath was another covering of what looked like dirty old felt. His hand noticeably began to shake as he gently tried to peel the hard covering back. Almost immediately, he stopped, sitting back and raising his hands.

"Och aye, this is indeed old!" he exclaimed, breathlessly.

"Aye, you see what I mean, I ken!" Douglas said solemnly.

"Could it possibly be … the Wallace blade?" Alex whispered. Standing to get a better view, Emma was surprised to see part of the hilt of what appeared to be a very long, heavy-looking sword. It was leather wrapped and in remarkable condition, if it was indeed that old. Alex mumbled aloud that it looked to be two-handed. Seeing the ancient weapon sent a cold shiver down Emma's spine.

"It is the freedom sword, it has to be!" Alex hissed in a deep state of excitement, rising to peel back another section of the felt.

Emma's own heart had missed a beat as she saw glimpses of the unquestionably large sword. It appeared to be still in its sheath and, even to her inexperienced eyes, the leather covering and belt were in remarkable condition, no matter what age it was.

"Stop!" she suddenly cried out.

Alex turned, cocked an eye at her, and, at the same time, pulled his hands away as if the sword was suddenly burning his fingers.

"We have no right to do this … it could destroy valuable evidence and you should know better!"

"Och aye, you're right; I got carried away by the moment!"

"If it is indeed a legitimate artifact," Emma interrupted, "it needs to be treated with extreme care and by an expert."

Again composed, Alex looked over at Douglas. "We'll take over for you now Douglas but we certainly appreciate your care and diligence. I think it best that we deliver this personally. I will contact John Dunstan."

"Amazing, to think we found it in the tunnel near those whisky barrels," Douglas commented, as Alex rewrapped the package.

"I agree it would be extraordinary if the Freedom Sword was found on Traymore land here in the Highlands," said Alex. "It's not where I would expect it to be but then William was thought to have taken part in a skirmish near Perth before his capture."

"Freedom Sword or not, it's time we were on our way!" Emma announced sharply, trying to hide the fact that she was indeed rattled by this discovery and just wanted to leave.

"I will expect you to keep us informed of any further discoveries Douglas," Alex added. "Carry this out to the car, will you?"

Emma followed the men outside into the rain and Alex opened the boot. She watched as they carefully placed the bundle in the car. As they drove out, workmen were already at the fence with the gate open, allowing them to swiftly pass through the geese enclosure. More

32

workmen were waiting at the outer gate but no geese were seen. They soon ran into a heavy downpour as darkness was coming on and, having no idea where they were, Emma leaned back and closed her eyes. She had almost fallen asleep when she realized Alex had turned onto a winding country road. He murmured that their destination was the lighted area ahead.

"Not interested," she objected. "I'm famished!"

The car's headlights illuminated a high, stone wall just before Alex drove between two stone gateposts onto a much-travelled dirt road. Around a bend, they came to a small well-lit village with a tavern.

"Maybe if I feed you ...," he teased.

Parking the car, he watched Emma run through the rain, jumping puddles as she hurried towards the entrance.

"Good evening, Sir Alex, marm," the barman greeted them, as the eyes of four old men intently followed the newcomers' arrival.

"It's probably better than snow, but it's a wet one, Peter!" Alex exclaimed going over to the bar while Emma found a chair by the fire. "What's on the dinner menu tonight?"

"Full menu if you order steak and all the trimmings," landlord Peter McEwan chuckled and Alex nodded. "Can I get you and your lady a drink, sir?"

"Two coffees and a wee carafe of your nectar, lad."

Minutes later, he returned with their drinks and asked if they had decided to have the steak. They agreed and Peter asked a myriad of questions before going away.

"Help yourself, Emma," said Alex, pointing to the carafe of whisky.

"I'll stick with coffee tonight, thank you, Alex," she replied, taking a sip and turning her attention to the room and its furnishings. She felt the heat from the enormous log fire and sensed the presence of a lively history in the blackened open beams littered with mainly odd-looking and unfamiliar artifacts.

Suddenly the familiar skirl of bagpipes caused her to turn around. Across the room; the four old men were busy removing musical instruments from cases, obviously getting ready to play. She smiled as a rhythmic rapa-tat-tat of drumsticks began to accompany the bagpipes.

"Do you mind if the boys play awhile, marm?" Peter came over to ask. "They'll enjoy the presence of a visitor."

Alex's eyes deferred the decision to Emma who was now clapping her hands while she shook her head enthusiastically to the beat.

An old squeeze-box accordion and a mouth organ now completed the band's array of musical instruments. Conversation ceased when Peter brought their meals and they ate while enjoying the entertainment. Half an hour later, when the performance ended, Alex sent a bottle of whisky over to the band. This drew a chorus of thanks unintelligible to Emma. It wasn't long before they realized the old gentlemen, each with a tartan shawl thrown over his shoulders and a bonnet on his head, were leaving. Two of the men held crooked walking sticks in knurled hands. Each one touched his forelock in an unexpected, respectful salute as they passed by, but the last man stopped in front of them. Straightening his back, he looked straight at Alex.

"That lassie is a Walters," he said, pointing at Emma with his walking stick, "maybe she's the one, lad!"

Emma's eyes danced with surprise and then amusement as she watched the man salute and then hobble away. She was hardly able to wait for the door to close before pouncing on her companion.

"How did he know I was a Walters and what did he mean I might be the one?"

"Easy now," Alex whispered. "I don't think we want to get into all this here Emma ... too late, here comes Peter!"

"Are you an American?" Peter asked, too eager for Alex's comfort.

"Hell no, I'm a Canadian from Victoria, British Columbia."

"I heard Duffy say you were a Walters, are you related to Trevelion Walters of Traymore?"

"He was mistaken, Peter," Alex interjected in as calm a voice as he could muster, pulling out his wallet and handing over his credit card.

"Why would he say something like that?" Emma asked Alex before turning to face Peter. "What did Duffy mean by saying, maybe I was the one?"

"They say old Duffy is psychic. Have you met him before?"

"No, I've only just arrived in Scotland. What was he talking about?" she murmured, wishing Peter would go away.

"He was probably referring to the Wallace prophecy," Alex suggested trying to look thoughtful and scratching his beard for effect. The prophecy says the Wallace relics were hidden by a woman and a woman would find them."

"I don't understand," Emma snapped. "I'm not a Wallace!"

Alex had played this charade long enough and stood up. "We'll be getting along now ... Peter, settle our account, lad!" He reached for

Emma's coat and Peter finally left them, albeit with a puzzled expression.

Emma's annoyance was obvious and he thought he would likely face an angry barrage but it was pouring rain and they drove away in silence. It was almost seven o'clock when they pulled into the yard of a large stone building. Dim lights glowed in many windows and rows of vehicles in the car park were evidence that something was going on inside. He pulled up in front of a door marked 'Office' situated under a large awning and turned off the engine.

"Is this the woolen mill?" she asked tiredly. When he didn't respond quick enough, she continued, "Talk to me; is there a shift working at night?"

"Sorry, I was in another century," he replied. "We're at the Highland Tartan Factory, where genuine Scottish tartans are designed and woven. Your ancestor, Jacob Walters, was instrumental for its rebuilding in 1810. The manager today is Alfred Holt, a Yorkshire man, and one of the world's leading tartan designers. Yes, there is no doubt a shift working tonight." He got out and came around to open her door. "Come on, you'll be glad to know this is our last stop tonight!" He abruptly left her to stride off towards the office door. Emma smiled and hurried to catch up.

The low hum of machinery became instantly evident as they stepped into the sparsely furnished reception area. A sign prominently displayed on the counter said, *Ring for Service* with an arrow pointing to a button. Within moments of pressing it, a middle-aged man arrived, smiling as he pushed his spectacles onto his nose and greeted Alex. Before Alex had a chance to introduce them, he turned to Emma.

"You must be Professor Emma Walters from Canada," he exclaimed. "Forgive us, Miss Walters," he chuckled, "we have a very good bush telegraph in the Highlands. Actually, both Douglas and Ruth called after you left them! I'm Alfred."

"Could I have my hand back please, Alfred?" Emma whispered. Trying to gently release his grip, she found herself gazing into the bluest, most penetrating eyes she had ever seen.

"Not yet, my dear," he whispered back, tucking her hand under his arm and patting it. He then led them back through the same door from which he had come. Now standing in a small office, she realized this room was partitioned off from the main work area by glass panels allowing full view of the work area beyond. Sitting at a desk, a young man was intently studying some paperwork; he acknowledged them with a slight wave before switching his attention to a ringing phone.

"This is our finished product room," said Alfred, gesturing proudly. "Nothing less than perfect leaves our factory."

"Are you always so modest, Mr. Holt?" Emma taunted, but she deftly managed to remove her hand from his arm and move away. Getting a better view of the large room, she was amazed to see so many tables of workers still busy at this late hour. "Will they work all night?"

"No, but sometimes when we have a large order, it's not unusual for us to employ two shifts," Alfred explained. He took them on a tour and presented Emma with a scarf in the Walters' tartan of blues, greens and a bit of red. Returning to the reception area, she noticed a rack of clothes.

"Do you sew these tartans into clothes?" Emma asked.

"One of our staff is a seamstress who does beautiful custom work. She's here tonight. Would you like to speak to her?"

Emma looked at Alex and he merely shrugged. "Yes, please."

"Wonderful, give me a moment," Alfred whispered, going to talk to the young man at the phone.

He returned in a minute and a woman of about Emma's age arrived soon after. She was introduced as Helen and immediately took Emma aside so they could speak privately. After a short, pleasant discussion, Helen took her measurements and said she would see that the skirt was delivered to her hotel by the end of the week.

As they left, Emma thanked Alfred for connecting her with Helen; he seemed almost too eager to accept her handshake.

"I'll look forward to seeing you again, Miss Walters," he said quietly. Emma shivered as their eyes met.

The rain had finally stopped and Alex soon had them back on the motorway. "You seemed quite taken by Freddy," he chuckled. "He's single, but I should warn you, all that man thinks about is the mill!"

"And what's wrong with that, may I ask?" Emma replied, somewhat sharply. "I thought he was a very intelligent man and quite attractive!"

Alex chuckled to himself in the dark. When they reached the hotel, he parked and went inside with her.

"I'll meet you at eight o'clock in the morning. I trust you enjoyed your tour today Emma, goodnight." He stifled a yawn and went straight outside without waiting for her reply, but he was not quite ready to go home. He couldn't get the sword off his mind and he didn't like it sitting in his boot. Before starting the engine, he called John Dunstan and made arrangements to drop it over at his office by eight o'clock the next morning.

## Chapter 3 – Tuesday 14<sup>th</sup> - Dorik Island

Groaning, she grabbed the ringing phone, thinking that she was at home in Victoria until she saw the display. "What the hell do you want?" she asked, trying to get her bearings.

"I trust you're awake?" Alex's voice purred into her ear. "Before you curse again, remember you're almost a Lady now! I'm running late this morning and I thought you might appreciate an extra 20 minutes!"

She began to say something but realized he had hung up. Now totally awake, she got up anyway. She left the room an hour later and found him at their table.

"May I join you, sir?" she whispered seductively into his ear.

"Only for a moment," he replied smugly. "I'm waiting for a dear, sweet lady to join me."

"Yes, you heathen and that dear, sweet lady will strangle you if you wake her like that again! I have news for you … from now on, I will use my own alarm clock and if we don't arrange a time, I just may sleep in until nine! So we have another adventure today, do we?"

"Will you forgive me if I tell you I've been to John's office to deliver the sword?" he asked, pouting at her. Without waiting for her reply, he continued. "You've wanted to see Dorik Island, so that's where we're going today. Let's order and I'll tell you about it."

"For once, you're not being evasive? Now I am suspicious!"

After they ordered, she cocked an eyebrow at him. "I'm waiting!"

Thinking about what he should divulge about this trip, he briefly explained where they were going and particularly mentioned that she would find it more relaxing than yesterday. He steered her into a conversation about the previous day's outing and breakfast soon arrived. Within the hour they were in the car and on their way.

"It's almost a two hour drive to the coast and the scenery will be quite different than what you've seen up to now," he informed her. "We're going to a little seaside village where we will meet our transportation." Fortunately, she was looking outside and didn't notice his smug grin.

Leaving the city on the A1 southbound, Emma watched with fascinated curiosity and realized he was right about the different landscape … one that was mainly flat. Alex jabbered away about the history of the area stating that to their left and closer to the Firth of Forth was an interesting hill which was part of a dormant volcano. "All that's left is a 600-foot bump that was the volcano's plug. Scientists say it's been there since before the Ice Age even surviving the glaciers. It's called North Berwick Law, probably named by the Lowland Scots as law is their word for a conical hill. Amazingly, they've found out that it was once a fort during the Iron Age and, more recently, was used as a lookout during both the Napoleonic and World War II."

"That's not very recent!" Emma commented. "I enjoy the new TV shows where archeologists study old rocks and find hidden cities under oceans and layers of dirt. It's all quite fascinating."

Alex commented on the dry roads, but dark clouds sweeping in from the English Channel did concern him. With some visitors coming for dinner, they might have a challenging trip to Dorik. "The coastline should be coming into view any time now," he announced, pointing out the front window as they passed the sign to Dunbar. Emma turned to look and, leaning back in her seat, caught her first glimpses of water.

"I do love the ocean," she murmured.

"Many of the villages along this coast are quite small, but each has its own individual character. They're fascinating places to visit if …."

"If I accept my inheritance," she finished for him. As more ocean came into view, she smiled and added, "How nice that the weather is co-operating so far; I do hope those dark clouds stay away."

Alex turned off the motorway onto a country road where farmland seemed to zip past on both sides of the car. Sea glimpses had turned into views of the North Sea which appeared and disappeared behind the low hills. The road twisted through a rocky area and, after a few tight bends, at last they reached the coast and Emma got her first view of the harbour below. A small sandy beach bordered by a narrow, cobble-stoned street, still wet from a morning shower, ran along the harbourside. White painted cottages were scattered about on a rocky hillside. The enclosed harbour contained a mixture of boats, fishing boats being the most common.

Emma gasped. "Lovely! It's like a postcard from another time!"

Slowing the car and pulling off the road, Alex reached under his seat, extracting a pair of high-powered binoculars. He handed them to her and pointed to a green mass of foliage that literally burst out of the sea a mile or two offshore. "Dorik," he announced, almost reverently.

Focusing the binoculars, Emma asked, "Which one is our boat?"

"It hasn't arrived yet," he replied, still looking at the island.

Driving down the steep incline into the village, Alex drove up to a small warehouse-type building that appeared to have several garage doors. Using a remote, he opened one of them and drove inside, explaining that Trev had these built so their parked cars weren't a temptation to anyone. An interior light went on and, after retrieving their suitcases and coats, he locked the car and they went outside. After locking the garage, he took her over to the village's only tavern. She followed him through the gathering of stern-faced fishermen, many of whom greeted him with such heavy accents their comments were totally incomprehensible to her. The barman helped them find a seat at a tiny corner table. After discussing what they would drink before going on the boat ride, Alex ordered a coffee and a glass of water for Emma.

"How old is this place?" she asked, frowning when she noticed that most of the men were smoking. Already there was a heavy grey cloud hanging above them and she soon understood why the blackened beams looked eerily like trees damaged in a fire. Then she spotted the large fireplace set into a wall that seemed to bend in many odd directions.

"They say it was built in 1250." Alex chuckled at her expression.

"I suppose you're going to tell me the toilets are out in the yard."

"You're very perceptive!" the big Scot murmured with a serious blank stare that left Emma not quite sure of anything.

When the barman brought their drinks, he also informed them in an unrecognizable language that their taxi was waiting.

"Drink up and we'll be off," Alex announced, grinning at the look of confusion on her face.

Minutes later, they went outside and, there parked in front of the door, was the most remarkable vehicle Emma had ever seen. She stopped and stared. It was painted a bright red, but it reminded her of the amphibious tank-like vehicles she had seen at a military display many years before. They were used by the army to move troops and vehicles from ship to shore, but this was somehow different. The top and windows were made of plexiglass and inside were three rows of luxury seating.

"Is this mine too?" she asked with a hint of excitement in her voice.

"It will be," Alex grinned, "if …!"

"Are we ready, sir?" a voice, with an unusual accent, interrupted.

Emma turned to see a short, bow-legged man wobbling from side to side as he came towards them flashing a wide grin.

"Yes, we are. Abe, meet Miss Walters. Let's get over there, shall we?"

Emma's eyes widened as the roof of the vehicle suddenly lifted and Alex opened an almost-hidden door so they could climb in. Abe got into the driver's seat, turned on the engine and called out, "Watch yer 'ead!" grinning mischievously over his shoulder at Emma. As the roof settled back down, the vehicle began to move down the hill, going across the road and onto a wide pathway. They followed the path across the lower part of the hill and along the side of the harbour, until they splashed into the water. Emma screamed, quickly covering her mouth with her hand, as the seawater and the engine combined to make a loud crashing sound, but the vehicle settled nicely and they surged forward. It took no time at all to leave the harbour and Abe now aimed directly for Dorik Island.

After a few minutes, Emma was afraid she was going to be seasick and closed her eyes briefly, but the feeling kept returning. She tried to take her mind off the movement by imagining what the island was like beyond the towering cliffs. The further they got from shore, the higher the waves became and she held onto her seat for dear life. After about 15 minutes, it became apparent that the cliffs protected the island from the ravages of the sea and beyond them stood a substantial forest of evergreens which were now bending in the wind.

"It's much like the West Coast of Vancouver Island, don't you think?" Alex shouted above the noise.

"Yes, somewhat, but how do you know?" Emma called back.

"I've been doing my homework!" he laughed.

Keeping an eye on the scene in front of them, Abe now turned southwards and followed the contour of the island staying on the westward and more protected side. Landing looked quite impossible to Emma, seeing neither a beach nor a ramp.

"There's where we're going," Alex shouted, solving her dilemma when he pointed to a break in the cliff face. The vehicle turned towards a narrow opening and soon they were rising out of the sea. Emma gasped, grabbing his arm.

"We're in shallow water now," he assured her. "Almost there!"

She could see a narrow strip of pebbly beach which they drove up and over, before setting onto solid ground. In front of them was a solid rock wall but somehow Abe had them safely through it and onto a rough track. Turning sharply to the left, they were now hidden from the sea. This provided an easier route that crossed a level grassy area. Through the front windows she could see the tall evergreen trees beyond.

"Sneaky," Emma exclaimed, holding her stomach again. Looking upwards, she watched as the trees lining the clifftop swayed wildly, warning of the impending storm. Her eyes clouded as she observed the craggy cliffs and, as her body shivered involuntarily, she couldn't help but wonder why she'd had such an odd reaction.

Bumping over uneven ground brought her back to reality as they entered the dark forest of evergreens. Emma saw daylight ahead and the vehicle moved straight towards that opening. She gasped with surprise as they left the trees and stopped, looking over a beautiful valley. The land rolled gently out before them like a lush green carpet.

"Is this real or am I dreaming?" she asked with such a look of wonder that Alex had to chuckle. He had seen this reaction many times, but this time made him the happiest. He opened the door and she almost tumbled out of the vehicle in her eagerness to get a better view. She asked Alex if he had his binoculars and he smugly took them from his pocket and handed them to her. Sweeping them across the valley from north to south, she swore under her breath. "There's a magnificent house over there!" she whispered.

"Traymore," Alex replied, the name catching in his throat as he realized the effect it was having on her. "That's Traymore House, lass, and tonight you'll learn some of its story."

Lowering the glasses, Emma turned to face her companion. Many questions raced through her mind and yet she was speechless. A strange gentle peace seemed to envelop her body as she stood watching highland cattle and sheep graze contentedly together in one of the stone-walled paddocks. She shook her head slightly telling herself she needed to think realistically, and then reminded herself she only had two more days to make up her mind before this could all be hers. *What an unimagineable situation*, she thought, handing the binoculars back to Alex and returning to their vehicle. Alex helped her get settled, closed the door, and then tapped on Abe's shoulder.

Turning back into the trees, Abe now followed a well-marked track; occasional glimpses of the valley were seen as he bounced the ungainly water taxi along the hillside. They left the forest behind and descended to the valley driving along the edge of a small lake before arriving at a group of buildings that comprised a barn and stable block. A hard, gravel road followed the contour of the lake going past white-railed paddocks with horses that inquisitively raised their heads. On past the farm's working yards they went until the manor house loomed before them.

"So this is Traymore House," Emma whispered in awe.

"The front door, please Abe," Alex murmured.

"It's wonderful, Alex," Emma exclaimed as she studied the large greystone manor house with three round turrets and many embellishments she had already noticed on other grand Scottish homes including Misty House. There was a more modern three-storey addition attached to the main house at the rear which, although builders had done a remarkable job of matching the designs, something gave it away. She wondered if it was the staff quarters. Turning her attention to the front of the house, Abe now stopped. Alex got out first, offering his hand. She found herself standing beside, what she could imagine to be a magnificent terraced garden which ran along the front and side of the manor house. She recognized heather and several rhododendrum bushes of various sizes, imagining the colours they might display in springtime. A wide expanse of three stone stairs cut from the manor's foundation led majestically to the grand front entrance. Her gaze fell on the most unique and splendid front door she had ever seen, framed by narrow, multi-coloured, stained-glass pieces depicting Scottish and Dorik Island scenes.

Alex ran up the stairs, spread his arms wide and, pulling off his cap, tossed it high into the air. "Welcome to Traymore, Emma!" he bellowed. As his voice echoed across the valley, she remained transfixed trying to take it all in.

"Thank you … did Trev live here, Alex?" she asked, now eager to see what the inside of the house was like.

"Be patient, lass, you'll be meeting some of our family tonight and all will be revealed. They can explain it much better than I, but yes, Trev did spend a lot of time here." He returned to her side. "We'll get some lunch now and you can just enjoy and explore."

"Oh no, you don't!" she said nervously. "You're going to be with me every step of the way." Seeing his understanding smile, she added coyly, "That is your job, isn't it?"

"As you wish," he acknowledged, although she thought he might be humouring her as he reached for her hand which he tucked under his arm before they mounted the stairs.

Suddenly, the great door opened and before her stood a tall, kilted gentleman, who so closely resembled Alex, she wondered if he was also a Wallace.

"Welcome to Traymore, Miss Walters," he said with a warm, genuine smile, standing back to allow them to enter. "Refreshments are served in the library. May I take your coats?"

*He even sounds just like Alex!* she thought.

Relieved of their outerwear, Alex took her arm again and they moved into a large foyer where a magnificent dark-stained staircase rose along one wall going almost to the top before it turned to meet the second storey. Two high windows on the same wall let plenty of natural light into the room even on this November day. A handsome chandelier with antique-styling hung from the middle of the ceiling. *So masculine*, Emma thought, frowning as her eyes danced from side to side, taking in a number of large, heavy-framed portraits hanging on the walls. Each of the portraits showed a kilted man, some wearing a blue/green/red tartan and others a blue/green/yellow tartan.

"Are these my ancestors?" she asked, but he seemed intent on guiding her towards an open doorway. "Alex," she insisted, not moving, "is Trev one of these men?"

"What … oh, yes," he replied, coming back to her. "This is Trevelion; these are all Walters' Clan Chiefs." He was pointing to the picture of a very good-looking man hanging near the base of the stairs.

"I'm in awe; I'll just have to come back and visit my ancestors later!"

Following him now, he beckoned for her to enter the room with the open door and she realized she was looking at the largest private library she had ever seen. Ten-foot-high bookcases filled with thousands of books lined two complete walls of this room. She noticed that some of the books had covers which were frayed from use and she knew she would have to investigate. She instantly appreciated the room's casual splendour, even though she felt it could use a woman's touch.

Two round tables flanked by a number of high-backed chairs, filled a corner and a large bay window looked out onto the terraced garden; other, more comfortable-looking easy chairs, littered the room. A huge, antique sideboard held a warming tray with a steaming jug of coffee and another with hot water. Nearby were other luncheon items, including a crystal cream and sugar set, a crystal dish with a selection of teas, a plate of sandwiches and a multi-tier stand with a tempting selection of biscuits and cakes.

She realized she was indeed ready for something to drink and, choosing one of the beautiful china cups, was about to reach for the coffee pot, when Alex came up beside her.

"Allow me," he beamed, pouring for both of them. "Shall we partake of a little extra special refreshment? Help yourself to some lunch."

"They forgot your whisky!" she declared.

"No, they didn't," he chuckled. "Come watch this."

She followed him over to a corner of the bookshelves where he must have touched something because instantly the whole section of shelf began to move.

"Very nice!" she proclaimed as a fully-stocked bar moved into view.

"A wee dram for your coffee, marm?" he asked mischievously. Selecting a bottle of Scotch whisky and hiding the bar again, Alex took the bottle over to the sideboard.

"The staff is very good about leaving a selection of food out for snacks," he explained, "and they will serve a regular meal any time you wish. They were mainly hired by Trev so it has been very sad and quiet since he went away. They're grateful to have visitors."

"Speaking of staff, that man who answered the door, I assume was the butler?" Watching him nod, she continued, "Is he related to you? The resemblance is uncanny!"

"No, he is not a relation of mine but Neville is a very nice person whom you can approach at any time. His family has been in service forever!" He cleared his throat and continued. "If you need anything, just pull that tasselled chord by the door." He went over to the door to show her. "You'll find one of these in most of the rooms. They were added when the house was enlarged and updated in the early 1900s."

"So, Trev did live here," she murmured softly, selecting a few sandwiches and putting them on her plate. She noticed the 'T' that was exquisitely embroidered by hand in gold thread on the white linen napkins. She rubbed her finger lightly over the monogram before placing the napkin under her plate. As Alex selected his sandwiches, he watched her splash a little whisky in her drink before going over to one of the comfortable upholstered chairs and sitting down. Holding her cup in both hands, she took a sip and leaned back contentedly. Closing her eyes, she began to review in her mind everything that had happened in the two days since arriving in Scotland.

"Don't go to sleep now," Alex warned, breaking into her thoughts as he sat down in his favourite leather chair.

"I won't," she chuckled lightly, "but I must admit, this trip keeps making me think I'm living in a dream. I don't want to wake up and find myself back in Victoria!"

"Trust me Emma; you are certainly not in a dream! We'll finish eating and then you can relax or do some exploring if you like. Dinner will be at seven o'clock and our guests will arrive sometime around six."

"What?" Emma came upright in her chair. "That means we'll be staying here overnight? That's not possible Alex; everything I need is back at the hotel."

"After we eat, I'll show you your room. Everything you need is waiting for you there."

"You had my things brought here?" she snapped angrily. "You had no right!"

"Stop," Alex ordered gently, "no one has touched your belongings."

"Then show me to my room!" she insisted.

Shrugging, Alex put his plate down and headed for the door, grinning when he heard her hurrying footsteps behind him. They went out to the foyer and up the grand staircase to the second floor. She followed him along the hallway until he stopped at the first door. Almost instantly, the door opened and a young maid came out, curtseying apologetically.

"I have laid out your evening clothes, marm," she said timidly before curtseying again and hurrying away.

"My evening clothes?" Emma repeated, pushing the door open. Instantly attracting her attention was a beautiful plaid dress on a dressing stand and a selection of lingerie and sweaters laid out neatly on the four-poster bed. Turning around, she looked at Alex who had hung back in the hallway, excused herself, and shut the door. The beautiful, full-length evening dress reminded her of last night's visit to the tartan factory. *This is the same tartan as the scarf Alfred gave me last night.* She grasped the hem of the dress and held it against her cheek, appreciating its softness and realizing the size seemed to be right. She then noticed a new pair of black shoes and sat down on the bedside chair to try them on. They were a perfect fit! *How could they know my sizes? Who did this shopping?* She cleared off the bed, putting the clothes in a drawer and went to see if Alex was still waiting. He was and she asked him to come in.

"Why are you doing …?" she began emotionally, but the sound of a motor vehicle caused them both to go to the window.

"It's Abe, probably bringing some last-minute groceries for tonight," he murmured, not having heard her question. "I hope you like the clothes and don't mind the effort we have gone to acquiring them without your permission. I promise no more surprises like that. I have to leave for awhile, but you're free to go anywhere you wish in the house or outside. Here," he said, handing her a little black remote-like device. She turned it over and saw a single button on one side. She was confused and looked up at him. "If you need me, just press the button and stay where you are. I'll be able to find you. Remember the bell cord if you need anything and one of the maids will come to help you. Don't forget lunch is still in the library, which, incidentally, has an excellent selection of books. The guests will be arriving around six o'clock."

"Alex, what exactly is going to happen tonight? Who are these people coming for dinner?"

"I'm sorry Emma. I don't know why I haven't been more forthcoming with you. I suppose I didn't want you to worry. There has been so much for you to take in, but now I see that my silence is having the opposite effect. There are two couples coming tonight: Bruce MacKray and his wife Jennie and George MacDuff and his wife Alfreda. They are descendants of the Wallace family and George is actually related to both families. They're lovely people, all very friendly and easy-going. I'm pretty sure you will feel comfortable with them. Rest assured they are coming to show their support and you can ask them any questions you like."

Alex smiled reassuringly, but seeing her expression, he continued. "Yes, they are aware of who you are and, of course, want you to make the right decision, for yourself, for the family and for everyone involved in the estate's various enterprises. They are looking forward to meeting you and hope they can make you feel more comfortable about the whole situation. Our families are good people, Emma. We also want you to learn more about the family history so Alfreda, who is a history professor, will fill in any of that subject you wish to learn about."

"Sounds like an ambush to me," she declared, "but I do appreciate how important this is to everyone, and to me. Thank you Alex."

"Now, please try to relax and rest; I need to go. I'll come for you after the guests arrive and you should be able to hear Phibbie outside ... that's what the staff calls the amphibious vehicle. If you could be ready by six o'clock, we'll meet everyone for cocktails in the sitting room and have dinner at seven. Try not to worry about anything, just relax and enjoy the evening." He took her hand and raised it to his lips, kissing it lightly before leaving the room. She could hear his footsteps hurrying down the stairs.

Emma turned back to the window. Her stomach was churning and her heart felt like it was a big lump in her throat. So much to think about, but something ... a feeling from within seemed to be screaming a warning. She pulled a chair over to the window and sat down. Something significant was about to happen at Traymore House, she could sense it. Unseen, behind a veil of curtains, she watched as Alex and another man unloaded boxes from Phibbie and then Abe drove it away.

A light knock sounded at the door and she went to see who it was. It was the maid she had met before. The girl asked if she would like her to bring the refreshments up from the library. Emma thanked her and assured her she would go down to the library to eat.

"Marm, Sarah will be along at five o'clock to help you dress and do your hair. She also has a supply of make-up and will be happy to help you in any way she can."

"Thank you, that would be most helpful … we haven't been introduced as you dashed away!"

"I'm Jayne. I'm new on the staff this week so please excuse me as I learn their ways," she explained, with a charming confidence.

"You're doing just fine Jayne. I'm new to this as well so we'll learn together, shall we?" she sighed. "I assume I'm to put on this lovely tartan dress for dinner?" Emma hoped she didn't appear to be as uncomfortable as she felt.

"Oh yes marm, you will look wonderful. I should let you go down and eat, can you find your way back to the library?"

"I believe I can and if I do get lost, Sir Alex explained the bell system. Are you here until I go for dinner Jayne?"

"Yes marm, we all live in the other wing of the house when we're on shift. I will be available any time you need me, just pull the cord!" She curtsied and closed the door quietly behind her.

Darkness had fallen over the valley when Emma decided she had better get ready for dinner. Having had an enjoyable time eating her lunch while curled up with a book on Scottish history, she now returned to her room. She was about to get dressed when the faint sound of bagpipes brushed the evening air and she went over to the window. It was dark already but she could still faintly hear the eerie wail even though it seemed to be some distance away. Looking up at the starless sky, she shivered with anticipation as she thought of the evening ahead.

As she began to dress, she murmured her appreciation at the extravagant selection of lingerie, and then blushed as she thought of someone investigating her sizes. She slipped her robe back on and poured herself a coffee. A smile crinkled her mouth when she looked at the small bottle of whisky on the tray and, although she did not touch it, she knew that Alex had talked to someone about her newly acquired alcoholic preference.

A knock sounded on the door and, expecting Sarah, she called for her to come in. The door opened and a young woman in her early 30s, pushing a trolley, poked her head inside.

"Hello marm, I'm Sarah. I believe you are expecting me!"

"Yes I am, come in Sarah," Emma called, resigned to enjoy the unfamiliar ritual of having someone help her dress.

"Sir Alex told me he will come for you around six o'clock, when your guests are expected to arrive."

"That means they will be travelling in the dark. I suppose they will have lights but it would be unnerving to me ...." Emma's voice trailed off as she envisioned a dark trip across the water.

"They'll be just fine marm. We prefer to travel in the daylight but Abe is well-experienced with Phibbie no matter the time or weather. No need to worry at all." Now let's get your nails done so they can dry."

As Sarah began, Emma found her to be gentle and efficient and she was soon enjoying the pampering of another manicure. She remembered that very occasionally, back in Victoria, she would treat herself by going to a spa, later cursing herself for being so extravagant. Now, here she was on an island off the Scottish coast being pampered by a maid who was a wonderful manicurist, snipping nails and gently massaging her hands before applying a red polish that matched her dress. Next was the hairdo, and Emma was surprised when Sarah asked if she would like a braid.

"You would look wonderful with your hair plaited marm! This was the height of fashion many years ago and it's becoming popular again."

"But surely my hair is too short for a braid?"

"Not at all, there is so much we can do now with hair extensions."

Consenting with a nod and closing her eyes, Emma felt Sarah's skilled hands weaving and twisting her hair until she was most eager to see the result. When Sarah handed her a mirror, Emma was astonished, obviously pleasing the girl. Next Sarah applied her make-up and Emma was ready to get dressed. Sarah left a few minutes before six, assuring Emma she was going to wow them all! Emma went into the bathroom to admire herself in the large mirror, using the hand mirror Sarah had left for her. *She's added a sort-of braided headband that encircles my head ... like a crown*, she thought. *I like it!*

Punctually at six o'clock, Alex arrived, hardly recognizable in his full-clan finery ... the Wallace kilt of mainly red, with gold and dark green stripes, a black Prince Charlie jacket and a vest adorned with silver buttons; a bow tie and knee-length black kilt hose with a small knife, he said was called a *sgian-dubh*, which was tucked into the top of the hose. A decorated sporran hanging from a silver chain around his waist and a white tuxedo shirt completed the picture. *He looks rather magnificent,* thought Emma. *A picture perfect Scot I'd say!* She suddenly felt her cheeks flush.

Standing rigidly to attention in the doorway, he announced in a very serious voice, "Robert William Alexander Wallace at your service, marm, please allow me to present you with a gift … several actually!" At that moment, she realized her bailiff was unusually excited about something and she watched him curiously. From his sporran, he produced a leather pouch, but suddenly realizing he had forgotten something, he stopped and simply gazed at her, his grin disappearing as his face went instantly beetroot red.

"Forgive me, Emma," he began, looking awkward for the first time since they had met. "I should have told you how lovely you look tonight. Your dress, your hair, everything, you look simply marvellous!" He looked down at his hand and realized he was still holding the pouch which he now unfolded. He opened it and emptied the contents into his hand. Emma stared at the items … an exquisite gold broach, a gold crested ring and a key.

"This ring is a wedding band signifying that you are wedded to Scotland …," Alex began, choosing the gold ring, and Emma watched as his face was transformed with such a concentrated expression of sincerity, tears came to her eyes. She shook her head in an effort to clear her emotions and tried to concentrate on what he was saying. "… and the crest is the Walters' family crest," he continued. Then he shocked her by descending onto one knee in front of her. She watched as if she were in a dream as he placed the ring on the third finger of her left hand and stood up again. "This broach is your clan identification as chief and the one mentioned in your list of *Conditions*. This key is the key to all the hearts in Scotland. Keep it near you at all times." He cleared his throat.

"But, Alex, I'm not officially …," she began, but he shushed her and pinned the broach on her dress.

"If the undecided Lady Traymore wishes to change her mind tomorrow, she can return these items and I hereby promise that no argument will be given," he solemnly stated, but she couldn't help but detect the emotion in his voice.

Finding it difficult to control her own rising emotions, she whispered "thank-you" and wiped away a tear with her finger then, taking the key from Alex, she placed it in her pocket as the overpowering urge to leave this room washed over her. Curtseying playfully, she gave him a brave smile and took his arm steering him towards the door. She could hear his sigh as he closed the door behind them. Walking together along the hallway, she suddenly realized she was now nervous of the evening's unknown proceedings. Suddenly, the skirl of the bagpipes in the foyer below beckoned, and they were piped down the stairs and into the sitting room. She was barely aware of the added tables dressed up for the occasion with Traymore-monogrammed silverware, glassware and Walters' tartan napkins. As the last notes of the bagpipes faded away, she realized the clapping had stopped and she and Alex were standing in front of two couples dressed in full-length tartan dresses and kilts which matched Alex's Wallace tartan.

"May I introduce Miss Emma Walters, the woman I anticipate will become the first Lady of Traymore and hereditary chief of the Walters' Clan," Alex announced. He introduced Bruce and Jennie MacKray and George and Alfreda MacDuff and, after greetings and hand shaking, the men welcomed Emma on behalf of their families. Standing well over six-feet-tall, Bruce MacKray was a powerful example of Scottish manhood, magnificent in clan regalia and with a deep brogue that rolled elegantly off his tongue. When it was George's turn, standing as tall as his short, stout stature would allow, he tried very hard to look serious as he smiled at Emma. He was a man with a lively sense of humour, who often poked fun at his own habit of overeating, and also at some little-known shortcomings of his friends. Tonight was different, however, because Alfreda had given him explicit instructions to behave himself.

Emma felt instantly comfortable with them all but especially with Jennie who had a lively sense of humour. By the time the meal arrived, they were all seated and eager to see what was on the menu. Formalities softened as Alfreda took charge of the conversation and as they ate, they all questioned Emma about Canada. Being especially interested in Vancouver Island, Bruce added his own personal knowledge as a naval captain who had visited the area on two occasions. By the time they finished, a comfortable friendliness had permeated the room.

At this point, Alex suggested they should retire to more comfortable seating around the fire reminding them of the selection of beverages on the sideboard. When everyone was settled, he raised the topic for the evening. "I have told Emma that you would all help her to understand how the combined history of the Wallace and Walters' families changed the course of history in Scotland 700 years ago. She is most eager to learn about her history and so, Alfreda, I invite you to begin."

## Chapter 4 – Tuesday Evening – Story of a Family

"Are you familiar with the story of William Wallace, Emma?" Alfreda asked, looking directly at her.

"Only slightly, I know he was a Scottish hero. Alex is educating me!" she proclaimed, hoping to hide her embarrassment.

Professor MacDuff smiled patiently at the Canadian being quite aware that her telling of this story was required to be so compelling it would persuade Emma to accept her inheritance.

"Well, it all began in 1286, over 700 years ago. This was the year Alexander III of Scotland died in an unfortunate accident. When his young granddaughter, his only heir, died on her way from Norway to claim her crown, a succession crisis was created and Scotland fell into a state of turmoil. Adding to this were 14 contenders who came forward with their claims to the Scottish Crown. The two main contenders were Robert Bruce 'the Competitor,' 5th Lord Annandale and grandfather of the Robert the Bruce we all know as Robert I, in the South; and John Balliol, the son of John, 5th Baron de Balliol, of the Comyn Family, and his wife Devorgilla, daughter of Alan, Lord of Galloway, in the North.

"When the nobles and guardians could not agree to a king, it appeared that civil war would erupt. Here, I must pause to explain that there was far more going on during this time than I can possibly convey in a few hours. You are well supplied with historical reading material here at Dorik and we trust your thirst for knowledge will increase after tonight!"

"To continue … King Edward of England, even though he was a distant contender, was asked to intervene and assist with their decision. This backfired, of course, only serving to widen the door for Edward who had already proven himself a ruthless warlord and now saw his chance to easily add Scotland to his realm.

"By 1292, Edward had amassed a much superior force, and he crushed the Scottish nobility into submission earning the name *Hammer of the Scots*. He finally agreed to allow John Balliol, to be crowned King of Scotland, but only if he agreed to be subservient to the English Crown. Many of the Scottish barons and nobles were tired of the fighting, having already lost family members and friends to Edward's barbarism. They gave in for the sake of peace and John Balliol was crowned King."

51

"What a mess," Emma murmured, as Alfreda paused to take a drink. "The Wars of Independence had begun. Peace reigned for awhile until the Scots themselves nicknamed King John, *Toom Tabbard,* meaning empty coat or a king without substance. King John rebelled in an attempt to prove himself, but his army was no match for the English and Edward took control of Scotland again.

"Now, the Wallace connection: Little is actually known of William Wallace prior to the Battle of Stirling Bridge. We do know he had an older brother Malcolm and John, the younger. Historians have been split for centuries in their belief of whether his father was Malcolm or Alan and whether he was from Elderslie in Ayrshire or the Elderslie in Renfrewshire. Recently, a letter surfaced giving his father's name as Alan, and other information seems to settle on Renfrewshire as his birthplace, but I'm sure the mystery will be argued about for centuries to come! William's schooling is another bone of contention. There is some agreement that he was probably, at least partly, educated in the church as a youngster and, as a teenager, went to live with one of his uncles who was a cleric. This was the usual vocation of a younger, untitled son. Which church is the question, but the teachings of our early churches often talked about country and freedom, as William will soon be seeking.

"It is thought that by the time he was around 30 years of age, he was a married man with at least two children. He already had a wild reputation with blood on his hands from the many minor, but successful, skirmishes against the English. With a small band of men, he then began fighting a sort of gorilla war escalating his efforts and agitating the enemy even more strongly. It was a bloody and brutal time as they attacked poorly manned English garrisons in Scotland, slaughtering the soldiers.

"He and Andrew Moray, pronounced Murray but spelled M-O-R-A-Y, whose father was from the baronial Moray's of Petty in northeastern Scotland, and his mother, the fourth daughter of John Comyn, gathered separate but enthusiastic armies, and in September 1297, they soundly defeated the English at the Battle of Stirling Bridge. A great number of English knights and nobles were slaughtered or drowned in the ensuing bridge collapse, making Edward even more enraged. "Wallace and Moray were made Guardians of Scotland but Moray had been fatally wounded and died of injuries shortly afterwards. Moray left an unborn son who later married Robert I's sister, Christina Bruce, but I digress. Meanwhile, Wallace's social standing had now been drastically changed causing jealousy among the aristocratic Scottish nobles. They left him with little support as he continued his fight against the English which did not bode well for Wallace's future."

Alfreda stopped to look at her watch.

"Almost a year later, Edward defeated Wallace's smaller, poorly equipped army in a surprise attack at Falkirk. Another bit of history worthy of studying, I might add. Soon afterwards, Wallace resigned as Guardian, in favour of Robert the Bruce. It is believed that Wallace went to France in a futile attempt to enlist King Louis IV's help and, also possibly to Rome, seeking the Pope's aid. The discovery of the "Lubeck Letter" in Germany in the 1970s was quite remarkable. It was a letter authored by Wallace and Moray as Guardians and showing Wallace's seal which said, "William, son of Alan Wallace." It offers possible proof of his father's name and of the fact William went to Europe. At any rate, by 1304, William was back and again leading raids in Scotland. On August 5th, 1305, it is said that he was betrayed by a Scot named Menteith who was a soldier loyal to King Edward. Turned over to the English near Glasgow, he was taken to London for execution on the 23rd of August, 1305." Alfreda reached for her drink and drained it.

"This is where your ancestors come into the story, Emma. In London, William was tried in a trial referred to as a mockery of justice and publicly hanged, drawn and quartered, but that's not where Edward's anger ended. When the English found Wallace's wife Mary, she refused to reveal the whereabouts of their three children, Flora, David and Malcolm, or the location of the royal regalia which William had held for safekeeping. So Edward did the only thing he was capable of, he ordered Mary's execution and a massive search for the children began."

Alfreda paused and bowed her head, viciously twisting her napkin.

"The bastard!" Emma's voice cut through the silence.

"Steady girl, there's more," Alex whispered, and then somewhat louder, he added, "Perhaps this is a good time for a short break. It looks like our dessert has arrived with fresh coffee!" Hearing his words, Jayne, who had knocked lightly and poked her head inside for Alex to notice, now entered pushing a trolley of sweets with fresh coffee.

"Join me for a special coffee, Sir Alex?" Emma asked.

"Me too," Jennie giggled. "I'm so glad to see Alex has got you addicted to his Highland Coffee, Emma!"

Bruce MacKray took advantage of the short break to question Emma about the naval docks in Esquimalt mentioning how much he had enjoyed visiting Victoria. They chatted for about ten minutes and then Alfreda called for attention.

"Time … we still have much to cover. Bring your dessert with you please!" she called. When everyone was seated, she stood up.

"Mary Wallace had known that, not only she, but their children would be hunted by the English if they ever got their hands on William. The story goes that when she received word that her husband had returned to Scotland, she put her plan into action. Dressing Flora in boy's clothes and separating her from her brothers, she spirited the children away to safety with her family. But Mary's worst fears came to fruition two weeks later when she learned of her husband's death. It didn't take long for them to come for her but her arrest had secret witnesses who sent reports of her mistreatment to her family. She kept her secrets right to the end, and when they hanged her from a scaffold in Elderslie, the soldiers loudly threatened the citizens, as a warning to those hiding the Wallace children.

"The children remained near Elderslie for a time but the family were terrified for, not only their lives, but for the children's as well. The boys' protectors feared the English were closing in and the lads were moved to the Augustinian monastery in Elderslie. Flora was moved as well, to other family. Thankfully, Mary had died believing the children were safe, but as often happens under these circumstances, when the boys were on their way south to another location, they were recognized and the English informed. Their escort was killed and the boys were captured and delivered to Edinburgh for public execution." The history professor paused, solemnly bowing her head for a moment. "Someone in power fortunately changed their mind and ordered the boys to be blinded instead … to set a frightening example. Once this terrible deed was done, they were taken out to the Highlands and left to perish. Those poor little lads were only nine and seven years of age. They needed a miracle!"

"Please stop!" Emma gasped. "For heaven's sake, must I know all of this sadness? I'm going to have nightmares … those poor children."

Alfreda looked over at Emma, realized she was quite overcome and wiping her tears, but she carried on. "Yes, you do, Emma," Alfreda somberly declared. "This is your heritage but allow me to continue because you will like the next part."

"Thankfully, the boys did not die!" she declared and Emma looked up in astonishment. "David and Malcolm were obviously strong and smart like their parents, because somehow they survived to tell at least some of the tale. Although suffering terribly and without food or drink, they were fortunate it had not turned unbearably cold and a sheep farmer sympathetic to the family saw them while checking on his mountain shepherds.

"Sending word to the Wallace family, it wasn't long before the boys were back with a much-relieved, but terribly saddened family who now had to help them live with their blindness. During the long, cold winter they continued to improve although they still feared being found. It was believed that a member of the Knights Hospitaller offered medical assistance and, fortunately for that knight who was fighting on the English side, the boys were too traumatized to remember and the family kept their silence.

"When Robert the Bruce came to the throne as Robert I in March of the next year, a cautious atmosphere of peace enveloped the country and more positive events began to occur. Having greatly respected William and his efforts for Scotland, after being told the sordid details of the suffering of Wallace's wife and children, Robert quietly sought to find and protect them. He also returned any confiscated land to their families. The boys went to live with their mother's cousin, Helen, who lived on a little farm called Misty House with her husband, George MacDuff, an ancestor of my George. Yes, it's on the same property as the present Misty House but it was then on the edge of a forest and perfect to help hide the boys. By this time, several additional family members had lost their lives helping the children, but the rest remained steadfastly silent.

"In early 1306, the king rewarded Mary's brother, Duncan Walters, for his service to Scotland by bestowing on him the hereditary title Lord of Traymore. This title included Dorik Island, a pristine and unique property which showed no visible signs of ever having been permanently inhabited. So the two families came together again, combined their talents and resources and built a home which could be added onto as the need arose. It was reported that Flora eventually found some measure of peace there, enjoying a new sense of freedom even though her guardians were ever watchful. The story was later told of how she had spent hours crying her heart out as she walked Dorik's seacliffs, at last able to release all the emotions she had held in for so long. Losing her parents in such a tragic manner and, now not knowing if her brothers were even alive, must have been almost too much to bear for the little girl.

"Let me interject here another piece of our history by going forward a wee bit in time," announced Alfreda. "Years later in 1346, following the Second War of Independence, one of young David's sons would fight alongside Robert I's son, King David II. He received the title of Baronet for his bravery. This is the title Sir Alex holds today." Alfreda paused to give Emma time to assimilate this information.

"So that's how it began," Emma acknowledged, "but please tell me what happened to the children? How did they meet again?"

"When all danger was deemed to be past, Flora at last left Dorik and was reunited with her brothers. She was instrumental in helping them heal mentally, even as she herself was healing. They were so happy to be together again and the boys eventually became more confident and able to more easily cope with their blindness," Alfreda murmured the last sentence with great emotion. "It was soon discovered that Flora had a gift for teaching her brothers. As she got older, word got around and other blind children began arriving at Misty House. So you can see how this was the beginning of what exists today at your wonderful school for the blind. Flora married Helen and George's son, Angus MacDuff, in 1318 raising their children as they continued to live and work at Misty House. To our knowledge, Flora never returned to Dorik Island although Malcolm married and then moved to Dorik to help his uncle with the farm. They would have five children. David lived on the Misty House Estate, helping Flora with their new school and enabling David to meet his future wife. They had a number of children as well. At some point in the future, due to the financial aid given by Lord Traymore over the years, the school was transferred to the ownership of the Traymore Trust.

"Emma," she said softly, pausing until Emma looked up at her, "in the next few days you will make a decision which will not only alter your life, but ours as well. We, as representatives of the family, feel we should inform you that we are very confident you are the person to fulfill the ancient prophecy."

"The one about a woman finding the regalia?" Emma asked, barely in a whisper.

"Yes, that the relics were hidden by a woman and will be returned by a woman," explained Bruce MacKray, jumping in eagerly. "You would become the first female chief of the Walters' Clan. Having descended from a long and ancient line, you are the perfect choice."

"Stories were passed down through the centuries; we all heard them as children," added Jennie. "I am one of your Walters' cousins and family tradition says Mary gave a package to Flora before she said goodbye but no one knows what happened to the package of relics after that. It was deemed hearsay and almost forgotten over the centuries."

"Eminent scholars have searched family and clan records for centuries," George added. "Others searched all the places Flora had lived during her flight and her lifetime but found nothing. Not one single clue has ever surfaced!"

"We desperately need you to be that woman, Emma!" Jennie pleaded.

"Oh Lord!" Emma mumbled, dabbing at tears which had long ago destroyed most of her make-up. "I didn't know there were such high expectations of me! I am honoured that you believe I could fulfill this prophecy, but I wouldn't want to disappoint you."

"We, and many others, are quite willing to help you, Emma," Alex added quietly and the others murmured their agreement. "There are two large journals in the library just down the hallway outside this room. These are the diaries which date from before the year 1300, written by those who searched for the missing regalia even while Wallace was alive, but in Europe. Each new search team has studied it from cover to cover but even the most eminent scholars have been unable to find any valuable clue hidden in its pages. We will look at them tomorrow."

"Forgive us for putting such a heavy responsibility on your shoulders, Emma," said Jennie, "but we have no one else to turn to."

"It's beyond our control," Bruce added, "the truth is, it's now or possibly never!"

"Give me a break; it's been lost for over 700 years!" Emma groaned.

"Aye, but you could more easily fulfill the prophecy because you're a woman!" George exclaimed loudly, drooling in his excitement and wiping his mouth with a napkin.

Alex reached over to touch Emma's hand before she could continue. "Do you remember what Gilbert Stuart said when he read the *Conditions of Acceptance* to you on Friday?"

"Yes, I do, but he did not say anything about blinding children!"

"He said one of the *Conditions* was that you would diligently continue the search." Alex looked at her patiently, and then grinning, he added, "I did briefly explain the relics at the time, although, on reflection, perhaps we should have added a small rider." Emma's expression suddenly changed to an interested frown and everyone turned to watch Alex intently. "We should have told you that the substantial Traymore Estate bank account would be at your disposal!"

At first her mouth dropped open, and then, when she managed to speak, she replied as only Emma could. "You mean I get a big fat bank account too?" she exclaimed, colour rushing to her cheeks. "I assume you held this information back because you didn't trust my motives?"

"Well, not exactly," he replied hesitantly. "Naturally, it was my responsibility as bailiff to ensure the estate was protected and you and I have had a limited amount of time to deal with such a massive amount of information. I felt it would be prudent to introduce you to the estate before speaking of the accounts. I confess, I fully expected you to ask for more detail about the estate's financial situation and when you did not, I became insensitive. Only tonight did I realize my error in judgement. I have some control of the accounts subject to board approval; this system worked well for Trev and it has continued to work well over the past seven years."

"Double talk!" Emma snapped. "I'm disappointed that by now you didn't feel you could trust me, Sir Alex. It's very plain to me and I find it a crock of bull!"

Spontaneous, but cautious laughter suddenly filled the room. Emma looked startled but seeing George's facial contortions made her laugh now and everyone relaxed a bit, although still tentatively watching her.

Jennie plucked up the courage first and asked, almost in a whisper, "What was that you said, Emma? Alex was a cracked bull?"

"Oh that, no!" Emma exclaimed, laughing. "*A crock of bull* is one of our sayings that means you're talking nonsense. I meant it too!" She turned to face Alex. "I will expect you to give me an explanation of the finances tomorrow, and in plain English, sir!"

"Yes, marm," Alex murmured, pretending to appear reprimanded.

"Could we continue now please? What happened to the children, Alfreda?" Emma pleaded.

"Forgive me for interrupting everyone," Bruce McKray interjected, "but I would just like to make a brief comment before we carry on." Seeing Emma smile, he turned to face Alex. "You've been more cautious than you realized Alex, but no doubt rightfully so under the circumstances. I wholeheartedly agree with a comment you made when you invited us here tonight. You said Emma was a fighter and tonight we have witnessed just how correct your assessment of her character has been. In my mind, Emma, you are definitely the right person for the job of keeping this clan together and for finding the missing Royal Regalia. We all hope to make this combined family so desireable to you that you will want to stay!" A resounding 'hear-hear' with cheers and clapping briefly filled the air, causing Emma to blush and then nod gratefully.

"Thank you Bruce for voicing our thoughts so eloquently," announced Alfreda, coming to her feet. "Now, I think we should finish up here; it's getting very late." Alfreda's voice had become happily emotional and the faraway look in her eyes had disappeared.

"So, where do I fit into all of this?" Emma whispered.

"You are a descendant of Duncan Walter's daughter, Mary's niece. Even though yours is a female line, some generations later, a marriage brought the Walters' surname back to you!" Alfreda chuckled. "You have to understand the importance of the commitment made between these two families so long ago. It became an unbroken and rarely discussed loyalty not often seen within any family unit, then or today. We want it to continue!"

"Our family's history is certainly a fascinating one … now tell me how the distillery comes into the story?" Emma asked, looking slightly bewildered.

"The children's uncle, Duncan Walters, initially had it built to provide additional income," Alfreda replied. "Over the centuries it has changed location and even disappeared for awhile during wars and political upheavals. Scotland has had too much of that over the last 700 years. The distillery always managed to be resurrected thanks to one ancestor or another. Many important records have been lost during these dreadful times but modern historians have miraculously been able to piece so much of it back together. Flora's descendants were nearly decimated at one time due to modern wars but, fortunately Trev's family survived and it was due to his efforts that your family was discovered. He was overjoyed when you were discovered alive! A few years before, he had been mortified to learn that he had no male heir as WWII had claimed the last three of his male cousins. He blamed himself for not making an effort to marry and have a family. It was shortly after that he received his devastating health news."

Emma, feeling suddenly lightheaded, covered her face with her hands, her mind in an uproar.

"Are you all right, Emma?" Alex's concerned and loud comment brought her back to the present.

Taking a deep breath, she gasped and nodded, looking over at him, her face grey and blotchy. In a weak and hesitant voice, she asked, "So I truly am the only one who can save this title?" Tears welled in her eyes and she knew she had to get out of the room. "P-please excuse me!" She hiked up her dress and ran to the door, fumbling with the handle.

In two strides Alex was beside her, his hand lightly on her arm as he opened the door and they went out into the hallway. He took her into the adjoining room and they sat down on a sofa in front of the fire.

"Do you wish to talk about it?" he asked gently.

She shook her head, still breathing heavily. He again laid his hand reassuringly over hers as she sat looking into the fire. Alex had a good idea what was going through her head but he knew she had to work it out herself. He had not been surprised with her reaction and he was actually relieved. It indicated how much she cared and that made him hopeful. Almost 15 minutes passed before Emma stood up and moved closer to the fire. "You knew Alfreda's telling of the story would do this to me, didn't you, you rotter! I guess I had it coming; I needed to hear it from someone else." She smiled ruefully, squared her shoulders and excused herself. "I'll meet you back in the other room shortly."

When Emma rejoined them, she looked surprisingly radiant with new paint, as Alex would say. He poured her a glass of wine and offered her a plate containing an assortment of refreshments. All chatter ceased and everyone made their way back to their seats.

"Who built the tartan factory?" Emma asked, now totally in control.

"The factory was a joint effort of almost every clan in Scotland who provided money or labour, sometimes both," Alex explained with a touch of sadness in his voice. "They said it was their penance on behalf of their ancestors who had not gone to William's aid when he needed them. It was closed numerous times due to local strife but always reopened. Remember I told you about your ancestor, Jacob Walters. He was instrumental for its rebuilding in 1810."

Emma had more questions and it was almost one a.m. before everyone was content with the outcome of the meeting. Jennie stood up and announced it had been a long enough day for her and she would see them all at breakfast. She went over to Emma and gave her a hug.

"Breakfast will be in this room beginning at seven o'clock," Alex announced.

"The four of us will be heading back to the mainland right after we eat as some of us have morning commitments. We must be away no later than nine o'clock," said Bruce, frowning at his wife standing by the door. "Thank you all for the informative and entertaining evening. It was lovely meeting you Emma and, speaking for the others, we want you to know that we truly believe you will be a perfect addition to this family. We eagerly await your decision." He hugged Emma and they left.

Alfreda and George came over to talk to her and Alex joined them. They thanked Alfreda for her history lesson and Emma gave her a tired smile. It was quite obvious she was absolutely worn out after the historically enlightening evening. Before the MacDuffs left, Alfreda surprised Emma by giving her a hug as did George, inviting her to visit them at Borthwick Hall.

## Chapter 5 - Wednesday 15<sup>th</sup> – Flora

Emma's alarm clock went off just as she was waking up so she quickly shut it off and dragged her tired body out of bed. Standing to put on her housecoat and slippers, she shivered and hurried into the bathroom to get ready. Splashing cold water on her face, she applied a bit of make-up, brushed her hair and went downstairs to meet the others in her housecoat.

She poured a coffee as Jennie told her they were leaving right away. A storm was expected and they had decided to forego a big breakfast. Before they hurried outside, the women hugged Emma, warmly assuring her they would meet again soon. When they realized the height of the wind, they all piled into the taxi and waved as they drove away. Alex was leaving the stable and waved as he walked towards the house.

"Setting a new fashion trend for Traymore House are you, marm?" he asked raising his eyebrows and shaking his head at her outfit.

"Are we leaving today?" she asked, trying to keep a straight face.

"We still have a lot to do, so we could stay until Friday morning, if that meets with your approval. This morning I want to show you the island and then we'll take a look at those journals."

"Yes, we should stay as long as necessary; I like it here," she said pensively. "Have you eaten, because I have not?"

"Let's go see if the breakfast is still warm and edible."

Before they finished eating, Alex looked over at her displaying a sly grin. "Do you ride Emma?"

Suddenly wary, she watched his face as she slowly replied. "Not since I was a schoolgirl. Why? Do you … no, we aren't!"

"Yes, we are," he chuckled. "You'll enjoy it! Your riding breeches are hung in your bedroom closet, boots too, and a helmet!"

"You've been a busy devil!" she muttered, silently admiring his efficiency … and gall. "All right, I'll go see how accurate you are with the size of this outfit!"

"You actually believe it was I who did your shopping? No, Emma," he laughed, "fortunately we are able to employ people for that sort of job!"

"I can never be sure of what's going on behind my back, can I!"

Making their way to the stables later, they were relieved that the wind had eased, although it now felt like rain. Emma's perfect-fitting riding clothes obviously impressed both Alex and the two stablemen. Two horses were already saddled and one of the men stepped up to assist her. She tried to hide her excited nervousness, remembering how much she had loved riding, so long ago. She nudged her horse to follow Alex.

"Just hold the reins loosely," he advised. "He'll follow me."

Cantering along at a steady pace, they crossed the fertile, green valley, avoiding fences and stone walls where small herds of long-horned cattle, and sheep, heavy with wool, grazed contentedly. They passed the lake and soon reached the other side of the valley. Alex slowed when grass gave way to a steep and rocky slope with the forest laid out in front of them. Allowing the horses to take their lead, he gave her a thumbs-up sign. *She'll do just fine!*

Partway up, they dismounted and picked their way over a rock-strewn area until they reached more level terrain. They rode on for another 10 minutes then left the horses to graze while they continued the climb on foot. He pointed out some dark red bushes which he said were heather.

"It is said that heather loves the Scottish climate so much, it covers five million acres of our moorland, hills and especially the wetlands which are its natural habitat. When it blooms in summer, it's an unbelievable mass of colour!"

Climbing even higher, she became aware that the steep pathway had taken them towards an area of tall, jagged rocks—like the ones she had seen as they arrived yesterday. She stopped to get her bearings and realized she could see the Scottish coastline. She looked down and quickly stepped back, seeing waves crashing far below. Alex called to her, asking if she was all right. She waved and something told him to go back, pulling her up beside him. They went through some very tall rocks and he stopped, pointing to the view.

"What an amazing sight … the mountains look so close!" she said.

"The closest are the Trossacks with the Highlands being the snowy ridges beyond. The distillery, where we were yesterday, is located on this side of the Trossacks. They do seem quite close from here, don't they?"

But Emma had stopped listening, unable to resist being drawn further along the path. Alex caught up to her, telling her to stop and look down. She did, catching her breath so sharply Alex grabbed her arm.

"Careful!" he warned.

The warning was well-founded as the wild tide, aided by strong winds, boiled angrily over the rocks far below. She reached out for support, and as her hand touched the rock, she instantly cried out as a shock wave rippled violently through her body. She screamed again, but the horrific sensation wouldn't stop and she began to cry hysterically. She was so relieved when she felt Alex's strong arms encircle her and pull her back from the cliff edge. As a feeling of safety washed over her, she tried to calm down clinging to him until she realized the sensation had stopped. She buried her head in his shoulder and sobbed.

"You felt her!" he whispered, but she didn't hear him. He held her protectively as his mind struggled with the realization that something very scary had just happened to Emma although he had no idea what it was. "You're all right, Emma. I've got you," he said in a soothing voice. Allowing her a few seconds and when she still didn't say anything, he suddenly made up his mind. "We're going down!" he snapped, grabbing her by the shoulders and turning her around. Looking into her eyes, he was gravely concerned when she seemed to look right through him. "Listen to me, Emma," he said loudly. "We're going down to the horses, right now!"

"Wh-what is this place?" she moaned, trying to sit down but he pulled her back onto her feet. He thought he might have to carry her but suddenly she spoke. "Why did you bring me here, Alex?"

Now feeling guilty and terribly worried, he looked into her blank-looking eyes and grabbed her hand trying to pull her along beside him. "Emma we must go! Come please, we must get back to the horses!" he said sternly but she barely moved. He tried again, pulling her harder and this time she seemed more aware, taking a couple of steps, then a couple more until they were moving slowly down the steep pathway retracing their steps. Suddenly, she began running, pulling him along with amazing strength until they reached a grassy area where they both collapsed on the ground, gasping for air.

She fell back against him moaning, but he grabbed her hand and they set off again. More slowly now, they continued to where the ground became more level and less rocky. Emma had stopped crying but was breathing heavily. Her silence was giving Alex time to think and his mind was now churning out questions that made him angry. *What on earth happened? Has anyone else had this experience before? No one had ever spoken of it. If not, why now? Could it be Emma?* Suddenly she began to shout angrily at him but he was too involved in his own thoughts to notice. When they passed the familiar patch of heather, he knew they were almost to the horses. Seeing them at last, they finally stopped and Emma slumped to the ground.

"Alex, w-what the h-hell was that all about?" she managed before coughing violently. He sat down beside her, relieved she was talking normally. When she stopped coughing, he wasn't expecting what came next for she began to hit him, punching him about the arms and chest. "W-why did y-you bring me up here? H-h-has this h-happened before? I need to know!" she demanded. He finally managed to hold her arms still and she slumped against him. Her heart beat wildly against his chest.

"I had no idea this would happen. Please believe me," he pleaded. "I am so sorry, but I realize that doesn't explain anything. I am way out of my depth here."

Her face held a pained expression.

"You're sorry? For what? Has this happened before? Tell me!" she demanded trying to hit him again.

He let her go and stood up, rubbing his hands vigorously over his face. His earlier expression of shock had now given way to one of sadness, which was enough to answer some of her questions at least.

"I promise you Emma, I had no idea this would happen ... actually, what exactly did happen? Tell me. Are you sure you're all right?"

"I-I think so. When I touched that rock, it was like something grabbed me and wouldn't let go sending shockwaves throughout my body. It wouldn't stop ... un-until you pulled me away. It felt ... painful at first and then ... I don't know how to describe it. It was just so frightening ... and you've never heard of this happening before?"

He had plenty of ideas, but he couldn't believe any of them at this moment. He just wanted to get them both back to Traymore where he knew Emma could feel safe.

"Let's go get some lunch and a drink. I don't know about you, but I can certainly use one!" he exclaimed.

She smiled ruefully and accepted his hand to pull her up. When they reached the horses, he helped her mount and then remembered he had put a thermos of water in his saddlebag. He got it and took it back to her, taking her reins. He began leading the horses down towards the valley, keeping a close watch on her. He was relieved that she seemed to be doing better so he mounted his horse and in minutes they reached the valley floor. He allowed her horse to come level with his and then handed her the reins. Riding side-by-side, they slowly retraced their earlier steps until they saw the lake and headed across the valley to Traymore. It began to rain as the horses moved into a steady gallop, but this time Emma welcomed the coolness beating gently on her face. She knew that something important had happened today and it made her feel strangely different and thoroughly Scottish.

Two farm workers, busy in the stable, were relieved to see them ride in and promptly took care of the horses. Alex removed his wet jacket and helped her out of hers, hanging them to dry. Grabbing an umbrella, they went to the house and headed straight for the sitting room. Meeting Jayne in the hallway, Alex asked for coffee and sandwiches then went over to the fireplace and threw on another log.

"Perhaps we should both go and get into some dry clothes," he suggested as they stood by the fire, grateful for the warmth.

"If I go upstairs, I might be tempted to climb into bed, pull the covers over my head and just sleep," she admitted, shivering.

He went over to a cupboard and brought out a blanket. "You felt Flora's presence up there didn't you?" he asked solemnly, putting the blanket around her shoulders and leading her to a chair.

"Why do you say that ... and why would it be Flora? You sound like you expected something to happen. What are you not telling me, Alex?"

Alex again felt a twinge of guilt and realized he was being unfair. "You may not believe me, but I didn't know anything for sure. It was all hearsay. Trev once told me there was a legend that said Flora cried for days up on those cliffs when she thought she had lost her brothers. It could have been told by someone who was with her but unless it's written down at the time, it's merely heresay. This story seems to have helped fuel the legend about the Wallace family. It must have been almost too much for such a little girl to bear. It is said her tears are embedded in those rocks. I hadn't believed it until today."

"Well, I certainly do!" She shivered again, pulling the blanket tighter.

"It's been called *The Place of Tears* for as long as anyone in the family can remember ... are you sure you're all right? I really think we should go and change. Lunch will be here soon ... I'll pound on your door if you don't come out, then you won't fall asleep!" When she smiled weakly, he held out his hand and she took it allowing him to escort her upstairs.

When they returned to the sitting room, they found lunch waiting. Alex rearranged the chairs and watched her make their drinks, coffee with somewhat less whisky than he would have added.

A smile crinkled his lips. "Well, you look none the worse for wear, thank goodness," he began, but then a grave expression appeared. "I still haven't answered your question about why I took you up to the cliffs. I simply thought you would appreciate the view … and it had been a special place for Flora. I was still trying to persuade you, I suppose." "It did have a lovely view and I'm grateful you took me there, Alex. I truly am. I suppose, under the circumstances, it was necessary for me to have that experience," she admitted. "If this was an example of the power of Flora's tears, you would think someone else must have felt it … sometime." She stopped and looked into the fire. "I really didn't want to leave there, you know, but you were so concerned. I thought you might know something you weren't telling me. It's strange, but I can already feel that place trying to pull me back.

"Something has happened to me, Alex; I need to know more about Dorik. Surely over the centuries someone must have found something referring to *The Place of Tears* … in a letter or diary perhaps. If they left it here in this house, the library would be the obvious place. You know, it's an odd feeling, but I think I've finally found where my heart belongs … found my purpose in life. Do you understand what I mean?" He nodded thoughtfully, being hopeful this was a good sign yet thinking better of making a comment. She continued to ramble on excitedly. "I would never have imagined this inheritance would lead to something so extraordinary. What is next? I can't help but wonder … and the strange thing is, Alex, I feel ready to tackle it!"

"It's exactly that, isn't it … extraordinary!" he said cautiously, passing her the plate of sandwiches. "You felt more than her tears, Emma, you felt her presence. You found a window that allowed you into the soul of this place, perhaps even Flora's soul! I doubt if more than a few people in 700-years have been so lucky and, whether they wrote it down or not …." He looked at her emotionally and shrugged.

Having her mouth full, she merely nodded and after they finished eating, she asked him to show her the journals.

"By all means, let's do that! I will have to leave you for a couple hours though, as I have some things to do."

"Do you have any knowledge of any other journals, diaries or papers that could help our search?" she asked. "Did Trev keep a diary?"

As she stepped into the library, she stopped briefly as a shiver went up her spine once again, as she viewed the rows and rows of books.

"An English professor's delight, no doubt!" Alex commented seeing the same look on her face as he had seen the day before when she first entered this room. Alex went over to a shelf and pulled out two large volumes, taking them over to the table. He also pointed out two shelves of books on Scottish history and Wallace, in particular.

"Now that you mention it, yes, he did keep a diary and I found several. I put them in the safety deposit box at the bank. I'd forgotten all about them, but these journals will keep you busy in the interim."

He left then and, going over to the table, she tentatively opened one of the journals and turned to a page at random. "Good heavens! I was afraid of this ... what a mess of writing styles. This is going to take a lot more than a couple of hours," she mumbled. Shutting the journal, she went over to stand in front of the book shelves and, starting at one end, scanned the rows until she just had to stop. She had discovered nothing more interesting than some frayed bindings on several well-used volumes comprised of mainly farming subjects. Her morning experience kept creeping into her mind and, to give her eyes a rest, she decided to explore the old manor house.

First, she went to get a fresh cup of coffee and a sandwich then, taking her drink with her, she went upstairs and wandered from room to room starting with the rooms adjoining her own. She couldn't help but wonder who else had used these rooms over the centuries! Had anyone famous stayed here? She lost count at ten bedrooms and wasn't surprised to discover several more rooms totally devoid of furniture. *I wonder how much work has been done on the house since Flora's time, other than the new staff wing? Trev might have written something about that in his diary.* She also wondered what a ten-year-old child would do with a valuable package, especially after being torn from her family and told that she would never see her parents again? What about the heartache when she was taken by rough strangers and separated from her brothers? How does a child survive a deeply traumatic experience? Surely it would have sent a little girl into a frenzy of uncertainty and despair. Missing her brothers for endless months and not knowing whether they were even alive would have been unimaginable. *I would have died of a broken heart.*

Considering her thoughts with the careful scrutiny of a university lecturer, she still could not find an answer. What would a child do under those circumstances, in those times? Would she transfer her affection and trust to an object like a doll or a toy or would she even possess such things in those hard times. Could she have discovered a secret hiding place somewhere, but it would have to be prior to arriving at Traymore or someone would have seen it. Could it be a wild stretch of the imagination to think a child would have concern for a parcel, even if she did know about its contents and had been told about its importance? *I definitely need to know more about the Wallace Family.*

Deciding to end her tour, she returned to the library to continue her search, she began where she had left off and almost immediately a large, old book with a much-used binding caught her eye. She stopped and studied the hard-to-read title but was unable to read the faded letters. Easing it gently from its snug-fitting position on the shelf, she picked up the heavy volume and set it down on the table. When she opened it to the first page, she caught her breath. It was in braille. Excited now, Emma searched the inside pages for a production date but could find nothing but braille. Knowing from her studies that braille was invented in 1847 by a teenaged French boy, Louis Braille, she remembered it had taken a long time to become officially accepted. Prior to this period in history, the raised Roman alphabet had been used for blind readers. Was it her imagination that was telling her this volume could be older or was it actually a possibility? Could a previous form of braille have been invented in Scotland years earlier and been kept hidden in plain sight among the books of Traymore House? *An interesting thought Emma*, she chastised herself. *Stop indulging in your romantic notions, you'll only be disappointed!*

Deep in concentration, she continued to check the titles on the remaining shelves, gasping when Alex's pager startled her. Taking it out of her pocket, she pressed the button.

"Found you!" he called bursting into the library seconds later. "Have you made any significant discoveries?"

"You left me with those journals on purpose, didn't you? Have you read them yourself? Can you read them?" she demanded. "I did find something of interest though, not that it has anything to do with our history but I do have a question."

"Why doesn't that surprise me?" he teased, crinkling his brow.

"There's a book open on the table over there, would you take a look at it and tell me who would have produced it and when?"

"Don't you mean who published it? It's dinnertime Emma, and I'm not a librarian!" he snapped. "Couldn't we discuss this later?"

Emma's 'no' was simple but direct and delivered with just enough intensity to send the Scot striding towards the table, muttering under his breath. Silence followed as she waited for his comment.

"This is in braille!" he exclaimed, looking blankly at her.

"I know that, but there's no publication date."

"How would I know, if you don't? Why is that important?"

"Damn it, Alex, just answer me," she hissed, "or tell me who can?"

"Ruth Oxley at Misty House would be the logical person or she could at least advise you. There are also various organizations for the blind in Edinburgh; otherwise, I have no bloody idea!"

"See," she snapped, "it's easy if you just answer the question!"

"I suppose if that's the end of that discussion, we may as well go down to dinner. Are you ready to eat now, my lady … Emma?" he asked, watching her eyebrows rise at his mistake. He chuckled and, taking her arm, escorted her down to the cozy little room where they had gone to escape during the family meeting the night before. A fire burned comfortingly and overstuffed armchairs beckoned, but they went to a small table which was immaculately set for dinner.

"Your personal hiding place, I presume," she commented.

"No, it's your personal place, Emma," he replied easily, "any time you want it to be."

The next morning's early hours would forever be stamped in Emma's memory as she was awakened by a dream so real she thought she was actually living it. Awake and, sitting up in bed staring into the darkness, an all-consuming fear clutched at her throat as she vividly remembered that ghastly smell. Then the vision of soldiers and stone buildings returned like a split-screen in a historical movie. A young girl with long, dark hair cried pitifully as she huddled in the corner of what looked like a straw barn with rough stonewalls, while in another scene, two little boys were being held by soldiers as their terror-filled screams rent the air.

Emma knew what was going to happen. She began to shake and reached for the light trying to stop the images. Covering her mouth, she held back her screams fearing she would wake Alex down the hall. She stumbled to the bathroom for a drink, trying to clear her mind. Putting on her housecoat, she went to the window and pulled back the heavy curtain to peer into the darkness. Hours later, her alarm sent a shockwave throughout her body, totally unaware she had returned to bed.

When Alex appeared at breakfast, she was already on her second cup of camomile tea.

"Good morning … or is it?" he murmured, studying her face.

"Sit down, your coffee is on the sideboard," she said quietly, "and yes, I had a wonderful night, those children kept me awake most of it!"

"What children?" he asked, noting her tea.

"Our children … who else? I'm not talking about it before breakfast!"

Puzzled at first, he now realized she must have dreamed about the Wallace children. He silently sipped his coffee as they waited for breakfast to arrive. After eating, he decided to revisit their earlier conversation before Emma changed her mind again. "So tell me about this dream ... the Wallace children, I presume. Was this the first one?"

"Don't you think I would have told you if I'd had any others? Yes, it was and not one I hope to repeat ... I could even smell the stench of burning flesh, at least that's what I imagined it was. It was horrible Alex."

"All right, that's settled then," he announced, standing up.

"What do you mean *settled*? Does this mean you are washing your hands of it all and leaving it to me?" When he didn't reply and seemed to be searching for words, she also stood up. She wasn't about to let him escape until they had spent some time on the journals. She grabbed his arm and told him they were going down to the library. Heading straight for the two journals on the table, she opened the first one at the beginning pages and almost immediately looked up at him, puzzled.

"Did you and Trev actually look at these? I've studied old manuscripts that were easier to discern ... this is about as clear as mud! Some of the writing is actually in Latin. I don't think it was ever intended for a layman to read."

"Well, if the truth be known, Trev did hire people to read it for him, translating as he listened."

"Come on Alex, give me a break. Trev would have listened to a synopsis and nothing more. This would take hundreds, no doubt thousands of hours to transcribe. I'll need my laptop for this, I'll be right back."

On her return, she noticed Alex had found a notepad, pen and white gloves. She sat down, opened her laptop and got to work. He watched her silently, admiring her confidence and efficiency as she put on the gloves and so carefully turned over groups of pages to speed up the process. He knew, from his own experience with the journals, she shouldn't be able to read anything at this point. She continued in this same manner for about 15 minutes, then sighing deeply, she closed the first book and pushed it away. Opening the second, her attention became immediately more absorbed and Alex watched as she leaned closer to the book and made some more notes. *She's reached the good parts!* he thought, moving to a more comfortable chair from where he could continue to watch her.

She began to find short passages she could decipher, but they weren't of much use being only entries that someone had found nothing. She noted the date and sat back in her chair to think. A few minutes went by and, having felt his presence earlier when she assumed he had left, she now swung around to face him.

"You've seen these records, what do we do now?" she asked solemnly. "They are still not easy to read and I'm up to 1610." When he didn't speak right away, she had an idea. "How many women have studied these journal entries?"

"You're the first I believe," he replied, frowning deeply as he rubbed his beard. "Are you thinking …?"

"Shh, don't strain your tiny brain, sir! Mary Wallace was a woman and *you* can't even suspect what a woman would do in her circumstances!"

The room was so quiet they could hear each other breathe, and then he murmured. "I'm assuming your course of action is about to take a sharp turn and you won't need me for awhile."

"I do believe you are correct, Sir Alex, so you may go now and leave me to my own devices. I will be right here if you are looking for me, but you may wish to check on me sooner rather than later, just in case I have slit my wrists. I'm sure you wouldn't want this lovely floor to be stained by my blood!"

He got up and went over to stand behind her. Gently gripping her shoulders, he whispered, "I don't want you to get *that* frustrated. You have the remote?" She nodded, patting her pocket, and without another word, he quietly slipped away.

She sat there for awhile, just mulling over her thoughts, and then she opened the first book again and started at the beginning. This time she turned the pages only a few at a time until just before she reached the halfway point, the writing became more legible and more readable than she had previously thought. Two hours later, her head spinning, she stood up and went out to the hallway. With no particular intent, she slowly climbed the stairs to her room. Noting that the bed had been neatly made, she poured herself a glass of water and drank half of it before dropping onto the bed. She fell back on the pillows and pulled the comforter up to her chin.

Seconds later, she was asleep and dreaming of her walk on the cliff, remembering every detail, but this time she was not alone for two people appeared … a young woman and a little girl were sitting on the ground beside the large rocks. The girl was prostrate over the woman's legs and her body heaved with crying as the woman lovingly stroked her hair. Even in her dream, Emma was completely aware she was meeting her long-ago ancestors, Mary and Flora. It took only seconds and, as the vision began to melt away, Mary looked up so Emma could see her tortured but lovely face. Mary pressed her hands together as if in prayer and then her expression changed as she seemed to look right into Emma's eyes. Her lips formed a word and her hands reached out as the vision melted away ... and Emma woke up! Sitting up quickly, she rubbed her face briskly and looked around her. She instantly remembered everything as if she had been awake. *I know you're trying to tell me something Mary, but what? Were you asking my help?* She sighed. *Silly, I wouldn't be able to understand her language anyway!* She got up and was surprised to find she still had her shoes on. Going into the bathroom, she splashed cold water on her face. *I must write this down before I forget!* But she remembered her laptop was downstairs. Feeling hungry, she freshened her makeup and returned to the sitting room. Pleased to see there was both fresh coffee and some tasty-looking sandwiches and cakes, she put together a selection to take to the library. Making room on the tray for her tea cup, she headed down the hallway.

*I must be careful around these books*, she told herself as she entered the library and went to sit at the table. It was a beautiful day with a mainly blue sky. *I should be going outside for a walk*, she told herself, but she took a bite of a sandwich and opened her computer. She reread her notes about her previous dreams and quickly added three new lines before pushing the laptop away. Gazing out of the window at the bedraggled plants in the garden, she tried to imagine what they would look like in spring. She knew she would look forward to returning here when the rockery and gardens were in bloom ... not so many months away. She finished eating and her mind went back to the children.

She wondered what Dorik would have looked like when the Wallace boys came here. *Thank goodness life had improved greatly for those poor lads.* She shook her head to return to the present and again looked out the window as she slowly finished her coffee. Her thoughts returned to her dream and her eyes strayed to the journals feeling herself being drawn inexplicably to those fascinating pages of old writing. She put away her dishes and set to work again. Three hours later, it was almost five o'clock and Alex arrived to tell her it was almost dinnertime.

"I don't see any blood on the floor, so you must be coping," he observed. "You've been in here a long time—dare I ask if you have found anything of interest?"

"I can't say *found* just yet, but I did have a visitor."

"A visitor? Abe didn't go anywhere, he was with me. Where is ...?"

"It wasn't that kind of a visitor, Alex," she giggled, "it was one of the heavenly kind!"

"What are you on about ... did you have another dream?" he asked. When she grinned, he shook his head and looked puzzled. "But it's daytime." She told him of going up to her room to rest and falling asleep. When she described Mary's visit with Flora, the blood drained from his face and he sat down across from her. "You and Mary seem to be developing quite a remarkable relationship! How do you explain two dreams in less than 24 hours? "Do you think they contain a message?"

"A message to me, of course they do!" she snapped. "Although other than conveying the real story, I don't know what else they could possibly have meant."

"Could she be seeking your sympathy?"

"Oh Lord, now you're telling me a dream can understand my thoughts?"

"Well, stranger things have happened. I guess it depends on your belief system. Do you believe in ghosts and spirits, Emma?"

"I suppose after coming to Dorik, I have to!" she admitted.

"Then we must assume that these 'dreams or happenings' are Mary's way of trying to convey a message to you, don't you think?"

"I hadn't thought of it quite like that, but you could be right that Mary and, possibly Flora, are both trying to send me messages. I suppose I should go on that assumption which certainly changes my thought process! I've had unusual dreams before but nothing as real as this. These people are my ancestors and without them I would not be here. I feel that connection and it thrills me to think I might be able to solve their mystery. I do realize though that Mary could not have said 'please' as she would be speaking a different language. However, enough said about the dreams which I am now diarizing, Sir Alex. I think I've done enough with the journals for now; I don't suppose I could take one of them back to Edinburgh?"

"Trev always believed they were safer here, so I think we should stick with those rules for now," Alex replied sympathetically. "I'm glad you've decided to write down your dreams, which may come in handy ... dinner at six?"

"Perfect, I'll just finish up here and put the journals away. I'm going to take one or two of the Wallace books with me."

Alex nodded and left her to get organized. She sorted out her papers and, with mixed feelings, put the journals away, and then went to choose her reading. Another Scottish history book by Nigel Tranter caught her eye and, remembering the author's name, she took that as well. Looking around, she gathered up her lunch dishes and took them down the hall to the kitchen, catching Sarah as she came out. Emma handed her the dishes, and received a puzzled expression.

"Please thank the kitchen staff for the tasty sandwiches and cakes. They really hit the spot!" said Emma, then turning around she went off toward the stairs. Sarah was so taken aback, she just stood silently and watched her, then shrugging her shoulders, she giggled softly and returned to her duties.

Just before six o'clock, they met in the hallway near their rooms and went down to dinner together. Alex noted that Emma was in a particularly good mood so he was eager to talk to her. Arriving in the small dining room, they found a bottle of wine chilling and once she agreed, he opened it and poured two glasses of the chardonnay.

"A toast," he announced, handing her a glass. "To happy dreams and solving mysteries!" She laughed and they touched glasses. "This dream hasn't seemed to have bothered you like the first one with the children."

"Because this one was quite different. It's puzzling though because it was a much more pleasant dream ... sad content, but certainly not scary. After thinking about it, I am very sure she is sending me a message, but I don't know what it is yet. I'm beginning to think you have enlisted her help to persuade me to stay!"

"She must be a very perceptive spirit ... or she's reading my mind!"

"Everyone seems to be making such a valiant effort to appeal to my heart," Emma whispered, "even the children and Mary have got into the act! Trevelion would be shocked but very proud. I can't thank ...," she stopped as Jayne arrived with the dinner trolley.

Alex looked at Emma and knew by her words and her expression that something serious was on her mind. He hardly dared breathe while Jayne set out their dishes.

"As I was saying," Emma continued after the girl left, "Trev would be very proud of all of you because you have played your parts so well. Your plan has worked ... for I have decided what I must do!" Alex's fork slipped out of his hand and clattered onto the plate.

"Yes?" he prodded, something warning him not to breathe as he waited anxiously for her next words.

"Exactly ... yes!" she laughed, the unusually happy sound of her voice mesmerizing him. "Yes, yes, yes, I have decided to accept my inheritance dear Alex, so you can stop worrying about your precious job!

I decided today that solving this mystery is exactly what I need to begin my life anew." She reached over and patted his hand.

"I am so relieved and pleased to hear this, my lady. Thank you for not making me wait any longer for this wonderful news! Quickly, a toast!"

"An excellent idea, Sir Alex, but I am certainly glad you don't have to drive tonight. I'm feeling a bit too happy already! Keep in mind that we have a very important meeting tomorrow morning!"

Refilling their glasses, Alex was grinning as he offered his second toast … "To Lady Traymore and her many heirs, long may they multiply!" causing them both to laugh so hard, they couldn't stop. When they calmed down and began to eat, he realized he was going to hear at last, all those harboured questions she had been putting aside.

"Will I live here, Alex, it's a bit far from anything and awkward to come and go, especially in a hurry. What about when we need to see each other? You haven't even told me about your home, I'm still waiting for that invitation!" She looked at him coyly, waiting for an answer which didn't come, so she continued eating. Minutes later, she had another thought. "Would it be proper to divulge our secret to the staff tonight? They've been so eager to call me, my lady!" she giggled.

"Yes, we can certainly do that tonight. In the meantime, don't worry about anything. We will work out the rest as we go. Oh, and one other thing, you are invited to my apartment at the earliest opportunity!" He patted her hand and they both laughed. "You can also visit Dorik as much or as little as you like … it's even lovelier in the summer. It will continue to be staffed no matter what you do. The same for your suite at the hotel or we can find another. Yes, I look after the finances, but you are allowed to use the money for personal expenses. Trev had a budget and we will discuss that as well. There, now let's forget business and enjoy our meal. Later, I'll have the house staff gather in the sitting room. I won't tell them why until we're all together. They will be delighted."

Later, after talking to the staff, Alex couldn't find Emma and surmised she had gone upstairs. He went to tidy up and by the time he returned, staff had cleaned the room and the butler was setting out glasses. A bottle of champagne arrived for the 'little toast' as Alex had described it. Alex went out into the hall to watch for their honoured guest and the butler uncorked the first bottle. The rest of the staff arrived within 10 minutes and Alex soon noticed a lot of whispering going on behind the door. He slowly climbed the stairs but only got partway as Emma appeared in her long tartan dress, looking absolutely radiant. Grinning broadly, he took her hand and they went to share their news. As she entered, some of the staff caught their breath not having seen her that first night dressed up in her Scottish finery. Alex nodded to the butler and he handed them each a glass of champagne. By then, a buzz was going through the group that 'their lady' was wearing her clan pin.

Alex made the happy announcement and everyone cheered, clinking glasses. She accepted their toast and comments gracefully and then Alex made a speech. The staff took their leave with curtseys and bows, although it was not necessary, calling her 'my lady' as they passed. The butler gave her an exaggerated sweeping bow, and with a large grin, told her how happy the staff are to have a mistress after all these years. Emma gently put her hand on his arm to prevent him from leaving.

"Could you wait a moment please, young man?" she asked with a smile. "Sir Alex, will you please introduce me to my butler!"

"By all means, my lady," he laughed. "I'm pleased to introduce Neville MacLeod, your butler and man-of-all-trades here at Dorik. His father and two grandfathers also served as butlers at Traymore and other Walters' residences over the years. You can ask him anything and usually get a satisfactory and often humorous answer!"

"How fascinating," Emma laughed. "I very much look forward to having some interesting chats with you, Mr. MacLeod. You may go now … thank you and goodnight."

When they were alone, she sat down by the fire, kicked off her shoes and tucked her feet under her long skirt. "Our appointment is at 10?"

"Yes, Phibbie will be here for us at seven a.m. We'll need two hours for the drive. We should eat some breakfast before we leave, but I have also asked the kitchen to pack us a lunch. We've covered a lot of ground this first week, my lady," he said, staring into the fire. "Are you absolutely sure you are ready to do this?"

"Yes and no," she replied, yawning, "but there's no turning back! This has been the most exciting week of my life, and I feel duty bound to take on the challenge, frightening as it may be."

"You sound more confident about this now, why?"

She spoke softly, closing her eyes. "I feel as if someone or something is tugging at my soul … like Mary's hands reaching out to me. It feels like pieces of a puzzle coming together. I've always enjoyed a challenge and it's quite thrilling that Mary has chosen me for this task."

They were both yawning when Alex suggested it was a good time to retire. At the stairs, he remembered the braille book and said he'd follow shortly. He watched the new mistress of Traymore slowly climb the stairs and smiled, before going down the hall to the library.

76

## Chapter 6 – Friday 17<sup>th</sup> – No Turning Back

Morning came much too soon for Emma and only Sarah's concerned insistence finally got her remotely mobile. She was in no mood for small talk when she arrived at the breakfast table. A cup of strong, black coffee was all she could manage before turning her attention on Alex. Staring disdainfully at his breakfast plate of ham, eggs, sausage and fried black pudding, she commented, "For goodness' sake, how are you going to manage to hold that down on the way back to the mainland?"

"Maybe you should try a simple good morning, my lady!" he growled.

"That's a matter of opinion!"

Conversation was minimal as she finally ate a slice of toast and jam. Sarah came to advise that the taxi was waiting and handed Alex the packed lunch he had requested the night before. He remembered the Braille book, asked her for a bag and went to get their coats.

"It's going to be a rough ride today!" Abe muttered under his breath as they climbed into the water taxi and he started the engine.

By the time they emerged from the shelter of the trees, Emma was shocked to see just how fiercely the wind was blowing. They soon reached the cliff track and before them lay the wildest spectacle of white-capped waves she had ever seen.

"Holy cripes, we're not really going out there, are we?" she asked.

"There's no other way," Alex replied apologetically. There was a hint of concern in his voice that he hoped Emma wouldn't notice. "Don't worry, my lady, I guarantee we're unsinkable!"

"Well, aren't you encouraging!" she exclaimed.

She waited for the lurch that indicated they had entered the water, but it still took her by surprise. She screamed as the waves splashed and rolled over their heads threatening to break them apart. Then, just as suddenly, they popped to the surface and assisted by the waves, they moved towards the mainland. It felt like an eternity to Emma, but 20 minutes later the sea calmed and their vehicle moved up onto the land.

"Would you like a drink?" Alex offered as they disembarked and went to their car.

"I sure would, but I'm not sure I could keep it down!" she exclaimed.

"All right, we'll stop at the first rest stop!" He was surprised when she agreed with a quick 'fine!'

As they drove towards the motorway, her thoughts were on their meeting with Gilbert Stuart in a couple of hours. *My big day and I will sure be glad to get this part over with.* She turned to look out the window and found herself savouring the sight of her newfound country with its wonderful green countryside, so much like home in some ways and so different in others. The narrow country lanes were another harrowing experience with a lot of early morning traffic zipping by. She hoped she wouldn't have to drive these roads any time soon.

When they reached the motorway, neither of them attempted any conversation until Alex pulled off at the Tranent Junction stop for petrol and they picked up a quick hot chocolate to eat with their lunch.

Friday morning traffic got even heavier as they continued towards Edinburgh and Emma smiled as Alex ranted about the other drivers.

"I suppose you think you're a perfect driver, Sir Alex!"

"Ah-ha, now I know you're back to normal!" he growled.

Luck found them a parking space not far from the solicitor's office.

"Just a minute, I had better check the war paint," she murmured.

Reaching over, Alex pulled down her sun visor and flipped the switch on the illuminated mirror. Emma frowned and he pointed to a blue button which she pressed. Silently, a tray slid towards her from under the dashboard and she laughed when she saw the make-up kit and a selection of nail polish.

"No way," she laughed, "next you'll have my manicurist pop out from under the seat!"

"I never did understand until now why Trev had all these things put into this car." Alex grimaced. "I rarely saw him with a woman!"

A chilling wind was blowing against them as they walked up the damp sidewalk to the solicitor's office. The receptionist told them Mr. Stuart was waiting.

Alex hung up their coats and heard Gilbert Stuart's loud voice calling to them even before they entered.

"Greetings, dear lady," he bubbled, his Adam's apple bouncing behind his tartan bow tie. "I trust you have come to a decision?"

Emma nodded stoically.

"Do you have the papers ready, Kelly?" the solicitor called to his secretary. "Perhaps Miss Walters and Sir Alex would like coffee?"

Kelly entered and as she placed a thick file on her boss' desk, she asked for their preference of drinks.

"Two coffees and …," he looked over at Emma who was frowning. "Two black coffees, Kelly!" He chose not to see Emma's smug smile.

"I take it you've read all the documents?" the solicitor confirmed without taking his eyes from the legal papers in front of him. "Now," he said forcefully, "you are about to tell me your decision."

"I have decided to accept my inheritance and yes, I have read and agree to its *Conditions*, but as to having read that pile of documents, no I have not. You did not have them ready on my previous visit!"

Kelly entered with a tray and set it down on the desk. Alex passed one of the china cups with saucer to Emma, took the other and handed the tray back to Kelly.

It took almost two hours to go over the documents, have them explained, signed, witnessed and duly sealed. When she was finished, her mind was such a blur of legalese she wasn't at all sure what she had read.

"I assume I shall be getting a copy of all these papers in due course?" she asked.

"Yes, that is correct, and let me say how pleased I am that you have decided to accept your inheritance, Miss Walters. Trevelion Walters would be greatly pleased and relieved. Now, our appointment with the High Court is next Friday the 24th at one o'clock," Gilbert told them. "My secretary will confirm the details by email and, Sir Alex, I am holding you responsible for bringing Miss Walters to the court promptly." He looked at his watch for about the third time and Emma and Alex exchanged glances. It was an obvious dismissal, so Alex was the first to stand up. They thanked the solicitor and left his office.

The wind was blowing even colder now and they were glad to have the car. As they hurried inside the hotel, Alex commented that it felt like snow. He suggested they have some lunch and discuss plans for the weekend. "We still have the third manor house to visit," he reminded his pensive companion.

"I'll be back shortly," she suddenly murmured and got up and walked away, past the lift to the stairs. She disappeared without looking back.

Frowning, Alex watched her and knew something was not right. He knew she was tired from not sleeping, to say nothing of all the surprises he had heaped on her including the ones at Dorik. He felt responsible yet he didn't want to interfere mainly because he didn't know what to say. He went to the stairs, opened the door quietly and listened for her footsteps. She was almost to the next landing but her steps were very slow and he heard the door close. *She must have gone to get the lift at the second floor. I'm sorry Emma, there's only one more chapter in my book of knowledge and then you will know it all!*

Letting herself into the room, she turned and stood with her back against the door. Closing her eyes, she sighed deeply and wished the court case could be over so she could just relax ... but would she continue to have the dreams until the mystery was solved? She had never had to deal with anything like this before and was suddenly overwhelmed. *What on earth did I sign today? Alex kept saying he would show me this and that, how many properties were there? More than I was initially told. Too much to comprehend ... me, a wealthy lady, oh my gosh!* She sighed deeply and then thoughts of Mary and the children began to flash through her head and she started towards the window. She was halfway across the room when the tears began to flow uncontrollably, choking her as pent-up thoughts and emotions incapacitated her ... albeit only briefly. She suddenly realized how utterly exhausted she was, but she had told Alex she would meet him for lunch so she needed to calm down. *I really do need to eat,* she realized, turning back to the bathroom to get a hand towel. Wetting it with cold water, she held it against her red cheeks and struggled to compose herself.

Going back to the window, she sat down on the wide sill and looked out at the magnificent view. The wind had blown the clouds away and, despite the cold, it looked to be a lovely winter's day with blue sky as far as the eye could see. Clearing her mind of personal thoughts, she surveyed the interesting skyline with its myriad of architecturally diverse designs and tried to put herself on Edinburgh's streets 700 years before. *How amazing that this Scottish legacy found me in Canada. Dad had not spoken of his Scottish family very much or else I just wasn't interested! The family tree only showed the last four generations ... but such fine Scottish blood coursed through his veins and mine! I'm sorry you're missing all the excitement, dad! In seven days my old life will no longer exist.* She wiped her face again and suddenly felt a strange peace envelop her. She could feel her old fierce determination return and heard herself vow that the new Lady of Traymore would leave no stone unturned until she had solved the Wallace mystery. Finally, able to release the frightening thoughts from her mind, she turned on some music.

*My students would never have believed it possible that their sharp-tongued professor could be so emotional,* she thought. Telling herself that emotional outbursts were not what she would have expected of Lady

Traymore, she went to re-apply her make-up. Thirty-five minutes later, she stepped out of the lift and headed across the foyer.

"You waited," she said softly when she found him.

"Of course, where would I go? I assume you're as hungry as I am!" he said gently, studying her face for some sign that would explain her absence. Seeing nothing unusual, he chuckled. "I don't know what you're going to eat because I'm hungry enough to eat a whole steer!"

Conversation was sparse as they ate, and even though Alex tried several times to talk to her, he received no reply. Finally, finishing his meal, he pushed his plate away and leaned across the table.

"Are you going to talk about it Emma or just keep it bottled up inside that pretty head of yours?" he asked gently.

"Dear Alex, stop trying to flatter me. You know it won't work!" Even though she sounded tired, the sharp edge was clearly present. "You have treated me kindly, shocked me and terrorized me in the past five days." She held up her hand to silence his objections. "I think the spirit of Trevelion has driven you to give me a crash course on 700 years of family history because you both truly felt I was the one to fulfill this blasted prophecy!"

Alex stopped breathing, raised his eyes and studied her face. "And will you, my lady?" he asked in a hopeful, deliberate tone.

"You know, you haven't even told me anything about these relics. What are they that make them so important?"

"They are the royal coronet, a chalice and a ring from at least as far back as the 12th century," he said heavily.

"You have pictures of them?"

Her question relieved their tension instantly and he laughed. "Yes, my lady, my ancestor took a picture of them in 1305 with his cell phone!"

"Oh, come now, Sir Alex!" He smiled smugly, assuming he was going to be chastised, but Emma's eyes were twinkling for the first time in days. "Sarcasm does not become you, Sir Alex!" she snapped. "There must be a painting or some drawings, an artist's concept perhaps."

Realizing she was serious, he took her empty plate and stacked it on his, moving them both to the side. She knew she had hit a nerve and he was considering his answer very carefully.

"You're right of course, but due to the internet it would be a nightmare trying to find such authentic artwork."

"All right, let's leave that for now. I would like you to tell me more of the story of Mary and the children, especially where they were last seen together … and who kidnapped them."

Sighing, Alex smiled ruefully. "Forgive me for being so bold, my lady, but you can't hope to find out the answers to those questions!"

"Why would you say that?" she asked, somewhat taken aback.

"Because of all people, you are the one who should be able to get the answers for yourself."

"I don't understand ... oh, you mean Mary!"

"Of course, all you have to do is ask her. I think she'll find a way to give you a clue!"

"Oh my," she giggled, putting her hand over her mouth as she began to laugh. "Whew, you may be joking, Sir Alex, but this is going to try my beliefs for sure. I guess we'll just have to see, won't we?"

"You know, I think we need a change of pace! I suggest you've been working too hard and it's time you took some time off! It's still early afternoon so why don't I give you a daylight tour of Edinburgh and if you'd like to go shopping I can drop you anywhere you please."

"That's a lovely idea Alex. You must have been reading my mind! I would like to go to a dress shop, and somewhere for toothpaste and face cream ...."

"That would be a chemist or a department store and both are close by. We should even have time for a dress shopping excursion," he chuckled.

It was an afternoon quite unlike anything they had done so far. Emma got her incidental shopping done at the mall and still had lots of time to drag Alex around to several dress shops. He complained a lot, giving her useless advice which she mainly ignored, and it was all good fun. By 5:30 she had apparently worn him out and they stopped to eat dinner at one of his favourite restaurants ... to save his feet, he explained. Emma had done a fine job rubbing in the fact he was no match for her in the shopping department! She had accumulated a large collection of shopping bags, now in the boot of the car. He'd even managed to go to the bank to retrieve Trev's diaries. After dinner, he asked if she would like to go to one of the night spots for a drink.

"No, I don't think so," she countered, "but I would enjoy a short walk in the fresh air." Seeing his weary expression, she repeated, "Just a short walk before you take me home Alex. My feet are tired too but a bit of exercise will do us both good, especially after eating! I am eager to take a look at Trev's diaries ... I hope he won't mind."

Leaving the restaurant arm-in-arm, they continued their conversation, taking a slightly longer route to the car. It was Friday and they soon realized they were about the only ones on the street who weren't rushing.

82

"I think you are safe there, my lady. Trev specifically said you were welcome to use his diaries to gain any knowledge you might glean from them."

"Oh my, I do wish I had had the opportunity to meet my cousin. He sounds like such a sensitive and thoughtful person. It's a shame he didn't experience having children."

"That's an interesting thing for you to say, my lady. Forgive my boldness but are your thoughts changing about marriage? We really don't want to have a repeat of this inheritance business, or lack of it, do we?" he asked, growing rather serious.

"I didn't think I had voiced any opinion about marriage, Sir Alex. You're hardly the one to talk; perhaps we should be helping each other find a mate."

"My lady, that's highly unusual, don't you think?"

"Think of the potential fun we could have! Oh goodness, I forget about protocol, we'll just have to sort it out somehow," she laughed giddily pulling him over to a beautifully decorated store window.

"I believe Christmas will allow me somewhat of a choice opportunity to hold up my side of the arrangement. We'll be able to utilize holiday parties to introduce you around to Edinburgh's most eligible bachelors!"

"Well, I believe it's getting rather cold, Sir Alex." She shivered for effect. "Let's go home."

It began to rain as noisy patrons spilled out of the open door of a tavern almost knocking them over. Alex pulled her to safety and they hurried back to the car.

"I thought we might go to Yorkshire tomorrow," he announced, as they warmed the car and caught their breath.

"Is this another of your surprises?"

"Not really, this is the third manor house. You will be surprised by this one. You have an army of helpers and thinkers on your staff!"

"I don't quite follow."

"Then say yes and you will find out for yourself tomorrow."

"Please Alex, I've really had enough of your silly secrets. I'll say yes, but you must tell me something good about this place. I don't want to encourage any more bad dreams!"

He pretended to pout, and then grinned. "All right, let's see … it will take us about 3½ hours of travel and then you'll meet a group of educated people. There will be no water vehicles, nothing worrisome, and you could nap in the car, although you would miss some nice North England countryside especially if the sun comes out. You should pack an overnight bag in case we decide not to hurry back. There you have it," he concluded, starting the car. When they arrived at the hotel and he unloaded her parcels, he put the package of diaries into one of her bags. "I'll come up with you; you have too much to carry."

"I can manage from here, Sir Alex, truly I can," she assured him as they stood waiting for the lift. She was very eager to unpack her purchases and look at the diaries without any interruptions. She surprised both of them when she impulsively kissed him on the cheek as he held the lift door open.

"What time do we need to leave tomorrow?" she asked.

"I think breakfast at 8:30 should be soon enough."

"Goodnight then, Sir Alex, and thank you for a delightfully different shopping experience!"

Leaving the lift was a bit of a challenge with all her parcels, but she finally got to her suite, only dropping one bag as she fumbled with her keycard. Taking the parcels into her bedroom, she dumped them on the bed and went to take her coat off. She thought of the diaries and remembered Alex had put that parcel into one of the bags. She returned to sort out her packages but the phone interrupted her. *Did Alex forget something?* She wondered, but it was the front desk saying a delivery had arrived while she was out. *My tartan skirt! I had completely forgotten.* They said they would send someone up with it right away. Within a few minutes there was a knock at the door and she looked through the peephole before opening it. Her new skirt was hung neatly in a clothing bag and she took it into the bedroom, laying it on the bed with her other shopping. Deciding to try on the skirt first, she was very pleased with both the workmanship and the fit. She hung it in the closet with her two new dresses and then put away the other items.

She took the parcel of Trev's diaries into the living room, laughing as she thought of her conversation with Alex. Almost afraid to open it, she took it to the table, found a knife and cut the tape. When she finished, five books with different covers and measuring about 5"x 8" each, were spread out in front of her. On the front of each were dates ranging from 1957-1999. The dates puzzled her but she picked up the most recent book, flipping to the last page. It was blank so she paged backwards, until back about 20 pages, she finally found Trev's last entry on September 16th, 1999. She was sorely tempted … but hastily closed the book. *Be fair, Emma, you need to read this in sequence.*

## Chapter 7 – Saturday 18<sup>th</sup> – An Unusual Manor

By noon the next day, they were well into Northern England on their way to Yorkshire. Heavy rain had accompanied them out of Edinburgh and continued until they passed through the outskirts of Jedburgh. Watching the rolling Scottish countryside move quickly by the window, Emma noticed that the scenery was different now and more hills were appearing on the landscape as they went south.

"Shall we stop there?" Alex asked, pointing to a large roadside sign that advertised, *Everything a traveller needs and more.*

"Good idea," she replied as Alex left the motorway at the next exit and found a restaurant.

"I'll just stretch my legs," he commented as she got out of the car.

She returned with two bottles of water, handing him one and silently noting his surprised expression. They continued on without conversation for a few kilometers at which time he began telling her about Northern England and how she would have to see it in the summer. Suddenly, he asked if she was hungry.

"It seems like we just ate, but I wager you have a place in mind."

"Yes, you'll enjoy this place in Bowburn; it's just down the road."

Alex was right, and after 45 minutes, he pulled off the motorway and followed road signs to a quaint little tavern named *The Black Swan*. Once again, he was greeted by name, and the innkeeper produced a whisky bottle and two glasses.

"No, no Harry," Alex laughed, "we're just here for lunch."

They ordered the special and it proved to be an interesting interlude as Harry told Emma there had been a hospitality house on this very spot since the time of William the Conqueror. He also explained that his family had continuously owned the tavern since 1265 and they could only pass it on … not sell it, to a family member.

"And if no one wants it," Emma asked, "then what?"

"The Crown takes it," Harry replied, "but that's not bloody likely!"

Back on the road, Emma inquired how much further to get to their destination. His answer was evasive, as usual.

"You'll know when we get there!"

She frowned but settled back in her seat and took out the map which had become her constant companion. She had grown to enjoy following their progress because the map showed historical points of interest. She had soon realized on this trip just how lacking her knowledge of British history really was. History had never been one of her favourite subjects, except for literature related works, and her own ambitions had kept the intricacies of learning another subject beyond her grasp.

It surprised her when Alex left the motorway to take a bleak moorland road where all vestiges of civilization seemed to disappear. "Where the devil are you going?" she asked in nervous anticipation.

Following the direction of her companion's pointed finger, the stark outline of a large stone manor rose above the landscape. A high wall surrounded it and above the wall Emma counted two storeys plus an attic. The massive roofline had dormers and gabled windows. It was an extraordinarily large building seemingly out in the middle of nowhere.

As they approached, Alex slowed to pass through a pair of impressive iron gates topped by a solid stone archway. A portal gate was built into the wall beside it and a Latin inscription caused Emma to think back to her Latin classes.

"*Deus vobiscum*, May God be with you … it's a monastery!" she gasped. "I own a monastery; you did surprise me, you devil!" She could hear Alex chuckle but the building clearly unnerved her.

Rounding the side of the house, the scenery changed dramatically as a shrub-lined entry gave way to large areas of neat, almost empty gardens. This seemed to indicate that some person or, no doubt persons, took much pleasure in their work. Alex commented on how beautiful the gardens would be by the summer.

"There they are!" she exclaimed as a group of black-robed gardeners appeared. Despite the cold, some pushed wheelbarrows while others worked amongst, what appeared to be, flower or vegetable beds. Not a single head turned to acknowledge their presence.

Alex pulled the car up to the front door and two black-robed monks appeared, standing like statues beside the entrance. Alex came around to open Emma's door and, apprehensively, she got out. Gripping his arm, they went to the door. The monks bowed their heads but not a word was spoken as they opened the door and motioned for their guests to enter.

"You've done it again," she quietly hissed, as they stepped into the hall. Alex took off his coat, helped Emma with hers and handed them to one of the monks.

He smiled reassuringly but offered no explanation as they were led down a short hallway past a wide staircase. Looking up, Emma saw several monks walking along the corridor above. They went into a well-lit sitting room with large windows that extended a broad view of the moorlands. Their escort left immediately and closed the door.

Emma spun around. "Who are these people and what is this place? What does this have to do with my inheritance?" she snapped. "And incidentally, you turkey, this is all very unnerving, so talk!"

"Please sit down, Emma," Alex ordered gently. He pointed to a comfortable chair by the window and went to put some logs on the fire. "I'll tell …," his sentence was cut short as a monk entered the room carrying a tray containing a teapot covered in a finely embroidered cozy, two china tea cups, sugar, cream and a plate of sweets. He silently set it down on the table and left.

"Pour the tea and I'll explain," he said. "This estate was built in the 14th century by a group of Augustine monks. They had hidden the Wallace boys for awhile before the English discovered them."

"Somebody must have tipped them off," Emma snapped.

"You already know what happened to the boys. Afterwards, the English soldiers vented their fury on the monks and the monastery. They stole anything of value then burned and destroyed the buildings, dispossessed them of their land and left those who survived destitute." Alex paused grim-faced as he stared off into space before continuing. "As a final act of senseless violence, apparently on the orders of that barbarian King Edward, the soldiers cut out the tongues of every member of the order, from the senior brother to the lowest novice. Hence, the Silent Order of Saint Augustine.

"Not a single word has been spoken by the brethren since that day as future generations vowed to remain silent in honour of those who suffered so dearly. The Walters' family provided this land in the mid-14th century and, over ensuing years, supplied necessary funds to build a new monastery and outbuildings. Parts of it have been renewed and enlarged several times over the centuries with help from your family, but the initial work to move the stones and build the first monastery at this location was done mainly by the monks over many years. Stories have been told of how villagers both in Scotland and Yorkshire came to their aid risking their own lives, even as Edward I was still in power. Fortunately, the library was never greatly affected by these misfortunes and it was enlarged when they recovered the collection from Elderslie somewhat later. The monks were, and still are, very proud and grateful to your ancestors, Emma. Their kindness renewed their faith in mankind and gave them the strength to become self-sustaining. As you can see, they are very hard workers and the Yorkshire people come to buy their extra plants and produce."

"So this is the last of my estates—no more surprises?"

"Yes, you know it all now. Look over there by the buildings," he said, pointing to a group of neatly arranged outbuildings well away from the house but still inside the compound. Black-robed workers seemed to be everywhere and, trying to keep a count, she estimated there had to be at least two dozen monks. One building was larger and had animal pens. Her eyes strayed beyond to the moorland where more monks working with dogs could be seen herding sheep.

"They supply all the raw wool for the Stirling Tartan Factory."

"Oh my, you said I would have an army of helpers, but how do I converse with them?"

"I said they don't speak," the Scot laughed. "I didn't say they were deaf and they are beautiful writers."

"Didn't you say the English soldiers burnt their monastery? I presume all their records were burned too."

"That's exactly what the English thought, but the truth of the matter is ...," Alex smiled at the excited, expression on Emma's face. "All their work in progress was lost in the fire or stolen by the soldiers, but in their haste to be destructive, the soldiers buried the entrance to the catacombs, and that's where the monastery kept all their original documents."

"You mean they were recovered?"

"Many years later, yes! Now let me tell you about tenacity, my lady. Every useful stone in the old monastery was brought here and rebuilt forming part of the ground floor you see today. Thousands of man hours were spent walking back and forth to Elderslie with horses and oxen-pulled carts. Is that not tenacity, my lady?"

"Yes, of course it is, and admirably so, they would have needed a lot of strong manpower as well, but tell me about the records!"

"They recovered them and they're all housed right here!"

"When can we see them?" she asked excitedly.

"We'll find Ebert after dinner," he told her. "You'll need to ask him specific questions but we'll do that later. While we have daylight and it's dry, I want to show you around the property. It's really quite remarkable."

Darkness was falling and there was a definite nip in the air as they finished their tour almost 90 minutes later and headed back to the house.

Alex was most pleased with Emma's reaction to the property, showing such a great interest in not only the farming and gardening portions of the monks' work, but also with a paper-manufacturing system, sheep-shearing barns and the dairy.

"That was wonderful, Sir Alex!" she exclaimed as they walked back up the driveway to the front door. Are we going to stay the night?"

"We can if you like. We still need to see Ebert and that could take awhile, perhaps overnight. We could go to a hotel if you feel at all uneasy about staying here."

"I don't feel the least bit concerned and I do want to meet Ebert."

"Then it's settled!" Alex agreed, opening the door.

Emma instantly felt a warm glow on her face as if many fires had been lit in the house. Removing their coats, they followed a monk along the hallway going the opposite direction from earlier and they arrived at a small dining room where lights were turned on and a table was set for two ... and, as she had thought, a fire burned brightly on the hearth.

"We shall be ready to eat in half an hour," Alex informed the monk who bowed slightly before letting himself quietly out of the room. "Would you like a coffee, my lady?" Alex asked, going over to the sideboard.

"Yes please. They are very efficient," she commented as Alex made their drinks. He passed one to her, grinning smugly.

"You're smiling, now what are you up to?" she asked.

"Well, to be honest, nothing, my lady. I was hoping we would have had a bit more time before coming here, so I could have surprised you."

"Surprised me with what?" she asked, her eyes moving to see what he was looking at. Above the fireplace hung a huge portrait of the same handsome man whose portrait hung in the foyer at Dorik. The way he was looking down at them, she instantly flushed, realizing she was staring at her cousin Trevelion dressed in his clan regalia as chief of the Walters' Clan.

"Dear Trevelion," she began, tears coming to her eyes as she addressed the fine-looking man in the now familiar tartan, "Alex wanted to replace you, didn't he? I suppose we'll have to make time for a portrait sitting when I'm official," she murmured, sounding a bit overcome. "I'm glad you didn't have time for your plans, Alex. We'll simply have to find a spot for him at Dorik where he belongs. He deserves to meet me from his real place of honour ... in his own home."

A knock at the door brought their attention back to eating as a monk entered wheeling a food trolley and waited for them to sit down. The service was first-class and the meal delicious. The monk returned when they had finished dessert and Emma sent their compliments to the chef.

"Can we ask Ebert about viewing their old records?" she asked Alex.

"Yes, but I warn you, they are very strict with allowing people into their library and you must be supervised. We'll write down your questions and send them over to the monastery librarian and see what happens," Alex replied sleepily from the armchair close to the fire.

Seated in the armchair opposite his, Emma leaned back to relax and think. Then *she remembered the question she had been trying to answer … did anyone know where Mary had last seen her children and had it been recorded? Did they have the relics with them? Who would know?*

A sudden noise caused her to giggle when she realized Alex had fallen asleep and was snoring. *If you don't ask, you'll never find out!* My mother used to say. She searched for writing paper and pen, finding both in a drawer. Writing a note to the monastery librarian, she signed it with her normal signature. *Now, how am I going to get it to Ebert?*

Folding the note, she tiptoed to the door and quietly slipped out into the hall. Not a sound could be heard in the building. *How can I attract their attention without waking Alex?* Then she remembered the bell pulls at Dorik and went back into the room. *Of course*, she thought, finding the long black chord. *How silly of me!* She pulled it and went out in the hallway to wait for results. Sure enough, within 30 seconds a monk was coming towards her.

"Thank you," she said softly, handing the note to the monk.

Reading the name on the front, he nodded and began to leave.

"Excuse me, I wonder if you might show me to my room. Sir Alex is taking a nap and I don't want to disturb him."

The monk nodded and motioned for her to follow him as he went up the main staircase and down a short hallway. He stopped at a door and opened it, turning on the light and motioning for her to enter. She saw her suitcase and felt the warmth from a small fireplace. She turned to thank him but the door clicked and she realized he had already gone.

Going over to the fire, she briefly enjoyed the heat then went to retrieve her suitcase. She lifted it onto a short-legged table and opened it. *I think our shopping trip yesterday was very fortuitous. I'm going to need to leave some clothes here and at Dorik or always be packing suitcases!* After hanging her clothes in the closet, she went out into the hallway to find Alex. She was almost at the sitting room when he appeared.

"I see you've made yourself at home, my lady. I apologize for my rudeness. I imagine you had to contend with my snoring!"

"If it was that bad, Sir Alex, I would have sent you to bed! Instead, I wrote a note to Ebert and one of the monks just came to pick it up."

"Good, but I don't believe we'll hear any news now from the monks before morning. Would you like to play a game of cards? It's a bit early to turn in for the night."

"I've not played cards very often, but I am certainly game to learn. I'll get my sweater and meet you in the sitting room."

A heavy mist swirled across the exposed moorland early that Sunday morning, blowing whatever remnants of autumn leaves had been left on branches after previous storms. Emma got her first real look at the unspoiled Yorkshire Pennine Range from her window and thought how wonderful the area must be for hiking. Dressed in her warm pantsuit and coat, she ventured outside but felt instantly chilled by the cold, clingy dampness. A few hardy monks were at work again in the gardens, and sheep bleated mournfully from the barns as a steer bellowed his reply. Shivering, and desperately in need of a coffee, Emma stayed outside only minutes before heading back inside.

She was surprised when a monk met her at the door, motioning with a hanger to give him her damp coat, and then she went to find her bailiff.

"Good morning, my lady," he greeted her as she entered the welcome warmth of the sitting room, returning his welcome. "Eager for some fresh air, were you? There's a letter for you on the sideboard."

"A letter?" she repeated, pouring a coffee before picking up the plain white envelope on which the words, *Lady Traymore*, were elegantly written in calligraphy. Turning it over, she was surprised to see it had been sealed with the monk's official seal … a crest with two praying hands.

"You have an admirer already," Alex commented, raising his eyebrows to tease her.

"I'll just be grateful to receive a straight answer to my question, unlike the answers I get from you, lad!"

The note was brief and she read it silently. *You ask*, it stated in bold pen strokes, *the exact location where dear Mary Wallace said goodbye to her children. The importance of this question escapes us. We believe, however, that the children had already been sent into hiding with various family members before the search for their mother began. As well, the Order known as the Knights Hospitaller, having their Scottish headquarters at Torphichen Preceptory in West Lothian may have given Mary some assistance. There is no substantial evidence to prove this and they were never involved in the English reprisals.*

The note was signed by Brother Ebert, senior research librarian.

"Did you get your answer?" Alex asked, as the door opened and a monk rolled the breakfast trolley into the room.

Allowing Alex to read the letter as they ate, soon created a lively discussion.

"How did you get to the head research librarian so easily?" he asked.

"Just like I get to the head of the Student's Union in Victoria ... I give a note to the first person I see and tell them to deliver it!"

"A monk?"

"Yes, a monk; who else?"

"So what's next; are you ready to leave?"

"No, not yet, I wonder if Ebert would be able to tell us when the boys arrived at the monastery in Elderslie?"

"I'm sure that's in the journals," said Alex.

"If it was, I couldn't decipher it. Brother Ebert may know, but if their current records were destroyed in 1305 ...," Emma began sadly.

"Then shouldn't we ask for an audience with him?" Alex suggested. "It would save us much time and worry."

"Wouldn't it! Let's do it," Emma giggled, going to the sideboard to get the writing pad and pen. A tap on the door revealed a monk with a tray of fresh coffee. He set it down on the coffee table. Handing Emma an envelope, he began clearing the breakfast dishes.

She chuckled as she read the note, handing it to Alex.

"An invitation to visit the library," he exclaimed. "There, I told you they were helpers and thinkers."

"Wait a moment," Emma spoke directly to the monk who was filling the tray with dirty dishes. "I am going to write a note back to Brother Ebert." Nodding, the monk finished his work and pushed the trolley over to the door, then standing with his head bowed, he waited.

Hurriedly writing a short note to the librarian, Emma suggested that they would be ready to visit at 10 a.m. and would wait for someone to come for them. She scratched her signature across the bottom, folded it and handed it to the monk who left immediately.

"It is 9:15 now, Alex," Emma announced, "just enough time to comb the breakfast crumbs from your beard ... I asked for an audience at 10."

Grinning, Alex saluted and left the room. Smiling at her bailiff's antics, she finished her coffee and also went to her room. At five minutes to 10, Alex was waiting in the sitting room when she arrived. Eyebrows raised, he stared in undisguised admiration as she stood inside the door, turning slowly for his inspection. The stunning red skirt of the Walters' tartan flared a little as she came towards him. She was also wearing her white V-necked blouse with ruffles and the Wallace broach. She carried her warm sweater over her arm.

"You certainly look like the Lady of Traymore, marm!" Alex exclaimed.

"I am Lady Traymore, sir," she replied, putting on an upper-crust air as colour rose in her cheeks. She giggled and dropped into her chair.

A tap on the door behind her brought their conversation to an abrupt halt and Alex called out to their escort that they were coming. They followed the monk through the foyer and down another hallway that led past the kitchen. Stopping, at what appeared to be a closet door, the monk knocked twice and waited. Emma shivered, reaching for Alex's arm. The door opened revealing a well-lit set of descending stairs and another monk who indicated they should follow him. Down, down they went until they emerged into a large brick-lined cavern containing what appeared to be hundreds of bottles of wine stacked on racks.

Shivering, they continued along a tunnel-like passageway which went past a junction with another tunnel. Emma peered inquisitively down the tunnel and saw small groups of robed figures busy at their work. Suddenly, it became evident that the floor was rising slightly and the leading monk stopped in front of a recessed door and tapped lightly. He paused briefly before opening it then indicated they should enter. He nodded and closed the door behind them.

Ahead of them was a brightly lit room and a monk was sitting at a desk. Emma's fingers dug into Alex's arm in nervous anticipation. The monk rose, motioning for them to follow him. Glancing around, Emma made the quick observation that this room looked like any normal office above ground. It was only a short walk before the new guide turned a corner and pointed to a short but wide stairway with a door at the top. There was no sign or indication as to where the stairs were leading, and yet, the monk indicated they should ascend. He stayed below.

Emma gripped Alex's arm again and when they reached the door, he opened it. Bare wooden floorboards polished to a gleaming finish stretched out in both directions of a wide hallway. There were several monks in this area, but these had no hoods to hide their faces. Every head and face was totally devoid of hair and different coloured skullcaps perched as if glued on top of each bald head. Many doors lined the walkway, each with its own nameplate. Not one face turned an inquisitive glance in their direction and no one challenged their presence.

"Are we invisible?" Emma whispered as two monks passed them.

"Shh, read the signs, we're looking for the librarian."

Squeezing Alex's arm, she pointed to the sign on the first door. Her expression indicated she was puzzled and she mouthed the word "Sacrist." Alex shrugged his shoulders and rolled his eyes. Suddenly a door opened a little further down the hallway and a monk in a yellow skullcap stood watching them. He lifted his arm and waved slightly, indicating they should join him.

"Ebert," Emma murmured, smiling as she extended her hand. Limply accepting, Ebert frowned but showed no emotion in meeting her. He indicated they should go into the next room.

Their first impression of the large, windowless room was one of amazement as books were everywhere ... lining every wall from floor to ceiling and then some rolling shelves which seemingly filled every spare inch. An enormous table ran down the centre of the only area that was not filled with books. Five monks sat on bare wooden benches; hunched over their books or papers in such deep concentration they didn't seem to notice the intrusion. Following Ebert to the far end of the table, he motioned for them to sit on a bench while he perched on a wooden stool facing them.

"I would like to discover the exact location that Mary Wallace last saw her children," Emma explained softly. "We know that the boys were caught at your monastery and Flora escaped with various family members, but that doesn't explain where Mary last saw them."

Ebert's face showed obvious displeasure and he scowled fiercely at the table before reaching for a pen and paper. Tapping the table with his knuckles brought a previously unseen monk scurrying to his side, as he wrote some instructions. Pursing his lips into a tight, narrow line, he handed the paper to the monk.

Alex and Emma watched in fascinated interest as the monk read the paper and walked away. A screeching sound caused them to turn sharply and watch as the monk pushed a rolling ladder along the high shelves until he came to the right place. Then he climbed the ladder to the upper shelf. Removing a huge ledger, he slowly descended—a dangerous action with his long robe. Emma expected him to deliver it directly to Ebert, but instead, he set it down in front of another monk near the opposite end of the table, placing Ebert's instructions inside the cover. Neither monk made eye contact. In the meantime, Ebert had turned his attention back to the work he was doing when they entered and was completely ignoring them.

They soon noticed the ledger was being moved from monk to monk each keeping it for a few minutes. He added a short note below Ebert's and passed it on. It was almost an hour before the ledger came in front of Ebert. With slow movements, he pushed his work aside and began to read all the notes which had accumulated under his original. He seemed to add a short notation at the end and then finally, taking a clean sheet of paper, he stamped it with what looked like his official stamp of office. Only then did he proceed to write.

Turning to face them about 15 minutes later, Ebert took one last look at the paper then handed it to Emma. He also tapped the table loudly. This appeared to be his dismissal, but it also served to summon a guide who entered to lead them back to the house. As with the initial journey, each monk passed them off to another until they reached the main hall.

"They were trying to get rid of us," Emma exclaimed when alone.

"Do you think you could have unearthed a hot potato?" Alex chuckled. "Let's go sit by the fire and read that paper he gave you."

The fire burned cheerfully as they entered the sitting room and Alex went over to the sideboard, asking what she wanted to drink.

"Tea please," she sighed, going to warm her hands at the fire.

Alex poured her tea and set it down beside her.

She turned around and lifted the back of her skirt slightly. "How the devil do these people communicate?" she asked in a whisper. "And don't tell me it's by letter or writing because it's too fast. They know too much too quickly, just like somebody phoned ahead."

"Now you're letting your imagination run wild, my lady! Let's read what Ebert had to say."

"*To Lady Traymore*," she read aloud. "*We, the Brotherhood of the Silent Monks, believe that Mary Wallace and her sons were met at an undisclosed location by a representative of the Knights Hospitaller. We have been unable to find any written proof, but if such proof does exist, it may be found in Hospitaller records.* The letter is signed by Ebert giving his official title."

"Well, it's almost the same as before," Alex muttered softly. "He's not about to budge is he? This could explain his displeasure."

"These Knights Hospitallers seem to have been rather important in their day ..." she mused, still staring at the letter, and then a smile crept across her face. "Can we go back to Dorik?" she asked rather loudly.

"Today?"

"Yes, straight after lunch. We could eat and be on our way in under an hour, if you could notify the monks."

Standing immediately, Alex glanced at Emma as he moved towards the door, hesitating when he saw the twinkle in her eyes. "You are serious, aren't you?" he asked, a puzzled expression turning into a frown.

Suddenly, there was a tap on the door, which Alex opened to reveal the lunch trolley pushed by a monk. "No need, they're here with it already," he exclaimed, opening the door to allow the monk to enter.

Emma giggled and went to sit in the chair by the fire until the monk had set the table and left.

"What?" demanded Alex, spreading his arms wide for an explanation.

Rising, Emma went over to get her notepad and pen, still having quiet outbursts of giggling as she wrote a message and held it up for Alex to read. *Don't talk, just watch what happens,* her note said.

A frown caused deep ridges on his brow as Emma began to converse normally. "I wonder if we could order a glass of red wine with our meal," she said, holding her finger to her lips to stop Alex from answering. Glancing at her wrist watch, she took a seat at the table.

The Scot followed her lead but not without an expression of frustration on his face.

"Mmm, it smells wonderful," she purred, lifting the tureen lids noisily and putting her finger to her lips to stop Alex from replying.

Suddenly, a tap on the door brought their attention to focus on a hooded monk who carried a basket into the room. Emma checked her watch again, smiling as the monk placed two wine bottles on the table, a red and a white, along with two wine glasses and a corkscrew. After the monk left the room, Alex held out his hands for an explanation.

"Could you tell me more about Dorik Island?" she purred, totally ignoring Alex's pleading eyes.

Unable to understand the way his companion was acting, Alex's frustration was nearing a breaking point and anger was beginning to take its place as they finished the meal and retired to their rooms in preparation for leaving. With little luggage to pack, they were soon at the front door and putting on their coats.

"Don't we have to tell someone we're leaving?" Emma asked.

"Don't need to," Alex muttered. "Here's your friend, Ebert."

Turning around, she saw Ebert, striding towards them. He made the sign of the cross and spread his arms in farewell, his face never slipping from its dark frown. Ebert did not display happiness it seemed.

Driving away, Alex's jaw was set in obvious frustration, remaining silent as they sped across the rain-swept moorland, stopping only when they were in sight of the motorway.

"Now," he snapped, "what the hell was all that nonsense about?"

"You're angry," Emma pouted.

"You're damned right I'm angry."

"Are you angry because you missed it or because I protected you?"

"I missed what?" the Scot demanded, stroking his beard.

"Those monks have a very sophisticated listening system built into that house. They can hear every word that's said, which is why they were always there to open doors and to help us when we needed them. They heard you say you were hungry and lunch appeared. Did you think I really wanted wine with lunch? I was testing what I suspected."

"Oh for goodness' sake woman, they're monks! So, you want to go back to Dorik, do you?"

"Not at all," Emma laughed, "that was only for their ears."

Joining the motorway, Alex was soon speeding north as conversation centred on the monastery. "It's possible they're not quite what they seem to be," she mused.

"Let me know if you wish to stop for anything."

"I'll be fine Alex. For your sake, it would be nice to get home before we lose the daylight." Daylight was already noticeably lacking due to heavy cloud cover. By the time Alex pulled off at the Jedburgh Rest Centre he was eager to stretch his long legs.

"You have a stretch and I'll get coffee," she called, hurrying away.

Alex got out and stood beside the car pondering Emma's suspicions about the monks. He was sure they were legitimately Wallace supporters, but that woman had now put a worrisome doubt in his mind. Why a religious order would need to listen to visitors' conversations was beyond him or was it merely part of their efficiency? Emma returned and they were soon on their way again. As darkness fell, it began to rain and she was glad it was Alex who was driving.

"That monastery is not sitting comfortably with me at all," she complained, as they neared Edinburgh.

"I've never heard anyone say a derogatory word about the silent monks, but you certainly have me thinking now," he replied.

"If the Hospitallers do have their own records, who would have safekeeping of them now?" she asked.

"One would think the archives but, as the Order is still active today as the Order of St. John of Jerusalem, we have discovered they possessively protect their records. Why don't I save you a bit of reading by telling you more of their story and introduce you to another very important Order?" She murmured her interest and Alex continued. "Shortly after Wallace's execution, an Order known as Knights Templar was having plenty of their own problems in France. From 1307 to 1314 many of the Templars were persecuted and burned at the stake in France."

"That's terrible, but who were these Templars and what made them so important ... or hated?"

"They began as a group of eight knights who received permission to protect the City of Jerusalem, and later, the pilgrims during the early crusades of the 11$^{th}$ century. They grew into an elite fighting force and about ten years later rose to become a military Order sanctioned by the church. The Templars were a fighting Order and became the world's first bankers ... and far too powerful for some of the European elite.

"The Hospitallers, on the other hand, began somewhat earlier although records are lacking in those medieval times, they looked after the sick long before the Templars came into the picture and they both became associated with a hospital in Jerusalem. This hospital was dedicated to Saint John the Baptist so the Hospitallers also became known as the Knights of St. John, primarily giving aid to the poor, sick or injured pilgrims going to visit the Holy Land. During the rise of Islam, they were forced to become a more militarized unit escaping to the Island of Rhodes then fighting for their lives against *Suleiman the Magnificent* of the Ottoman Dynasty in 1522. They gained his respect and he allowed them to escape. They eventually ended up in Malta, adding the title Knights of Malta until they were ousted by Napoleon. Today, recognized as the Order of St. John and the St. John's Ambulance in our British Colonies, they continue doing their good work around the world.

"During the period immediately following Wallace's execution, the tables were turned on the Templars and they were put on trial in France. As a result of King Phillip's power over the pope, they were prosecuted, imprisoned and disbanded. But this was only the beginning of their problems for they suffered terribly during those years. Hundreds were killed, tortured or burned in the beginning and finally their leader, Jacques de Molay and about 60 others were imprisoned and finally burned at the stake in France while others managed to escape, travelling to distant corners of the world and mainly disappearing as they aged. The Templars held lands in Britain and when they were disbanded, all their Scottish lands and more were given to the Knights Hospitallers. The Templars disappeared for a long time but the Order is again active with a different role. The Hospitaller story has continued for many centuries as already mentioned. There, now you have the short version of their history, but I will add that the religious history of the knights is as intriguing as their battles and many books have been written on the subject."

"I thought you were going to save me some reading! I assume you can loan me a book or two?"

"Any time you're ready, my lady, and there are many books in the Traymore library as well. I have only touched the surface of this story. We need to talk to Alfreda again and they live close by at Borthwick Hall," Alex said quietly, pulling off the motorway into a lay-by.

"Now what are you doing?" Emma asked.

"I'm going to call them; they really are not far away!"

Leaving the engine running, Alex pressed a button on the dashboard and a cultured female voice asked, "What number would you like to call?" Emma giggled then heard Alex say, "Borthwick Hall."

"Hello?" George's breathless voice answered seconds later.

"It's Alex, George, are you at home to visitors?"

"Of-of course, old boy," George stammered. "Come on over."

"We'll be there within the hour. Tell Alfreda to put the coffee on, Lady Traymore is with me."

Dark country roads now slowed their progress and after awhile Emma began to search the darkness for lights. Suddenly, Alex turned onto a gravel driveway hidden behind some trees and a house appeared.

"You've obviously been here before," she said dryly.

A cold wind blew across the front of the stately old manor house as they stood at a large front door. Welcomed warmly, George took their coats and Alfreda led them into the sitting room where a great log fire burned. Emma smiled when a maid arrived with coffee.

"Where have you been?" Alfreda asked with an interested eagerness.

"I took Emma to the silent monk's monastery," Alex informed them. "I think our Lady of Traymore shook Ebert up a wee bit!"

George clapped his hands. "That sounds like you have come to a decision, Emma!"

"Yes I did, you knew I could hardly do otherwise, didn't you!"

"We're so happy we were successful," Alfreda laughed. "Did you meet Ebert?"

"Yes we did," Emma sighed, glad to change the subject, "he's such a cold fish."

"I've only been there once and did meet him at that time," Alfreda chuckled. "I found the silence difficult to deal with."

"Ebert said the Hospitallers may have aided Mary and the boys," Alex offered, "but there is no known proof. Obviously the Order needed to keep this secret from the English. Show her the notes, Emma."

Thoughtful concentration showed on Alfreda's face as she unfolded the two notes and glanced at Emma curiously before reading them.

Frowning, she raised her eyes and asked, "Why do you want to know where Mary and the children parted?"

"It's just my intuition," Emma replied. "Would a mother who knew she was going to die, turn over such a valuable package to a child who could then be linked to Wallace?" Both women stared at each other intently. "It's a woman thing, what would you do, Alfreda?"

"I never thought about it from that angle before," Alfreda said thoughtfully. "Now I understand your question to Ebert. Dinner is almost ready; I do hope you two are going to stay the night with us."

"That would be lovely Alfreda, thank you," Emma replied. "Ebert was an unusual one, but then the whole situation and history of those monks is unusal. I'm afraid he's left me with another problem ... how do we access the Knights Hospitaller records?"

"I doubt the Scottish National Archives will have them as the Order continues today," George replied. "The Knights' Hospitaller have always been very protective of their members."

Alex was about to ask a question but the maid entered and announced that dinner was ready to be served.

"We'll continue after we eat," Alfreda announced, brushing the conversation aside as she led them next door to the dining room. "We decided not to dress for dinner tonight. I trust you don't mind, it will be lovely just to relax and chat, rather than your going out in the dark again!"

"I think Emma should definitely see this house and the area in daylight!" Alex replied, winking at her.

"Aye, take her over to the castle for tea, Alex," George suggested.

Moving towards the beautifully decorated dining room table, Emma's eyes flitted from corner to corner, impressed and delighted at the sight of the magnificent antique furniture and the dark-stained open-beam ceiling. Emma assumed the lovely candelabra, the table's centerpiece, was a collector's item.

*This is just like stepping back in time*, she thought.

When the meal was over, Emma offered her compliments to the chef causing their hosts to look at each other and chuckle playfully. They admitted that they had ordered the meal from a local village publican who often provided meals when they had guests. "We don't have the staff any more," Alfreda chuckled.

"And we never have to fire the cook!" George added brightly.

Moving back into the sitting room, Alex explained that he and Emma had been talking about the history of the Knights Hospitallers and the Templars. "You can cover it much better than I, Alfreda. Do you mind?" Alfreda nodded thoughtfully, waiting until everyone was settled.

"Both of these Orders began at the time of the Crusades in the early 11th century; they were military religious orders formed in Jerusalem to protect and care for the travelling Christian pilgrims. The Hospitallers gave care to the poor and sick pilgrims while the Templars, being fighting knights, protected the city and later the road to Jerusalem. They were hired by rulers who needed people with certain skills and were paid either in property or with large sums of money becoming the bankers of the Crusades. Eventually the Templars became the second largest bank in the world, leading to their ruin. The Hospitallers used a great deal of their money to build large temple-like buildings that were used for hospitals. Some of these still remain today."

"If the Templars were the second largest bank in the world, who was the first?" Emma asked.

"That was the Vatican," George replied, "and they still are!"

"The Catholic Church?" Emma gasped.

Alfreda held up her hand to silence her husband and Alex grinned at the mystified expression on Emma's face.

"It's all about money," the history professor noted. "Religions have always been at war, but we digress. Ebert told you he thinks Mary Wallace was aided by the Hospitallers. I can see that happening ... being the go-between for important families of the day, including the Bruces, but they would have had to be very cautious. Danger was everywhere."

Emma listened attentively for awhile. "Ebert never mentioned that English soldiers attacked any Hospitaller but surely it happened."

"Money and influence," Alfreda said coldly. "King Edward may not have wanted a confrontation with the knights so he could have told his men to simply follow them."

"If that's what happened," Emma said thoughtfully, "where could they have chosen to meet the monks to enable them to safely transfer the children?" There was dead silence from the MacDuffs.

"No thoughts at all? Come on, I need help here."

"Finding a safe and neutral location would have been very difficult in those days. The Hospitaller's Scottish headquarters was at Torphichen

Preceptory but that was no secret and the area would have been crawling with soldiers. Edward had been in control of Scotland for years and he would have had his spies everywhere with sizeable rewards being offered for the Wallace children. I can't honestly offer a logical suggestion," exclaimed Alfreda, looking to her husband who shook his head.

The conversation lasted well into the evening and Emma enjoyed it all immensely. When George yawned, he was the first to announce he was going to bed. Emma excused herself a short time later and Alfreda took her up to her room. When Alfreda returned, she asked Alex how Emma was making out with her new situation.

"Alfreda, that woman is a true Crusader. She is taking this all in stride as if she was born to the title. I truly believe she is enjoying almost every minute of it. I can only hope that continues as we try to solve the prophecy!" he said ruefully.

## Chapter 8 – Monday 20th – Archives

Sleeping in later than usual, Emma remembered it was Monday as she woke to sunshine streaming through the opening between the curtains. Stretching, she went to the window and looked out across the valley. It was almost 9:30 when she ventured downstairs and heard the voices of Alex and their hosts in heated conversation. Hesitating for a moment before entering the room, she observed the Scottish professor pacing the floor gesticulating to emphasize her point. Moving into their line of sight, conversation abruptly ended.

"Good morning," a trio of voices greeted her.

"The coffee's fresh," Alex commented with a wink.

"Please, don't let me disturb you," she said, going to pour her own.

"Alex told us," said Alfreda, now showing her snobbish side in her tone, "you don't believe the silent monks are what they appear to be."

Emma contained herself from giving Alfreda a piece of her mind but listened instead as a wealth of facts and figures poured forth from the professor's mouth. Seven hundred years of silent monks' history was now unleashed upon them. Alfreda was apparently unstoppable, a relentless force in defence of the religious order.

"Right, now that you've got that off your chest Alfreda," Alex laughed, winking at Emma. "I'm starving so I think I'll go see how breakfast is coming." Moments later, the maid arrived with the food trolley and Alex followed with a pot of fresh coffee.

Emma looked surprised and Alex sent a frantic signal her way. It was noon by the time they managed to get away, waving goodbye through the closed car windows as Alex turned on the heater.

Driving leisurely along the dry country roads, he soon broke the silence. "Did you speak with the maid?"

"No, should I have?"

"You had that questioning look in your eyes when the maid promptly turned up with breakfast as soon as I said I was hungry."

"Yes, I'm sure I did. It did remind me of the monastery."

"It's not that sinister or even mysterious actually. That lecture Alfreda gave us was her regular university lecture on the silent monks. Her maid must have heard it a hundred times and knew as soon as the professor got to a certain part, she could deliver breakfast."

"Alfreda MacDuff sounds like North America's Unsinkable Molly Brown! I imagine she could be a valuable ally," Emma mused thoughtfully.

The rest of the way to Edinburgh was driven mainly in silence accompanied by bright sunshine and a blue sky, and what a difference it made to the landscape and Emma's spirits.

"What would you like to do for the rest of the day, my lady?"

"I'd like to go to the hotel to change my clothes and then, seeing as it is Monday, I think we should visit the archives."

By the time they were ready to leave the hotel, under one of the hotel's large umbrellas, they walked over to the Scottish National Archives on Princes Street. It was a rather large, stately building and once inside the great door, Alex checked their coats and went to speak with the receptionist.

"Would you please inform John Dunstan that Sir Alex would like to see him," he requested, smiling at the older woman.

"Certainly, Sir Alex," she replied with an eager smile, reaching for the phone. After a short conversation, she replaced the receiver. "Mr. Dunstan will see you in his office."

"I presume you know your way," Emma commented as he indicated the direction of the lift.

The polished brass nameplate on the door said, *John A. Dunstan, Director of Archives*. Pushing it open, Alex held it for Emma, and then grinned at the young woman behind the desk. "Hello Katie."

"Go right in, Sir Alex," she blushed. "Mr. Dunstan is waiting."

Emma didn't miss the girl's interesting reaction but her attention was soon taken by the office they entered. She could feel the power as she entered John Dunstan's domain. Tastefully decorated for a long ago period, it was difficult to hide the fact that the room had not seen many changes since the building was first built in the 19th century. The best part was the huge bay window furnished for sitting because it enjoyed a direct view over the Princes Street Gardens.

Introductions were made, making it quite obvious to Emma that the two men were not strangers. Coffee was ordered and delivered soon afterwards by a girl in uniform.

Once the girl had left, at Mr. Dunstan's invitation, Emma began to outline her problem. Before she had gone very far, he interrupted.

"You're trying to unravel the Wallace mystery," he stated.

"I'm trying to establish a series of facts that are covered by 700 years of historical dust and I'm begging for your help, sir."

"Can you help, John?" asked Alex.

"Many people have already tried to find the lost regalia. You know that, Alex, it's all in the Dorik records."

"Has a woman ever tried?" Emma asked coldly.

A grin slowly spread across the director's face as he watched her expression. "No," he said somberly, his eyes twinkling with amusement, "but I have the feeling you would like to be that woman! *Hidden by a woman and returned by a woman*, said the prophecy. Maybe you are that woman, Lady Traymore!"

"Can you help or not, sir?" Emma asked stoically.

"I can, just tell me where you would like to start."

"Do you have any Hospitaller records for that period?"

"No, the Knights Hospitaller kept their own records; they guard secrets with their lives. Tidbits of information are sometimes found in personal diaries and family ledgers, but it's not often possible to piece them together."

"Did the Hospitallers fight for Wallace?" asked Emma.

"Not that we know of, they were busy at the Crusades and fought for money while Wallace fought for his ideals."

"Then why did Ebert say a Hospitaller may have helped the Wallace boys? There must have been some indication of this."

John Dunstan smiled. He could feel the frustration in Emma's questions and agreed with her. "There could be written proof locked away in the records somewhere, but where? The Hospitallers would not have wanted it known they were helping an outlaw and, besides, they were supposed to be fighting on the English side. Actually, I would think the Order was much too busy in Europe to have had many of their members in Scotland during this time." He felt the cold intensity of her eyes as she scrutinized his every word and facial expressions. Standing up, John began to pace the floor. Suddenly, he stopped and turned to face her. "Why are you so interested, Miss Walters?"

"Obviously it's because I have inherited this mystery whether I want it or not!" Emma replied sharply, his question taking her by surprise. "I hate what the English did to those little boys and to the whole family."

"Tell me a little about yourself?" he asked, cocking his head with interest, freeing a greying curl which slipped down onto his forehead.

"I was born in Canada to a Canadian mother and a Scottish father, both of whom died well before their time," she said with only a hint of emotion. "I have a PhD in English Literature from the University of Victoria, British Columbia, and I'm the heir to the Traymore estate."

"You're Canadian?"

"Yes, and proud of it: Are you a Scot?"

"No, actually I'm English." He laughed at the look of astonishment on her face. "Does that alter things?"

"Not if you're prepared to give it your best shot."

"Miss Walters," John's voice now had an authoritative ring. "I'm a professional archivist, and a searcher of the truth who likes to dabble in archeology. Nothing less than my best shot is acceptable."

"How long will it take to get some results about our sword, Mr. Dunstan?" Emma asked watching the handsome director's reaction.

"Alex brought it in only last week, so it's much too early to form an educated opinion on either its alleged owner or the period of its origin. I'll keep you up to date on any information I receive."

A bell sounded somewhere in the background causing Emma to glance inquiringly at the door.

"It's just the 4:30 bell," John explained. "We close at five."

"I'm afraid I must have more time with you to discuss this matter, Mr. Dunstan," Emma informed him, as she stood up. "Would you have dinner with us at the *Courtyard Inn* at 6:30? It would be far more relaxing."

"Yes, I would like that, thank you, Miss Walters. It's been a pleasure, until 6:30."

They shook hands and made their way back to the entrance. The rain had stopped, but a bitterly cold wind was sweeping along Princes Street. Emma shivered and, taking Alex's arm, they walked briskly back to the hotel. Just before reaching the door, a thought struck her.

"Where the devil do you live? It can't be very far away if you walk." As they entered the hotel foyer, Emma jerked the Scot to a halt and turned to face him. "Well, where?" she demanded impatiently.

"Two blocks away on Rose Street, overlooking the bus station."

"Great view," she said sarcastically. "Are you ever there?"

"I'll be there in five minutes," he chuckled, "and I shall see you in the dining room at 6:30, my lady!"

Smiling to herself, Emma turned towards the lift, but she glanced back as she waited and saw her companion walk quickly through into the restaurant. Puzzled, she waited for a moment and, when he reappeared, she commented, "I thought you were going home?"

"Reservations had to be made, my lady," he said, winking at her mischievously before heading for the door.

Watching Alex leave, she couldn't help but wonder why he was being so evasive about his apartment. She let the lift go and, instead, walked over to the receptionist whose name badge said Megan. "Megan, do you know where Rose Street is located?"

"Yes, my lady, it's one block west of here."

"If someone lived on Rose Street overlooking the bus station, do you know of such a building?"

"It would be a very expensive one in that area, my lady!" Megan replied peering over her glasses. "It would probably be one of the flats on a top floor, a penthouse perhaps."

Satisfied with the young woman's answers, Emma thanked her and returned to the lift, smugly chuckling. Now, at last, she knew a little more about her bailiff and protector.

Darkness had fallen over the Scottish capital as Emma looked out her window at the lines of traffic going back and forth below and in the distance. Reflecting on the events of the past few days, she smiled to herself as she thought of Sir Alex's humour and the pleasant, tolerant way he accepted her sarcasm. *His efficiency certainly cannot be faulted*!

Taking her time getting ready, she walked into the *Hunting Bar* at 6:15. As expected, Alex was already there with John Dunstan.

"Would you like a drink, my lady?" John asked.

"No, thank you, Mr. Dunstan, I'd prefer to eat."

"Please, call me John."

Alex suggested they go right into the dining room and the maitre d' was waiting, leading them over to a private corner. The subject of the claymore was raised again by Emma immediately after they were seated and Alex posed his theory that the distillery sword could be the Wallace blade. John smiled even as he shook his head, glancing at Emma who had produced her notebook and a pen from her handbag and was poised to take notes. A waiter arrived with menus and a wine list interrupting their conversation. Emma selected her meal quickly then waited impatiently for her companions to stop bantering about the merits of every item on the extensive menu.

"Relax, my lady," Alex laughed, "we're just having a wee bit o' fun!"

"Then don't," Emma rebuked him with a hint of anger in her voice. "I'm deadly serious about this subject and you should realize that."

John smiled like a schoolboy caught by the headmaster, but he got back on track after the waiter left. "In simple terms, Miss Walters, that sword could not be Wallace's claymore or broadsword, because there was no such weapon at that time."

"Oh, come on, John," Alex objected. "History has even spoken of that sword."

"No it hasn't, Alex," the archivist said firmly. "Blind Harry didn't even mention it in his 12-volume poem from 1477. Historians now believe this work was a partly imagined tale of Wallace's life written 150 years after his execution. The fact of the matter is that the broadsword was not seen or written about until around 1600 so it's most unlikely that Wallace could have acquired such a weapon. Does that answer your question, Miss Walters?"

"Up to a point sir, but who was Blind Harry and how could a blind man write anything, let alone 12 volumes of work?"

Chuckling at her bluntness, John continued, "It was originally thought in early modern times that he was not blind, but history now believes they have enough proof to say that he was blind and these were some of the stories he sang as a minstrel. The text of the Wallace stories were quite possibly gleaned from a book known to be written by one of Wallace's childhood friends, Father John Blair, although no copy of this book has been found in modern times. Monks would have probably been responsible for transcribing Blind Harry's songs into a book, but that involves a great deal more speculation."

"Next, you're going to tell me there were no children, that they are also a myth."

"Now, that is another story," John chuckled. "There is actually no record of William Wallace ever having been married and so, my lady, your bailiff is an imposter!"

Alex roared with laughter; John's statement was obviously a standing joke between the two men.

"Are you serious?" she gasped. "They must have been married!"

"Why must they?" John asked.

"The library at Dorik has records of the children."

"Yes, but that doesn't mean they were legitimate."

"My word, there is one mystery on top of another, isn't there? I thought the church kept good records?"

"Oh yes they did, but travelling ministers performed services too, as did ordained monks and ship's captains."

"What about the Walters' family records?" asked Emma.

"Their family Bible lists the birthdates and names of Mary's children as do your Dorik records. It also lists William Wallace as their father, yet it doesn't list a marriage date."

"Are you sure there isn't a page missing?" Emma asked doubtfully.

"No, we thought of that and checked it out."

"Where is Mary buried?" she asked.

"In Elderslie, so it's claimed."

"Have you seen her grave?"

"No, I haven't. Grave markers are practically non-existent in the old burial grounds and although church records have been thoroughly checked, no records can be found."

The banter with John was obviously beginning to bite at Emma's patience and she suddenly turned silent. Having tried every avenue she could presently think of, she now pursed her lips and frowned as her mind searched for the right question. The men waited, silently watching her and, after a minute or so, she knew what it was.

"Why would the monks pay such a high price for helping the children and, why did the English King order them blinded, if they weren't the children of Wallace? Also ... why did Robert Bruce, upon gaining the throne of Scotland, restore the Wallace lands back to the children, if they weren't actually of Wallace blood?"

Alex smiled. He had listened and watched every second of this surprisingly intense banter between these two learned strangers who were his friends. At this moment, he was very proud of Emma and he realized that if he still harboured any doubts as to her sincerity in wanting to solve the Wallace mystery, they had absolutely been erased with this conversation. He knew that Lady Traymore was going to work tirelessly to keep her promise, no matter how long it took!

John raised his hands in mock surrender. "I totally agree, my lady. It would appear that everyone close to Bruce and the Wallace family had to have known, but where is the proof? We need proof!"

It was after 10:30 when they stood with John in the hotel foyer as he retrieved his coat. He expressed his enjoyment of their discussion and enthusiastically suggested they should do it again when Emma had further questions. "As to your sword, I would carry on with plans to have the museum look at it. It could still be a historically valuable artifact. Find out who Douglas talked to there and take it to him. Goodnight."

"I need to clear my head so I'm going for a walk," Emma murmured after John had left. "Are you coming?"

"Go get bundled up and we'll walk up to the castle," Alex suggested. "It's well-lit and an amazing sight even in the dark!"

On their way 15 minutes later, they walked hastily to combat the cold. Emma linked her arm through Alex's and listened to his commentary on the statues and history of the area they were passing through. High above them stood the massive lighted silhouette of Edinburgh Castle, a daunting image of the past looking very cold, harsh, and impregnable. Breathing laboriously from the effort of walking up the hill in the cold night air, at the gates Emma went over to the lookout and surveyed the remarkable sight of the well-lit ancient city below. Alex pointed out some visible landmarks of both modern and old Edinburgh but a stingingly cold wind tore across the ramparts, quickly convincing them to return to the hotel.

"I would like to go to Elderslie tomorrow," she told him before they reached the hotel.

Alex took the request in stride and instantly arranged the morning's itinerary in his mind. Upon entering the warmth of the hotel foyer, he took her hand and kissed it.

"I'm very proud of you, Emma … breakfast at 8:30 and on the road by 10 o'clock, my lady?" he added quietly. "We should be in Elderslie by lunch time." She nodded. "Good night and sleep well."

Smiling, and feeling somewhat like a princess of old, she touched the hand he had kissed and, as she waited for the lift, she watched him stride across the parking lot on his way home. Suddenly feeling drained of all energy, she headed upstairs. Knowing sleep was an urgent necessity, it wasn't very long before she was crawling into bed. Thankfully, sleep came easily to her that night although her last thought, as she drifted off, was of Mary and the children.

Fitfully tossing about inside her cozy envelope of blankets sometime later, her subconscious began it's now normal evening ritual. Conjuring up the image of a young woman, it appeared to her as if it were daytime. The woman was sitting on an unpretentious gravestone as the wind blew through her hair. She looked so peaceful; it wasn't until she waved for Emma to come closer that Emma was shocked awake and realized it was Mary. Sitting bolt upright, Emma fully expected to see the churchyard and Mary right in front of her.

"Where are you?" Emma asked, hesitantly, peering into the darkness.

"Elderslie … monastery graveyard … waiting," came the soft reply before it faded away.

Staggering out of bed, Emma stumbled towards the bathroom, swearing profusely as she tripped over her slippers and bumped into the chair. Finding the bathroom light switch, she splashed cold water over her face and viewed herself in the mirror. For a moment she actually thought she was seeing Mary standing behind her. Sweating profusely, she returned to her room and sat down on the bed, elbows on her knees and cradling her head in her hands.

"It was a dream you fool," she moaned, "only a dream!" Recovering a little, she checked the time on the bedside clock. "Only two!" she groaned, getting up and going out to the kitchen. Turning on the kettle, she got out the camomile tea and then remembered she was keeping a record of her dreams. She got her notepad and sat down in her favourite chair to wait for the water to boil.

She woke with a startled yelp when she heard the nagging beep of the alarm clock in the distance, realizing she was in her chair and chilled to the bone. She shivered and then remembered the dream and putting the kettle on for tea. Finding her notepad on the floor, she realized she had indeed scratched out two sentences and she read them. She shivered again, went to turn the kettle on, then changed her mind and went to take a hot shower.

Angry with herself for reacting to the dream and ruining a night's sleep, she hurriedly dressed and proceeded downstairs. Selecting a window table, she was having her first coffee by 7:45. Alone, wide awake and now thinking straight, she tried to make sense of her dream. Sipping on her coffee, she closed her eyes, intensely focusing her mind on the image of Mary Wallace she had seen in her dream.

"Are you all right, my lady?" the young waitress asked gently, touching her arm.

"Yes, I'm fine," Emma snapped, "why do you ask?"

"You were groaning and you hadn't moved for 20 minutes, are you sure you don't need some assistance?"

"No, I do not," Emma hissed, and the girl frowned and left her. Glancing at her watch, Emma realized it was already 8:15 and knew Alex would be arriving soon.

"You're early," he said, taking her by surprise a few minutes later. "I'm sorry, my lady, I've startled you. Were you somewhere else?"

Ignoring his question, she summoned the waitress. Alex raised his eyebrows at Emma's shortness and noted that the girl came to stand beside him, not looking at Emma as they gave their orders. As he prepared his coffee, he commented gently, "Are we a little testy this morning, my lady?"

"I'm annoyed, irritable and angry," Emma retorted. "I had a visitor last night and almost froze to death by falling asleep in a chair. It would serve me right if I finished up with pneumonia!"

"You had a visitor?" Alex was suddenly alert. "Who was it?"

Emma kept her eyes glued on the table top as she tried to keep control of her emotions. Biting her lip, a tear suddenly escaped, rolling slowly down her cheek and she made the mistake of looking up at Alex. Quickly covering her face with her hands, her body began to heave with silent emotion.

Alex never knew what to do when a woman cried so he waited patiently for her to regain control, thankful there weren't many people around. When he could no longer wait, he challenged her in a stern whisper.

"Tell me Emma, you'll feel better for it!"

"It-it was M-Mary ... Mary Wallace," she whispered.

"A ghost ... again?" he asked incredulously.

"No, in a dream ... but ... yes, a vision too ... I think, in the bathroom mirror. Oh cripes, I can't think."

"Oh my, this is really getting to you, isn't it?" Alex patted her hand sympathetically and her shoulders slumped. "Your imagination is apparently running wild."

"It's not my imagination, Alex. This is real life, even though it is in a dream. I can't possibly expect you to understand or believe me, not yet! One day you will see it for what it is. Right now, for some reason, I really need to go to Elderslie. No, I do know. I wrote it down. She's waiting at the burial grounds. We have to go!"

"We will, after you eat ... and I don't want you to get hurt."

"It's too late for that," she declared. "I'm totally consumed by this mystery, Alex, and nothing is going to alter that now."

Welcoming Alex's patient understanding, Emma recovered her composure and felt much better after eating. As they left the hotel, she noted that the earlier promise of sunshine had now disappeared behind some ominous-looking clouds.

"The rain seems to have found us," he quipped, as large drops splashed onto the windshield. "We just follow the signs to Paisley now and then it's not far to Elderslie. He began to talk to her about Paisley's famous abbey. "It's a wonderful example of how a building can survive due to the will of the people. I'd guess you don't have structures like this one in Victoria! The most recent abbey dates back to the 14<sup>th</sup> and 15<sup>th</sup> centuries but even in more recent centuries the abbey has been plagued by fires and collapses so it has gone through many restorations. Inside is an effigy of Marjorie Bruce, the daughter of King Robert I. She was pregnant when she fell from her horse while riding nearby. She was taken to the abbey where she gave birth to the future Robert II. Sadly, she did not survive and was buried there. We'll stop only briefly and we won't be getting out of the car." Glancing at his passenger, he watched her thoughtfully nod.

Reaching Paisley, he drove slowly through town until the majestic old building loomed ahead, eliciting an expression of wonder from his passenger. He pulled into the parking area and they sat quietly studying the magnificent old church. It seemed completely appropriate to Emma that it was pouring with rain.

"Even the heavens are weeping," she whispered. "The abbey looks so sad on such a miserable day. When you think of the history that has taken place around this church over so many centuries …." Then, as if suddenly realizing something, she exclaimed, "It's a magnificent structure, much larger than I imagined … but please, we must get to Elderslie."

"I do believe Mary could have chosen a better day to summon you to the burial grounds, my lady."

"You're saying it would be preferable to return on a sunny day aren't you, Alex?" she sighed, looking outside again and making a face as the rain bounced on everything around them. "I do believe you are right for once! I'm sorry Mary, but we can't do anything in this rain so why don't you find a coffee shop, Alex?" she suggested, sounding disappointed.

He grunted and started the car, taking only minutes to drive to the Paisley Shopping Centre. He pulled up in front of a cute little shop that looked like a restaurant until she noticed the sign, *Tartan Tea Shop*.

"I suspect you are already familiar with this place, am I right?" she asked, seeing the smile on her companion's face.

"Best cream cakes in the world are made here!" he exclaimed.

"Just go!" she prodded and they both left the car and bolted towards the door. He held it open for her as they laughed and tried to brush the rain from their coats. Once inside, she noticed there were six square tables set with red, chequered tablecloths. All were filled with patrons.

The happy waitress beamed a welcome, wiping her hands on her floral apron and apologizing that they would have to wait for a table.

Very quickly they were noticed by a minister who was sitting alone at the window. He waved them over, gathering his papers into his briefcase.

"Thank you sir," Alex murmured as they sat down.

"Are you tourists?" the minister asked in a kindly tone.

"Sort of," Emma replied, eyeing the religious man suspiciously. "Are you from the abbey, sir?"

"Yes, temporarily at least, my name is Monsignor Jason Sharp and I'm part of the restoration team with the Scottish National Archives."

Alex smiled to himself; he had seen that glint in Emma's eyes and knew this man of the cloth had innocently offered himself up for scrutiny. "We're pleased to meet you, Monsignor Sharp," he said. "This is Professor Emma Walters from Canada and I am Sir Alex Wallace."

Reaching across the table, Alex offered his hand and felt the soft, clammy touch of someone who was nervous. The waitress arrived with menus and they ordered soup and a sandwich, with coffee and one cream cake. Emma murmured that she was going to share the cream cake with Alex, but whether he heard or not was immaterial, the waitress had.

"You're a scholar from Canada ... what is your field professor?"

"English Literature ... not nearly as interesting as your field of study. I assume you are a religious historian, Monsignor Sharp?" she asked.

"That would cover it admirably," the minister admitted.

"Would you mind giving us a brief synopsis of the abbey's history?"

"I would be happy to do that. The abbey was founded by 13 Cluniac monks from Shropshire, on the site which had long been an ancient Celtic church and a 6th century priory," he began, obviously delighted by the request. "The church was raised to the status of an abbey in 1245, answerable only to the pope."

"Benedictine," Alex whispered to Emma.

A raised eyebrow from the monsignor was the only visible indication that he had heard Alex's comment, then he carried on with his much-rehearsed recitation of abbey history.

"Enjoying royal patronage, the abbey prospered and became very influential and a celebrated centre of learning. William Wallace is believed to have been educated there." Pausing, he took a sip of tea. "Much of the original abbey was destroyed by fire in 1307 and it took until the 14th century before it was rebuilt. King Robert II was born at the abbey in 1316 when his mother, Marjorie Bruce Stewart, was riding in the area and fell from her horse. The heir to the throne survived but his mother did not. Thus, the abbey lays claim to be the location of the beginning of the Stuart Dynasty. Parts of the building collapsed in the early 16<sup>th</sup> century and the monastery was disbanded in 1560 during the Reformation. In the late 19<sup>th</sup> century repairs began that eventually returned the abbey to its former glory and it became a national monumental treasure." Pausing briefly, he then asked, "What brings you to Paisley, Professor Walters?"

"I'm working on my family history and I seem to have lost the trail of one of my ancestors. I'm trying to unearth them."

"Not literally I hope." Monsignor Sharp made an attempt at humour, forcing himself to smile, albeit weakly.

"They were Knights Hospitallers or Templars, I'm unsure. I've only begun to study the history of these old Orders."

"I doubt you will find a Templar in the abbey's hallowed ground!" the monsignor proclaimed with only a hint of emotion, but his actions and flashing eyes gave away his annoyance. Alex tapped on Emma's toes, but the damage had already been done. The cleric stood up immediately and, without a word, threw some coins on the table, picked up his briefcase, and left the restaurant.

Emma looked at Alex in astonishment as the door closed behind him. Alex laughed, but Emma put on a show of innocence.

"Are you really Sir Alex Wallace, sir?" the waitress murmured self-consciously, arriving with their meals. "I heard you introduce yourself to the monsignor ... I believe you have come in on previous occasions."

"Yes, you are correct in every way. This is Miss Walters."

"Welcome to the *Tartan Tea Shop*; I'm Moira, the owner. Forgive me for hearing snippets of your conversation marm, I was particularly interested in the research you said you were doing on your family. There is a burial ground in Elderslie that once belonged to the Augustine monks. My grandfather was sexton and later the caretaker of the grounds." She lowered her voice even further. "He retired about 15 years ago and still talks about it. He used to be able to remember every grave and their occupants. Sometimes he would even scare us kids to death when he talked of seeing ghosts ... 'long dead warriors who rose out of the ground' he told us. He said they talked to him! As little kids, we didn't know whether to believe him or not!" She laughed self-consciously and a touch of pink coloured her cheeks. "He might be able to help you trace your relative marm."

A customer wanting to pay her bill drew Moira away briefly and Emma whispered to Alex. "We need to investigate this."

They waited patiently for the young woman's return.

When she came back to their table, Alex asked her why she thought here grandfather could help them.

"He had some boxes of records in his shed. He always said he had to take them to the monks but it was too far away for him to go."

"Would you mind if we talked to your grandfather?" Emma asked.

"That would be lovely for him marm, he doesn't get much company these days, all his friends have died. It's so sad and he so enjoyed having visitors. He lives with my parents in Elderslie on Hillview Road. Their garden gate opens right onto the old monastery property."

Obtaining her parents' address, they thanked her profusely and went outside. The rain had stopped and it took only minutes to reach Elderslie and find Joe's council house.

Sitting on his little porch nursing his well-worn pipe, Joe watched the large, black car through his billowing smoke and frowned suspiciously as it stopped in front of his garden gate. At 80, Joe had lived all his life in Elderslie, and he once knew every path and lane for up to a day's walk in any direction. Joe adjusted his tam and then he noticed a man and a woman walking towards him.

"My name is Sir Alex Wallace, Mr. Thornton. Your granddaughter, Moira, gave us your address. This is Miss Walters and she would like to speak with you."

"To me, sir?" the old man spluttered, snatching his tam from his head and trying to come too quickly to his feet. Alex helped him get balanced using his walking stick.

"Yes, Mr. Thornton," said Emma, "we are trying to find the grave of a relative and Moira told us you were familiar with all the graves in the monastery grounds and have even spoken to some of their occupants!"

Old Joe chuckled, causing him to start coughing and Alex watched him closely as he kept his balance.

"Moira told you 'bout my old ghost stories, did she lass? Ah've noo worked for 15 years … noo burials yon 40 years an memory's noo so good any more. I wouldna think ah'd be a help to ye now."

"You might be surprised sir," said Emma, suddenly having an idea. "I have a ghost story of my own. Her name is Mary and she's lost an artifact of some sort. She often visits my dreams."

"I found some artifacts in a hole I was digging. They just popped up and I almost lost me teeth in the hole!" he cackled, looking towards the graveyard. "I put 'em in the dugout, but they belong to the monks."

Alex and Emma exchanged raised eyebrows and Alex continued the questioning. "Moira said you have some old burial books and records."

"No, sir, I don't have any, she must mean the ones in the dugout."

"Can you show us where this dugout is located?"

"The shed …," he mumbled, looking around and seeming confused.

"Shed's gone … all tumbled in, lost me tools and I want 'em back!"

"Where is the shed, Mr. Thornton?" Alex gently persisted, smiling as the old man rubbed his unshaven chin. Helping Joe as he moved towards the front door, he then beckoned for Emma to join them and Joe led them into the house. Moving very slowly, he led them through the house, out of the back door and partway down a garden path. They could see a fence with a gate at the bottom of the yard.

"There," he pointed with his stick, "it's right there in the corner of the monastery property."

It was obvious the old man was either incapable of walking that far or had lost interest for as they were busy looking for the shed, Joe walked back to the house seemingly oblivious of their presence.

Emma took the lead and strode eagerly out across the wet grass, even though she could see there was no obvious sign of a building.

"There should be some evidence of it … stones or building material, roof or something," she muttered loudly enough for Alex to hear.

"Perhaps the boundary lines have changed," he suggested. "We should be able to find out from the municipal office."

"John Dunstan would know?"

"Yes, and if we ask him he'll want to know what we're looking for."

"All right, we need to think this out rationally," Emma suggested. "If we actually find some old records, it's more than probable they will have been written by the monks of the monastery … and be in Latin!"

"More than likely," Alex nodded thoughtfully, and then he added hastily, "the silent monks could translate them for us but …."

"I'm not so sure about that, I don't trust them yet."

"Is there anyone you trust implicitly, my lady?" he muttered sarcastically. Knowing not to expect an answer, they started back up the path and when rain spots suddenly reappeared, they found a way around the building and hurried to the car as it turned into a downpour. Alex handed her a towel and, after drying their hands and faces, they both started laughing. Then they just sat watching the rain.

"How the devil are we going to find it?" she asked in frustration. "We can't dig up the whole blasted graveyard!"

"How did Joe describe his dugout?" he asked pensively.

"He said it was all tumbled in, but how could that happen? What is a dugout and how does it differ from a shed? He seemed a bit confused."

"And now you have me confused Emma! Just slow down a minute. A dugout would have sod walls and a tin roof. I remember my grandfather talking about air raid shelters built like that during the war."

"Ok, what's on your mind? You've got that glazed look in your eyes so I know it's working! Can you just come out with it!" she prodded.

"Joe said he lost all his tools when it collapsed and they would be garden tools … spades, forks, rakes, shovels, more modern tools made out of Sheffield steel. All we need is a metal detector to find them."

"We can certainly do that ourselves," Emma chuckled. "We don't need John Dunstan yet!"

The weather was awful as they drove back to Edinburgh and, eager to put her feet up and relax, Emma suggested they have dinner in her suite. "We really have a lot to discuss tonight and my chairs are so much more comfortable than the ones downstairs. Besides, thanks to you we will have a wonderful view!"

"An excellent idea, my lady. We can also order our beverages."

"If you like but I have both a coffee maker and a kettle in my room!"

When they arrived at the hotel, Alex parked and Emma suggested they go and find out about the dinner special. They went to look at the menu and were happy to see the special was Roast Beef and Yorkshire Pudding. Speaking to one of the waitresses, they explained that they were going to have the meals delivered to Emma's room and she went to check on the delivery time. Returning to tell them it would arrive in 30 minutes, they headed upstairs.

True to the staff's word, the dinner trolley arrived on time and their coffee was right behind. During the meal, their discussion eventually came around to finding the site of the dugout.

Alex was still adamant that a metal detector would locate it expeditiously. "I'm actually wondering if the old man might be mistaken. Trev and I found ourselves on many a wild goose chase over the years, as we depended on the memory of others."

"I suppose we could ask around but that would add another problem."

"Yes, and have a host of people knowing what we're doing. I believe it is best we keep this to ourselves, Emma, at least for now."

"I agree wholeheartedly … incidentally, I am ready for some more reading material. Could you bring me something on the Knights Hospitaller, the Templars and another book on William Wallace?"

When he yawned, Alex got up and put on his coat, suggesting they meet for breakfast at eight a.m.

## Chapter 9 – Wednesday 22nd – A Bomb

As she woke up, she turned to look at the clock ... 10 minutes before the alarm. She sighed gratefully and slipped out of bed, but before her feet hit the carpet, she groaned and stopped, cradling her head in both hands. Having vague memories of getting up earlier, she tried to recall her dream ... no doubt the cause of her headache. The vision of Mary sitting on the gravestone, just like the previous night, came back vividly.

"Is something wrong?" Alex asked, when she joined him.

"I had that dream again," she snapped, "and I also have a splitting headache ... is that enough?"

"You dreamed of Mary again? You're back to normal, I will say that ... crotchety as hell and no doubt have a whisky headache. I'd say it's a normal start to the day!"

She threw him an icy stare, making a face. "I don't suppose you even noticed I was drinking tea last night? I don't know why I've allowed you to persuade me to drink so much, I rarely drink alcohol at home."

"Oh, now I'm going to get a holier-than-thou speech!"

"Please spare me your theatrics, Alex, and let me suffer in peace!"

"Perhaps my gift will change your mood," he said slyly, but he received no reaction. "Instead of buying you some books, I decided to loan you copies from my library. He brought out a bag from under the table, extracted a selection of books and placed them on the table. He studied her as she read the titles and her facial expression softened.

She looked up at him and beamed. "I've so enjoyed that book on Wallace. This is perfect, thank you Alex."

Selecting a light breakfast, she picked up one of the books and grimaced, rolling her shoulders. Alex got up and went to stand behind her, surprising her by massaging her neck and shoulders. Emma's first reaction was to object, until she felt the tension begin to release under the soothing touch of his fingers. She groaned softly as the pain began to lift. "That's wonderful, where did you learn to do that, or do I want to know?"

Grinning, he was saved by the waitress wanting to refill their coffee and breakfast came soon after. They ate silently for awhile and then Alex broke the silence. "I'm going to buy a metal detector," he announced.

"Then we'll go back to Elderslie to check on Mary and find that dugout, if you feel up to it."

"I feel much better, but shouldn't I go to the local archives and try to find an early map of the area. I could be a tourist interested in the Augustinian monastery. You said yesterday the boundaries of the monastery land may have been altered. An old map could be useful."

Alex nodded thoughtfully. "Elderslie and Paisley are actually a village and a town in Renfrewshire County. The archives are at Renfrewshire House in Paisley. We could also visit Moira again. Can you be ready in half an hour?"

"I'm not rushing today and I want to take a look at these books. Why don't you go and buy *your* metal detector and I will be ready in an hour."

Smiling, Alex studied his watch. "One hour it is, my lady!"

Leaving Emma finishing her coffee, Alex approached the receptionist.

"Good morning, Megan, do you happen to know of a shop where I may purchase a metal detector?"

"Well, let's take a look, Sir Alex." As her nimble fingers brought up a list of items on her computer screen, she turned the monitor so he could also view it. "Here's a hobby shop and not too far away," she informed him, writing down the address and handing it to him.

Taking the note, he thanked her profusely and went out to the car. It wasn't difficult to find and soon he'd parked and was walking the block to the shop. A young man behind the counter greeted him. "I'm looking for a good metal detector," Sir Alex told him, "and a little instruction."

"Well, sir, you have come to the right place, we have several brands. Come through to the showroom." The young man stopped in front of a display and immediately began rattling off facts and figures.

"Stop!" Alex protested. "A demonstration, please."

The young man threw a coin on the floor and reached for a blue and silver model. Covering the coin with his foot, he swung the detector over the area and a high-pitched noise suddenly erupted and the meter's needle swung wildly.

"This machine has both audio and visual alert signals," he explained, after switching off the sound.

"Very good, I'll take it!" Alex announced, grinning at the shocked expression on the young man's face.

Emma was ten minutes early when she stepped outside the hotel to wait for Alex. The breeze was cool and she was glad she had chosen to wear her warm pants. Alex arrived within minutes and as they drove, she realized that after only 10 days in Scotland, she was already thinking of the country as her own. Having a driver meant she was able to get used to the scenery and even the roads, although she was certainly not ready to drive herself. She asked Alex how he had made out with the metal detector and listened with vague interest as he described his acquisition.

"So we're going to stop in Paisley first to see Moira?" she asked.

"Yes, she could be a wealth of information for us."

"I agree but we must be careful how much we disclose. There are ears everywhere just like in Wallace's time! Not to mention, Moira herself could easily be tricked into talking to the wrong people."

Alex grunted. It seemed only minutes before he turned onto the motorway to Paisley and they soon reached the *Tartan Tea Shop*.

They found an empty table close to the cash register.

Moira came and greeted them. "Good morning, Sir Alex, and Miss Walters, lovely to see you again. My grandfather said you had called to see him yesterday. Will it be tea or coffee this morning?"

"We had breakfast so just a coffee for me and I'll let Miss Walters give you her complicated order!" Alex laughed.

"A lemon herb tea, please Moira ... not so complicated at all!"

"I'll get them for you right away, won't be a tick!"

By the time they'd finished their drinks, the restaurant had cleared and Moira returned to sit with them.

"Thank you for visiting with my grandfather. Did he tell you his ghost stories?"

"Not really," Emma replied, "but we did chat briefly. He seemed tired so we didn't stay very long."

"He does have his off days, to be sure," Moira admitted, shaking her head sadly. "He gets a little befuddled with his memories. Now that he lives with my parents it's lovely to see him more often. I called last night and he knew he'd had visitors but couldn't remember who you were!"

"That's all right, we understand, dear," Emma replied.

Paying the bill, Alex left a generous tip and Moira waved her thanks.

"Next stop the Land Use Department at Renfrewshire House," Alex announced. Little did he know that his pleasant mood was about to be put to the test.

It began when Emma asked to see the oldest known map of Elderslie. The clerk questioned her on her reasons for needing this particular map and when she replied that she wanted to view the original boundaries of the monastery land, this apparently caused quite a stir in the department.

She went away and, soon afterwards, they were informed by a junior clerk that this was archival material and would have to be acquired through the national historical offices in Edinburgh. Emma first eyed him coldly and then, in her most scathing manner, sent him scurrying for his superior. He soon returned to escort them down the hall and into a private office where a man of about 50 years, sat behind a desk, scowling over his dark-rimmed glasses. A small sign on his desk said *Rodric Brodie* but he made no effort to introduce himself. Motioning for them to sit down, he indicated two uncomfortable-looking wooden chairs.

Wasting no time on niceties, Emma attacked. "Are you an employee of the people, sir?" she asked sharply with that icy glint in her eyes. "Or are you merely here to make life difficult for ordinary citizens?"

Alex, trying very hard to control his facial expressions, had to turn away when Mr. Brodie sat bolt upright, his disinterested demeanor gone.

"Marm," he replied hesitantly, "we shall do everything possible to satisfy your wishes."

Calling the clerk, he issued muffled orders at the door and then returned to clearing everything off a nearby table. He selected a large map from a wall rack and lay it out carefully on the table. Looking pleased with himself, he suddenly turned to them and smiled wanly.

"Perhaps this is a good time to introduce ourselves," he stated. "My name is Rodric Brodie, Supervisor of Land Use for Renfrewshire … and you are?"

"Sir Alex Wallace and Professor Emma Walters from Canada," Alex replied, each accepting his cold, limp handshake.

"This," he explained, with heightened interest in his voice, "is the oldest map we have of the Village of Elderslie. It goes back to 1300, the time of Wallace and Bruce when forests covered much of the area. "This is the monastery land you referred to." He pointed to the map. "These monks were quite self-sufficient and much of the land was farmed."

"Could I have a copy of this map please?" Emma asked.

"No, I'm afraid it's much too fragile to be copied."

"I could take a photo …," Alex offered, producing his cell phone and quickly snapping a series of photos, all before permission was given.

"I'm relieved you didn't use a flash, as they are also prohibited … in an effort to preserve the historical documents you understand."

"It would appear," Emma sighed, raising her head from studying the map, "that most of the monastery land is no longer in existence."

"Yes, you are absolutely correct. Even as recent as the end of WWI, this area was mainly barren land yet our information indicates that portions had been farmed over previous centuries, despite the fact that the monastery no longer existed. Today it is all part of a housing development scheme. I can show you on this modern map," he announced, going over to look on a bookshelf and returning with a pamphlet entitled *Elderslie Burial Grounds*. "The area comprising the burial grounds is all that remains of the old monastery land. You may keep this pamphlet."

"Then you know exactly where the boundaries were at that time?" she pressed.

A tap sounded on the door and the young clerk returned carrying a thick folder which he handed to his superior. Waiting until the young man had left and the door closed, Mr. Brodie proceeded to flip through the contents, extracting several pages.

"This one," he said, handing the first sheet to Emma, "is a copy of a survey of the monastery land in 1920 which shows the barren land. There has been a burial ground in that location from at least the 8th century. We also have a copy of what the survey team assumed was the original land grant to the monastery. We cannot, however, verify its date or its accuracy." He handed that page to Emma as well as another. "This one is believed to be a line-drawing of the monastery after it was destroyed. You may take pictures of these pages."

"Thank you," said Alex and, after taking his photos, he added, "it would be very useful if we could also get a photocopy of these two maps Mr. Brodie."

"Certainly, Sir Alex." He immediately called to a clerk, giving her instructions.

"Well now, Professor Walters," Mr. Brodie said with an eager smile, "I do hope I have put your mind at rest that my department is not trying to make it difficult for ordinary citizens. Is there anything else you need?"

"Actually there is, and then we must hurry off to another appointment," she replied. "Can you tell us what year the monastery was abandoned?"

"Well yes, it was plundered and virtually destroyed in 1305, about the time of Wallace's execution. The English were looking for Wallace's family and suspected the Augustinian monks had given them refuge." Emma tried to react suitably as he told the silent monks' sad story, one very similar to that told by Alfreda. He finished up by saying that due to a lack of official information about those turbulent years, it had been thought the monastery was destroyed during the Reformation. However, these papers and drawings had come to light in more recent times. "It is now believed this line drawing was made immediately prior to the time of Robert I ... before the stones were carted away to rebuild the Augustinian monastery in Yorkshire."

The girl returned with the copies and, containing her excitement, Emma now graciously thanked Mr. Brodie for his assistance. Alex stood up and ended their visit with a handshake.

As they drove down the motorway, she began to mumble to herself.

"What's wrong?" he asked.

"Remember I told you Mary said she was waiting for me at the Elderslie burial grounds! Didn't you hear what I just heard? Our silent monks did originate in Elderslie! This would give more credence to the assumption that they were familiar with the family, especially if William had grown up in this area and been educated by local monks.

"And it would certainly explain why Mary would be comfortable leaving the boys at the monastery," Alex said thoughtfully, "but did she?"

"Didn't Ebert's letter indicate there were possible ties to the Hospitallers, and could the Templars be involved as well? It wouldn't surprise me if both the local monasteries and the knights weren't all tied together in some mysterious way."

"Ebert's message only mentioned the Hospitallers, but it certainly looks like what you suggest could be possible," Alex agreed vaguely, his mind obviously not on what she was saying. "But now, there's another problem!"

A look of dismay crossed Emma's face. "And what problem is that?"

"It's just struck me, and it should have been obvious to us, that Joe is no longer living in the same house as he did years ago when he worked at the monastery. Moira said he lives with her parents now so his shed or dugout can't be where he thinks it is. We should go back and see Moira, but first let's go do a little exploring using these maps."

There were only a few people on the streets of Elderslie when they drove into Abbey Road and parked the car with a view over the old burial grounds. The wind was picking up when Alex suggested they look around using the 1920 survey to see if they could work out if the boundaries had changed. It soon became apparent that the houses north of the burial grounds were too modern to have been there in 1920.

"This map is very difficult to read with few roads and no labels. This here looks like a small graveyard and could be this cemetery," said Emma pointing to the page. Then she turned around and walked a

124

distance away looking at the monuments and graves as she went. Surprised to see a large sign initially hidden from their view, she went to investigate. "Oh my, look at this Alex; it's still called the Burial Grounds. This cemetery is huge and appears to be used even today. The neighbourhood is all built up now but this must have been the monastery property. I wonder who looks after it? Suddenly, she stopped and looked inside her handbag, taking out the pamphlet Mr. Brodie had given them. "I don't suppose it's very important to us but this pamphlet says the burial grounds are managed by the County of Renfrewshire. So, the monks are no longer responsible for the upkeep. Which direction did it spread beyond this area? If there were any old graves ...," she began thoughtfully, looking all around.

"Look across the street," Alex murmured, turning to face her, "there's a farm over there and it's also bare land in this survey. There couldn't have been anything left of the graves when the county allowed houses to be built ... unless the cemetery didn't spread that far. I'm going to get the metal detector and quickly check out the area Joe Thornton indicated so we can rule it out. We might just find something that will be useful and we don't want to alert anyone needlessly."

By the time Alex returned with the detector, it was beginning to rain so they hurried over to the farthest corner of the burial grounds near Joe's house. Now in the shelter of trees, he moved the detector across the ground and the gauge suddenly went wild, swinging erratically as the machine produced a loud buzzing noise. Emma grabbed his arm and mouthed "shut it off" while moving her hand back and forth across her throat until it went quiet.

"For goodness sake, Alex, you've just alerted the whole neighbourhood!"

He rolled his eyes, yet he was obviously excited. "At least we know there is something down there but we can't just start digging. We'll be arrested!"

"What on earth are you thinking?" she hissed. "This isn't even the right location; you're like a little boy with a new toy. Now you know that it works, I think we should go talk to Moira and find the right area."

At that moment they heard a small voice and turned to see a tiny, white-haired woman come from behind the shrubbery at the fenceline. "Are you looking for the water main?" she asked.

"Possibly," Alex replied hesitantly, looking to Emma for help. "Do you know where it is marm?"

"No laddie I don't but Tommy Campbell's the waterman. He and his mother live next door and he's home today. Tommy knows everything about the local water. I'll get him for you."

Emma smiled and thanked the old lady, who then turned away very slowly and they realized she was using a walker.

"Well you were a great help," accused Alex, "now what do we do?"

"We play it by ear, what else can we do?" Emma replied, shrugging. "It would be nice to just leave but that could look somewhat suspicious if this waterman finds out who we are."

Leaving little opportunity to discuss the problem, they soon heard a man hailing them as he jumped the fence and came towards them.

"Hello, I'm Thomas Campbell, the Paisley and District water engineer," he called, looking at them curiously. "Mrs. Watson says you need some help finding the water main."

"Oh, I think we're all right thanks," Alex said cautiously. "We have a metal detector."

"You wil'na find a water main there," Thomas stated adamantly. "Let me see that machine." Muttering to himself, he threw a coin on the grass and checked the detector's reaction, and then he began to sweep it back and forth over the area, just as Alex had done. He soon had the dials jumping erratically. Then, more slowly moving the detector, he made heel marks in the dirt, outlining the anticipated object's position. A serious expression appeared on his face. "I think you might have found a bomb," he announced, but seeing their shocked expressions added, "It's really not so unusual; we've found a few of them in recent years."

"You're joking, of course," Emma said haughtily. "Who would bury a bomb in a cemetery?"

"The Germans during the last war, Miss. My guess is you're not from around here … they bombed the shipyards in Glasgow and didn't always make it! Harassed by the British fighters, they sometimes dropped their bombs and ran for safety or crashed. The army cleared most of them but they missed a few! I shall have to request a disposal unit to come and take a look." Suddenly, Thomas stopped and scratched his head. "Why were you looking for the water main?"

"We were not looking for the water main," Alex replied, "we were looking for Mr. Thornton's dugout where he kept his tools."

"Joe, the old sexton?"

"Yes."

"Could I ask who you are and why you are interested in Mr. Thornton's tools?" he asked, frowning.

126

Alex sighed and raised his eyebrows at Emma before he spoke. "This is Professor Emma Walters and I am Sir Alex Wallace," he replied using his best pompous manner. "Mr. Thornton has asked me to locate his tools which he left here."

Taken aback, the young man stammered an apology, then blushed as he handed the metal detector back to Alex. "W-well, if it is a bomb, there will be an inquiry, sir," he stated quietly. "The police will also require a statement from you both. May I ask for your contact information?"

They both got out their business cards and handed them to Thomas. Reading them, he failed to disguise his surprise and then turned to Emma. "You're a Canadian, Miss Walters!"

"Does that bother you, young man?" she snapped.

"Not at all. Now if you'll excuse me for a moment, I believe I should contact the police." He got out his cell phone and walked a few strides away. They couldn't hear his quiet conversation, but he was grinning as he came towards them.

"They're on their way," he chuckled, "and not very happy about it!"

"Well, I'm going to sit in the car," Emma muttered, "or maybe we should go find a coffee shop, Sir Alex."

"I don't think you should leave," said Thomas, displaying a hint of nervousness.

Ten minutes passed but still there was no sign of the police and Alex went to speak to Thomas.

"We are going to find a coffee shop, young man," he announced. "You have my cell phone number so call me if you need me, although I can't think why."

"But they're on their way, sir," Thomas argued as Emma joined them.

"On their way from where," Emma snapped, "Edinburgh?"

Walking away from Thomas, they got into the car without looking back, but Emma had noticed a man watching them from behind the shrubbery.

"We're being watched," she told Alex, keeping her voice down, but still keeping an eye on the man.

"I know," Alex replied, "and he's not the only one."

"Let's go to Moira's," Emma suggested, once in the car.

Alex started the engine then glanced over to see if her seatbelt was fastened. "Hang on!" he called and stepped hard on the accelerator, shooting out of their parking space and around the corner. Emma screamed, reaching frantically for something to grab as the car leapt forward, careening towards the shrubbery when a man's face popped up.

Alex skidded to a stop just as the scowling figure of the monsignor stood up waving his arms at them.

"Doing a little spying, monsignor?" Alex asked coldly, getting out of the car to face the shocked cleric.

"N-no, not at all," the monsignor stammered, stumbling as he hurried away.

"Now for the next one," Alex declared, grinning at he got back into the car.

Frowning, she remained quiet but watchful as she wondered what Alex was going to do next. Driving slowly up Abbey Road, he came to a stop at the end of a pathway. A small roughly-dressed man walking a white terrier dog could be seen hurrying away. Alex got out of the car and called him.

"Do you need to borrow my binoculars, Mitch?"

"No, Sir Alex," the man replied, removing his cap and looking hurt.

"Then who were you watching … me, the waterman or the minister?"

"I wasn't watching, sir; I just happened to be passing."

"Mitch, don't lie to me!" Alex barked and the little man cringed.

"I just wondered why the minister was hiding behind the bushes watching Tommy talking to you and the lady."

"We were looking for a water main."

"No, sir, Tommy knows there ain't no pipes under the monastery lands. That minister is always creeping around when anybody goes on that property … either him or one of those monks who don't talk."

"Have you actually seen the monks here?"

"Oh yes, sir, many times."

At that moment, Alex's cell phone began to ring and Mitch escaped.

"All right, we'll be there in five minutes," he said curtly to the caller, then put his phone away again. He climbed back into the car.

"Police?" Emma asked, watching him nod. "Who was that funny little man? He seemed quite happy when your phone rang!"

Alex started the engine, and as he drove he answered her question. "That's Mitch Pooley, the poacher. He was caught poaching rabbits awhile back and the nickname stuck. He's harmless and quite a nosy little man who can be useful at times!" he explained. He pulled in behind the police car where two policemen were seen talking to Thomas. They noted that the monsignor was back and hovering near the trees where they had used the metal detector.

"You left the scene, sir!" Sgt. Mackie growled.

"The scene of what?" Alex replied sharply.

"The bomb you found."

"Don't be ridiculous," Emma snapped, "it could be an old wheelbarrow or a farmer's plow, and besides, we gave our ID to the young man."

"You're not helping the situation, my lady." Sgt. Mackie turned to give Emma a withering glare.

"Sergeant!" Emma snapped. "I should warn you I'm a university lecturer well versed in the art of intimidation!" She turned away, but not before a splash of telltale colour crept onto the sergeant's face.

Trying not to smile, Alex made a suggestion. "Sergeant, why don't you just ask your questions so we can leave? You have our names and contact information and I see no legal reason for you to detain us. Perhaps I should call the police commissioner to help sort out this mess."

In the background, Thomas and Cst. Falconer were looking distinctly uncomfortable. Sgt. Mackie had a reputation for intimidation and a temper to match, but it wasn't being very effective on these people.

"Could I have a word with you, sergeant?" Cst. Falconer asked quietly.

Red-faced and glowering at the young police officer, Sgt. Mackie nodded and followed the constable out of earshot. A whispered conversation took place and the sergeant squared his shoulders as he returned to stand in front of Emma and Sir Alex.

"Exactly what were you doing when you found the underground object, sir?" he asked.

"I was testing a new metal detector."

"And what were you looking for?"

"I was looking for the monastery's collapsed dugout which Joe Thornton used as a garden shed."

"Old Joe who lives over there?" Sgt. Mackie asked, in obvious surprise, pointing towards the row of houses where they had met Joe. When Alex nodded, he asked, "But why?"

"His garden tools were still in the shed," said Alex, "and he wants them back."

"How did you know where to look?"

"Joe told us. He said it was near his house in the far corner of the monastery property."

Sergeant Bill Mackie's mood changed instantly. "This isn't the right place, lad," he laughed. "Joe lived in a cottage up near Main Street at the corner of what is now Moray Road. All that land was redeveloped some years back and Joe's Council house was torn down to make way for new houses. He moved in with his daughter. His shed could have been torn down with the rest of it but the property where his old house stood is going to be made into a park. I can show you where it is, Sir Alex. And you, lad," he continued, turning to Thomas, "can get the Renfrewshire County Council to investigate your little bomb and then you can have it as a keepsake! Come constable, let's show these good folk where Mr. Thornton's shed used to be!"

Thomas Campbell looked completely dismayed at the sergeant's admonishment, kicking angrily at the dirt as he returned towards home. Meanwhile, Monsignor Sharp, although eager to hear more of what was going on, hurried away in a different direction. Alex caught Emma's attention with his mischievous wink as they returned to the car.

"You are a devil, how did you manage that!" she exclaimed out of earshot.

"Just goes to prove, honesty is still the best policy!" he replied smugly.

It only took a few minutes to drive around to Moray Road, stopping in front of an empty lot where five foot high bramble bushes grew rampantly along one side.

"I believe this is where you should be looking, Sir Alex," called the sergeant, coming over to their car. "Old Joe lived in a cottage over there." He pointed right at the tangle of brambles. If you talk to him on one of his good days, he might even remember. He gets a bit forgetful now and then. I hope we've been a bit helpful, sir."

"Thank you sergeant, you have," Alex replied, keeping a straight face.

"My name's Bill, Sir Alex, you can dispense with the formalities now that we know each other."

Alex nodded and began walking towards the back of the property until the police car had driven away.

Emma walked up behind him. "How on earth are we going to find anything under that mess? What did he call them, brambles? They look like our blackberries; do they grow a fairly large black berry in the summer?"

"They sure do and they make lovely pies! I think we should be heading back to Edinburgh," Alex suggested, raising his eyes to the darkening sky. "It looks like more rain and we've almost used up the daylight; aren't you hungry yet?"

"Well, now you mention it, I'm starving!"

They were back on the motorway when the big raindrops began thundering on the roof as darkness enveloped the countryside.

"That was pretty clever the way you bullied that policeman into helping us find the right place," she said, raising her voice over the noise.

"I didn't bully him!"

"Yes you did, telling him you would ring his superior ... and name dropping!"

"Oh that, when I mentioned James, and you think I was bluffing?"

"Of course you were, but no matter, it worked. How can Mitch be useful?"

"He's the local busybody; he sees things, knows things. He can be a right fountain of information!"

"You have some incredibly interesting friends," she muttered, yawning. Putting her head back on the seat, she closed her eyes.

Grinning, Alex peered through the window, straining to see the sign to Newhouse where he turned off the motorway.

"Where are we going?" she asked sleepily.

"Right here, my lady," he said, pulling into the yard of a public house.

"Are we eating here?"

"No, just stopping briefly."

Using the umbrella, they hurried inside, removing their wet coats as they entered. Emma took in the quiet scene and, noticed that the man behind the bar reading the newspaper had raised his head and grinned at Alex.

"A coffee for the lady and a wee dram of the dew for me, Jack."

"Which way are ye going, Sir Alex, east or west?" the barman asked without taking his eyes off the drinks he was pouring.

"East."

"Ye've been to Elderslie." It was more a statement than a question and Alex nodded as the barman placed Emma's coffee on the bar. Allowing their eyes to lock for a moment, he added, "A toast, lad."

Alex raised his glass. "To the rebel of Elderslie!" they whispered and downed their drinks in a single gulp, banging the empty glasses on the counter.

"Jack Cameron meet Miss Emma Walters, the soon-to-be Lady of Traymore," Alex announced, surprising Emma with his rather jubilant manner. "She's a Canadian professor with a tongue like a claymore and totally unafraid of using it!"

"A rebel ... welcome, my lady!" Jack responded with obvious delight.

Sipping on her coffee, Emma wondered why they had called at the out-of-the-way tavern but, in the next breath, she got her answer.

"Do you still have a backhoe, Jack?" asked Alex.

"No, but I can easily get the use of it."

"On short notice ... like tomorrow?"

"Aye."

"Can you meet us at the empty lot at the corner of Main and Moray at ten in the morning?"

"Och aye," the barman nodded solemnly, "anything else you need?"

"Six to ten builder's planks and a wood pallet would be helpful."

"I shall be there, Sir Alex, pleasure meeting you, Miss Walters."

Leaving the country tavern and rejoining the M8, Alex grumbled at the rain and waited for the inevitable barrage of questions. The first was not the one he expected.

"Who was the rebel you and Jack drank to?" she murmured.

"William Wallace, of course!"

"Does Jack know what we're doing?"

"How could he, *we* don't know what we're doing, do we?"

"But how can he come up with all that equipment so easily?"

"He was a builder and his son, Allan, now runs that business. Jack retired to become a publican but he still has access to the equipment. We'll eat at a nice little place near the airport."

"Do you think that policeman will give us any trouble, Alex?"

"No, but the monsignor might, he seems to be quite a ferret."

Her questions stopped as Alex drove off the motorway at the next exit and followed well-lit signs to the appropriately named, *Airport Restaurant*. Music was playing softly as they entered the old stone building and were shown to a table; Alex explained that it was once a manor house. A low murmur of voices emanated through the room as Emma glanced around at the décor of the busy restaurant, locking eyes with a gentleman in a nearby room who nodded in recognition.

"John Dunstan is at a table to your left," Emma murmured.

"Och, is he alone?" Alex asked.

"No, with a woman and he's seen us. Here he comes!"

"Hello, you two beautiful people," John gushed, resting his hand lightly on Emma's shoulder. "Have you ordered yet? If not, please come and join my sister Anne and I. She's visiting from Sussex."

Not particularly pleased to be interrupted, Emma turned to Alex and they wordlessly decided they had no choice. John led them over to their table, ordering drinks from a passing waiter. When he introduced his sister, Anne Dunstan, he made sure to add Emma's and Alex's titles.

"Are you really a descendant of William Wallace?" she asked Alex.

"Well it's debatable really," he laughed, "your brother says I'm not, yet I hold the family title. Our family Bible says I am, yet offers no proof!"

Anne laughed, but realized she was none the wiser.

"Are you making any progress?" John asked.

"We could be very soon," Emma replied, "with a little bit of luck!"

"What exactly are you looking for?" Anne asked.

"Our quest is for the items referred to as the royal regalia which William Wallace was keeping for the rightful heir of Scotland. It went missing about the time of his death," Sir Alex explained, sporting a serious expression. "Finding any proof of William and Mary's legal union will be a bonus and, of course, make me legitimate!"

"Good gracious me," Anne gasped, "what an enormous task you've set out for yourselves."

"Oh no, they didn't set the task, Anne," John corrected his sister. "It's a 700-year-old mystery they are trying to solve. The Wallace family's prophecy says a woman hid the regalia and a woman will recover it. Emma is the first woman to inherit the Traymore title, which is a Walters' title."

Anne pursed her lips and frowned. "But Emma is not a Wallace; she's the chief of the Walters Clan isn't she?"

"Correct!" the men chorused loudly, causing some disapproving glances from people at nearby tables. Alex leaned forward and quietly added, "Mary Wallace, Emma's ancestor, was born Mary Walters and married William Wallace."

Anne was in a high state of excitement for the duration of the meal, chattering incessantly as she picked at her food. Relief crossed Alex's face when John announced they had to leave, generously offering to pay the bill which they refused.

"Anne's voice made my ears ache!" he said when they were alone.

"You have to admit she was definitely interested but I'm so glad the sword wasn't mentioned!" Emma murmured. "It's my turn now. I want to know what we're going to do in Elderslie tomorrow?"

"You will just have to wait and see, Emma," Alex murmured, coyly winking at her as he set down his empty cup and pushed his chair back.

133

She shook her head in exasperation, watching him walk to the cashier. She got ready and followed him taking her time. Seeing the car was at the door already, she sauntered outside.

"I'll bet ye were a wee brat as a young laddie, because ye 'aven't changed a great deal!" she exclaimed, trying out her Scottish accent.

"Very good Emma, at this rate we'll 'av you turned into a real Scot befur ye knoow it!" All he received back was a grunt.

They both sat silently, each in their own thoughts as they waited for the foggy windows to clear. Once on their way, she broke the silence.

"Were you serious with what you said about that minister?"

"Of course, he's a nosy buzzard; he could cause us some trouble. "Maybe we should give him another interest in life."

"A decoy you mean?" asked Emma. "Now *that* could be a very interesting manoeuvre if we could pull it off. What are you thinking?"

No matter how she tried, Alex resisted all attempts to coax more information out of him, further infuriating her with his sporadic chuckles.

"Would you like a nightcap?" he asked, pulling up to the hotel.

"No, thank you, laddie, I believe I've had quite enough of you for one day!" she said wearily, forcing a smile. "My batteries need recharging to face it all again tomorrow. Thank you for a most interesting day and good night, Sir Alex." She turned and went towards the lift.

"Breakfast at 7! We want to be in Elderslie by 10 and I would suggest wearing your most casual clothes for muckin' aboot in the mud!" he called after her.

Emma was relieved Alex had not given her an argument and she was happy to reach the solitude of her suite. Kicking off her shoes, she called room service, ordered a decaf Irish Coffee and picked up the Wallace book from the table. Turning on the TV, a local news program was showing pictures of some lowlands' flooding around Stirling and several rivers far too close to overflowing. The forecast was for sunshine.

"Maybe I won't be muckin' aboot in the mud tomorrow after all!"

Her coffee arrived partway through the news so when she found herself yawning, she switched it off and went to the bedroom window. She finished her drink as she studied the intriguing silhouette made by spires, domes and the castle. She couldn't help but think of the similarity to her view back home … albeit not so grand!

134

## Chapter 10 – Thursday 23rd – The Dugout

The next morning, she joined Alex and, before she had a chance to even think about breakfast, the waitress arrived with a cup of coffee.

"Your Irish Coffee, miss," she quietly announced at her elbow before asking if they were having their usual. Once confirmed she left quickly.

"Hmm, trying to butter me up this morning, are you, Sir Alex?"

"Simply doing my best to turn you into a sweet-tempered lady, my lady!"

"You're going to have to try a lot harder than that, m'laddie!"

They smiled wanly at each other and traded comments on the weather until their breakfast arrived. Emma cast suspicious glances his way realizing something was troubling him. She waited until they were on their way to Elderslie, however, and then began to quiz him.

"Do we have a problem?" she asked as the car moved slowly through Thursday morning traffic. Alex merely grunted.

Once the city was behind them, he finally spoke to her. "The monsignor said he was working at Paisley Abbey, didn't he?"

"He said he was with the restoration team for the National Archives. If that were true, John Dunstan would know about him. You could have given him a call."

"I don't want to alert him just yet. We really need to see Moira."

"Good idea, but we won't have much time before meeting Jack."

It was just past nine o'clock when Alex pulled up at the little tea shop. Moira saw them first, greeting them like long-lost friends. They ordered coffee and waited for a chance to talk to her.

"Moira, how well do you know the minister we sat with the other day?" Emma asked as the young woman passed by with a loaded tray.

"Don't know him at all, my lady. I had never seen him before that day. Why, what has he done?"

"Oh, nothing, dear, we just wondered, you carry on." Emma tried to make light of the question as she tapped urgently on Alex's foot under the table and made signs with her eyes that they should be leaving. Nodding, he left money on the table and they waved to Moira.

"Who could have put Monsignor Sharp onto us?" Alex asked as they drove towards Elderslie. "He had to have been waiting for us to return to

Moira's." He was grinning as they reached Main Street, seeing the truck and trailer carrying a backhoe already parked on Moray Street. Jack was getting ready to move the backhoe as they went past to park in front of his truck.

"Good morning," he greeted them loudly. "So that must be your problem over there by the fence—what are your plans, Sir Alex?"

"I need the pallet in the middle of those brambles," Alex replied, pointing it out. "Then lay out the planks like an octopus, so we can walk all over that area."

Jack nodded, understanding perfectly. He lowered two ramps, then started the backhoe and, in no time at all, he had it ready.

"Now what?" he shouted, shutting off the noisy machine.

"We have company," Emma called, pointing to the side of Main Road where Mitch Pooley was watching.

"Oh, that's only Mitch Pooley," Jack laughed, "the local busybody."

Alex waved at the man, calling him over. He approached nervously, the little dog at his heels. Emma watched as Mitch pulled his cap off and stood humbly before Alex, his lip trembling in anticipation of a reproach.

"I have a job for you, Mitch," Alex said gently, "go and find that minister, watch him for awhile, then come and tell me what he's up to, but don't talk to him. When you report back to me, I'll give you some more of this." He put a folded bill into Mitch's hand. "We'll probably be here all day."

"Right, Sir Alex, I will do it, sir!" He backed away quickly, putting his cap back on and hurrying away.

Removing the metal detector from the boot of the car, Alex checked his batteries, adjusted the handle and climbed down onto one of the planks. He jumped up and down a couple of times to make sure the board was stable enough over the brambles. Swinging the detector into place, he focused his attention on the dials and turned it on. When he got to the middle section, a loud squealing erupted and he turned it down.

"Found it!" he called excitedly.

"Found what?" Jack snorted.

"Well, something metal … hopefully the shed or some tools."

"Hold on a minute," Jack laughed, "let me do a little fishing. You'd better move yourself."

Removing some of the planks, he attached hooks and chains to the bucket then started the motor. Driving the machine closer to the edge of the brambles, he swung the chain out into the tangled mess, lowered his bucket and began backing away. Suddenly, two of the chains snapped tight, the hooks had found an object. Revving the power on the machine jack, he began to lift the bucket and, out of the brambles, came an iron bedframe and a rusting bicycle.

Jack had the machine deposit the trash in his truck and sat shaking his head. "Don't move, I'm going to try it again," he yelled at Alex.

Twice more Jack raked his hooks through the bramble patch, each time coming up with more trash, adding a rusty motorcycle frame and numerous bicycle parts to the pile of rubbish on his truck.

It was soon after one o'clock when Emma asked their intentions for lunch. Jack yelled back that he'd packed a lunch and they could share it. Both men agreed they were having too much fun to be hungry.

"It's a shame you can't drive on the 'wrong side' of the road, my lady," Alex called.

"My lunchbox is on the seat of my truck, hot black coffee too, my lady!" Jack called. "Help yourself and come back. I have a feeling we're going to come up with something a bit more interesting now that we've cleared this rubbish!"

Knowing there was coffee was all Emma needed to be persuaded. When she returned to join Alex, he was leaning over the hole watching Jack intently.

"I'm going to move some of these planks," Jack called from the digger. "I believe I can see a bit of corrugated. It could be the roof of your shed. Listen, why don't you two go and get some proper lunch and leave me mine so I can have a coffee. By the time you get back, I'll have this all cleaned up and made safer so we can have another look."

Deciding to follow his suggestion, Alex and Emma left and Jack ate a bit of his lunch before returning to work. He always enjoyed this part of a dig and was too occupied to notice that both Mitch and the monsignor had returned. They continued to secretly watch him from separate locations as he rebuilt the walkways and lowered the pallet into the brambles. The monsignor kept glancing over his shoulder nervously and Mitch, who could make no sense of any of it, took his dog for a walk then returned minutes before Alex and Emma drove up. The watchers both became alert when the car returned and the monsignor moved further away. Split between his own inquisitive nature and Sir Alex's orders to follow the monsignor, Mitch stayed where he was and continued watching from his hiding place. His interest peaked when Alex picked up his metal detector again and began to slowly sweep it over the brambles.

"I just saw Mitch's little dog again, over in the trees," Emma alerted Jack and he nodded.

Jack went out on one of the planks until he was near Alex. Suddenly, the detector began to squeal with the indicator bouncing erratically and the noise increasing. Alex turned it down but Mitch was now forgotten as Jack hurried back to his truck, returning with a can of yellow spray paint.

"Spray some paint on that area," he ordered, tossing the can to Alex. There was excitement in the air as Jack started the backhoe shouting to Alex to get out of the way. Brambles were swept aside as the backhoe dug into the ground. He stopped to inspect his work when he saw bits of wood and more rusted tin sheeting.

"Looks like we've found your garden shed!" he called, laughing.

Assisted by Alex, Emma walked gingerly along a 12-inch wide plank and peered into the hole.

"See there!" Alex pointed. "That looks like the corner of the shed all right. Jack's pulled part of the roof off."

"I'm surprised the old thing is still recognizable," Jack muttered, "but now we've disturbed it, it could collapse at any time."

"Can you dig down the side of it?" Alex asked.

"Yes, but I can't guarantee its safety."

"Dig, Jack!" Alex snapped. "If that old man's right, I need to get in there before the authorities find out we're here and shut us down."

Emma watched fascinated as Jack gently used the mechanical arm of the backhoe like a delicate finger, digging carefully as Alex directed his effort. Peering into the now six-foot-deep hole, Emma could see rotting wood along the side walls with layers of black soil and old leaves still covering the roof. Alex scrambled down and Jack followed. Jack pulled away bits of rotting wood, cautiously making a hole in the old wall. They extracted two very rusty spades and a rake in deplorable condition.

"I don't think Joe is going to want these any more!" Alex shouted, pulling out another rake and a few smaller items, taking them topside. "Can you see inside? It's larger than I imagined."

"No, it's as dark as the devil's heart in there, but there's a flashlight in the truck under my seat."

"Got it!" Alex called, already halfway there. Unable to contain his excitement, Alex found the light and returned to the dig, climbing back down to join Jack.

"Careful!" the builder warned. "It's mighty fragile!"

"What can you see?" Emma called impatiently.

"It doesn't look good," Jack muttered. "The roof's all bent in. Come a wee bit closer and I'll hand you some more of these garden tools."

Making a face, she did as he suggested and one by one, he handed the tools out of the hole. Emma's hands soon became wet and grimy causing her to grimace and grumble to herself.

"Throw them in my truck," he ordered, chuckling at the withering look she sent him.

When she returned, the muttered conversation from the men drew her even closer to the edge of the hole, peering down just in time to see Alex step through the now larger hole in the wall and disappear.

"Careful lad," Jack warned again.

Emma suddenly screamed as the rain-soaked ground gave way underneath her, sending her sliding towards Jack. Gasping as he caught her, she laughed self-consciously.

"What's happening out there, Jack?" Alex's panic-stricken voice called from the hole.

"Oh, it's only Lady Traymore. She jumped into the hole with me; you know how irresistible I am with the ladies, Alex!"

Now angry with herself and covered in mud, Emma punched his arm and watched the light, shuddering when she saw the dangerously sagging roof structure with broken pieces of metal hanging over top of Alex. Suddenly, a loud creaking sound made her grab hold of Jack.

"Get her out of there, Jack. Now!" Alex shouted in obvious panic.

Eager to comply, Emma attempted to scramble upwards on hands and knees in the soft mud, only succeeding when Jack pushed her from behind, then he followed. Once out of the hole, and both very muddy from head to toe, Jack asked if she was all right. Receiving her wordless wave, he slid back down the bank to assist Alex. Emma watched Jack and looked for Alex but couldn't see him. Concerned, she waited until she heard them talking before turning her attention onto her clothes. She swore under her breath as she surveyed her new jacket and shook her head sadly. *Well, one consolation, I heeded Alex's warning and worn my jeans!* Looking up, some movement caught her eye over by the trees and she suddenly remembered seeing the dog earlier. She stood up and peered in that direction and, sure enough, Mitch and the dog were moving through the bush slinking away thinking they had not been seen.

Her thoughts were interrupted when she heard Jack calling excitedly. Going as close as she dared to the hole, she reached down to take an oblong-shaped dirt-encrusted package from him. "Alex said to put it in the boot of the car … quickly!" He was practically whispering but she got the message. Eight more of these packages were handed out to her before both of the men climbed out of the hole and joined her at the car. Looking down at the dirty objects, they silently looked from one to the other and smiled smugly. Alex slammed the lid shut as a rumbling and cracking sound emanated from the direction of the hole. They turned just in time to see the muddy sides of the excavation collapse on top of what was left of the dugout, leaving a gaping hole of rotten wood, leaves, debris and corrugated iron where Alex had just been standing.

Emma shrieked and they all ran closer to take a look with Jack warning them to stay back. They gazed horror-struck down at the hole, realizing how close Alex had come to being hurt or buried alive. While they stood talking, a police car turned the corner and slowly drove towards them, stopping behind Jack's truck. The men exchanged sheepish grins before turning to face the familiar officer.

Constable Jim Falconer stepped out of the car, adjusted his hat, and walked past them to view the hole. Scratching his head, he addressed the builder, whom he recognized.

"What in heaven's name happened here, Jack?"

"You're too late, lad," Jack chuckled, "but our excavation found old Joe's tool shed!"

"That's the shed you were talking about yesterday, isn't it, Sir Alex?" Cst. Falconer inquired.

"Yes, that's right. Once we had the correct location, Jack was able to find both the shed and the tools easily," Alex explained.

"Where are the tools now?"

"They're in the back of Jack's truck."

A puzzled expression again spread across the constable's face as he turned to Alex. "I assume you acquired the appropriate permission, Sir Alex?"

At that moment, a second police car nosed slowly in beside the first and Alex relaxed. He flashed a relieved glance at Emma and Jack, as the constable's question was forgotten, momentarily at least. Both front doors of the police car opened and the driver stepped out ... a police officer they had not seen before. Accompanying him and looking rather agitated, was Rodric Brodie. Cst. Balfour McLean came over and introduced himself.

"What seems to be going on here?" asked Rodric Brodie, greeting Alex and Emma. "My office received a call from a neighbour complaining of some loud equipment that seemed to be working where they didn't think it should be!" He walked towards the hole and peered down. "What do we have here?"

Between Alex and Jack, they again explained about Joe's shed, making no excuses and hoping for the best.

"I didn't know there was a garden shed on this property. It must have been very old," Mr. Brodie commented. "I've been head of the County Lands Department for almost 20 years and I'm sure it isn't marked on any plan. How did you know it was here under these brambles?"

"As I explained to the police officers," Alex began, "Joe Thornton asked me to find his tools, but we realized yesterday that Joe had shown us the location near his present home instead of his former home. It was Sgt. Mackie who set us straight. Joe apparently lived this side of the burial grounds when he worked here and then some years later, moved into a home over there with his daughter." He pointed to the other side of the burial grounds.

"I dare say, many years ago!" mumbled Mr. Brodie and they all silently waited for his next comment. "So, you have now finished with the shed, I presume?" he asked with an inquisitive frown.

The men nodded.

Looking past Jack at Alex, who was now whispering to Emma a few meters away, Cst. McLean spoke loudly enough for all to hear. "Who's going to be responsible for cleaning up this mess?"

"The Traymore estate will pay all the expenses," said Alex, "and it will also pay for your rhododendron garden!"

"Cst. Lister, did you hear that assurance?" Mr. Brodie asked, smiling.

"Yes, sir, I did, so I assume you don't need me any more?"

"No, I think we can leave these folks to get on with their work and the next time any of you get notions to start digging up our county," Mr. Brodie declared, glaring at Jack and Alex, "please notify me beforehand!" He chuckled to himself as he and Cst. McLean walked back to their car and drove away. He had been meaning to clean up that patch of brambles for years and now he would be able to report to council that it was being done at no cost to the community.

Constable Falconer started his car but suddenly changed his mind and got out, walking back towards Emma. "Lady Traymore," he began, blushing profusely, "forgive me, my lady, but I suggest you might like to take a wee look at yourself in a mirror!" Seeing the horrified look on her face, he quickly returned to his car. He was speeding away before either of the men was aware of what had happened.

"What did he say to you?" Alex asked sharply, seeing her expression.

"He said I looked a frightful mess!" she snapped, trying to see herself in the car's side mirror. "And he's right, just look at me!"

"A little mud and dirt never hurt anyone, my lady," Jack assured her trying to keep a straight face. "Have a bath, buy yourself a new outfit and you'll be as good as new!" He then hurried over to the backhoe.

Alex, stifling a smile, silently backed away from her, holding up his hands as Emma sighed deeply; her eyes shooting arrows at him.

Starting the backhoe, Jack got to work removing his boards and pallet then dragging out the rotten timbers and rusted corrugated iron sheets of the shed. Finally, the space that had been the floor of the old garden shed was exposed. When Emma suggested they should continue digging for another two feet, both men argued against her but she held firm.

Jumping off the machine, Jack grabbed two shovels and scrambled into the hole. Alex joined him and, they had no sooner begun to dig, when Jack stopped, as the corner of what looked like a wooden box appeared. Pulling the box carefully out of the dirt, they commented on how old it looked and remarkably well-preserved. Emma watched, not sure what to think. Jack set it into the bucket of his backhoe, returned topside and brought it up close to their vehicles. As she watched, the men tried unsuccessfully to open it, so Jack put it in his truck.

"It's too late to do anything more today and I believe we're finished here anyway. As far as I'm concerned, it's tea time and in her ladyship's state of dress I'd better take her home with me so she doesn't mess up your precious car!" Jack announced, winking at her. "You, my lad, had better visit the shopping centre and buy your lady a new pair of trousers. Come on over to the house when you're finished and I'll cook you both a good old-fashioned meal while she's soaking in the hot tub!"

"Alex, I wear size 10 pants at home, jeans or black slacks, also dark socks … please!" she shouted as Jack opened the truck's door for her.

Alex waved and they drove away.

Chuckling to himself, Alex changed into his shoes and stashed his muddy wellies in the boot, but not before he noticed his own mud-caked trousers. "Looks like I need a change, too!" he muttered, getting a blanket from the boot and covering the seat before getting in.

Finding a small shopping centre a mile or so down the road, he located a ladies' dress shop and a gentleman's clothier. Dealing with his own shopping first, he soon found what he needed from their limited selection. Now he was ready to tend to Emma's wardrobe and went a couple doors down to the ladies' shop. By the time he was finished, he had created an uproar in the ladies' shop, but he thought Emma would be pleased with his choices. Blushing, he paid the cashier.

Jack laughed when Alex arrived with his shopping bags.

"She's out in the stables," his friend advised, "enjoying her soak!"

"How do you know she's enjoying her soak, have you been peeking?" Alex asked, reaching for the drink Jack offered.

"I had to check on her, didn't I? She might have needed me to scrub her back!" Jack chuckled, ducking as Alex let fly.

Walking through the kitchen and taking in the delightful aroma, Alex followed Jack's directions to the back door and found himself in a short enclosed walkway between the buildings. He knocked gingerly on the next door and when no one answered, he slowly began to open it.

"Shut that blasted door!" Jack shouted from behind him.

Alex went through closing the door behind him, then gazing in wonder at Jack's imaginative development of the large, old stable block. The floor and walls were decoratively tiled in the style of a Roman bathhouse and chairs and a table stood off to the side near a large built-in and vented barbecue. It was all set into an exterior alcove surrounded on three sides by sliding doors opening onto a large outside tiled patio. His eyes fastened onto a counter with a coffee pot, whisky bottle, cups, etc. At the far end of the room, he noticed steam rising and then heard Emma's voice calling to him.

"Come join me, Alex, but first pour me one of your special coffees!"

Somewhat shocked at her request, he poured her drink and started warily towards the hot tub.

"There are swim trunks and a towel in the cubicle to your right," she said with a giggle, pointing to two nearby doors. As she reached for her coffee, he caught his breath and stepped back, then realized she was wearing a light-coloured bathing suit. "Fooled you, did I?" she laughed.

Blushing profusely, he began to walk away. "I left your new clothes on the table," he shouted over his shoulder as he went to join Jack. Not long afterwards, Jack announced that dinner would be ready in 15 minutes and he went to call Emma.

Returning to the other building, Alex was surprised to see she was already dressed in her new clothes.

"You're quite an expert on women's clothing, Sir Alex," she murmured, as she put on her shoes. "I don't know why I am so surprised!"

"I see your shoes have been cleaned," he said, ignoring her teasing, and then remembering why he had returned, he added, "I was sent to tell you dinner is almost ready."

"Oh, thank goodness, I'm famished … Jack graciously offered to clean my shoes and jacket while I was in the hot tub!" she giggled.

Minutes later, they were feasting on roast pork with apple sauce and all the trimmings, complete with Jack's special fiery mustard sauce.

Meanwhile back at the dig, Mitch Pooley had not followed Alex's orders but instead had watched them from a hidden vantage point until they had left. He was puzzled and making wild assumptions as to the purpose of the hole. Monsignor Sharp also appeared after Mitch had left.

"Did you bring that box inside, Jack?" Alex asked.

"Yes, I did," he affirmed, "and I cleaned it too, very carefully!"

"You opened it?" Emma whispered, hoping she was wrong.

Jack grinned, shaking his head. "We'll take a look after dinner."

They, no doubt, finished the meal more quickly than they would have without the incentive. They all helped with the cleaning up and Jack invited them out to his workshop. When they saw the box, they realized it was a good deal cleaner as a design was now clearly visible.

"Can we open it?" Emma asked eagerly, moving closer to look at the fascinating symbols carved into the wood. "What is this?" she asked, touching what looked like a metal band running completely around it.

"It has no way of opening that I can see, unless it's under that metal band," Jack growled. "Someone will have a grand time dating this!"

Alex silently walked around the saw table, viewing it from all sides. Jack tipped it over so Alex could view the underside, but he finally agreed with him. There didn't seem to be any easy way to open it.

"Why would somebody make a box that won't open, and then bury it in secret under a garden shed?" Alex muttered. "It doesn't make sense."

"How old is it, do you think?" Emma asked, thoughtfully. "I wonder how long the garden shed had been there or could the box have been buried prior to the shed being built?"

"Good questions, my lady, but how do we find that out?" asked Jack. "You heard Rodric say he'd never seen the shed on any plans."

"John Dunstan," Alex murmured.

"Could we ask John without telling him what we found?" Emma asked doubtfully.

"Not likely, he'd be instantly suspicious," Jack agreed.

"How about a library or a small museum where we could do some research?" Emma suggested.

"Don't include me in that," Jack muttered. "I don't go much for that book stuff."

"We have those leather pouches, too," Alex said quietly. "Perhaps I should go and get one of them."

"Why do you call them pouches, Alex?" Emma asked.

"It just slipped out because that's what they remind me of. Leather pouches were a common item used to store old papers and easier to acquire than a box. There was no plastic in those days! Many have been found in old houses and archeological digs, and the contents are often in amazing condition.

"Joe might remember if the shed was there when he took the job at the monastery," Emma suggested. "Perhaps Mr. Brodie is mistaken about the records. The monks do appear to record everything, yet they may have thought this was insignificant!"

Suddenly, Alex got up and left.

"Now what's he up to?" Jack growled.

"I think he's gone to get one of the leather pouches."

Her assumption proved correct as Alex returned, carefully carrying one of the grimy objects. "Do you have some old newspaper, Jack? This thing is not only dirty but it feels as hard as a rock," he muttered, setting it down beside the old box. "We'll never be able to open it without damaging it," he stated sharply, his frustration apparent.

Jack also examined the pouch, muttering to himself when his glasses kept slipping off his nose. Suddenly, he stepped back and ran his hand through his hair. "We haven't thought this out very well, Alex; you should be taking these to Misty House. I'll make a bet Tom and Charlie have seen artifacts like these before. They are quite the wizards with their tools. They'd be the first I would go to and they're under your employ so wouldn't have to tell anyone!"

"Have you met them, Jack?" asked Emma.

"Oh yes, I've done some work for Ruth over the years."

After some more discussion, they agreed with him.

"Gentlemen, I believe we've forgotten what we came here for today … those horrid tools!" she exclaimed. "Joe's not going to want them back, Alex. "If we don't see him again, he probably won't even remember them … or us!"

"I believe she's right, Jack," Alex agreed. "Och, get rid of them with the other garbage and add it to our bill!"

They finished loading the artifacts into the car and Emma thanked Jack for his kindness and the use of his hot tub.

"I'll finish clearing that site and get it ready for planting your rhododendrons, my lady!" he laughed, waving as they drove away.

As they drove home, Emma was quietly fascinated by the sliver of a moon as it played hide and seek with the stars in a partly cloudy sky. They could now laugh at their brush with Rodric Brodie and the police and they began discussing the artifacts and Jack's suggestion of taking them to Misty House.

"Do you feel like joining me for a nightcap?" he asked as they pulled up to the hotel. When Emma nodded agreeably, he cocked a surprised eyebrow and they went directly to the *Hunting Bar*.

"Over here!" the familiar voice of John Dunstan called from a darkened corner table, waving them over.

As they went to join the archives director, Alex and Emma's eyes met, exchanging suspicious glances.

"I ordered you drinks," John said with a grin. "I hope you don't mind; I saw you drive in."

"You would have been in a wee bit of a bother if we had said noo, wouldn't ye, John!" Emma said solemnly, trying to mimic his accent.

The drinks arrived and their waiter placed them in front of the correct person, handing John the tab and, at the same time, telling the director, "There's a message at the bar for you, Mr. Dunstan."

"Was he waiting for us?" Emma whispered while John was away.

"I think so, but why? Does he know something or is he just fishing?" Alex frowned as he sipped on his whisky and watched as John now talked to the barman.

Long athletic strides brought John back to the table. "Well now, was your trip to Elderslie successful, Miss Walters?" he asked. "Did you find any clues you'd like to share with me?"

"Mr. Dunstan, sir," Emma cooed, "you know where we've been and my guess is Rodric Brodie has already informed you of our little adventure!"

John nodded amiably, readily admitting he had talked to the Paisley land supervisor. "One thing has me puzzled, though." He stopped to look at each of them in turn, but getting no obvious reaction, he went on. "I cannot understand why you were looking for a gardener's shed, or even how it was found."

Neither Alex nor Emma offered any explanation, following the archivist's conversation with silence and innocent expressions.

"I could easily have your dig shut down, you know," he said. This time his frustration was laced with a threatening tone.

146

"Oh, please do," Emma taunted him, "but Paisley Council will be awfully upset with you."

"And why would that be, my lady?"

"Because we hired a contractor to clean up the site, remove the brambles and garbage, and plant rhododendrons ... at our expense."

"Even that could get you into a lot of trouble," John suggested. "The site could now be described as an archeological dig and then my office must be notified. We are obligated to inspect such sites."

"Alex, would you order me another drink, this conversation is making me thirsty," she snapped. "Then, please tell him what he wants to know!"

"I'll order," John murmured, signalling the waiter. "I never meant to upset either of you. I really just want to help."

"We were merely trying to help Joe Thornton by finding his garden tools," Alex began. "We weren't having any luck until Sgt. Mackie came along and told us we were looking in the wrong place. He took us to where he knew the old garden shed should be and we investigated. We found the broken-down shed today with all the old gardening implements under the rubble. Rodric Brodie came and gave us a lecture about disturbing municipal property without permission and our lady generously offered to turn the rubbish heap into the garden they wanted."

"Would you like the garden tools?" she asked sarcastically.

"I imagine they could be somewhat interesting, but I doubt they're of any significant historical value," John replied.

"Jack Cameron has them in the back of his truck, along with two old bicycles, a rusted bed frame and some other junk we took out of the brambles," Alex informed him, without smiling.

"I can give you a plan of the original burial grounds," John offered.

"If you really want to help, we could use a map that includes the original gravesites and a list of occupants," Emma suggested boldly.

"We do have a gravesite plan but no list of occupants exists pre-1370. Some have old headstones or markers, many of them damaged, but the interment documents identifying those early graves have never been found," John admitted. "There is, however, plenty of forensic evidence that the graveyard was used pre-1100.

"On another subject," Emma pressed, "have you received any word on our sword?"

"The museum did say they were busy and short-staffed, so I am not very hopeful that your mystery will be solved in short order." Soon afterwards, he finished his drink and said goodnight.

"Was he warning us that he has eyes everywhere?" Emma asked.

"I think he was saying there are many mysteries surrounding the old monastery lands. At least we're now more aware of interested parties."

"Are we going to investigate that wooden box tomorrow or take all the artifacts to Misty House? We can only hope that Tom and Charlie can come up with a method to open those leather pouches without damaging the contents, if that's what they are."

"More importantly, you have to be in Court at one o'clock tomorrow so we won't have much time to do anything else. Misty House will have to wait until Monday."

"Oh my goodness, I had forgotten all about my big court date. I guess there is good reason for you to look after me!" Emma yawned, leaning over to gently tug on his beard as she wished him goodnight. "Don't expect me to be down here before 10 o'clock!"

Standing at her window in her nightclothes awhile later, Emma looked out over the rooftops. A cold draft rushed in as she opened the window briefly, and her body flinched as she breathed in the chilly air. Closing the window, she knew she should be tired, yet her mind kept thinking of the secrets their ancient wooden box could hold. *How can we open it without causing damage and what will the leather pouches reveal?* "Forget all of that tonight," she admonished herself aloud. "Tomorrow is the day that really changes my life, and if I think of that I surely won't sleep!"

It was almost dawn when her soundly sleeping mind settled restlessly on a vision of Mary Wallace. Once again, the woman was calling her from the monastery graveyard and beckoning her closer. Sitting upright with a startled gasp, Emma stared into the darkness.

"Mary, dear Mary, I really am coming to find you!" she whispered, before collapsing back onto her pillow.

## Chapter 11 – Friday 24<sup>th</sup> – She's a Lady!

The effect of her dream ruined all chance of sleeping, but she tried nonetheless, tossing and turning until the first grey light of dawn crept through the cold streets. She got up and then felt much better after a hot shower. When she was ready, she started towards the door but hesitated before opening it, deciding to go back for her laptop.

The night clerk glanced up as she went past him.

"Having an early start, Miss Walters?"

Emma shook her head. "No, only an over-active mind!"

The smell of coffee drew her towards the partially open door of the not-yet-open dining room. "Would you like a coffee, Miss Walters?" called a male voice from inside the room. Peering around the corner, she recognized one of the young cooks.

"Black will be just fine, thank you," she called to him. He motioned for her to come inside and disappeared briefly to return with a large mug almost full to the brim. "Now all I need is a corner to use my laptop and I'll stay out of your way!"

"You wouldn't be in my way, marm, but that corner over there has a power outlet if you need it," he advised before leaving her.

Sitting down at the suggested table, she opened her laptop and soon found her way into the Internet. Searching for *ancient box image*, she selected a number of appealing links and went through page after page of pictures but nothing seemed to match the unusual box they had found. Frustration began to gnaw at her brain. *Think Emma!* she told herself. Trying *religious artifacts*, she watched as another long page of hopelessly unrelated images appeared. She tried again, adding a date and changing the words slightly. Another long page of pictures came up, many of which she had already seen. With her eyes focused like laser beams, Emma began to scroll down through the lengthy list, stopping excitedly when she saw an image of something that quite closely resembled their pouches. Clicking on the image led to a wordy description. Clearly, they were typical folders, often formed into a cylindrical shape as used by long-ago monks and nobility to hold or pass on important papers. Losing all sense of time as she read the fascinating descriptions, she was brought back to reality upon seeing a pair of men's legs arrive in front of her. Looking up, she grinned at Sir Alex. Bookmarking her page, she closed the laptop.

"You're early this morning!" he exclaimed noticing her empty coffee cup. "How long have you been waiting for me?"

"Good morning to you, too! I wasn't actually waiting for you at all, Sir Alex," she grinned. "I couldn't sleep, so I got up early and just had to get out of my quiet, claustrophobic room, and decided to bring my laptop with me. Would you like to know what I've been searching for?"

"Naturally, I'd be happy to peek into your private world momentarily … what are you doing so secretively, hiding in the corner?"

"I wasn't hiding and the young cook was very friendly and helpful showing me this corner so I could plug in. To answer your first question, I've been here long enough to find out those leather pouches are likely to contain important records from the monastery."

"And how did you accomplish that?"

"Well, I had a devil of a time at first, but finally hit on the right word to describe them. Do you want to see?"

"Not right now, I believe you, my lady, and besides, our breakfast is arriving. I ordered when I saw you were already here and absorbed!"

"When do we need to leave for court?" she asked, as they ate.

"I called a taxi as parking is at a premium there and it's much too far to walk in this weather. It will arrive at 12:15. We may have to wait for our case to be called; we'll just have to be there on time and hope we get through quickly. The judge will probably only want to verify your name and relationship to Trev but there could be some conversation between the judge and Mr. Stuart as well. I have nothing else planned for the day, but we should be early enough to do something, unless you're exhausted from being up half the night!"

As they finished their leisurely breakfast, Alex again realized that Emma's mind was being quite distracted and he speculated she was thinking about her day in court. When asked, she admitted he was correct, but she was also concerned about the possibility that one of the pouches held the missing interment lists which John had mentioned.

"Will John send the monastery maps to me?" she asked as they left the dining room.

"I doubt it. If I know John, he'll make us come to him. He'll be testing us to see how eager we are. If you feel like it later, we can go see him."

It was a mild, dry morning so they mutually agreed to go for a brisk walk. Returning to the hotel they had tea and Emma went upstairs to get ready. At 12:15, the taxi came and they arrived at the courthouse in plenty of time to find their courtroom. They didn't have long to wait as Mr. Stuart appeared in the lobby to meet them. Sharp at one o'clock, they were called into the courtroom and so it began. Within 20 minutes, it was all over and the three of them were back in the lobby. Emma breathed a sigh of relief and Mr. Stuart shook her hand and congratulated her. He handed her a large envelope, heavy with papers.

"Here are all your documents, Lady Traymore. I'm sure we will meet again relatively soon but, in the meantime, I have great faith that Sir Alex will continue to do an excellent job orientating and looking after you. Goodbye." He bowed slightly and, with heels clicking on the marble floor, he disappeared around a corner.

Alex stepped forward and took the envelope from her, tucking it under his arm. He also offered his congratulations, taking her hand and holding it in both of his. "Well, Lady Traymore, how does it feel to be a legal lady of means?"

"It feels quite extraordinary, Sir Alex, unbelieveable actually," she laughed. "That part was much easier than I anticipated!"

"How would you like to celebrate your auspicious day, Lady Traymore?"

She couldn't help but be aware that he was repeating her new title for both of their benefits and she giggled. "Now that you ask, I feel like doing something rather silly. Where is the closest ice-cream parlour?"

"In the winter, my lady? An unusual request this time of year but there is one not far away, Lady Traymore."

"Lovely, there is no time that I can't enjoy ice cream. I've used it to celebrate special occasions since I was a child!" she replied, breaking into a giggle. "I won't even expect you to join me, if you don't want to!"

When they returned to the hotel by taxi an hour later, Emma felt quite giddy. "I can't get those papers off my mind. We'll have to go visit John on Monday and see if you're right about his having them. Oh cripes, now I know all of this has boggled my mind… it's still Friday, isn't it? Will he be at work? It's not even three o'clock yet!"

Alex took out his phone and, within seconds, John's secretary was on the line and he was told John was in the office until four o'clock. He put the phone away and stood up. "Let's go!"

The large hotel umbrella sheltered them from the rain as they walked down Princes Street to the National Archives.

Katie was waiting for them at reception. "Go right in, Sir Alex, Miss Walters. Mr. Dunstan is ready for you."

Looking up from behind his immense desk, John came over to greet his visitors, smiling as they shook hands, and then he called to Katie to bring three coffees. "Now, how can I help my two favourite sleuths?" "No doubt you've come to your senses and are ready to open your hearts and divulge those dark secrets you're harboring!"

"That's exactly what we'd like to do, John," Emma whispered seductively, "except we're still working in the dark and finding garden sheds. We offered you the tools last night."

"Yes, you did," he replied, "but I'm not sure you revealed the true purpose of your excavation."

"Oh, John," Emma scolded in her most innocent voice, "you're so distrustful!"

Dunstan looked at her and realized he was beginning to finally understand this fascinating and intelligent woman. He had always felt he must be cautious when speaking to her—he was never quite sure if he could trust her. A smile now tugged at the corners of his mouth as he remembered the news he had received only minutes before their arrival. He stood up and extended his hand. "Lady Traymore ... I believe it's appropriate to use your title now. Please accept my congratulations."

"Thank you, Mr. Dunstan, you truly have spies everywhere, don't you!"

"Oh, come now, it's just that I have so many well-trained staff you never know when they will be in the right place at the right time. Let's say they have a knack for knowing when information could be important to me, especially if it relates to our fair country!" he chuckled. "Sir Alex requested a survey map of the original consecrated land of the monastery. I have that for you complete with a modern-day survey so you can identify whether the boundaries have changed. I've had them enlarged for you, but I fail to see the significance of this request. Perhaps you would take this opportunity to enlighten me."

"Of course, Mr. Dunstan," Emma murmured, accepting the two rolls. "I am trying to form a picture in my mind of what it was like in William Wallace's time, but any maps we have found appear to be incomplete."

"And just how is that going to help you fulfill the Wallace prophecy?"

"It may not help at all; it's merely another small piece in the large puzzle. Are you any good at jigsaw puzzles, John?"

"Certainly not," he sputtered, "but I hope you'll show me the finished picture someday. I have a feeling it will surprise the hell out of me!"

"You can bet money on that, laddie," Emma whispered flippantly. "Can I treat you to dinner for being such a good fellow?"

"Thank you, no, but I will take a rain check!" he laughed, as they left.

"Are you really hungry or were you trying to bribe a county official?" Alex laughed. "And those tools ... they're probably in the county dump by now, my lady!" Their laughter seemed to match their mood tonight, turning heads as their jaunty steps took them over to George Street.

Almost to the hotel, she remembered his question. "I'm actually not very hungry, Sir Alex, what I really am, is impatient to get to the bottom of this! I knew John wouldn't accept and I'm glad, because I just want to get back to the hotel and begin a weekend. Oh my, I haven't thought of a weekend since I arrived! It's actually Friday and we have nothing urgent to do for ... so long! I'm thinking how much I would like to just veg out for a couple of days ... clear my head and relax. I hope you don't mind, Alex. Surely, you can use a break. I've been very demanding of you since I arrived. I should be here most of the time and, if you haven't made other plans, we could have dinner on Sunday."

"I think that's an excellent idea. Use room service and watch some TV, pamper yourself, you deserve it, Emma. Read your books and try to get your mind off this mystery for at least a few hours ... although I'm not sure how restful any of that will be for *you!*" They both laughed.

Later, feeling tired by 10 o'clock, Emma decided to go to bed early and, heeding Alex's comment, she found a magazine, rather than a book, to read. Unable to fall asleep, she got up an hour later and paced the living-room floor in front of the window as all manner of images raced through her mind. She stopped often to gaze out over the dark city, still unable to quiet the myriad of thoughts that raced through her brain. She turned on the TV and was surprised to find one of her favourite old musicals was playing. It was 2 a.m. when she finally went back to bed, remembering to turn off her alarm. This time sleep came readily.

She had almost forgotten the luxury of sleeping in on a Saturday morning. She watched a Christmas movie and wrote a brief email to one of her friends before ordering brunch from room service. She promptly fell asleep until a loud knock on the door announced that her meal had arrived. She felt somewhat refreshed when she looked outside to discover it was snowing. It was so pretty she ate watching TV with the curtains open, feeling relaxed for the first time in days. She revelled in the long-absent feeling but, by the time she had eaten, she knew she was fooling herself. She went to get a glass of water and to locate her journal notes.

"It's useless, useless!" she ranted aloud an hour later, getting up and pacing the floor. "I can't make head nor tale of any of this! I should have listened to Alex and put it out of my mind; so much for my relaxing day!" Turning the TV back on, she went to make some tea.

On Sunday morning, feeling remarkably rested despite feeling guilty about her lazy Saturday, Emma opened her bedroom curtains and looked out at Edinburgh Castle and below to the Princes Street Gardens. Some distance to the left was Holyrood Palace and, beyond, the ancient hill called Arthur's Seat. She was surprised to see that much of the snow had melted from the roads and sidewalks.

"So like Victoria," she mused, and then her glance strayed back to the castle and she laughed. "Not quite!"

She looked towards the city centre and realized something was going on in that area. It was too far to see much but she thought white tents were being erected. After eating, she surprised herself by deciding to go for a walk. She asked Megan what was going on down Princes Street and was told that tonight was *Light Night,* the beginning of their month-long Christmas celebration.

Not far from the hotel, the castle loomed ahead as she walked towards Princes Street. Awestruck at the view, she stopped and then realized she was feeling too much like a Canadian schoolgirl rather than a titled woman. She knew the gardens ended at Lothian Street, a block or so distant, so she set out. She remembered seeing a large church over there and wanted to check out the architecture. She walked briskly through the grounds feeling like she was in another era visiting an old outdoor museum with church buildings, statues and breathtaking architecture.

On her return to the hotel, Alex was waiting to see her.

"Good morning, Sir Alex, are you looking for me?"

"When you didn't answer your phone, I decided to come over. Megan told me you had gone out for a walk an hour ago."

"Did you realize there is a street market and fireworks going on today?" she asked. "Megan told me about it."

"That's what I came to tell you, my lady. I had neglected to tell you and I do apologize. It's called *Light Night* and George Street is already full of street vendors. I was going to find some lunch there and thought you might join me. At five, there are fireworks and all the Christmas lights are turned on simultaneously. It's quite a spectacle to start the Christmas season. Have I persuaded you to join me?"

Much later, looking back, she realized what a marvellous time she had had and neither of them had even mentioned the Wallace mystery.

## Chapter 12 – Monday 27<sup>th</sup> – Rumours

The next morning, she did a few stretches to try to erase the tiredness caused by her dreams, which she knew had woken her several times. Just before leaving her room, she opened a window, breathing deeply of the cold, crisp Scottish air and smiling at the fresh dusting of snow. Heavy clouds still covered the city and she wondered what their trip to Misty House would be like.

She nodded politely to the doorman who commented on the inclement weather but she hastily pointed out that it had been perfect for *Light Night*.

"You didn't sleep very well," Alex murmured, after they had ordered.

"Oh dear, is it that obvious!"

"Not physically, you're as beautiful as ever Emma, but your eyes …."

"Hmm, you got out of that quite smartly, didn't you?" she chuckled. "Do you have any plans for us today besides Misty House?"

"It will depend how the roads are and what we encounter there … but I also have a surprise for you," he said, looking quite serious.

She watched him suspiciously as he reached under his coat on the other chair and drew out a large but fairly thin box. It was wrapped in the type of parcel wrap from an expensive store. "What is it for?"

"No questions, Emma, just open it please."

She carefully unfolded the wrap already feeling there was something unique and special about this gift. Lifting the lid revealed the most exquisite brown leather briefcase. Inside was an envelope with her first name handwritten on the front. She looked at Alex and opened it.

It was from Trevelion and with tears in her eyes she silently read: *Dearest Cousin Emma, If you are reading this note it means you are my successor. I congratulate you and send you every wish for a wonderful life, Lady Traymore … and please don't make the dreadful mistake that I did. Find a nice gentleman to help you produce an heir to our amazing title and estate!*

*Fondest regards, Lord Traymore, Trevelion Walters 1959-1999*

Speechless, she wiped her tears and handed the note to Alex, mouthing the words, 'thank you.' Their breakfast arrived, and later, Alex told her about the day Trev had purchased the briefcase, leaving it in his care.

With breakfast over, she stood up and patted his hand before heading towards the lift. As soon as the lift door closed, she looked in the mirror and checked her make-up. She smiled, remembering his comment. *You're a devil all right, my dear Alex, and now my eyes do need a repair!*

Leaving shortly after 10 o'clock, as they reached Edinburgh's outskirts, Emma commented on how lovely the farmlands were with their dusting of snow. It was also easier to see the small wooded areas when the landscape was no longer completely green. Alex referred to them as forests and she laughed, telling him about Canadian forests. It did serve to set her imagination spinning with thoughts of what this land might have looked like centuries before. Alex told her that she had not travelled this particular part of the country before and, after following the bypass west, he pointed to a sign for Bathgate.

"We're going to take a little detour today," he said secretively.

"Another of your surprises?" she asked, looking at him expectantly.

"It depended on the road conditions, but I thought you might like to visit the Hospitallers' ancient homebase at the Torphichen Preceptory. She was so surprised it took a few seconds to react. She took the map out of the glovebox and and asked Alex for directions. "Look for Bathgate and follow the road north. Torphichen will be well-marked as a historical site," he instructed. "It's a pleasant drive through sheep country and then we can simply go north to Misty House."

Emma was much more interested in talking history now and she soon had him discussing another of his favourite topics, the Knights Hospitaller. It was as if being in Hospitaller country, Emma's mind now opened, albeit with cautionary thoughts, of Wallace and the Order. Very soon they were turning onto a narrow country road and went past Bathgate. Seeing a sign for *Torphichen Inn,* her excitement grew.

Alex drove up to a small parking area in front of a fairly large stone church with a small, very old, graveyard. He got out but Emma was definitely mesmerized as she looked upwards at the interesting rooflines.

"Well, I thought you'd be more eager that this!" he teased, shutting his door and going around to her side.

His words soon brought her back to the present and she opened her door just as he got there. "How old is this church, Alex?" she asked.

"Come, this is fascinating and so important historically," he said, walking toward a pathway on the east side. "It's wet, so stay on the path. This is the ancient side of a large complex built by the Hospitallers as early as the mid-12<sup>th</sup> century on the site of St. Ninian's 1<sup>st</sup> century AD church. It was said to have been visited by King Arthur in 500 AD. The tall building was added in the 13<sup>th</sup> century. This is all that remains of the medieval compound comprised of buildings, covered walkways, galleries, and a great wall which formed a quadrangle filling this grassy area and beyond. There's a modern drawing of it inside the Preceptory. The church on the other side was rebuilt in the 18<sup>th</sup> century."

"Can't you just feel the souls of the knights here?" she exclaimed.

"You're actually quite correct! Just think about it, Emma. William Wallace set up his base here and held his last parliament right here in this building in 1298 prior to the Battle of Falkirk. But alas, no, I can't feel them! You're the one who talks to ghosts! It's too bad we can't go inside. You'd love to see the worn stairs and the amazingly low doorways. Your imagination would have a field day but we'll come back for a summer tour. If you think it's spooky …."

"Who said anything about spooky, this is our history and I love it!"

Returning to the car, Alex suggested they go over to the *Torphichen Inn* for lunch. As they entered, they were greeted loudly by the barman.

"I heard you were having a little trouble in Paisley, Sir Alex!" the waiter murmured slyly, pouring their coffee.

"What kind of trouble, Ken, who told you that?" Alex asked.

"Tom Campbell's dad, he said you'd found one of the war bombs."

"Damn, I thought we'd kept that a secret!" Alex muttered, appearing to concentrate on the menu. "Do you enjoy barley soup, my lady? Their Scotch Broth with fresh-baked bread is excellent."

"My mother made Scotch Broth. I'd love that!" Ken took their order and went away. She looked over at Alex and whispered, "I can't believe how easy it would be to start a rumour! If you were to tell him it's true and they have the bomb locked in the council office at Paisley …!"

"Are you out of your mind, my lady, it could cause a riot in Paisley."

"Yes and council would deny it," Emma replied, "but if we did that two or three times, nobody would believe anything they hear!"

"Och, you may be right!" They talked until Ken brought the soup.

Alex winked at her before setting up their plan. "Don't worry, it wasn't a very big bomb, Ken, it's locked up safely in the council office."

Visibly shaken, Ken hurried away without another word.

"Let's see how long that takes to get back to Paisley!" Emma whispered.

As they left Torphichen, light snow was falling and, before long, the size of the flakes turned much larger and Emma grew concerned.

157

"Under normal conditions we would be at Misty House in about 35 minutes, but I'm getting a bit concerned about this myself," he said, peering through the window. "The forecast was for light flurries but I think we're beyond that. Try not to worry, we have a big, powerful car with excellent tires and I'll take it easy. You have to admit it is pretty!"

"Yes, it's pretty if you don't have to leave your house!" she said testily. "I'm not used to driving in it, living in Canada's tropics!"

When they arrived at Misty House, he parked closer to the Studio than usual so they could unload. Getting out of the car, Alex heard Ruth calling from the partly open doorway.

"I told Tom and Charlie you would come, snow or not!" she shouted. "They're waiting for you in the Studio. Come for tea later!"

Alex waved and she closed the door. It was still snowing, so he told Emma to stay in the car while he organized the artifacts into some cloth bags. When he was finished, he alerted her.

"Did you bring the braille book?" she asked, coming up beside him.

"Of course, but it's too large to carry around. I'll come back for it."

"I put the rest of these in a box last night," he explained, taking out a second bag which she could see held the wooden box. "I'll bring them shortly. We don't want to overwhelm the poor lads!"

The Misty House carpenters were easy to find as laughter was heard as soon as they entered the Studio. Jessie, the dog handler, was with them standing in front of a door frame set in the middle of the floor.

"Hello, hello, come in!" Tom called.

They took their bags over to the work table and went to watch.

"What are you doing?" Emma asked, frowning as Jessie stepped through the mock door frame and yelped softly.

"We're testing a new system for training the dogs," said Charlie, "and the settings need to be just right. Jessie has offered to be our guinea pig."

"You're crazy," Emma snapped, "that's dangerous!"

"Oh no," Jessie laughed, "it doesn't hurt. It's very low voltage. I was just having some fun. It has to be perfect for the dogs. Come and try it."

"Not on your life!" Emma muttered, hastily stepping backwards.

"One more try and I think we've got it," Tom called. "Okay, Jessie."

In one quick movement, Jessie stepped through the door frame, gave a thumbs-up and left through the door to the dogs' area.

"Now, Sir Alex and ...," Tom began turning to their visitors.

"Hold it!" Emma interrupted. "I do want to try that doorway!" She went over to the frame, received a thumbs-up sign from Tom, and hesitated only briefly before stepping through.

"It was only a tickle," she said in surprise, "would that stop a dog?"

"A small animal will feel it more," Charlie explained. "It looks like you and Sir Alex have brought us another project."

"We'd be very happy if you can tell us what these are," she explained, as they took the two dirt-encrusted artifacts out of the bag. "We thought you might know how to open and clean them."

The men's interest was obvious and after a cursory examination, they carefully turned over one of the items.Tom looked at his co-worker.

"Och, these are raw leather message pouches once used by the army, governments and ministers. We haven't seen one of these in years."

"Can it be opened without damaging it, Tom?" Alex asked.

"Oh yes, but it takes time; reviving leather is a very slow process, and I presume you want the contents intact."

"Most definitely, if at all possible," Emma replied. "I'm afraid we have some more of those in the car. Are you familiar with this box?"

"Oh yes, my lady," Charlie replied. "This is a monk's biographia box. There have been many of these found around Paisley. I assume you want it opened? How many pouches do you have?"

"There are seven more," Alex replied.

"How can you open the box without damaging it?" Emma asked.

"Same way they put it together, my lady," Charlie said casually. "We have to remove that iron band first. It serves as a lock; see how it holds the lid closed. How soon do you need it?" Seeing her uncertainty, he glanced over at Tom. Going over to a bench, Tom cleared a space and opened a cupboard door. Mumbling to himself, he noisily moved some material around before pulling out a jumble of wires. He wrapped them around the box, being very particular as to how the wires were situated on and around the metal band. Next, he got an odd-looking frame contraption from another shelf and set that on the table, too.

Alex and Emma watched in fascination as they joyfully went about their work, placing the box into the frame and then plugging it in.

"Now watch and listen," Tom proclaimed secretively.

Suddenly, the wires around the box began to change colour, sending a wisp of smoke into the air. Low crackling noises emanated from the frame and Tom moved quickly to work two clamps. This motion slowly pushed the wooden box out from under the iron band.

"Don't touch anything!" Tom warned. "It's hot!"

"Will it open now?" Emma asked eagerly.

"No!" both Tom and Charlie answered in unison.

"Now we have to break the seal," said Charlie while Tom mumbled unintelligibly to himself.

"What seal?" Emma snapped impatiently, "how long will that take?"

"Come, my lady," Alex coaxed, "let's go have tea with Ruth and give them a chance to do their work. I'll get the other pouches from the car."

"She has some photos of a box like this in her office," Tom called, as they started to leave, "ask her about it."

Tom's comment piqued Emma's interest and she thanked him as she took Alex's arm and hurried him to the door. He delivered her to the manor and then returned to the car to deal with the other packages. Joining the women inside, he found them chatting. Unable to contain her inquisitiveness, Emma mentioned the box Tom had told her about.

"So," Ruth murmured, "you're interested in a monk's box? They really are quite fascinating. The one Tom told you about was a fine example found in someone's garden. John Dunstan insisted it had to go into Edinburgh's Scottish Heritage Collection along with the box's original contents. Opening a drawer in a filing cabinet, she took out a file folder and handed it to Emma. "This contains a photo of the box and a copy of the manuscript found inside the box."

Ruth poured tea as she watched Emma remove her coat and then pick up the file. Alex took a sip but neither of them took their eyes off her. ·

Emma opened the folder and almost immediately moaned as if grief-stricken. "They're written in Latin!"

"Turn the page over," Ruth suggested. "I translated it before contacting Mr. Dunstan. Would you like a homemade apple turnover with your tea? They were freshly made by our students this morning."

"That would be lovely, when I finish," Emma murmured, without looking up. "This reads like a résumé."

"You're right, it is a résumé," Ruth replied, "a religious résumé for a monk's entry into the Kingdom of Heaven."

"My goodness, do all the boxes have one of these?" asked Emma.

"Yes, but some are more detailed than others, it depends on their perceived accomplishments, but why are you so interested?"

"Before you answer that question, my lady," Alex interceded. "I think we had better tell Ruth your exciting news. She obviously doesn't have the right spies around to inform her that you are now Lady Traymore!"

"That is wonderful news for all of us ... at last!" Ruth exclaimed, joyfully getting up to come around the desk and shake Emma's hand. "Congratulations, Lady Traymore, now you can truly feel a part of all of this ... and your splendid estate ... as well as the Wallace mystery!"

"You are quite right, Ruth, but it will take awhile to sink in. I think I'm still in a state of disbelief since my court appointment. So let's get back to the story of a biographia box, shall we? Tell me, where would you find one of these boxes?"

"They are buried beneath the body of a monk," said Ruth.

"So, if one of these boxes is found, you can be assured that the body of a monk was buried above it?" Emma asked thoughtfully.

"To my knowledge, yes," Ruth replied.

"Would any evidence be left of a body after 700 years?"

"Not often, my lady. If Scotland's naturally acidic soils didn't do the job, then certainly time would."

"Even metal?"

"No metal was allowed on a monk's body before burial. Any rings, clasps, crosses and jewellry were put into his box, and remember, monks usually did not possess valuables such as jewels."

Emma had run out of questions for the moment so she took a sip of her tea and continued to read Ruth's translation.

"This man was at the Battle of Stirling Bridge," she whispered, with her eyes focused intently on the papers before her. That was September 11th, 1297, the day of Wallace and Moray's great defeat against the English. This monk blessed a union, between Mulin and Agnes at Caplaw in 1303 and another one between Angus and Mary in 1307, but he doesn't list any of his own family names."

"They were probably peasants, forest folk," Ruth proffered. "The use of surnames was generally still in the future unless you were highly born, but why do you find this so interesting?"

"We found a monk's box in Elderslie, Ruth," Alex admitted, joining the conversation. "We left it with Charlie and Tom today, but that's not all. We also found some ancient monastery records in leather pouches."

Ruth set her tea cup down as it rattled against her saucer and they realized the colour had drained from her face.

"It all happened quite by accident, or perhaps it was luck, when we called for tea in Paisley on Tuesday," Emma murmured gently, allowing the matron to recover. "We had a nice chat with Moira, the owner."

"Yes, I know Moira," said Ruth, looking as if she wanted to ask them questions but, before she had a chance, they began to tell her about the bomb and their dig.

"Who told the council you were digging and who had the backhoe?"

"Jack Cameron had the backhoe," Alex interrupted. "I believe he works for you when you have need of his machinery."

"Oh yes, I like Jack, he has a delightful sense of humour!"

"He has … it must have been a neighbour who complained," Alex replied.

"That's not your only problem," Ruth sighed. "What is going to happen when John Dunstan finds out?"

"Oh, don't worry, we told John," Emma quipped, "and we offered him all the rusty garden tools we had found. He turned us down!"

"You didn't tell him you'd found a biographia box or the monastery pouches?"

"No, not yet, but we will. I would like to see the contents of that box before John spirits it away like he did with your biographia box."

"I agree. Now let me refresh your tea and you must sample the children's baking." She brought over the plate of apple turnovers. They would very much appreciate your opinion."

Handing the folder back to Ruth, they both accepted a turnover, expressing their delight at the tasty treat.

"Please tell the chefs we enjoyed their turnovers immensely," Emma chuckled. "Could I have a copy of those papers, please Ruth. They make fascinating reading and I would like to finish them."

"Certainly, my lady. I'll get them before you leave."

"We have one more thing to show you," Alex announced, coming to his feet. He lifted the heavy book onto the desk, took it out of the bag and turned it to face the matron. "I'll let Lady Traymore tell you about it."

"When we were on Dorik Island two weeks ago, I came across this book in the library," Emma began. "I realized it was written in braille, but it looked very old. I wondered if it might contain something about the missing relics. It was strange to me why it was in the Traymore House library and not here, so Sir Alex suggested we should let you take a look."

"This sounds like a mystery in itself and you're right, it does *look* old and it is rather large, isn't it?" she exclaimed. "I doubt it's a children's book though!" She silently scanned the first few pages, her fingers expertly skimming across random sections. Then, twice, she turned a group of pages, going further into the book, until she stopped and gently closed it. She looked up at them and smiled. "I'm so pleased you found this, although I highly doubt it will help you with your Wallace mystery. This is a Scottish history book of short stories featuring our well-known kings and heroes. It's simply a braille edition of an old classic and not as old as you may think. With your permission, Lady Traymore, it will be an excellent addition to our library. Perhaps the staff will be able to interest some of the older children to read it aloud to the others."

"Well, that solves one mystery, a shame they weren't all that easy!" Emma laughed, coming to her feet. "This is a much better home for the book. Thank you for your assistance and for tea, Ruth."

"And for your time," Alex added. "We are so lucky to have you and the boys to call on when we have a problem. I want to talk to them before we leave." The technicians were not surprised to see them again, saying they would have the box open by Wednesday.

As they drove away from Misty House, Emma put her head back and relaxed, looking outside at the snowy scene and wondering what Tom and Charlie would find in their artifacts. Hearing Alex talking to himself, she looked up and realized it was snowing heavily and they were no longer on the motorway.

He had taken the exit to Ratho and the unplowed country lane made her nervous. Alex drove cautiously but Emma had lots of time to imagine getting stuck in a ditch. At last, the rooftops of a small village appeared and she breathed a sigh of relief. They drove up to the doorway of an unpretentious building which sported a small sign that was so covered in snow she couldn't make it out.

"You seem to know all of these out-of-the-way pubs!"

The grin on Alex's face was neither agreement nor denial, just a mischievous show of amusement as he came to open her door. He asked if she had brought the envelope Ruth had given her; she looked at him and frowned, but decided not to ask. *I'll find out soon enough!* She took his arm and they walked carefully across the snowy car park to the door. Emma's eyes widened as they stepped inside and she allowed her eyes to adjust to the light. The luxurious modern interior was totally unlike any other pub she had seen since arriving in Scotland. She felt the unusually thick carpet underfoot and knew it was expensive. A tall, tartan-vested man with a broad smile, came towards them.

"Good evening, Sir Alex, marm, let me take those wet coats!"

"Thank you. Frank Costello, I'd like you to meet Lady Traymore, Professor Emma Walters from Victoria, Canada. Frank is the owner of this establishment."

"Welcome, Lady Traymore, I'm honoured to meet Sir Alex's new boss!" he replied with a broad smile, shaking her hand and then indicating they could sit at the bar. Frank set a glass in front of each of them on the well-polished countertop and chose a bottle of premium

Scotch whisky from his extensively stocked bar. She covered the glass with her hand causing both men to frown.

"Are you hungry enough to eat a Texas steak?" Alex asked.

"It's only lunchtime, Sir Alex, a steak is hardly on my midday menu, but what exactly is a Texas steak? I feel you are dying to tell me!"

"It's one that fills the plate!" Frank replied, laughing.

"Oh no, you didn't actually think I could eat that large a meal, did you," she groaned. "You're pulling my leg! What I would appreciate is a black coffee and a glass of water with lemon," she said to their host.

"I thought she'd be hungry!" Alex murmured, shaking his head.

"Right away, ma'am, and my apologies about the steak," Frank replied, surprising her with his Texan drawl. "Would you like to order now? We do have a regular lunch menu ... and please, inside these walls, call me Tex!"

Emma shook her head and grinned. "So you really are a Texan. It's fun to hear your accent, especially here in Scotland. I have a Texan friend who is a professor and I see him at the occasional conference. He's a real character. Let's see, do you have a chicken wrap on your lunch menu, Tex?"

"Sure do, you have a choice of Thai Chicken or Greek Chicken wraps. I'm told they are equally delicious! Sir Alex, are you having the steak?"

"Well, I'm going to have the Thai wrap with chips!" said Emma.

"I'll have the Greek wrap, also with chips," Alex laughed.

"So, you're a Canadian, Miss Walters?" Tex asked when he returned with her beverages. "In all my travels, I've always thought your city was one of the most beautiful in the world."

"Really," she replied, "so you've actually been to Victoria?"

"Sure have. I stayed at the Empress, saw the whales, fished for salmon and I've had afternoon tea at your famous Butchart Gardens."

"It sounds like you were in my fair city for awhile," she replied. "Now tell me how you met Sir Alex?"

"Alex is merely a customer who sometimes secured my services for Trev and his business affairs." He became silent as he waited for the inevitable question, but when it didn't come, he continued. "I'm a former policeman, my lady, and a handwriting expert."

"Ah, I wondered why we were making this horrid trip in the snow! Your friend has a bad habit of not explaining things ahead of time. I guess we can use a person with your skills, eh Sir Alex?"

"I think we might," her bailiff agreed, nodding thoughtfully. "Last week we dug up a biographia box in an unusual place. With no sign of a coffin or a body, I became suspicious that it could have been planted."

"A decoy, but it's hundreds of years old?" Emma argued.

"That doesn't prove the contents are authentic, does it?" asked Tex.

"No, but most people would expect them to be; I would think John Dunstan's department could carbon-date the box if we asked him." She looked closely at Tex. "It appears you know what we're talking about, Tex?"

"Slightly," he replied evasively.

"So what would carbon-dating prove?" Alex asked.

Emma then realized the men were both serious, but she was puzzled why Alex hadn't mentioned this possibility of a decoy to her before. "Should I let Tex take a look at Ruth's papers?" she asked, looking at Alex who shrugged his shoulders. "These are just copies of documents found in another monk's box, one that Mr. Dunstan has given to the museum," she said, opening her purse.

"It could be an interesting read but without the original parchment I can't do my usual assessment," Tex admitted. Your meal is ready now, so I'll take a look while you're eating, if that's okay."

Handing him the envelope, Emma followed Alex into the dining room where a formally attired maitre d' showed them to a table.

"Your friend can't possibly be making the kind of money this place requires to make it lucrative," Emma commented, a bit too loudly.

"I wondered when you'd get around to that, my lady!" he whispered.

Conversation ceased as the waiter approached and asked if they would like a bottle of wine. Emma declined and Alex made excuses saying he was driving, and the waiter left them.

"Well, I'm waiting," Emma hissed impatiently.

Lowering his voice, Alex tried to explain. "It's a front, a cover to hide from the world and still make a living."

"Hide from whom?"

"From everyone, those whose fraud he exposed, or those who know he will, if he ever comes in contact with them again. The Mafia would, no doubt, kill him if they found him, and I've already told you too much."

"And you expect me to believe that?" she whispered.

The meal wasn't long in coming and they both commented on how glad they were not to have ordered steak. Half an hour later, they sat back to relax and wait for Tex, who returned shortly afterwards.

"I've actually seen the parchment for this ... some months ago in John's office," he said, when he rejoined them. "He was evasive but asked me to take a look and give my opinion. I felt they were authentic and that's the last I heard."

"Well, as I mentioned, they're apparently in the museum now," Alex told him. "Lady Traymore was fascinated and asked for a copy as Ruth had translated them."

"Why would John suspect they could be fake?" Emma asked.

"Let me explain," said Tex, pouring himself a drink. "It was John who told me of his suspicions, awhile back now ... possibly three years ago," Tex declared. "With Trev's illness and the lack of an heir, he had confided in John before his disappearance, or whatever it was ... John and I have our own theory on that subject!" Emma looked sharply over at Alex and was not surprised to see that he was as shocked as she was by Tex's admission. He continued his story and she listened even more closely. "Trev was concerned with who might make a claim on his estate, but no one did, to my knowledge. The other concern was that someone would try to find the relics for their own profit, but if that was the situation, they had been very secretive. These documents would have been the first indication that something was amiss, so I'm now very relieved. When you came into the picture, my lady, John feared that if someone had the relics or knew where they were, they would simply go underground for awhile. So he kept his ears and eyes open and began snooping around. He wouldn't give me any details, saying it was for my own protection. I'm quite sure he knows something he's keeping to himself. John is an extremely smart man with many resources at his fingertips and friends in high places. He also has a keen interest in anything Scottish, despite being born English. If anyone thinks they can pull the wool over John Dunstan's eyes, they will be sorely mistaken!"

Realizing this answered her question about Alex's concern eased her mind somewhat and they left shortly afterwards. The roads improved and Alex became talkative. He told her he'd been thinking that he'd like to take her to a concert or something musical for a change.

"We've become so wrapped up in Traymore intrigue, neither of us has had any real time off. Christmas is coming and there is always so much going on at the theatre with special Christmas shows and the like. You need some fun in your life, Emma, not with me necessarily, perhaps with Alfreda or Jennie MacKray. Edinburgh and Glasgow are famous for their music and theatre. Is that something you would like to do?" Not getting any interest, he added, "Or, we could go on a pub crawl through

Old Town and visit some of the oldest ale houses in Scotland." Seeing a glimmer of interest, he continued. "Pub crawling in this city is phenomenal; music and booze, a perfect combo for the young, my lady!" "All right, that did it! That's exactly what I feel like tonight, but the theatre is a favorite of mine also! We'll get some exercise at least," she added. "I'm feeling better already! You're right, Alex; I really do need something to take my mind off all this, even if only temporarily."

By the time they reached the city bypass, the roads were clear, and traffic was moving well despite the rush hour.

"Will it snow tonight?" she asked, looking at the starless sky.

"You can tell me about it," he growled, feeling a bit uncomfortable.

"The snow?"

"No, my lady, the feelings you are attempting to hide from me again. I'm not very experienced with the mystery of female emotions and yours are a challenge, but if I can help ..."

"I'm not sure I can even understand my own feelings, as you call them, Alex. Every part of this mystery is drenched in pain and suffering and it often feels as if I can't shake them. I believe Mary is pulling at the strings of my very soul and it hurts like hell."

"We've made more progress solving this thing since you came to Scotland, than Trevelion and I made in the whole time I worked for him. What's more, Emma, I'm confident you're going to fulfill the prophecy. Be warned though, that there will be more pain before it's over. We're literally unearthing the most violent and murderous time in Scottish history. Edward I unleashed a spiteful, furious bloodlust on anyone he imagined had offended him. William and Mary were not the first, nor were they the last to suffer his wrath. And now we have this new revelation about trickery and we're drawn into another plane."

Hearing Alex's emotionally charged words unleashed a tear that slowly trickled down her face, thankfully unseen. After he parked, she sat so still he turned, concerned, to look at her aided by nearby lights.

"Are you all right?"

"Can we just sit here for a few minutes please?" she whispered, dabbing at her eyes. Ten minutes later, her emotions now in control, she walked into the foyer ahead of him. She nodded when he said he'd see her at six o'clock in the dining room and carried on to the lift. Once in her suite, she changed into her housecoat and sat down at the dresser, staring at the image in the mirror. She was shocked with what she saw. Her hair was a mess and make-up was almost non-existent. She immediately set to work and, when satisfied with her effort, she went to the window and looked out at the castle.

"I'd love to hear some of *your* stories!" she murmured.

Precisely at six, she stepped from the lift and walked regally towards the dining room. Wrapped around her neck was a brightly coloured scarf of blue, green and golden hues, magnificently setting off her brown hair and blue eyes against the white background of her skintight thigh-length sweater. Her glitter make-up assisted with the façade that she felt somewhat younger than her years. She approached the dining room with a confidence and eagerness she hadn't felt in years. Seeing Alex stand up to greet her, she smiled brightly ... a smile he hadn't seen since Dorik.

He, however, had merely stood up stoically because he was having trouble believing that the vision approaching him was Emma. As the realization passed from his eyes to his brain, his newspaper slipped out of his hand and fell to the floor, and then his mouth dropped open.

"What the hell?" he murmured under his breath.

Summoning her courage, she stopped before reaching his table to give him the full effect. Turning slowly, he realized that the long white sweater that fell loosely about her upper-body, clung seductively to her skintight designer jeans; and her fashionable, very high heels, made her appear taller, slimmer, and even sexier than he had thought possible! Confused over his feelings, it was fortunate that he noticed the Walters' broach pinned to her sweater.

"What the devil are you doing?" he hissed, glancing furtively around the room. Several people dropped their eyes under his glaring gaze.

"I'm going pub crawling with you and I dressed for the occasion!" she whispered, as he pulled out her chair.

"My lady, this is Edinburgh, not some university campus!" he hissed.

"Go to hell sir, I'm not bound by your stuffy collar and tie code," she snapped at her bailiff who now slouched mortified in his chair. She saw a glint of refrained anger flash briefly in his eyes. "Don't worry, I conform to the stipulation of my inheritance," she pointed to the Walters' broach. If my appearance displeases you, Sir Alex, I'll go out on my own!"

Alex sat up straighter, took a deep breath and glared at her. "I'm glad to see you're enjoying yourself, my lady!" Then, he leaned across the table. In a lowered voice, he continued, "Your sharp tongue is working brilliantly tonight, my lady, and is only outshone by your colourful and totally inappropriate attire!"

A waiter arrived with menus, two coffees and a small decanter of whisky then left them to make their selection. Silence reigned as each examined the menu and took a drink of coffee.

"All I want is an appetizer so I can handle this booze you've promised me!" she proclaimed. "We'll no doubt eat as we go."

Not wanting to admit that he was thinking along the same lines, he looked at the appetizer selection and asked if she would like to share the seafood plate. She agreed and he summoned the waiter explaining they were having a light meal and ordered.

While they ate, his mood began to relax and he described some of the pubs they would visit. When they finished eating, they stood to leave and he looked down at her feet. "None of these pubs are very far away but I doubt you will make it in those ridiculous high heels!"

Without a word, she left him; she had to get her coat anyway. As she rode the lift, she considered Alex's unusual behaviour and decided that she must be overdoing her outfit. For the first time a suspicion crossed her mind that he was unused to dating. She changed her shoes, brought out her recently acquired black cape and pulled on her Canadian felt hat with the tiny red maple leaf logo. Checking her image in the full-length mirror, she smiled and went to meet him.

"Where are we going first?" she asked, linking his arm as they went out onto George Street.

"*Breck's Bar*, it's a very famous old pub. It will be packed, but it's a friendly atmosphere. We'll have one drink there and then move on to the *Auld Hundred*."

When they arrived at Brecks, the sight of the many old windows with their small panes of glass made her smile as she thought of a restaurant at home. Hearing the loud, happy sounds of revellers inside, she kept close behind as he pushed his way to the bar where they patiently waited their turn. When they finished their drink, the push through the crowd was repeated until they reached the sidewalk.

"What a mad house," she laughed, "not the sort of exercise I was envisioning! I've never seen a pub so busy but then I rarely go out at night, especially to pubs!"

"I'm glad I'm giving you a new experience then," he chuckled. "Are you ready for the next one?"

"No, not yet, find me a nice quiet place this time."

"Right, we'll go to *The Grape*, it's where the newspaper reporters gather and always proves to be entertaining, perhaps moreso than quiet!"

The night air was chilling rapidly as they walked a few blocks and Alex pointed out the sign of their destination. When the door opened, the noise from inside was little more than a murmur. Alex noticed the admiring glance that an exiting older gentleman cast in Emma's direction as he held the door open for her. Luck was with them as there was one small, empty table, probably vacated by the man at the door. It quickly became obvious that everyone knew each other as names and jests were shouted between tables, often with spontaneous bursts of laughter.

"Are you a visitor?" a dour-looking older woman called to them.

"The lady is from Canada," Alex quickly replied, recognizing the outspoken columnist, Eliza Burns.

The reporter's eyes swept over Alex like a flame thrower, scowling fiercely as she slipped heavy glasses onto her face from a bejewelled chain hanging around her neck. Emma realized the nearby conversations had all but stopped and eyes had turned her way.

"Sir Alexander Wallace," the woman hissed. "I'm sure Lady Traymore can answer for herself!"

Ms Burns was a long-time columnist for the oldest Edinburgh newspaper in the city. She was a well-known and unyielding feminist who championed the cause of equality and the Women's Rights Movement. Opinionated and always provocative, she was a force to be reckoned with and one to be avoided in an argument.

"You know who we are?" Emma coldly levelled her eyes on Eliza.

"Yes, the media are normally informed when a titled person dies. We especially take note when the title goes to a foreigner." It was a thinly veiled insult aimed squarely at Emma. Glances of mixed surprise and horror passed quickly around the area of the pub within earshot and patrons now waited to hear the Canadian's reply.

Inwardly, Emma was seething, but to all present her manner portrayed that of a genteel lady. Smiling at Eliza, she spoke somewhat louder than her sparring partner. "In Canada, we have a saying, my dear … you don't need to be born in a stable to be a horse's ass!"

Polite laughter was heard, warning her there was some dissention in the ranks. Notepads appeared and questions were soon being thrown about with everyone talking at once. Alex ordered their drinks then sat back to watch how Emma expertly handled this group.

"Ladies and gentlemen," she called, banging an empty glass on the table, "please sit down and be quiet! I am not going to shout, but I will answer your questions one at a time." She shrugged out of her wet coat and Alex took it from her, giving her a quick wink, before she stood tall, pushed up her sleeves and glowered at her audience.

Alex held back his smile. He was fully aware that she had now reverted to her professional persona ... there would be no doubt who was in control during this interview.

"Are you really the legal heir to the Walters' estate?" the first questioner asked.

"Look it up for yourself sir ... when the new Debrett's Peerage is published!"

"That won't be until 2008, I'll take that as meaning you are or will be!" he grunted and sat down.

"Are you going to solve the Wallace mystery, Miss Walters?" Eliza Burns sneered.

"Yes, I am," she replied unemotionally.

"Is the regalia thought to be in Scotland?" asked a portly gentleman.

"No, sir, I believe it's in Yorkshire."

Thirty-five minutes went by quickly, and then she pushed down her sleeves, clapped her hands and declared the question period over. Drinks were offered and refused as she and Alex put their coats on and left.

"Well, that was both informative and profitable!" she declared smugly, taking his arm. With wind and snow blowing in their faces, they hurriedly returned to the hotel.

Feeling cold, Emma chose a table near the fireplace in the *Hunting Bar* and Alex excused himself, saying he would be right back. Ordering their drinks from the bartender on his way out to the foyer, he also informed the man that he would find Lady Traymore sitting at a table near the fire to which he nodded.

She looked relaxed and full of life when he returned and the drinks arrived soon after. Alex waited until the waiter was out of earshot before he turned to her and whispered, "Do you realize what you may have achieved at *The Grape* tonight, my lady?"

"Yes, sir, I surely do," she murmured coyly, as flickering sparks of amusement danced in her eyes. "I sent all those reporters scurrying for a story on the silent monastery and, by the weekend, all eyes watching us will be focused on the monks."

"John Dunstan won't fall for it, you know."

"Oh yes, he will. He'll have to because those reporters won't disclose their source of information and they'll research every story concerning the monks. They'll probably rewrite some of them and add a little fabrication, but it's going to be a mighty interesting week, don't you think, Sir Alex!"

"And just where shall we be?"

"I'll divulge that tomorrow for I'm now calling it a day! Let's meet at 7:30; it looks like we will have a very full week ahead of us." She raised her cup, flicked her eyebrows coyly, took another sip of her coffee, and with a playful air of mystery, walked jauntily away.

Unknown to either Emma or Alex as they visited Misty House earlier that day, Monsignor Sharp was blatantly stirring up trouble by contacting both Paisley Council and the Scottish Heritage Office in Edinburgh complaining that Jack Cameron was desecrating old gravesites. Referred to the Land Use Department, Rodric Brodie assured the cleric he was well aware of the work being done and any further concerns should be put in writing. The Heritage office then notified John Dunstan.

Later, as Emma climbed into bed, she thought of Tom and Charlie unlocking the secrets of the artifacts. Just before sleep overtook her, she had the remarkable, but fleeting thought, that her rumour would soon be travelling around the country and she giggled.

It was too late of course, but she would soon realize the consequences of her rumour ... for those too had already begun.

## Chapter 13 – Tuesday 28<sup>th</sup> – Suspicious Events

Rising early after an unusually restful night, Emma groaned as she watched the weather report. Wind, rain and snow at higher elevations did little to excite the Canadian and she quickly adjusted today's plans, at least in *her* mind. Going down to the dining room, she poked a small hole in her newspaper to spy on the door. She felt smugly superior, like a spy queen in a James Bond movie.

Disaster struck when she saw Alex and John Dunstan walking towards her. Lowering her newspaper, she stared in disbelief. *Has John already heard about the mass confrontation with the press at* The Grape?

"Good morning, my lady," Alex greeted her. "Look who I found lurking in the foyer. John would like to join us for breakfast."

"Only if I'm not intruding, Lady Traymore," the national archives director interjected, flashing Emma a charming smile.

"You are most welcome to join us Mr. Dunstan, but why so formal? I thought we were friends."

"We are," John assured her. "I called Alex from the office but he wasn't answering his phone. I then called this hotel and they told me you had just come down for breakfast."

"You were in the office early," Alex noted.

"I was. Have you seen today's newspaper?" he asked.

"Not yet, but I see Lady Traymore has a copy. Why do you ask?"

"Look in the Scottish History section … I can find it for you," John began, reaching across the table, but Emma was quicker. She flipped to the correct page, found the article and slowly folded the newspaper. At the same time, she managed to scan the article for her name, hoping he wouldn't notice the hole. John pointed to the article she was already reading and when Alex reached for it, she gave it to him.

"Read it aloud please, Sir Alex," she directed.

"Rumour says there's evidence of the Wallace treasure in Yorkshire," Alex read, looking over at John. His voice trembled slightly when he asked, "You have this evidence, John?"

"No, have you?" John replied, looking stern-faced from one to the other. Since receiving the phone call from the Heritage office regarding Monsignor Sharp, he had been having difficulty getting these two amateur sleuths off his mind. His immediate reaction was to laugh, and yet, he could sense the undeniable intention of someone who was determined to impede the search for the Royal Regalia. His next thought was: *Who would want to do this and why? This mystery has prevailed for hundreds of years, so why now is someone afraid it could be resolved by Lady Traymore?* At that point he had decided to pay more attention to the activities of Sir Alex and his lady!

"Of course not, you would know about it if we did!" Alex countered. "We were at the monastery just over a week ago and my lady was sure they had a listening device because they knew our every move."

"Listening to you and Lady Traymore?" John asked, as the waitress arrived to take their orders. Holding their conversation until she had gone, John repeated his question.

"They listened to our conversations in various rooms and as we ate. I actually proved it to Alex," Emma exclaimed. "It was very upsetting."

"And just what does that prove, my lady? We have security cameras all over our building. Does that make me a suspect too?" John argued. "And what about your actions? You've been in Scotland two weeks and you've already upset at least two government employees and several policemen. Doesn't that seem rather thought-provoking to you, it certainly does to me!"

The discussion continued as they ate and Emma was fairly sure she had managed to calm John down and see the problem from her perspective. When John's cell phone disturbed the dining room's quiet ambiance, drawing a look of derision from other customers, he checked the display and angrily put it away. Gradually showing signs of frustration, as soon as he finished eating, he claimed he had an appointment and left.

Guilt touched Emma's consciousness as she watched him go.

"I think we will owe John an apology when this is over, my lady."

"It did seem like a good idea when we started," she whispered, a sad tone in her voice. "I suppose it went too well ... do you think?"

"I believe so," Alex replied, "everyone with the slightest interest will be swarming over the monastery this morning but the press won't find that they make very good interviewees!"

"I am a bit disappointed that we didn't make the front page though!"

"But we did, my lady!" he refolded the paper with the front page showing and pointed to the top headline with teasers of the day's stories. She broke into a grin and he leaned closer to whisper to her. "If the authorities ever find out we started this rumour, Emma, they'll lock us up and throw away the key!" She almost choked on her coffee.

Silently finishing their meal, they became aware of various conversations from nearby tables and Emma frowned as she heard the words *Yorkshire, monastery, regalia* and more. When Alex looked at her and winked, she knew he had also heard.

"Did you feel like doing any reading last night?" he asked.

"Did I feel like it? I couldn't bear to put the book down! You devil, you knew that would happen, didn't you? I suppose you were just waiting to see how long it would take me to ask for books!"

Alex merely smiled and stood up, going over to pull out her chair. "Now tell me, have you some plans for today, my lady?"

"Yes, I would like to go over the survey maps John gave us and compare them to those we received at the land department."

"Could we do that in your suite? It will be much warmer there ...!"

"Oh Alex, I didn't mean go to Elderslie! It will do no good going out in this weather. We've missed our chance at the burial grounds for now."

Half an hour later, with their maps spread out on the table and chairs, they matched the modern survey map to the ancient map of the monastery lands. It was soon obvious there were many discrepancies; old boundary lines now passed through housing estates and cut across modern roads. A shopping centre even stood on what was once monastery land and modern boundaries included all the old burial grounds, but clearly marked on the old map were some paupers' graves close to the western perimeter.

Emma let her trembling finger trace the outline of these ancient graves. Although much was faded on the old map and there were no identifying codes or captions, there were tiny marks which she and Alex felt could relate to the number of bodies occupying a grave.

"She's here!" Emma suddenly whispered, stabbing her finger at the group of plots near, but not as far over as the western boundary. She swallowed to hold back threatening tears as her hands went first to her heart and then she leaned on the table. "I can feel her Alex! Oh my gosh," she exclaimed, moaning, "it's ... that feeling I had ... *Place of Tears*. My heart ... it hurts so much ... please stop!"

As soon as Alex realized she was in trouble, he went instantly to stand behind her, putting his arms around her shoulders. Speaking softly and gently, he eased her into a chair and tried desperately to prevent another breakdown which he knew would frustrate and even debilitate her, at the very least. Slowly, she gathered her wits and her body stopped heaving, weeping softly as she returned to normal. All of a sudden, the phone rang, taking them both by surprise. She stood up in panic.

"You answer it," she told him, going slowly towards the bedroom.

It rang again as he watched her go in and close the door. When he picked up the receiver, the desk clerk said, "You have visitors, Lady Traymore, shall I send them up?"

"This is Sir Alex, Lady Traymore is busy. Who are these visitors?"

"Mr. and Mrs. MacDuff, Sir Alex. May I speak to Lady Traymore?"

"Lady Traymore asks that you please send them up," he replied, hanging up before she became more insistent.

"What is it, Alex?" Emma called.

"George and Alfreda are on their way up," he replied. "Are you all right?" He quickly gathered up the papers and put them out of sight.

Composed and looking somewhat repaired, Emma emerged from the bedroom just in time to answer the door.

"Have you read the newspaper today?" Alfreda asked excitedly.

"Yes, John Dunstan met with us for breakfast."

"Well, do you actually have such evidence?" Alfreda queried.

"Hold on!" Alex interrupted. "It doesn't say we have the evidence."

"Oh come now, Alex, who else would have it?" George asked.

"Possibly Monsignor Sharp or his superior?" Emma suggested. "You know he is extraordinarily nosy. We're sure he's up to something. It could be any number of people, even the Knights Hospitaller, but we have no idea who they are and they would never disclose willingly. What about Dunstan himself? He could be running a bluff to force the monastery into revealing their records."

"We agree somewhat, of course," Alfreda assured them, "but George and I think there could be several secret organizations with some perceived interest in the Wallace mystery. We have no doubt they are all watching each other very closely. When you came into the picture as the heiress accepted by the family, Emma, someone must have expected you to make a greater effort at fulfilling the prophecy than anyone had ever done previously. This was no doubt sufficient concern to get the attention of everyone interested in the Wallace mystery. I'm afraid you've begun to attract a great deal of interest from concerned parties who feel they could be affected to their detriment by the discovery of the regalia. Everyone is watching you and we all know how Sir Alex feels. He proved his loyalty many times to Trevelion Walters, and there has been no reason to think he would not continue to protect Trevelion's successor as his title stipulates. The mystery deepens," she proclaimed. "You're an educated woman and Mary Wallace has now lit a fire in your belly. I can feel it in my bones. You're simply going to have to solve this mystery and fulfill your destiny as laid out by the prophecy. I feel very strongly about this, Emma."

"That's all very nice, Alfreda," Emma replied, "but I'd like to know who these groups are, or what you suspect, at least."

Alfreda nodded in deep thought. "We find it hard to believe that the Royal Regalia could remain hidden for so long and I believe the silent monks have a lot more information than we know. They were present at the start of this mystery; in fact, I wouldn't be surprised if they haven't already found the regalia!" She looked pensively off into space for a moment, and then took several sips of her tea. Lowering her cup onto the saucer, she continued, "The Knights Hospitaller could have been involved and, perhaps a number of Templars as they fled France and annihilation, but the English took no action against any of them. Balliol's cohorts were suspected of being involved in the boys' betrayal as the Balliol faction was always a known thorn in Wallace's plans. I'm sure the descendants of that family would love to get their hands on the regalia!"

George had listened patiently until his eyes closed and his lips wobbled in time with his breathing. Suddenly, he spoke. "I believe you're right in suspecting local political authorities. My feeling is John Dunstan, for a mere archivist, gets too readily involved in Scotland's political scene, and he certainly keeps a wary eye on Renfrewshire!"

Alex winked at Emma before dropping his key question. "And are you willing to tell us who keeps you informed, George?"

"You cheeky devil," Alfreda chuckled. "We all know your source of local rumours. Every ale house in the country keeps you informed!"

"That hasn't answered my question, Alfreda!"

"All right, Alex," Alfreda replied, grinning. "I know Maggie at the post office is a good talker and believe it or not, so is Bill Mackie. I also know they both talk regularly to John Dunstan, and that crazed, Monsignor Sharp, seems to always be poking around. He must be working for someone, but who is the question."

"Somehow, we are going to find out," Emma announced firmly. "If you get suspicious of anyone else, we would be grateful if you could contact us. We know we can count on you and George; we feel you are the only ones we can trust explicitly."

It was almost one o'clock when Alfreda looked at her watch and coming quickly to her feet, went to waken George. Emma invited them for lunch but Alfreda said they had another engagement. Within minutes Alex and Emma were left giggling at the door as a still half-asleep George was dragged away.

"Did that seem a wee bit contrived to you?" Emma asked.

"I think they were fishing, we hadn't talked to them for awhile. The news story gave them the excuse, but I'm relieved you were cautious. Are you all right now?" he asked.

She sighed. "Having them barge in on us was probably a good thing!"

He let it pass, yet felt her mind must think otherwise.

They went downstairs for lunch but normal table conversation was severely restricted as Susan, the waitress, hung around their table seemingly eager to get their private attention. Finally, she came to ask if they wanted a coffee refill, and then blatantly inquired if they had heard 'the wonderful news that the Wallace treasure had been found at the silent monks' monastery in Yorkshire.'

Saying that they hadn't and trying to appear unconcerned, she left.

"A perfect example of how rumours are spread!" Emma hissed.

"Perhaps we should show a bit more interest as Scots." He frowned, beckoning to the girl. "Are you sure about your information, Susan?"

"It was in this morning's paper, sir, but I also overheard the minister over there in the corner, talking about it with his two lady guests."

"Thank you, Susan," Alex whispered, flashing a smile that caused the girl to blush before scurrying away.

Soon afterwards, Alex excused himself and went out to the foyer. When he returned, he told Emma that the minister and his ladies were still at the corner table and he wanted to get a photo of them. He took out his cell phone and made sure the flash was turned off before handing it to her under the table. He warned her that one of the staff would no doubt come over and try to stop her due to their privacy rules. "Try to get both the minister and the ladies in the photo."

Without standing, Emma began taking pictures of the elaborate ceiling, the candelabra and another of a nearby floral display, soon drawing the attention of the assistant manager who rushed over. "I'm so sorry, Lady Traymore, but we can't allow photos to be taken by the public in this room. I, however, could take a few pictures for you."

"I'm so sorry Mr. ...," she strained to see his nametag. "Mr. Fellows, I didn't realize," she apologized. "Would you mind? Your lovely dining room reminds me so much of the Empress Hotel in my hometown." She smiled brightly, handing him the phone. Making it look like an afterthought, she stood up shyly with her back to the minister's group.

Alex couldn't help but feel she was overdoing it but the assistant manager took two photos and then waited while Emma made another show of turning to a different position and then coyly asking him to take a couple more. When finished, he handed the phone back to her.

Eager to look at the photos, they finished up quickly and went to Emma's room. Alex checked the pictures but only one of the shots she had taken included the minister and he had contrived to hide his face behind a menu.

"Blast," he growled, but then broke into a grin, for in the background of two of the last photos was a full-face, perfect image of the minister and good side views of his companions!

"I don't recognize the minister, do you?" she muttered. "The woman on the right looks a bit familiar though."

"Och, you're very clever, my lady," Alex said drolly. "The minister dropped his guard when the assistant manager took the pictures. It seems I misread your clever manipulation of the situation. Well done!"

"Thank you kindly, sir," she replied coyly, "but now we need to identify these people."

"Moira may be able to help us," he suggested. "Right now, I want to have another look at those maps." He went to the kitchen, gathered together the maps and spread them around the counters and table again. Emma watched him and laughed as she remembered the MacDuff's arrival.

"We need to locate the paupers' graves," he said thoughtfully.

"I agree, but by the look of the ordinance map, they could be under this road. It's difficult to be sure as the map is faded so badly."

Again they studied the maps together, comparing their thoughts until suddenly Alex pointed to the river. "Look at that!" he gasped. "This area is much larger than we thought, perhaps a thousand acres! One of the kings must have given them a grant."

"You think, but this ordinance map must be incomplete. It doesn't even show the outside boundaries of the burial grounds which we've seen on other maps," said Emma. "It seems like every time we take a step forward we find another problem!"

Alex shook his head, muttering so softly she had to strain to hear. "Perhaps, this is a good problem to have. If the size of the land grant changed, the size of the consecrated land surely wouldn't alter, do you think … unless it got larger?"

Emma looked up and stared at him, then broke into a smile.

"Share it with me," he prodded.

"It has just occurred to me that if we go back and start to dig up that hole again, Rodric Brodie will have a heart attack!"

"You're right but I don't think that is the right place. We need an ally in Paisley, someone above suspicion like a police officer."

"You seem to know the police commissioner personally or were you just blowing hot air to impress me?" she asked, cocking an eyebrow.

"Now that would be a good thought, except Jim doesn't live or work in Paisley but ...," he stopped to look at her. "If Jim would tell Sergeant Mackie to help us, he could be the perfect connection."

"What? You didn't answer my question. Is *Jim* a personal friend?" When Alex grinned, she looked shocked. "You're kidding me! He could do that? You can simply ask him to help us?"

"Slow down." He pulled out his phone and speed-dialed a number while Emma sat back and watched him with a questioning frown.

"May I speak to the police commissioner," Alex asked. "Tell him it's Sir Alex Wallace." Within seconds, he was grinning and making a comment in broad Scots. He chuckled at the muffled reply. "I need a favour and I have a lady with me who wants to meet you." He listened again briefly. "We'll be there in 10 minutes."

Taken aback at the sudden turn of events, Emma went to freshen up while he put the papers away. As they walked to the car, she suppressed her urge to ask him about this fascinating friendship. Alex turned into Princes Street and, for the first time, she noticed the bus station and the glorious buildings surrounding it. She shook her head in disbelief when the street changed its name to Waterloo and then suddenly it was Regent, reminding her again of home. It surprised her when Alex turned off Regent into the car park of a large, official-looking building.

"Is this the police station?" she asked. Alex nodded. "Then hadn't you better be careful where you park your car, this spot says it's *Reserved!*"

"It's Jim's spot, he walks to work," he replied, getting out.

"How do you know that?"

"He's my neighbour!" he exclaimed, closing the door.

She turned to face him as he opened her door, but held back the curse that came to her lips and, merely whispered, as people passed nearby. Entering the building, Alex stopped at the information booth and discovered his name was not on the appointment list. The senior sergeant had to phone the commissioner's office to verify. Before he put the phone down, he made another call and a young officer appeared asking them to follow him.

The commissioner was waiting and Alex stoically made the introductions. Commissioner MacDonald greeted Emma as if he already knew all about her, even holding her hand somewhat longer than usual. As he led her to a comfortable armchair, he offered tea or coffee. She chose coffee and he alerted a nearby staff member. He further proved beyond a doubt that he and Alex were friends when he told her he would prefer to offer her a Highland Coffee but it was against the rules. He laughed when Alex shook his head disapprovingly.

James proceeded to expertly question Emma about her background, obviously impressed with some of her flippant answers, especially when she mentioned her male faculty friends and their highbrow, pompous attitudes. He listened particularly intently when she gave a short version of the history of the Wallace and Walters' families as it pertained to her personally. Finally, she touched on her search for the final resting place of Mary Wallace.

"How do you believe I can help you?" he asked.

"We think there are others involved in trying to locate the Royal Regalia, but up to now they've been highly elusive. They are no doubt secretly working through local contacts and, we believe, they are stirring up trouble as they wait for some perceived opportunity."

"Are you referring to Monsignor Sharp, my lady?"

"Oh yes, of him I have little doubt, but we believe there are others."

"If they don't break the law, there's really not much we can do."

"Perhaps you could ask Sgt. Mackie to … help us if he sees the opportunity."

"Yes, I could, but I must warn you, Bill Mackie would arrest his mother if she broke the law!"

"We don't want to break the law; but we may be able to use his presence to keep certain others away from us."

"All right, that sounds reasonable under the circumstances. Let me write you a Letter of Cooperation for assistance in historical matters. That would help open some doors for you."

"You would do that commissioner … we are grateful."

A sudden knock on the door and a constable stepped into the room. "You're wanted immediately at Station 23, sir."

"Stay here," the commissioner ordered and hurried away.

Draining her coffee, Emma began to fidget, going over to the window. "Can we see the hotel from here?"

"It's to the left, behind those buildings."

Tapping lightly on the door, another constable came into the room with two fresh coffees on a tray. Emma frowned before addressing the young man. "How did you know we wanted more coffee?"

"The commissioner asked me to check on you for coffee refills. I simply watched the surveillance camera, my lady." He pointed upwards.

"Can you also hear what we say?" she asked warily.

"Yes, my lady."

Ten minutes later James returned.

"An emergency?" Alex asked.

"Not really, just an unusual situation in Yorkshire that has stirred up the press. It should interest you both as it's at your monastery."

Alex and Emma looked at each other briefly and frowned, now knowing James was watching them.

"What's going on, James?" asked Alex.

"It seems the silent monks have a problem. News reporters from Scottish TV, various radio stations and many newspapers from who knows where, have their reporters trespassing on the property. Haven't you heard about this today? It's all over the news."

"Not a clue," said Alex. "We've had meetings and haven't had the news on. Do you know what caused this situation, James? Perhaps we should go down to Yorkshire?"

"You wouldn't say that if you saw the TV; rumour says the monks have found the Royal Regalia!"

"Oh no, it will be a madhouse ... what do the monks say?" Alex rolled his eyes as he realized what he had just said.

"Not a word, of course!" James laughed. "Maybe it will blow over in another 24 hours. At any rate, you can pick up my letter to Sgt. Mackie at the security desk as you leave." Having been dismissed, Emma shook James' hand before they left.

Conversation was almost non-existent as Alex drove back to the hotel. Intermittent chuckles were heard as Emma silently conjured up a picture of the Yorkshire monastery swarming with news media. Several phone messages were waiting for her at the hotel ... Douglas at the distillery, Alfred Holt at the tartan factory and even Ruth Oxley. Surprised, Alex checked his phone and realized it needed charging.

"Och, I'll have all those messages too! They've all heard the rumours now and want our input. Why don't you go upstairs and call Ruth and I'll call Douglas and Alfred. We'd better follow the pattern we set up with James. We know nothing and only heard about it this afternoon from

James. Would you like to go somewhere quiet for dinner?" he asked, reading Emma's mood.

"I certainly would," she murmured tiredly, "it's been a most eventful day. I'll meet you in the bar in about 20 minutes."

She returned Ruth's call and tried to keep it short, saying she was just seeing it on TV for the first time. The news channel showed pictures of the Yorkshire monastery. Police were everywhere and cameramen and news reporters were climbing walls and wandering all over the property. Monks were trying to chase the trespassers away as they came too close to trampling the gardens ... difficult when you don't speak! She sighed sadly and was almost ready for leaving when the commentator announced that the army had been called out to restore order.

When she found Alex, bar chatter was buzzing with the story of the day and she found Alex near a TV monitor.

"I think we've got what could be called 'a situation,' my lady!"

The biting wind made her grasp Alex's arm as they left the hotel and walked up George Street. Turning a corner, they entered a small restaurant. A bell signalled their arrival. A jovial lady in her middle years wiped her hands on a red-checkered apron and hurried over, beaming.

"Good evening Molly," Alex greeted her as he found a table and helped Emma with her coat. Emma turned to greet her, but realized that Molly had disappeared through a curtain into the kitchen.

"Now you've surprised me," Emma whispered across the table just before Molly returned carrying a tray with three coffees.

"I'll join you shortly," she announced turning back to the cash register where two of her customers waited. When she was finished, she stopped to poke a few stray hairs back under her hairnet, then came over to join them.

"So this is your lovely lady from Canada, Alex? I was wondering when you'd get around to introducing me!" Her voice had a lovely, lilting accent that Emma couldn't place. Molly didn't give her time to ask as she continued with the compliments, reaching out to gently lay her hand on Alex's as she smiled at Emma. "You were right, she is lovely. If I were you, I'd marry her quickly before she finds out about you, Alex!"

"And you Molly Dugan can behave yourself when you're in the company of respectable people," Alex replied.

Emma didn't miss the fact that his cheeks were now a bright shade of pink and the colour increased when he glanced at Emma and noted her raised eyebrows and the mischievous grin spreading across her face.

"You two obviously know each other," she chuckled.

"We grew up together," he admitted. "Molly's father was our Irish gamekeeper."

"Are you eating or just calling to show off your lady?" Molly asked, winking at Emma.

"Have you got two of your steak and kidney pies in the oven?"

"Just came out, must have known you were coming, lad. I also have fresh-baked bread just waiting for somebody special." She threw a smile at Emma and went off towards the kitchen. She stopped before reaching the curtained door and tossed a comment over her shoulder. "I don't mean you, my lad. I'm talking about your lady!"

"Isn't she wonderful?" Alex whispered. "She's like a breath of spring in a world too often full of misery. She's not trying to be funny, it just comes naturally, I have never seen her sulk or be miserable, always happy." Watching Alex closely, Emma saw his eyes cloud a little as he continued, almost inaudibly. "Molly is family, the sister I never had!"

Thoroughly enjoying the simple home-style cooking, it was Emma's turn to shower Molly with comments of appreciation.

"Please come again, my lady," she insisted, accompanying them to the door and taking Emma's hand.

"It's only 7:30," said Alex as they stood on the sidewalk outside. "Is there anywhere you would like to go?"

"Yes, there certainly is. I want to go see a place in Rose Street."

"What place in Rose Street? I live there!"

"I know, now take me there! Your time for promises is up, lad!"

They walked only two blocks before entering the controlled entrance of a large, beautifully gardened, white stone building and Alex used a swipe card system to open the door. They entered a lift that silently whisked them to the top floor. Not a sound reached her consciousness as they walked across thick carpet to a door displaying an ornate number '2.' Alex swiped his card again and the door opened, lights came on, and once they were inside, the door closed silently behind them.

"My goodness, this is truly Fort Knox … don't you British call it 'posh'?" she asked, looking down her nose at him and making a face. He took her coat and hung it on a coat rack that mysteriously appeared.

He motioned for her to go into the living room and waited for her reaction. Before taking two steps she saw the stunning white, stone fireplace and swore. Dominating the outside wall and surrounded by a very pleasing collection of artwork, he knew she'd be eager to examine everything at close range. She sat on the white leather sofa which had two matching chairs encircling a spherical, etched glass coffee table upon which sat the inevitable tray containing glasses and a matching etched glass decanter of amber liquid.

"Which way is your bathroom … toilet!" she giggled, moving quickly to follow his finger. The bathroom was like something out of a movie, also white with lots of glass and gold accents. When she rejoined him, the smell of coffee and sounds of clinking china drew her into an exquisitely modern kitchen which was almost totally white.

"Your toilet is wonderful, Alex. I'd have difficulty leaving it but I couldn't find your magazine collection! Why have you been hiding this from me? It's quite delightful—did you design it yourself?"

He picked up the coffee tray and, telling her to go ahead of him, they returned to the spacious living room. She sat down and waited for his reply.

"So, you approve of my humble home? You might say I assisted with a few architectural details! It pleases me that you like it."

"Well, humble it certainly is not! You don't spend very much time here, at least not since I have arrived. That's a shame."

Suddenly, part of the wall above the fireplace moved, sliding smoothly aside to reveal a TV monitor showing a picture of Alex's front door and hallway with James MacDonald stepping out of the lift.

"Good evening, Jim," said Alex, chuckling when Emma's mouth dropped open. "Would you join us for a drink, the coffee is fresh!"

Looking directly into the camera, the policeman nodded his acceptance and winked, knowing it had to be Emma who was with him.

"Shall I open the door for the commissioner?" she asked.

"No need, my lady, I'm already here!" She turned around in surprise to come face-to-face with the Commissioner of Police. "So you've finally discovered the wonders of Alex's real home?" Oh, and please call me Jim or James."

"I've never seen anything like it; it's really quite unexpected. I would have imagined Alex to be an old-fashioned kind-of-guy. I obviously haven't moved in the right social circles to see this modern decor … yet!" she laughed as Alex brought Jim's coffee.

"Actually, Jim helped me with the technology features," Alex admitted. "We had quite a lot of fun doing it up!"

"We certainly did," Jim declared. "Alex is finally getting quite used to penthouse life and seems to enjoy being the Lord of Wallace Manor!"

They all laughed and soon conversation inevitably turned to the subject of the Wallace mystery and Emma's involvement.

"It must be quite a transition for you, my lady, from a university lecturer to a detective trying to solve a 700-year-old mystery in Scotland," said Jim. "If I can be of further assistance, you now know my favourite places!" He finished his coffee and said goodnight.

"Does that fancy television also play news, Alex?" she asked.

"It does and we should just catch the BBC News at 10 p.m."

Instantly, the large picture switched to a TV monitor and the British National News was just beginning. A well-groomed announcer with a plum-in-mouth accent began giving his report. She noticed a hint of excitement creeping into his monotone voice and her interest was heightened when pictures of the monastery appeared. She heard Alex chuckle as photos of the bleak Yorkshire moors showed not only an unusual number of police vehicles but military activity as well. A closeup shot showed the main road with cars parked along it and crowds of people approaching the monastery. Police had now cordoned off the area to vehicles but it all looked quite hopeless.

"It is rumoured," the announcer droned, "that the ancient Scottish Royal Regalia has been found, although neither the police nor the Scottish National Archives will confirm or deny this."

"I can't believe this. Look at all those stupid people, they have no respect for private property at all. Surely they can find something better to do with their time. I've heard enough, all this publicity is giving me a guilt complex. Those poor defenseless monks." She looked sadly at Alex and shook her head. "Before you walk me home I'd like to look at your library, Alex, and see what other treasures you are hiding there."

"Of course, come on then," he said, shutting off the television."

He led her down the hallway and when he opened the door, she gasped. "Why do you need such a massive private collection when Dorik has one?" He just shrugged and pointed to the Scottish selection. As she looked, she changed the subject. "We're going to Misty House tomorrow, aren't we? I'd also like to go to Paisley and talk to Bill Mackie. I might have an idea how to expose Monsignor Sharp's contact!"

"The sergeant may have gone to Yorkshire but we'll go and see," Alex mused, only half-listening as he handed her a book by Nigel Tranter entitled, *The Story of Scotland*. "This book is short but excellent. Tranter wrote many wonderful novels, too. Some of them about your favourite Scottish heroes! Now let's get you home, my lady!"

## Chapter 14 – Wednesday 29<sup>th</sup> – Biographia Box

By 9 a.m., they were leaving the rain-soaked streets of Edinburgh and heading up the M9 towards bluer sky. The radio warned of backed-up traffic due to some accident on the M8 and Alex chuckled. By-passing the problem by cutting off near Falkirk, it was then only a short hop to Misty House where they discovered unplowed country roads and Emma commented on the beautiful Highlands with their fresh snow.

Upon arrival at Misty House, they saw a group of the children using their white canes and carefully crossing the plowed road from the manor house to the studio. Alex waited until they were inside the building before driving up to the front entrance.

As he got out of the car, he heard Ruth's voice and saw her waving from behind the partly open door. "Hello, Sir Alex and Lady Traymore! Och, we don't like ice and snow here at Misty House!" she called, waiting for her visitors to come closer. "Ice makes it very difficult for the children, such a danger for the blind." When they arrived, she opened the door a bit wider. "I'm so sorry to greet you with complaints. I really am pleased to see you both. Did you see the children? They're going over to train with the dogs. You may like to go and watch, my lady."

Alex, seeing Emma's smile, told Ruth they would both go over and return to see her shortly. Ruth nodded and closed the door.

Upon entering the Studio, she noticed that an area of the large building was now set up with benches and room dividers. They went closer as ten children of varying ages, mostly girls, lined up in front of their teacher. She told them to sit on the floor and then she and Jessie talked to them about what they were going to do.

Emma was very impressed that the ten dogs, left alone by Jessie off to the side, still remained laying quietly on the floor. They rarely even raised their heads or wagged a tail as they patiently watched the proceedings. Prompted by their teacher, the first girl called out a name and her dog immediately trotted over, sat down, and nuzzled the girl's hand. Emma caught her breath knowing the affection between a dog and a child was certainly genuine. The girl then gave her dog a hug, talking quietly as she attached its lead and then allowed it to take her over to stand in front of Jessie. As the rest of the children linked up with their dogs, Jessie started the first ones off and the dogs led each child around the obstacle course. They went in and out of the benches, only stopping when Charlie put something in their path. Some of the younger children had difficulty keeping up from time-to-time but it was an amazing demonstration. It also did not escape Alex's attention that Emma, although delighted, was having some trouble with her emotions.

She suddenly turned to him and pointed to the door, turning away from the display. She was impressed with the staff's dedication to their sight-impaired residents, but she was also eager to see Ruth. Alex informed Tom they would return in awhile and went to catch up with her.

At the manor, Ruth met them at the back door. "Do come in, I have some news," she informed them secretively.

Following Ruth into her office, Emma beamed when she saw the biographia box on the side table. Unable to contain herself, she went over to look at it.

"Our biographia box … is it open?" she asked breathlessly. Without waiting for an answer, she reached out and tentatively touched the box as if it might give her an electric shock. She had had one of those already on Dorik and wasn't in a hurry to repeat the experience. But nothing happened except a growing excitement as her fingers caressed the ancient box and she considered the possible age of this wonderful artefact they had found. Her mind was suddenly alive with pressing questions.

"Have you read the resume, Ruth?" she asked. "Was it in Latin? Could I see it please? Oh my, I so hope it will be pertinent to our search."

"Steady, my lady," Ruth declared, holding up her hand. She looked over at Alex and noted his similar, yet more restrained reaction. "Please, sit down, both of you. I've ordered tea and then I shall endeavour to answer your questions."

Alex watched Emma as she tried hard to control herself, rubbing her fingers in her lap as he'd now seen her do several times before when agitated. The tea arrived and after she'd poured, Ruth produced a file folder and opened it painfully slowly, handing both Alex and Emma two sheets of handwritten notes. She sat down to observe their reactions.

"Och aye!" Alex gasped. "This almost makes me legitimate!"

Emma frowned, not realizing or even caring what he was on about at that particular moment. Almost oblivious to everything else, she slowly began to translate the Latin copy.

188

"Brother Martin ...," she whispered raising her head to look at Ruth. "Everything here suggests the monk was buried, but we found no sign of a body, why is that?"

"It also says he was going to be a witness at the wedding of William and Mary," Alex added, "and that could be the proof I need except ...."

"Careful now," Ruth gently advised. "I think you have simply discovered another set of questions with very few answers including surnames. The biographia is dated 1300 A.D., a bit too late for their marriage, Sir Alex, but nonetheless a time of great unrest in Scotland. Let me first offer you a simple explanation as to the missing body of the monk. If he was badly wounded and expected to die, his friends would have made preparations, and if he didn't die, or they had to move on in a hurry, what could they do with the grave? Leave it, naturally, and someone else would come along and fill it in or use it. They could be unaware the grave was prepared for a monk or that the biographia box was already in place. It may be just that simple." Ruth looked over at Alex. "I'm sorry, but making plans to go to a wedding to be a witness is not proof that that wedding ever took place. I'm afraid you're still on the wrong side of the blanket!"

"He was close to Wallace at least," Alex argued hopefully. "The paper mentions the skirmishes and the battle at Stirling."

"Your explanations are fascinating, Ruth, and help us to stay objective," Emma mused, glancing at her bailiff. "It would be wonderful if the interment records could help us out, but I don't see how that's possible. They don't belong with this box. We were told the pouches were found in another area of the burial grounds and had been stored and forgotten for many years. We simply unearthed them from their storage place in the same dugout as the biographia box."

"Have Tom or Charlie talked to you about our pouches, Ruth?"

"I think we should go over so you can talk to the boys directly. The children will be finished with their class in a few minutes. Do you wish to take the original parchment or would you prefer a copy?" Ruth asked, turning to point to a white plastic container on the sideboard.

Emma went over to look and as Ruth removed the cover she was shocked. The writing on the parchment could only be described, as scratches of something that looked like dreadful ... or perhaps hurried writing. "How can you possibly read this, let alone translate it?" Emma asked in disbelief. It looks like chicken scratches! Oh my, we have certainly given you all a greater challenge than I could have imagined! To answer your question, Ruth, I would like both please!"

189

The astonished expression on Ruth's face surprised Emma. She seemed to wait briefly for an explanation, but with none forthcoming, she picked up the tray and left the room.

A wink from Alex told her he approved. When Ruth returned, she handed Emma two labelled envelopes, one of them was quite bulky.

"I've left the parchment in the tray so it won't receive any more damage than necessary," Ruth explained. "Remember to use cotton gloves if you must touch it. Pertaining to your question, yes, I believe the boys have opened one pouch so far but that is also slow work." Ruth got her coat and put it on as she talked. "The leather of the pouches is very fragile. We've had a few discussions and now realize that we need more information on the monastery's land grant. Without that knowledge, it is virtually impossible to find the paupers' section."

A light snow was falling as they went across to the Studio.

"We have something that may help you with that problem," Alex declared. "Give me the envelopes, my lady, and I'll go get them."

"Is it a map?" Ruth asked Emma as they carried on walking.

"Yes, I think you'll be pleased. There are actually two maps."

"Oh goodness, that's wonderful! The boys are working so hard on this project," Ruth exclaimed, as Emma held the door open for her. "It seems like you have this mystery well in hand."

"We truly hope so, Ruth," Alex commented, rejoining them, "but it's far from solved yet."

Ruth was busy watching the children as they worked with the dogs. She turned slightly to put her finger to her lips before leaving them and going closer to watch. It was now remarkably quiet in the Studio as the children and their dogs went through their final paces. Emma and Alex kept out of the way and just watched, intently. A few minutes later, the class came to an end and Jessie instructed the children to take the dogs back to their kennels. Ruth followed them.

"That's a wonderful way to train those dogs," Emma commented.

"You've got that wrong, my lady!" Charlie laughed, "It's the children who are being trained now. The dogs already know what to do. What brings you two out here today?"

"I believe we mentioned earlier that we had visited Rodric Brodie at the land office," said Alex, watching Tom nod. "He gave us some original copies of the old survey maps. Last Friday, John Dunstan gave us a similar but enlarged copy of the original consecrated grounds. It has much greater detail than the other maps and indicates that the area is far larger than we originally believed. Sadly, portions of it are quite faded in some pertinent areas, naturally those areas are the ones in which we are most interested. We have already studied it and have some ideas, but we thought you might like to have a look.

The men watched as Alex began to unroll the first map over an empty table and they went to clear a second table. Tom grew excited and soon they were all talking at once as they searched the maps. By the time Ruth joined them, the group was sharing their thoughts more quietly.

"Och, this shows the paupers' graves," Charlie exclaimed. "If only it was possible to see the numbers!"

"Look!" Tom pointed eagerly to another area on the oldest map. "The burial plots are divided into two sections!"

"Religion!" Emma exclaimed. "Even the monks pushed the poor into the farthest corner. Are either of you knowledgeable with the western boundary?" She watched as the men both shook their heads.

"Remember, my lady, we have no proof that Mary was intered in the paupers' section," Ruth reminded them, "it's merely an assumption."

"We understand, Ruth, but I am almost certain she'll be found in that area. She's there!" Emma murmured curtly. "You can call it intuition, spiritual guidance or whatever you like. I know she's there!"

"Lady Traymore, you're going to like this!" Charlie shouted, beckoning from his own area where they were working on the pouches.

"It's one of the interment documents!" Emma gasped, now realizing that Tom had also gravitated away from the maps and joined Charlie. They had both put on their white cotton gloves. "Ruth told us you had one of the pouches open."

"Actually we have two open, but this is the only one that has been translated," Tom explained, obviously eager to show her.

Emma smiled. "Now that theoretically we know where the paupers' section is, all we need is a clue that will lead us to Mary's grave."

"You make that sound so simple, my lady," Tom commented. "I assume you mean a clue in the interment records?"

"I believe that is what she means, gentlemen!" Alex laughed.

"All right, let me tell you about the type of information that is coming out of this first pouch," Tom announced as Emma and Alex moved closer. He was looking at a piece of parchment slightly smaller than a modern letter. It was sitting in a plastic tray identical to the one Ruth had given her. "This one is dated the first quarter of 1302. The parchment is actually in amazingly good condition for its age and the information is fascinating. Come look for yourselves, but please don't touch any of the original artifacts as they are very fragile in this state. This family was a forest family, charged with killing the king's deer and they were put to death by the king's soldiers. So, this is in the right era and we're hoping that some of the other pouches hold information from this time period as well.

"I can read the translation if you have something else to do Tom," Ruth volunteered. He thanked her, handing her the page of handwritten notes. "It says," she began, adjusting the light, "that Isaac, Petra and three children were put to the sword for stealing the king's deer. They're buried in Paupers' Plots Numbering 73 and 74 on the western boundary. The clergy were forbidden to read them their last rites ... barbaric savages!" Ruth added venomously, turning away to hide her emotions.

"Can you guestimate how long it will take to open and translate all the records from the pouches?" Emma asked.

"It's going to take some weeks, my lady," Tom replied, "unless we are able to spend more time on them."

"It would save time if you could quickly scan through the documents to see if the dates are what we need ... if any Wallace or Walters' names are included, in particular Mary's."

"Yes, we can do that, my lady," Tom agreed. "I'm sorry; we should have thought of it ourselves. We'll call you if we find anything important, otherwise, why don't you come back out on Monday? We should have a few of them open and translated by then."

"Listen, all of you," Ruth got their attention. "I believe I can safely say that both myself and these men are very happy to be able to help you on this historical project. We're going to make every possible effort to free up our time to speed up this translating."

"Oh Ruth, that would be wonderful, if it's possible," Emma exclaimed, looking surprised and happy about the new development.

"I promise we will do our utmost," Ruth added. "Charlie, we'll talk about this immediately and see how we can re-arrange work schedules to help Tom with the translations, but it still could take a few weeks! We're excited about this too! It's a very special honour to help you, my lady."

Before they parted company, Emma thanked them all for their hard work. "I feel so confident that the key to the Wallace mystery will be found in these records. I hope you can prove me right!"

"We'll leave the survey maps here for a few days," Alex offered.

As they were saying goodbye, Ruth reminded Alex to drive carefully.

Driving away from Misty House, they turned on the radio and the announcer said it was snowing heavily between Falkirk and Linlithgow.

Stirling had also experienced a cold snap around noon which caused several vehicles to go off the road.

"That's all right, they can have their weather," he scoffed. "We're not going that way today, anyway. We'll be able to use the M8. It takes us right past Tex's pub," Alex assured her. "Would you like to drop in and say hello to Alfred at the tartan factory?"

"That's a great idea," she replied, completely taking Alex by surprise. "I could talk to my seamstress, if she's there. I am getting hungry though.

"All right, we'll see if the road to the mill is passable and not stay long. Then we'll find a place to eat. I hope this storm is going to end soon. This is not the Scotland I know!"

"Could it be you're travelling more now because I'm here?"

"You're right, I am going into the interior more than usual for this time of year, but it's nice to have company Emma."

"It is, isn't it?" she said pensively, thinking of her quiet life at home.

The roads were actually clear with only a fresh dusting of snow, so they soon arrived at the mill. Alfred was very pleased to see Emma, congratulating her on becoming Lady Traymore, and the staff cheered when they entered. She had a nice, but short, chat with Helen telling her she needed a formal dress for her portrait and for Christmas. Helen brought out an album and showed her a photo of 'the perfect style for my lady with a few slight adjustments to make it unique' and a much-relieved Lady Traymore told her to go ahead with it and they left.

Tire tracks in the snow led them straight to the main road. Alex checked the outdoor temperature and was confident they were missing any dreaded cold snap. He stopped at the first Services Stop where they had soup and a sandwich before getting on their way again. Roads were almost dry and Emma marvelled at the county's response to the poor highway conditions.

"They do a better job than our crews in Victoria!"

"We've no doubt had more practice than you colonials in Canada's tropical belt!" Alex quipped.

"Shouldn't we call to see if Sgt. Mackie is available?"

"We'll find out in a few minutes anyway. The station is only five minutes away."

The young desk constable watched with interest as they came towards him. He asked if he could assist them and Alex introduced himself, asking to speak with Sgt. Mackie. The constable nodded, disappearing through a nearby door. Within minutes they were standing in front of a desk occupied by a familiar, bearded sergeant.

"Lady Traymore, Sir Alex, it's nice to see you again," Sgt. Mackie greeted them, extending his hand. "Please take a seat; can I get you a coffee?" They declined, explaining they had just finished lunch.

Emma glanced around her in surprise. All the furniture was from a long ago era, reminding her of an office where her father had worked.

"How may I assist you?" Sgt. Mackie's voice broke into her thoughts.

"We have a letter from Commissioner MacDonald," Emma replied, handing it to him.

"Yes, I spoke with the commissioner this morning, my lady, but I will not allow you to break the law," the sergeant warned. He rolled his chair back and opened the letter, looking up at them partway through.

"So, what is it you want from me?" he asked, dropping the letter on the desk.

"I want to know what you can tell us about Monsignor Sharp and his superior. Why is he always snooping around Elderlie, and watching us every time we come here?" she demanded.

"I'm sorry, but I don't know about this and I couldn't tell you if I did, my lady. It used to bother me too," he replied, "but he never breaks the law, even though he's been a nuisance for years."

"Are you saying, this began before I arrived, sergeant?" Emma asked.

"Oh, most certainly, he's been seen skulking around for years and apparently mailing dubious and unusually regular letters to his family!"

"Is he right in the head? Couldn't you get a warrant to view the letters in the interest of national security?" Alex asked.

"Definitely not, Sir Alex!" Sgt. Mackie looked shocked. "A judge would never let me tamper with the Royal Mail for any reason ... the authorities would arrest me!"

"Then what do you know about his letters? Who does he write to? Does he use the same post box?" Emma persisted.

"I-I don't know any details that I am at liberty to divulge, and what good would it do for you to know?" he replied, somewhat agitated now.

"This is getting us nowhere," Emma snapped, standing up in frustration. "Maybe we should just ask Monsignor Sharp ourselves!"

"I-I'm very sorry I can't help you," Sgt. Mackie muttered but she left without another word. "Sir Alex, I don't want to hear that you or Lady Traymore are getting into any trouble with the monsignor!"

"Don't worry sergeant, we'll be model citizens," Alex assured him, shaking the policeman's hand then hurrying to catch up to Emma.

"Well, that was an utter waste of time!" Emma exclaimed when they were outside. "They're the police, but they're absolutely useless!"

"Not totally, Emma. Don't you realize what you said in there, and incidentally, you're absolutely correct ... we're going to have to deal with the monsignor directly and be very careful in doing so. I think we've been asking the wrong questions of the wrong people, and you just proved it!" Alex proclaimed, opening her car door. Emma hesitated and he began to laugh, putting his arm around her shoulder. "You're wonderful, my lady, Trevelion would be so proud of you!"

"Why?" she asked, pushing him away.

"You're possibly the only person that ever made that policeman feel inferior. But he did his job well nonetheless."

"I thought police were supposed to help the public?"

"He did."

"But he wouldn't tell us if he knew the answers, so what do you suggest we do now?" she asked.

"Get in and I'll show you."

"What are you talking about?"

"I believe I know how to find the information we need!"

"You rotten swine, why didn't you say so?"

"You didn't ask me! Calm down, I'm going to show you."

Driving slowly through Paisley, he went on to Elderslie and the old burial grounds, pulling up to the curb and turning off the engine.

Emma eyed the Scot suspiciously. "What are you up to, Sir Alex?"

"Hat and gloves, my lady. It's cold out there and we have some bait to spread!"

"Bait to spread? That definitely sounds intriguing!"

Opening the boot, Alex silently walked around to the rear of the car, took out the metal detector and handed Emma a spade.

"Ready now?" he asked, winking at her before walking away.

She held back, shook her head and then followed. *Is he really planning to dig somewhere? Why does he need the metal detector?*" Next, he stopped at a monument, bent down and fiddled with the dials. She frowned and went to join him.

"What are we looking for?" she asked.

"There, it's there!" he yelped loudly, pointing to an ancient grave where she now realized he had placed his monogrammed money clip. He waved the metal detector over it again and the detector screamed an ear-shattering warning. Instantly switching it off, he glanced furtively around the area, crouched down and seemed to be looking for something on the ground.

"Are you nuts?" she hissed.

195

"Probably, come and take a look," he whispered. When she did, he continued. "Now, stand up and look around, and tell me what you see."

Puzzled, but fascinated, she complied. "I think I see Monsignor Sharp watching us from a hedge behind you and Mitch is coming with his dog."

"Excellent, bait taken!" Alex murmured, picking up his money clip and slipping it slyly back into his pocket as he stood up.

"Good afternoon, yer worships," Mitch greeted them, as he made an exaggerated effort to read the monument they were standing beside. Unfortunately, he stumbled on the raised edge of the grave and fell down, grazing his head on a nearby grave marker.

Alex moved quickly to his assistance, as a trickle of blood ran down the poacher's face from his eyebrow.

"My goodness, are you all right?" Emma cried in alarm as the dog came to investigate.

After wiping the blood away, Alex coaxed Mitch onto his feet, supporting him as they walked back to the car and he helped him sit in the front seat. "Sit down for a moment," Alex insisted, before asking Emma to get his whisky flask. Three tots later, Mitch was quite a bit more talkative and seemed to be feeling better.

"I think your friend, the minister, is waiting for you," Alex commented, glancing across the graveyard.

"He ain't no friend of mine!" Mitch replied sharply.

"Is he a lonely man?" Emma asked. "Sgt. Mackie says he writes unusually often to his family.

"Mackie don't know nothin!" Mitch growled. "He posts a letter just about every day outside the drug store at the shopping centre at precisely 4:55. The post van collects at five. I watched him many times and he don't even put a stamp on it, he just writes zero HMS in the corner."

"Letters to his mother every day," Alex joked, "now that's a dedicated son!"

"Oh no, sir," Mitch argued. "They go to Edinburgh."

"Come now, Mitch," Alex teased, "how do you know that?"

"He showed me … offered me £5 just to watch somebody."

With that said, Mitch staggered to his feet, wobbled a little as he regained his balance, and then shuffled away without a backward glance.

"Right, time to go, mission almost accomplished," Alex declared. "You may as well go sit in the car while I collect the tools." Emma watched from the car as he loaded the items into the boot. When he slipped in behind the steering wheel, he sat quietly waiting for Emma's anticipated comment.

She didn't disappoint. "Okay, Mr. Super Sleuth, show me your next move." Concentrating on his driving, he didn't answer right away so she tried again. "Are you going to explain this to me or am I supposed to be a mind reader!"

"We have an hour to kill. Do you want to do some shopping or should we have coffee at Moira's?"

"Oh, you can be so aggravating! An hour to kill? *Why does this man always speak in riddles?* Is that all you're going to tell me?" Looking at her watch, she cocked an eye at him as the puzzle pieces began to click together in her mind. Instead of watching the monsignor and Mitch, Alex had enticed them into the open and Mitch's fall had been an act of providence making the little man more talkative. "All right, I get it! You're going to check Mitch's story about the letter. Yes, I will do some shopping and you can go to see Moira, perhaps tell her about finding the tools. I don't know how long I'll be but I'll join you as soon as I can."

They had now arrived at the shopping centre and Alex backed into a spot across the car park from Moira's, away from any lights.

"All right," he said solemnly. "I'll see you in a little while." He watched her go and then got out himself.

The tea shop only had a few customers so he easily found a window table with a pretty good view of the postal box, assisted by a nearby light standard. He sat down in the chair opposite the window and Moira came to offer him coffee.

"Thank you. Moira, do you remember when we first went to talk to your grandfather about his knowledge of the graves he used to tend?

"Yes I do, was he able to help, Sir Alex?"

"Actually, not really, but he did mention that he would like the tools back that he had left in the shed. I told him I would try to find them. I should have known better because they would have been at least 15 years old and in poor condition by then. As it happens, we found them last week and they were in such bad shape—rusty with rotten handles, etc., that I thought it best not to complicate life for him or your parents. So I had them garbaged! I trust you will agree with my actions. Oh, and you might like to know that Miss Walters is now Lady Traymore."

"Oh my, that is wonderful news, and yes, I'm sure my parents would be grateful. Thank you very much … now please excuse me, Sir Alex."

Meanwhile, Emma had found a store which had all the items she needed and by 4:35 she was heading back to meet Alex. She looked around for the monsignor, realizing he could be anywhere in the darkness

197

out of range of the street lights. With no obvious sign of him, she walked nonchalantly to the tea shop.

Moira fussed over her when she arrived, curtseying deeply before going to get her order. Alex laughed, suggesting she sit in the chair beside him where she could see the post box.

"You told the poor girl I was a lady now, didn't you? Now she's going to fuss. Have you had a chance to show her your photos?" she asked.

"Photos?" he asked, somewhat puzzled.

She smiled, cocking her head at him. "The ones we took in the hotel dining room."

He nodded and rolled his eyes, taking out his cell phone as Moira came with Emma's tea. He asked for a refill of coffee and, by the time she returned, he had located the photo. He quickly checked the time.

"Moira, do you know any of these people, are they locals?" he asked, showing her the photo.

Moira took the phone and studied the photo until the image went off.

"I'm sorry, Sir Alex, I don't believe I've seen them before." She looked over at the door as new customers arrived, excusing herself.

"It's almost time, Alex," whispered Emma. "I hope you can see better than I can; it's very dark."

"I can, here comes someone in a dark overcoat. He's wearing a hat and walking slowly," he noted, glancing at his watch.

"I see him but I can't tell who it is."

"Right on time! It has to be him, it's exactly five minutes to five and he's just dropped his letter into the box!"

"Mitch was right then," Emma whispered, "but he's not leaving. What is he waiting for?"

"He's probably waiting for the pickup; here comes the mail van."

The van left and the man vanished into the darkness. They waited a few more minutes finishing their drinks. Moira came to see if she could entice them to stay for her just out-of-the-oven steak and kidney pies.

"We're sorry, but not tonight, Moira," said Emma, trying to look disappointed. "We have a dinner date elsewhere."

They left immediately and one of the topics of conversation was that Alex had remembered to talk to Moira about her grandfather's tools. Almost an hour later, they reached the *Rogue's Inn*.

"It's very aptly named," said Emma, "who would think this old building was the home of such an unusual policeman!"

"It will save us a trip if Tex can look at those papers today and we definitely need to eat," Alex commented as they went inside. The restaurant was quiet but Tex appeared as Alex hung up their coats. "You have something for me?" he asked, following pleasantries. "Yes, we have the papers we mentioned on our last visit," said Emma. "After your warning, we're very eager to get your opinion," Alex added, "if you have the time, that is, and we'll also have dinner." "Well, I have the time, so let's get you dinner menus ... and coffee?" "Please," Alex replied.

After taking their order, Tex came to sit with them and Emma took the envelopes out of her briefcase and carefully put them in front of him. He chose the one labeled *Copy* and opened it. "Parchments are so fragile I hate to have to handle that one, but I will need to see the original handwriting." He was clearly interested and immediately began to skim the translated page. Looking up at them, he let out a sigh and stood up. "I'll take these into my office where the lighting is better. One of the staff will look after you while I'm gone."

Enjoying their dinner, the waiter had just cleared the plates from the table when Tex returned. Striding over, they both saw that his smile had disappeared and been replaced by a grim intensity. They were not particularly surprised, for during dinner they had agreed that his demeanor had changed after his initial scan. Now, he stood over them holding the envelopes in one hand and a magnifying glass in the other.

"So folks, you wondered if this parchment was genuine. What do you know about this biographia box, Lady Traymore?" Realizing that he had unfairly put her on the spot, he continued, "Nothing, I would wager and, in my learned opinion, that's exactly what this is!" He paused briefly waiting for their reaction and it was Emma who spoke.

"You think this parchment is a fake?" she whispered, wide-eyed.

"I don't think, my lady, I'm sure of it," he replied. "Whoever wrote this wanted someone to believe he was a fighting monk and possibly wounded; he or they were being chased and no doubt afraid of being caught. I would have said they were in hiding and wrote the document by the light of a single candle or a small fire. It has three different sets of handwriting and, in my experience, this indicates a fake. I'm very sorry."

"Are you for real Mr. Costello, you can actually read this supposedly old document handwritten in Latin and figure out whether it is fact or fiction?" Emma asked with a hint of doubt in her voice.

"Well, usually I can, and many people have put a lot of money on my talent and opinions in the past," he growled. "Someone is trying to make you believe in something that shouldn't be possible. If you can trust my judgement, you have the information with my compliments. Now it's up to you to use your heads and your own common sense!"

Sparks in Emma's eyes alerted Alex that something was going on in her mind. She bit her lip and carefully put the envelopes back in her briefcase, before turning to Tex.

"Damn you, Mr. Costello," she snapped, wagging a finger under the smiling Texan's nose, "you have a mighty unusual method for getting one's attention!"

"And it apparently worked for you, Lady Traymore!" he chuckled, taking her hand and raising it to his lips—totally defusing her. "But that is exactly what you need to do. You have to outfox the fox and I know you two detectives will come up with something, so good luck!"

"That's it, you have nothing more to offer us?" she exclaimed.

"Oh, I could have lots to say, if you'd like. This work is my life, my favourite pastime and it doesn't come my way very often. All right, my lady, I've the time … what would have been my next question?" He thought for a moment, looking from one to the other of their serious faces. "I'm assuming this is the original parchment from the biographia box you found in the dugout, is it not?"

Emma looked up to the ceiling and sighed, deep in thought. "It has to be, the only people who have had access to it other than ourselves are the Misty House technicians and Ruth. Would they not be suspicious of the box's authenticity?" She stopped to gather her thoughts. "Surely, with their experience they would have noticed something? I'm positive Ruth has no idea this is a fake and, besides, we didn't tell them about the dig until we took the box to them. The area of the dig definitely looked like it had not been disturbed for *many* flippin' years, had it, Alex?" She was getting frustrated but trying desperately to think this through logically.

"I agree with everything she has said, Tex. But there is one thing you've forgotten, my lady … there *were* people who saw us there and we didn't know how long they'd been watching us."

"Oh no, Alex, you're right, the monsignor and Mitch! Not Mitch surely, I don't think he's bright enough to figure it out, but the monsignor always seems to be watching us, as if he knows we're coming. Unless Mitch is his gofer, he said he'd been paid to watch someone. Sgt. MacKie said the minister had been nosing around for years. Why? Could there be something else going on in this area, with or without the Wallace mystery? Tex, you said John Dunstan had been suspicious for a few years. It frightens me to think that someone could be watching our every move, but could there be?" She stopped to take a deep breath, looking from one to the other. "This is ridiculous, isn't it? I'm becoming paranoid and suspicious of everyone! I can't seem to think straight sober; perhaps I should have a drink!" She laughed self-consciously.

"It's very easy to be fooled and let your imagination run away with you, my lady," Tex began, "especially when you are not an expert in this field. I'm impressed and I would be very tempted to hire you if I needed staff!"

"You're kidding me; I'm an English professor!"

"You're also a very bright lady and I think you and Alex make a great team. Now, to carry on ... I don't think you need be concerned with the integrity of your long-standing Misty House employees. Alex knows them well and for many years. I believe radiocarbon-dating of the parchment should be your next step and John could advise you on that. This would give you some peace of mind, especially if they can prove that this parchment is really centuries old.

"I have something else to tell you, he continued. Jim MacDonald is my personal friend and he is also aware of John's suspicions and interest in the mystery of the relics." Emma and Alex exchanged surprised glances. "I realize he is your neighbour, Alex, and that's probably a good thing. When you turned up so very motivated to solve the Wallace mystery, we thought it best not to say anything to either of you as our suspicions were only speculation. We didn't want to alarm you needlessly or have you telling anyone. We hoped that by allowing circumstances to present themselves naturally, in time, this would flush out the enemy! Of course, none of us knew you yet, my lady!" Tex laughed and reached for the thermos of coffee, refilling Emma's cup, leaving enough room for some whisky, which he added, with her permission.

"Do they think I have something to do with the conspiracy?" she asked.

"Oh no, certainly not, but you've brought a new slant to the mystery, my lady. Your acceptance of the title has stirred up a renewed interest in the old legend, apparently making someone very nervous. My opinion is that it could be time to get closer to ... John, perhaps. As I said, he can help you out in many areas, and is much better connected than I am! Tell me, has anything really struck you as odd or out-of-place since you arrived in Scotland."

"Only the silent monks," she said, without hesitation.

"You were at the monastery?"

"Yes, we stayed overnight; they gave me the creeps. I'm sure they have recording devices, at least in the public areas."

"I was doubtful at first," Alex admitted, "but then I got to thinking it could be quite feasible for this day and age. Their actions became very suspicious to us."

"How else would they be able to know when we were hungry or that I had told Alex I wanted a glass of wine?" added Emma.

Their host was definitely surprised. "Well, I'll be damned!"

"Well, personally I still think the monsignor is one of our key figures to watch," Emma continued, pronouncing his name with an exaggerated French accent. "I have no doubt he is capable of causing trouble."

"I agree he's a nuisance and you could be right, my lady," Tex added. "I happen to know he reports regularly of the local goings-on in and around Elderslie, to somebody by mail, so we don't believe he is self-appointed."

"Reports to whom?" asked Emma.

"We don't know, but Bill Mackie told me the monsignor posts a letter nearly every day."

Emma laughed nervously, wondering how much to divulge. She glanced at Alex and a sudden thought came to mind. "Has it crossed your mind, lads, that it might be the postman he's informing?" She smiled ruefully as startled expressions spread across their faces. "Tell me, Mr. Texas policeman," she asked, "what is your own interest in the Scottish regalia?"

"It's merely a fascinating mystery to an idle policeman, my lady," he said seriously, "but, of course, I don't know all the details and I'm not a Scot with a vested interest."

His attention was drawn to a cook beckoning him from the kitchen and he stood up. "Please excuse me, my chef calls."

"Tex, we're going to be off now," Alex exclaimed, getting up to shake his hand. "You've been more than generous with your time old friend and we're very grateful. I'm sure you'll see us again very soon!"

Tex nodded and hurried off as Alex took some bills out of his wallet and dropped them on the table. Emma looked up at Alex who had sighed deeply as he held her coat. *If he's thinking along the same lines as I am, we could be in dire trouble and have some important thinking to do!*

Hard snow crackled under the car's tires as they drove away. No new snow had fallen, although dark clouds threatened anything could happen … and it did, as a sudden shower of icy rain pounded them as they entered Edinburgh and got into traffic. Emma had lapsed into silence even as they left Tex, and Alex had plenty to keep his mind occupied.

Emma's mind was in turmoil as she looked into the darkness and considered the list of people who might have an interest in the Wallace mystery. A chill went down her spine as her thoughts drifted to the silent monks and the secrets a modern monastery could hold. *Who would be devious enough to plant a misleading biographia box and how long ago?* "A penny for your thoughts, my lady?" Alex asked finally.

A stern expression remained on Emma's face and her hand tightened on the armrest before answering. "I thought we would be able to quietly conduct a logical investigation when we began this search, Alex, but it seems we've alerted every interested party in Scotland, perhaps beyond. I can feel them quietly hovering and secretly watching us to see what we do next. We're like fish in a glass bowl and, may I add, this is the first time I have ever heard of a phoney grave!"

Arriving at the hotel, Alex noticed a familiar vehicle. "John Dunstan's here, that's his sports car. Give me 10 minutes or so before you come down. I'll be in the bar."

Going into the bar, Alex stood for a moment before seeing John. "I thought you were down in Yorkshire?" Alex almost had to shout and, as he sat down, he noticed a second glass of liquor on the table. "Who are you with?"

"Jim, your neighbour," John replied, attracting the attention of the waiter. "Two coffees, Alex, or something stronger? Is Emma ...?

"Only one Highland Coffee, Lady Traymore will join us in awhile."

James returned and greeted Alex. "Was it snowing in Paisley?"

"Of course, it's almost December, so it snowed, rained and blew in and around Paisley, what else would you expect?" Alex embellished it a bit, knowing Jim was fishing, probably after talking to Sgt. Mackie. "So, to what honour do I owe this ambush?"

"Ambush, come now, laddie! I just want to know what you did to Sgt. Mackie today?" James asked. "The poor man was crying in frustration after you and Lady Traymore left him!"

"Oh that," Alex laughed. "It was merely Lady Traymore giving him the third degree. We first met Sgt. Mackie when we were looking for Joe Thornton's garden shed. At the time, he came over a little strong and she put him in his place. My lady won't stand for any nonsense, you know. He was being nice to her at the police station, but he had no answers to her questions and she walked out on him, poor man!" Smiling at his thoughts, he continued, "Take a little advice, gentlemen, she uses her tongue like Wallace used his broadsword but it's twice as sharp!"

"I think it's you, Alex," James commented thoughtfully, "you always were a bad influence on people, look at the friends you have!"

"I agree," John muttered, "except, I think Emma outshines all of us and will make an excellent heir to dear Trevelion once she gets used to us! Oh, speaking of ... hello, my lady!"

"That's flattering, John, I think ... did you see me coming! Could I have my man back please, I'm famished!" Emma had manoeuvred her way through the crowd unnoticed, she thought. She had heard enough of the conversation before entering at the most appropriate moment.

"Please sit for awhile," John pleaded, leaping to his feet and finding another chair. "Just long enough to have one coffee!"

Emma shrugged and sat down while John called the waiter. She ordered herbal tea. When she'd taken a couple of sips, Alex noticed her face light up and he waited to see what mischief she was up to.

"So, John, did you manage to recover the regalia in Yorkshire?"

"No, my lady, we didn't," he admitted tersely, "but this has certainly stirred up a hornet's nest at the monastery. There will be a government inquiry to find out what precipitated it all and the court case will drag on for a longtime, especially because the monks don't talk! Mark my words, we haven't heard the last of this thing yet."

"How did Mitch Pooley get hurt?" James asked.

"How on earth did you hear about that? He fell over a gravestone while being nosy," Emma chuckled, "but Sir Alex kissed it better with three drams of whisky!"

"If I had to kiss Alex, I'd need three drams of whisky, too!" said Jim.

As if this reminded him of something, John reached into his chest pocket and handed Emma an envelope. "Here's a little information about Paisley," he said. "Don't worry about the envelope, it's just an old one I recycled. Now, why don't you two go and eat?"

Emma thanked him and slipped the envelope into her bag without looking at it and followed Alex to the foyer. She suggested they get the meals sent to her room so they could talk in private.

"I want to talk to you about some of the things Tex said today, while everything is fresh in our minds, Alex," she whispered. His expression told her he agreed and he conveyed their wishes to the maitre'd. They decided on the special and she went on ahead to the room.

Ten minutes later he arrived with his own coffee. He immediately noted the tension on her face. Even her normally bright eyes were dull as if from deep concern. *This is bothering her more than I imagined.*

While they ate, she commented how nice it would be to just sit and put their feet up and watch a movie, and then she snapped herself out of it, knowing they would both probably fall asleep.

"I'm concerned that this search could get very dangerous from here on, Alex," she suddenly announced, lowering her voice.

Alex sat up straighter, pursed his lips and picked up his drink. He stopped before it reached his lips and held it tightly in his hands, looking off into space. It was as if he thought he could gain some useful knowledge from warming his hands on the hot liquid. Finally, lowering his eyes and fastening them on Emma, he took a long, slow sip and then put the cup down.

"Are you ready for quitting, my lady?"

"Hell no! You must never think that of me, Alex! I'm merely preparing my mind for a fight and also beginning to realize that we don't know friends from enemies. That frightens me to death!"

Not having seen her in this sort of mood before, Alex studied her face for a few moments before speaking. "Maybe we'll find a clue when Tom opens more of the pouches. They seemed more authentic than the box but that's only my thought in hindsight."

"Well, it certainly looks like we've been duped by a grave with no body and a fake biographia box. I shall be very interested to hear Tex's comments when we show him the contents of some of the pouches."

"And what if the pouches are empty or hold nothing of consequence?" he suggested, looking at her sympathetically.

"Oh Alex, don't even go there!" she groaned. "Who would go to all this trouble then make it obvious it was only a decoy? No, m'lad, whoever we are matching wits with is much smarter than that, if they belong to this century!" She was now whispering as she leaned towards him. "I have a question niggling at my brain that we're missing something very important. We should have known there was never a body in our grave. Why is that? How could we know?"

"You do know the answer, Emma, think of Tex's words … 'use your brain.' How should we have known there was no body in that grave?"

"There was no crucifix in the box!" she whispered. "Holy cripes, what idiots we are! Ruth told us. Did you remember?"

205

"Not me, but you're absolutely right; once the box was opened there was only a resumé. Only when a monk dies would his crucifix be removed and put into his biographia box."

"That leaves me with a burning question," she added. "Could Ruth have been right that the monk didn't die? Or was the box planted as a decoy as Tex suggested? Either way it's one more mystery to be solved. We're going to have to talk to John, there's no way around it."

"Are we going to have our dessert?" he asked.

"What dessert? What did you order?" She went over to look and groaned. "What on earth is that? It looks sinful!"

"I suppose it is. It's treacle sponge pudding, covered in a caramel custard ... simply heavenly when hot!"

"Well, you can have yours, it would keep me awake. Put mine in the fridge and yours will need nuking, Alex." Then, she remembered ... "Oh cripes, we've forgotten to look in John's envelope!" Going to get her handbag, she studied the envelope briefly before giving Alex the papers that were inside. He was watching her unusual intensity.

"What is it?" he asked, putting the papers down on the table unread.

"The postage stamp," she said, showing it to him, "our monsignor is reporting to a government official! How could we have missed this?"

Alex frowned, looking briefly at the envelope. "John?"

"No, I don't think so. Mitch said he saw the monsignor's letter and he didn't have to put a stamp on it. He wrote zero HMS on the corner."

"Ah!" Alex said thoughtfully, picking up the envelope again, this time looking more carefully at the postmark. "OHMS," he said slowly. "On Her Majesty's Service! Aren't we red-faced? We're going to need to trace one of the monsignor's letters."

"And how do you propose to do that, Sherlock?"

"By asking Tom and Charlie, they're smarter than I am!"

"I believe you," she whispered, grinning. "So we'll put that on tomorrow's schedule." A short while later, yawning, she exclaimed, "My brain is shutting down Alex; I must get to bed."

They agreed to meet at 8:30.

## Chapter 15 – Thursday 30<sup>th</sup> – Postal Mystery

Waking early and unable to return to sleep, Emma realized she had slept like a baby, only receiving a brief visit from Mary. She made herself some herbal tea as she got ready and then, as it was still early, she curled up in her easy chair and read. She was so engrossed in reading about the Knights Hospitallers she hadn't realized it was time to go and meet Alex. She looked out over a now-waking city and hoped the weather was more promising a bit further north. Ominous dark clouds streamed overhead and the staccato of wind-driven rain now pelted her windowpane, making her shiver. She reluctantly bookmarked her page and put on her warm boots and a sweater. Carrying her coat, she went downstairs. Alex had just started his first coffee when she arrived.

"Good morning, my lady," he murmured, moving his newspaper to make room for her.

After ordering, they began their usual conversation like two thieves after a night of mischief. He asked her about the papers John had given her yesterday but she hadn't read them either. They only lapsed into silence when their breakfast arrived and then, as they finished, Emma mentioned that Mary had again visited her dreams.

"I think we should retrieve our maps today," she added, "if the boys will let us. They'll think we want to spy on them."

"They won't be wrong!" he laughed. "Should I go warm the car?"

"I'll come with you; I'm ready!" she replied flippantly, standing up and handing him her coat.

By the time they reached the motorway, the driving rain seemed to propel them towards Stirling. Radio reports weren't any better, forecasting more snow in the Highlands.

The rain had stopped by the time they hit Falkirk and Alex turned west toward the only blue sky around. Sunshine bathed the Misty House property when they arrived and the snow had completely melted. Looking tired, Ruth met them at the door and offered her usual welcome, showing them quickly into her office.

"You're working too hard, Ruth," Emma said gently. "Sorry we've had to come back earlier than expected. How is the translating coming?"

"It's proving very stressful for all of us reading about these terrible things that went on in those days. Are you here to see me or the men?"

"We actually came to talk to all of you but first, we want to ask the lads for their help with a little problem," explained Emma.

"I'll come with you if you don't mind," Ruth sighed. "I could use a break from this torment."

Charlie was using the electric saw when they arrived and didn't hear them until they were almost upon him. Grinning, he switched it off and pointed to his partner huddled over a table partly hidden by a shelving unit. Charlie's shrill whistle reverberated through the building, startling them and bringing Tom's head up with a jerk. He came over to join them.

"I haven't found anything but bloody heartbreak in these hellish papers," Tom growled. "Excuse my language, my lady, but it tears at a person's soul."

"Thomas!" Ruth's voice held a noticeable edge of displeasure. "Please control yourself!"

"I'm sorry, marm," he apologized half-heartedly then turned back to their visitors. "Can I help with something?"

"Yes, we need to get our maps and we have a little problem we thought you could help us with. We have to find a way to identify an envelope in a letter box so we can find it later."

"Whose letter box?" Tom asked.

"A normal, post office letter box," Alex replied.

"That is a problem … just one letter, sir? I presume you have no chance to touch it before it goes in the box?"

"You're quite right, we don't!"

"How do you propose to follow it, Sir Alex?" Charlie interrupted.

"We don't really have to. We just want to know the address on it."

"That's fairly easy, but messy!" Tom chuckled, walking over to a wall cupboard and taking out a small blue jar. Then he opened a drawer and removed two items, grinning as he came back to join them. The items were a plastic bag with a zipper seal, a small hessian bag with a drawstring and the blue powder. He first put the hessian bag into the plastic bag and handed it to Tom. Charlie produced a spoon and carefully took a small amount of blue powder out of the jar and put it into the hessian bag. Tom closed both the bags, handing it to Alex.

"Be careful not to touch this stuff," Charlie warned. "It will turn everything it touches blue, but it should serve your purpose! Just empty the plastic bag into the post box, dropping the hessian bag inside. Incidentally, we know nothing about this!" He looked at them dubiously.

"It's not dangerous, is it?" Emma asked anxiously.

"No, my lady, even though we've not used much powder, it's going to make the postal service and a whole lot more people very angry. It will, no doubt, make the news! I hope you're sure about this and not many letters are mailed that day!" Tom warned, watching both of them nod, albeit with rather reluctant expressions.

Glancing at her watch, Alex's voice broke into her thoughts.

"Yes, I know," he said. "We'll have time today if we leave fairly soon.

"Would it be all right if we kept the maps until Monday, when you come back?" Tom asked. "Would you like to have another look at them?"

Alex and Emma looked at each other.

"Why don't you take a photo of the parts we might need, Alex? That could do us for now. Are they still on the table?" she asked, looking around.

"They're on my work bench. Come with me." Tom directed them to his table. Alex took a number of photos and then they had another quick look at the map.

"We had better be off," Alex commented, looking at his watch again.

The car's clock registered 3:30 p.m. as he turned the key in the ignition.

"With traffic, we should make it to Paisley in less than 45 minutes, just pray for no extra hold-ups."

"Can I add to that?" she asked, making a face. "I'm praying for no rain, no speed cops, no accidents and no other complications for the rest of the day! At least it will be fairly dark, except for that lamp standard."

Turning on the local radio, little conversation passed between them until they reached the shopping centre.

"Great, you have lots of time," she said as Alex pulled up near the tea shop. Looking around and knowing it was rather early for the monsignor to appear, he noted how quiet the parking lot was and decided to get on with it. He told Emma to set out for Moira's as he opened the postal box and got ready to do his deed. Thinking of something, he made sure he had both of his gloves on and switched the plastic bag into his outer left coat pocket. Next, he grabbed some tissues, stuffing them into his outer right coat pocket. She watched curiously at first, and then told him how brilliant he was. When he arrived at the box, she left the car, making as much noise and fuss as she could before heading over to the tea shop. She didn't dare look in his direction. After he had emptied the bag into the post box, being careful not to get any blue dust on himself, he returned the plastic bag to the same pocket and put his right hand into the other pocket, strolling over to the tea shop as casually as he could. He went straight into the toilet and checked his clothes for any telltale sign of blue dye. He rinsed the plastic bag carefully in the sink, wiped it dry and flushed the soiled paper into the toilet, putting the bag back into his pocket.

*Och aye, I feel like a crook!* He experienced such a feeling of guilt he thought he was going to puke. *Calm down and think!* he scolded himself. He remembered to carefully wipe off his gloves, putting them into his coat pocket as well. Breathing a sigh of relief, he left the toilet.

Going to join Emma, he interrupted Moira who was just leaving their table. She was curtseying again to Emma and he stopped her.

"Moira, you don't need to curtsey to Lady Traymore, she's not the Queen!" he explained in an agitated manner. "I'll have a coffee, please."

"It's already on the table, sir; I'm sorry, Sir Alex," she whispered, hurrying off into the kitchen.

"Now you've gone and hurt her feelings, I thought I was the one who was supposed to do that to people! Why do you suppose I didn't say anything?"

"You didn't because you liked it, my lady!" he snapped, sitting down and looking out at the post box.

"What's got your knickers in a twist?" she asked.

"Oh, here he comes," he muttered looking at his watch. "What is …?"

Emma kicked him under the table and glared at him. "Don't look!" she hissed.

Alex realized she was right and picked up his coffee, so he didn't see the monsignor drop his letter into the box.

"Let's have a bite to eat before we leave, Sir Alex," she commented.

"If you like," he said curtly.

One more person posted a letter before the postal van arrived, pulling up in front of the post box and stopping. The young driver jumped out with a mail sack in his hand and selected a key from a big brass ring chained to his belt. He flung the door open, reached in and scooped the mail into his sack. It was then, as he jerked the bag shut, that he noticed the bright blue stain on his hand and on the cuff of his uniform. Not realizing what it was exactly, he held the sack away from him, swearing loudly as he returned to the van. Dropping it, as usual, onto the floor, he sped away and the onlookers who had seen his little tantrum, merely moved on. No one inside the tea shop seemed to have noticed and Emma ordered a piece of apple pie for them to share, although Alex claimed he wasn't very hungry.

"Did you see what was happening outside?" asked Moira, looking out of the window as she delivered their pie on two plates.

"Happening? No, what did we miss?" he asked, trying to sound only vaguely interested as he turned to look outside.

As they were eating, a car with postal colours on it pulled up to the box and a man dressed in a suit got out and opened it. The man quickly took a step backward, scratching his head and then pulling out his cell phone. He talked to someone briefly and, after hanging up, he took several photos of the inside of the box, relocked it and drove away.

When finished, Alex paid the bill and they said goodnight to Moira. Emma went ahead of him, but Moira called him back.

"Sir Alex, something interesting happened this week ... Monsignor Sharp asked about you on Tuesday and I said I hadn't seen you. He said he thought you were both in Yorkshire, but then I saw you yesterday. There has also been an American gentleman wandering around Elderslie. He came in Tuesday and sat with the monsignor for a short while."

"Did the monsignor tell you why he thought we were in Yorkshire?" Alex asked.

"Oh no, sir, he doesn't talk very much, so I assumed it had something to do with the monastery news on the telly."

"Thank you, Moira, we must be off," he declared, opening the door for Emma who called her thanks and followed him to the car.

"So, now we have another twist, Alex," she muttered when they were inside with the door shut, "an American joins the cast!"

"He could simply be a tourist. Elderslie is a famous place now!"

They were not far down the road, when they passed a police car going in the opposite direction. It turned into the shopping centre.

"Would you please remind me to get rid of this plastic bag before we get to the hotel," mumbled Alex.

"You've had second thoughts about this, haven't you, Sherlock?"

Heavy traffic near Glasgow and a sudden shower kept Alex occupied until they arrived at the Bargeddie Junction and turned towards Edinburgh.

"We'll be home in about half an hour," Alex told her as the rain stopped and the complete darkness of a Scottish winter evening obliterated the land.

"Why did you rush us away from the tea shop?" she asked.

"I thought it was best not to stay any longer in case they found out."

"*They* meaning John Dunstan and Sgt. Mackie?"

"Yes, I don't think Monsignor Sharp saw us either."

"Moira knows we were there."

"If anyone thinks to ask her or question us, we were inside the restaurant when the commotion started and we didn't see a thing."

"Yes, that was clever, and, you lie so beautifully, sir!"

"Meow," he responded, and she giggled.

He made a quick stop to empty his garbage and the next hour passed uneventfully. After eating dinner at the hotel, Emma decided to have an early night, leaving Alex to join his friends. After getting ready for bed, she found the papers on Paisley that John had given her in the OHMS envelope, and turned on the evening news. In between commercials, she read about the history of Paisley until she suddenly became aware that the silent monk's monastery was on the screen. Media vehicles, army tents and trucks littered a snowy field next to the monastery.While out on the road, caravans and media trailers shared the area with almost a dozen police vehicles. Shocked, she felt a measure of regret, and changed channels.

Downstairs, Alex was still in the bar when someone announced that the postal sorting office had been the subject of a bizarre prank. It seemed that several of the sorting staff and a letter collector now had blue-stained hands and uniforms! The announcement created much laughter from the drinking fraternity and many humorous comments were bandied about; sympathy, however, was definitely lacking.

## Chapter 16 – Friday, December 1ˢᵗ – Clans

No arrangement had been made for meeting Alex the next morning so Emma took her time going down to breakfast. When she entered the dining room a little after nine, he was, at first, unaware of her presence. She found him deeply engrossed in the newspaper, obviously enjoying his reading.

"Look at that!" he laughed, and then suddenly sat up in his chair when he realized Emma had arrived. "Good morning, my lady, I have some news!"

"What's so funny?" Emma asked as the waitress poured her coffee.

He showed her the front page with its colourful picture and waited for her comment. The photo was of a group of postal workers and a postal official was examining the hands of a letter-sorting clerk who apparently also had blue dye splattered over his uniform. The caption read, *A Job that Makes You Blue.*

"Have you read the entire article?" she asked.

"Yes, and we now have the answer to our question." He pointed to the bottom of the article and handed her the paper.

Emma read the details and a smile played on her lips. There had only been four letters to catch the blue dye. Two were personal letters to English addresses, one was to the Scottish tax office and the other was addressed to a local individual with a P.O. Box.

"A rental box, Sir Alex!" she whispered excitedly, "it shouldn't be hard to find out that location."

"Read on," he prodded.

It appeared that each piece of blue mail was put into a plastic bag for personal delivery by a post office official who would offer an apology.

"It doesn't say how the receiver is going to read their mail without getting the stain on their hands," she laughed. "The recipient of the monsignor's letter does seem to be a local person."

"We still have to find out who it is though," he muttered, looking off into space. "Tex! That's what I forgot to tell you. He knows a bit of everything. That's whom we should talk to about the paupers' graves. You haven't even scratched the surface of this guy's knowledge."

It was almost noon when Alex pulled the car alongside a luxurious tour coach in front of his friend's pub. A light rain was falling as they read the bus' banner, *American Scottish Heritage Society*.

"It looks like he has a private party tonight. My goodness, you don't think word has reached them this quickly to organize a bus tour?" Emma asked as they entered. Noisy conversation could be heard even from outside as they approached the establishment but no sign warned that it was a closed party. The Texan's voice rose above it all.

"Come on in, Sir Alex," Tex's barman called to them.

As they went to the door of the dining room, they saw it was quite full of tartan-clad people all talking and laughing together. On a raised dias at one end of the room, Tex was attempting to speak amid the noise.

"Ladies and gentlemen, a moment please," his voice boomed out of the speakers. "I see we are being honoured by the presence of two of our regular customers who apparently didn't realize we were hosting a private party tonight. I think you will be very happy to hear about these people. Come in! Come in! Let me introduce Lady Traymore, Professor Emma Walters of Canada and Sir Alex Wallace, Baronet."

Polite, but generous clapping followed, however, the level of conversation returned quickly to its boisterous intensity. Tex beckoned them to join him. Offering Alex the microphone, he whispered. "Just a few words please, Sir Alex."

Beaming at his audience, Alex rubbed his chin and winked mischievously at Emma before he began. "Ladies and gentlemen I presume from the many tartans you're wearing you all have a connection to Scotland. How many of you are descendants of Clan Walters?" Several hands shot up as he reached for Emma's hand and pulled her up beside him. "Then you folks are in for a thrill," he said dramatically, "because Lady Traymore will soon be named the new chief of Clan Walters. She's the only woman in 700-years to hold that title. Is anyone here from my clan ... Clan Wallace?" Two hands went up. "Then you may be aware of the very special connection of these two clans and the mystery of the missing Scottish Royal Regalia. He gave them a brief history lesson on the two clans including the prophecy. "Our families believe Lady Traymore is that woman—the one who will solve the mystery of the missing regalia! Meet Lady Traymore, Emma Walters!" There was more polite clapping in the room as well as some boisterous cheers from her clan members.

There was nothing she could do. Alex had trapped her and he now chuckled quietly at her discomfort. She gracefully took the microphone.

"You do realize I've been tricked into this," she said bluntly, but not without a smile. "I only recently became the heir to what has been an unsolvable mystery. You see, I'm a Canadian from Victoria, British Columbia and I knew nothing about my father's family until a few weeks ago. I'm just beginning to understand what I've let myself in for!" She smiled as she heard a few sympathetic sighs. "I'm simply a Canadian university lecturer in English Literature. My life was often a dull routine as I attempted to teach an increasing number of layabouts who thought the government owed them an education at their expense and convenience! I prefer the challenges Scotland has now given me!"

There were a few snickers and expressions of shock over her comment but she ignored them and continued. "I deem the privilege of inheriting the Walters' estate and title of Lady Traymore a remarkable honour. I am learning a great deal more about Scottish history than I ever dreamed possible."

"Shall we invite Sir Alex and Lady Traymore to our party?" Tex shouted. A chorus of 'yeas' couldn't help but make Emma laugh.

What had started out as a private visit to see Tex was now turning into a delightful afternoon. Later, they had many interesting conversations with amateur genealogists who had found long-ago relatives due to a family bible or a faded baptism or marriage certificate.

It was when she talked to a Seattle couple, a retired coroner and his wife, that a snippet of useful information came to her attention. Emma asked the coroner if he had ever been involved in re-locating part or all of a cemetery. The question raised the old coroner's eyebrows.

"Oh, my goodness," he said shaking his head solemnly, "to remove for any reason, a previously intered body, is nothing but trouble. Everyone becomes involved, clergy, police, coroner, undertaker and the Lands Office. All must keep specific records. No, my dear, it's not an easy operation to move even a small portion of a cemetery."

The time passed quickly and, after dinner Alex was coaxed into giving an impromptu lecture on the history of Paisley and Elderslie. Emma was delighted and settled down to relax and enjoy herself. It was almost 10 o'clock when they left the inn, just ahead of the others. Through the misty darkness, the land seemed to possess an air of mystery, but that was just Emma's imagination at work again. Paying little attention to the road, she focused on the blackness, willing her mind to give her a clue to Mary's whereabouts. When she opened her eyes again, she knew she and Alex needed to talk.

215

"We simply must find out if and when the monastery boundaries were changed and if they relocated all the bodies," she suddenly announced.

"Oh, you are still with me!" he laughed. "Didn't we have this discussion at breakfast?"

"Yes, but I was talking to a retired coroner and he gave me a list of the officials involved in this sort of matter. Perhaps a simple search of the newspapers would turn up something. If they were moving bodies, surely someone would report it. Newspapers would have a field day."

Alex was quiet for awhile before answering. "First things first, my lady. We have to find out the year the boundaries were moved and that's a simple call to the General Register Office."

"We already have those maps from John."

"And how will they help?"

"Do you remember when the maps were dated?" Emma asked, but he shook his head.

Conversation took a different turn as they entered the city limits and Alex began relating some of the humorous questions he had been asked.

There was a lady who asked when men first began wearing trousers and, oh yes, a young man wanted to know why we wear a dagger in our socks."

"I'm surprised none of the women asked you what you wear under the kilt!" she giggled.

"Oh, they did ... someone always does!"

"And what did you tell her?"

"Nothing," Alex chuckled.

"You could have told her the truth!"

"That was the truth!" Alex laughed. "I quite embarrassed them, I believe, but it was their own fault!"

"You're quit embarrassing this lady also!"

It was almost midnight when Alex left her in the lobby of the hotel. She was still giggling as she caught the lift; totally unaware Alex was making an urgent cell phone call.

## Chapter 17 – Saturday 2<sup>nd</sup> – Alex's Crisis

Vague sounds and a hazy image returned to darkness for a tome before he slowly regained consciousness. Alex tried to move, sending a searing pain through his leg and hip. It was then he became aware of being in a small room with people in green clothes.

"W-where am I?" he mumbled, still unable to think or see properly.

"You're in an ambulance that is taking you to hospital, sir. You've sustained some injuries due to being hit by a car," the emergency technician seated beside him explained.

"Och noo!" Alex whispered. "That must explain why my leg hurts like hell! I sure hope I haven't broken anything ... blast it!"

"Just stay calm and, as still as possible, please. We'll find you a bed very soon and you'll be getting some x-rays of that leg."

At the *Courtyard Inn* that morning, Emma enjoyed her leisurely start to the day not having arranged a time with Alex. By nine o'clock, she began to wonder why Alex had left her undisturbed. *Could he be waiting in the restaurant?* Glancing outside before going downstairs, she watched snowflakes falling gently to the already white ground of the car park. The view made her shiver; she hadn't turned the heat up thinking she would be going out. As her eyes became accustomed to the dull light, she realized it must have been snowing for some time.

Before Alex had left the hotel the night before, he wrote Emma a note and left it with the reception clerk. In the note, he advised her he would meet her for dinner at six o'clock, giving no other details. He hastily scrawled his cell phone number on the envelope. Knowing she was always greeted by the receptionist as she went to breakfast, he asked the staff to make sure the note was delivered to her room if they had not seen her by 10 o'clock that morning.

As a result, Megan handed her the note as she passed by that morning causing Emma to frown when she recognized Alex's handwriting on the hotel stationary. She kept the note in her hand and continued to the dining room.

By the time the waitress came to take her order, she had read the message and, feeling it was of no particular importance, put it into her

217

handbag. Engrossing herself in the newspaper until her meal arrived, she soon wished she had put the Hospitaller book she was reading into her bag. Eating alone was a new experience since arriving in Scotland three weeks before. She tried to ignore the feeling of being abandoned, although she would never have admitted to Alex that she missed him.

Emma would have been horrified if she had realized the real reason Alex had not shown up that morning. After leaving her the night before, he had used his cell phone to contact an old friend and clan member who worked in the postal service. Feeling duty bound by clan affiliation, the man agreed to meet Alex on his coffee break that very evening. Determined to find the answer to the monsignor's letters, Alex drove through the night and the inclement weather, to the central sorting station in Stirling. A superior car, a goodly amount of luck, and his own driving skills, had taken him safely to his destination. As he parked, he was unaware that a sudden freeze had struck the region and black ice with a light covering of snow had now enveloped the area turning driving into a nightmare. After quickly explaining the details of the search for the body of Mary Wallace utilizing the blue-stained letter, his friend needed little convincing to help him.

Luck, however, had deserted the bearded Scot by the time he left the building. Engrossed in crossing the ice-covered car park, he didn't see the car sliding uncontrollably around the corner towards him.

Emma, totally unaware of Alex's predicament, had finished a relaxing breakfast and picked up the newspaper again. Minutes later, she noticed the familiar, uniformed figure of James MacDonald striding towards her.

"May I join you, my lady?" he asked quietly, pulling out the chair opposite her.

"Of course, James, good morning. To what do I owe this pleasure?" Remembering the note, she took it out of her bag. "Sir Alex left this for me and I was wondering if this was your telephone number?" She passed the note to him.

"No, that's his cell phone number. Sir Alex left this for you this morning, you said?" he asked, returning to his police persona.

"Well yes, I suppose it was this morning. I assume he stayed in the bar for awhile. We were very late last night and something must have come up. I can't imagine what it could have been. It was after midnight when he left me and he must have written this note before he left the building. The desk clerk gave it to me just now."

"Have you finished your breakfast, my lady?"

"Yes, I was just contemplating what I was going to do today. Sir Alex is apparently away until six o'clock; he didn't send you to look after me, did he?" she asked. "Would you like a coffee, James?"

"Yes, I will have a coffee," he said, turning to beckon the waitress and then waiting until she was out of earshot. Then, he turned to Emma. "I'm afraid I have a bit of bad news for you, my lady." He reached out to rest his hand on hers. "Sir Alex has had an accident."

"Oh no! Bad news must mean he's hurt, please tell me that's not so, James? Is he all right?" Emma's voice had decreased to a whisper as the colour drained from her face.

"He's in Stirling Hospital; his leg is broken and he has a few bumps and bruises, that's all. I'll take you to see him as soon as you wish to leave."

"That's all? What on earth happened? You say you'll take me … I must go to him at once. Oh, I need to go upstairs and get my coat. How terrible, poor Alex!" The words fell over each other as she started to get up, but James grasped her arm gently.

"He's going to be fine, Emma. I suspect his pride will cause him to suffer much more than his injuries. You go upstairs and get ready, there is absolutely no rush. He'll, no doubt, be resting after his eventful night. I'll finish my coffee and have the car at the door when you come down. Then I'll give you all the details I have, but please don't worry. He truly is going to be all right and I've already made arrangements for you to have the use of a vehicle and a driver."

James' voice had an authoritative, yet calming edge to it. Emma nodded then, smiling weakly, signed the bill and hurried away.

Reminding herself that James had assured her Alex would be fine, she tried to calm herself as she waited for the lift. Getting ready only took a few minutes, but she suddenly felt exhausted and sat down to gather her wits. *What will we do now? I can't have someone around me all the time.* Taking a deep breath as a picture of him lying in a hospital bed flashed through her mind, she got up and went to get her coat. Putting it on, she picked up her hat and scarf and went back downstairs. Going straight to the hotel's main door, she looked out, not realizing that James was right behind her. He spoke to her softly indicating the police car was parked right outside the door. She was surprised to find that the unmarked police car came complete with a driver who was introduced as Sgt. Simon. James opened the rear passenger door for her and then went around the car and got in beside her.

Twice James answered his cell phone, breaking into their conversation as Emma tried to hear his explanation of Alex's accident and his injuries.

"Damnit James, will you please tell me what happened!" she snapped.

"He was run over by a police car," James said too bluntly, cursing himself afterwards. "Apparently it was unavoidable due to last night's icy conditions."

"A police car!" Emma repeated warily.

"It happened in the early hours of this morning, in the car park of the central sorting station of the postal service in Stirling. Do you have any idea why he had gone to Stirling at such a late hour?"

"What the devil does it matter why he was there? You ran over him!"

James turned his head towards the side window to hide his smile. "It wasn't me, my lady, and it was truly an accident. Road conditions were treacherous in Stirling with a snap freeze surprising everyone."

"Now that you have your excuses neatly arranged, tell me again what injuries he has?"

"A broken leg, a few stitches and bruises, and a very bad temper, I was told!" he chuckled, shaking his head. "I think you know Sir Alex well enough now to understand."

"Now what am I supposed to do? One of your men has crippled my driver, ruined our investigation and left me stranded in a foreign country. Nice going, sir, are you sure you're not the Scottish mafia?"

"He should be home within the week, my lady. I will arrange a little time off and drive you wherever you wish to go," he said patiently.

"*You* will?" Emma snapped. "You expect me to believe you can take Sir Alex Wallace's place. Let me tell you something, Mr. MacDonald, that man is irreplaceable!"

"Och, I wish someone had that much faith in me!" he retorted.

Conversation ceased as Emma withdrew into a worried silence, wondering how she could continue the investigation with the police commissioner as a constant companion.

Arriving at the hospital, their driver ignored the obvious *No Parking Signs* as he pulled the car in front of the main door. Emma opened the car door and began to get out, but their driver was quick to help her. James MacDonald's loud, authoritative voice caught her by surprise as he, too, hurried to her aid.

"Wait, my lady, remember it's been very slippery here this morning. We don't need any more broken bones!" He mumbled the next sentence under his breath. "This I have to see for myself!"

Too busy with her own thoughts and emotions, Emma obediently took his arm until they were safely inside. She followed close behind him as he led the way to the main desk.

"We are here to see Sir Alex Wallace," James stated firmly, showing his identification to an obviously weary receptionist.

Instantly, she picked up the phone and murmured some sharp instructions. A uniformed young man arrived within seconds and the receptionist directed him to escort them to Dr. Greare on the second floor. Emma's stomach was in a knot as they moved towards the lift and then along a corridor to a door that was partly open. Already warned of their approach, their escort directed them inside and left. Dr. Greare rose from his desk to greet them. Inviting them to sit down, he began to detail all of Sir Alex's injuries. He noticed Lady Traymore's apprehension and allowed himself to smile as he assured them Sir Alex was going to be fine and would be home in a week. "At the moment he's very worried about your plight, Lady Traymore, being alone in a strange country. Seeing James' expression, he added, "Oh yes, and he is harassing the staff for a good cup of coffee with whisky, I understand ... which is not allowed, of course!" Dr. Greare shook his head in what could only be construed as disgust or sadness. "I'm sure you're wanting to see him. Why don't we do that right now?"

Following the doctor through a maze of grey-and-white hallways, Emma suddenly thought she could hear Alex's voice. Even from a distance, she could hear the word *coffee*!

"What did I tell you? It sounds like he's making a right nuisance of himself," James commented with a chuckle.

Dr. Greare turned into a private room and was almost knocked over as an unhappy nurse ran out cursing under her breath. Dr. Greare forced a smile, shrugged, and indicated they could go in. When they looked for him later, they realized he had escaped.

Pausing for a moment, Emma hurried into the room, trying to keep calm as she went over and kissed Alex lightly on the cheek, hugging him stiffly. Alex looked at her apologetically and returned the hug, whispering, "I'm sorry, my lady, I've made a mess of it, haven't I?"

Emma sat down on the chair James had moved closer to the bed. She silently surveyed her friend and bailiff from head-to-toe before speaking.

"He needs a coffee, Mr. MacDonald; please go find one and don't forget the whisky!" she snapped, her eyes glinting, but James was unable to discern her emotion. Even before she finished speaking, he had moved quickly towards the door, knowing full well he'd been dismissed.

Alone at last, Emma sat down and began to bring Alex up-to-date on what she'd been told. As they talked, her eyes flitted about the room, then to his leg which, although partly covered by blankets, she was able to observe a long, white, plaster cast which appeared to encase his left leg from his toes to his upper thigh. She also noticed scratches on his left cheek and a bandage covering part of his forehead. They had shaven a section of his beard to expose another sizeable cut on his jawline. There was also a bandage on his right palm and another visible beneath his unbuttoned pajama top. He was obviously pleased to get her on her own, so after quickly discussing his injuries and, fearful James would return too soon, he got straight to the point. He told her that Duncan Bruce, whom he'd gone to see at the sorting station before his accident, would be expecting her. Lowering his voice, he explained what she had to do.

"Duncan will give you the information we need for that PO Box." Emma had a question on her lips but a knock at the door indicated James had returned. Trying to raise the mood, he came in carrying a tray of coffee in paper cups, balancing it like a waiter. Laughing, he set it down and handed each of them a cup. Producing a small whisky bottle from his coat pocket, he stood at attention, winked at Alex and then somberly offered it to Emma.

"Mission accomplished, my lady!"

Emma added as much as there was room for into Alex's cup and a small amount into her own. James pulled up a chair and sat down, taking the whisky bottle from Emma and returning it to his pocket. They toasted Alex's health and James then asked how he was feeling.

"You should have asked me!" Emma retorted. "I think he looks like he has tried to stop a runaway train! Next time you'd better wait until I give you permission to do something that stupid, Sir Alex!"

"Excuse me, my lady," the police commissioner intervened. "I think your bedside manner is a little rough on the patient."

"Oh, stop whining James, Alex is a big boy," Emma snapped. "Do something useful and go find that doctor. Tell him I need a nurse in here around the clock. Sir Alex requires better attention."

"They won't do it," James began, but he suddenly stopped himself when Emma swung quickly around to face him with that familiar look.

"Be gentle with him, my lady," Alex murmured after James had gone, "he's not used to answering to a woman … especially one like you!"

"Quit making excuses for him, Alex; he's a cop, not a choirboy!"

"And you've watched too many American movies, my lady!"

James returned with Dr. Greare, leaving him to deal with Emma while he escaped to the far side of Alex's bed.

"There is no way I can spare a nurse to babysit Sir Alex, Lady Traymore," he told her, posturing officiously to emphasize his point.

Smiling, Emma raised her hand to stop his tirade.

"I would think that a man of your stature, sir, could easily arrange for a private nurse, for which I would be happy to pay."

"Yes, I suppose *that* is possible," Dr. Greare agreed.

"Then I shall leave it up to you to make the necessary arrangements," she purred. "You have my gratitude, sir." She held out her hand which the doctor took, bowing slightly and backing out of the room. Watching the doctor leave, she turned back to face the men. With a twinkle of mischief in her eyes, she exclaimed, "Mission accomplished, gentlemen!"

They stayed until Alex's lunch tray arrived and she promised to come see him every day. He looked confused by this and James told him he was looking after her and that he was not to worry. They said their goodbyes and left.

"We should go get some lunch as well," James announced as his driver waited for instructions, "take us to our usual place, Simon."

"You don't have to eat meals with me, James. I'm sure you have another life besides policing. It is Saturday. Will your postal sorting station be open today?"

"I believe so, now don't tell me you want to see where Alex's accident happened? I told him I would look after you so if you don't want to do something I suggest, you had better tell me."

"All right , I would like to go to the sorting station."

"We will do that following lunch, my lady," James replied as Simon pulled into a small shopping mall and parked near a coffee shop. "We're hungry and we outnumber you, my lady!"

They went inside and Simon found a small corner table for himself while James led her to a booth. He recommended the soup and sandwich and it arrived quickly.

"I can now appreciate why you like this restaurant, James. The soup was excellent. I would liken it to what we call a truck stop in Canada. You can always count on their food being excellent and plentiful!"

When they returned to the car, Simon already had the car warm.

"Take us to the postal sorting station, sergeant," James instructed. As the car moved off, he turned to face her, "Why do you want to go there?"

"To complete the business Sir Alex began yesterday."

"And what might that be, my lady?"

"Don't be so nosy, Commissioner MacDonald, if you think I'm going to explain everything I do to you, you're deluding yourself!"

"Then maybe I won't take you!" he chuckled.

"Threats won't work either," she quipped. "I could easily rent a car and driver."

"I can open many doors for you, my lady," he said, grinning.

"Now that's the best argument you've come up with yet. I'll take that under consideration." Noticing they had stopped, she looked out and saw the sign announcing their destination. "So this is where you ran over Sir Alex," she teased but he did not rise to the bait this time.

It was just after two o'clock and the long, single storied building with five truck bays seemed busy with trucks coming and going at irregular intervals. The sergeant parked near the office but Emma had already noticed that the exterior lights had already come on in the parking area. Emma opened her door before either of the men could get out.

"Are you sure you don't want me to go with you?" James asked.

"No, thank you James, I shouldn't be very long," she replied.

Pulling her coat tightly around her as a bitterly cold wind swept across the car park, she walked to the main door. It was unlocked but inside was obviously a security zone with a sign that announced in large, bold letters, *RING BELL*. Grateful for the instructions, she smiled, pushed the button and waited. It took about five minutes but suddenly a small sliding window opened and a uniformed, middle-aged male security guard with a dour expression asked gruffly, "What do you want, Miss?"

"I would like to see Mr. Duncan Bruce."

"Wait there," he replied, slamming the window shut.

Ten minutes passed slowly as Emma paced the tiny holding area.

Suddenly the window opened again, this time framing the face and shoulders of a younger man who muttered, "Is this a family emergency, Miss?"

"No, but it's important."

"We don't allow visitors during working hours; this is a secure building. Good day, Miss!" The window was slammed shut again.

"Hey, come back here!" Emma yelled at the closed window, banging on it with her palm, but nothing happened. Going back outside, she slammed the main door so hard the wall shook, causing another security guard, who was talking to Simon, to look at her suspiciously as she stormed back to the car.

"The lady seems to need me," James murmured matter-of-factly keeping a straight face as he climbed out and went to meet her. "They wouldn't let you in, would they?" She nodded and he motioned to the security guard. "I will give you just five minutes to comply with Lady Traymore's request or I shall personally have your ass placed in a toaster! Now go before I lose my temper!" he snapped.

Shocked by the police commissioner's blunt methods, Emma's anger melted away. *Here is the man*, she thought to herself, *who can open doors to anywhere.*

"This time, my lady, I shall be going with you," he said firmly.

Within minutes the security guard came hurrying back, panting as he delivered his message to the police commissioner. "The shift supervisor is waiting to personally escort Lady Traymore, sir, and he's extremely sorry for any misunderstanding."

Taking Emma's arm, they followed the security guard as he led the way back into the building. This time, they were greeted with smiles, handshakes, and the white-coated supervisor's complete assent when James suggested they must have a private office where she could conduct her meeting in privacy. Using the supervisor's office, Duncan Bruce arrived and nervously took a chair, his eyes meeting Emma's.

"Are you Lady Traymore?" he quietly asked after James had left the room and closed the door.

"I am, Mr. Bruce. Are you aware that Sir Alex was hurt last night?"

"Yes, my lady, I heard about it after he had been taken to the hospital. I couldn't believe it happened right here in the car park after he left me."

Lowering her voice, she asked, "Do you have the information Sir Alex needed?"

Producing a folded paper from his trouser pocket, Duncan Bruce nervously handed it over the desk. Emma immediately deposited it in her handbag. They shook hands and he conveyed his greetings to Alex before he hurried away.

"We can go now?" James asked through the open door.

"No, now I want you to ask the supervisor to step in here for a moment, and you can come with him. He may need a witness."

"Careful, my lady, don't you go stirring up a hornet's nest."

"Would you please do as I ask?" Emma demanded haughtily, staring hard at the police commissioner.

In under a minute, the supervisor timidly opened the door and asked nervously, "You wanted to see me, my lady?" She nodded and then beckoned him inside. Her icy glare was already doing its job.

"Mr. Whoever you are," she began coldly, "your attitude requires an urgent adjustment. I warn you, if you need me to help you, you won't enjoy the experience. Do I make myself clear, sir? I want to make it clear that there will be no reproach whatsoever for Mr. Bruce," she continued, waiting for him to nod his agreement. Then she looked over at James. Grasping her bag, she rose, delivering her final blow to the confused man. "Now sir, I hope you feel competent enough to show us out of your establishment!"

There were neither handshakes nor goodbyes as she and the police commissioner were shown to the door. Quickly crossing to the car, they were soon speeding towards Edinburgh.

"Do you have any plans for dinner tonight, my lady?" James asked. It's a wee bit early for a Canadian to eat, but I'm ready for a cup of tea."

"Don't tell me you have a long list of watering holes, too?" Emma replied. "I thought Alex was unique."

"Was that a yes or no?" James asked.

"That was a no and a yes, I am also ready for a cup of tea."

"Simon," James addressed the driver, "you can take us to the academy."

"Now that *is* a new one for me!" Emma commented dryly.

Her comment drew no response from the commissioner, but she could hear his driver chuckling softly, and tried not to smile.

Dusk was showing signs of arriving an hour early as they drove off the motorway and onto a country road in a sparsely inhabited area outside Edinburgh. Emma had no idea where they were until they finally halted in front of two tall iron gates with a security gatehouse and a large sign that said, *Police Academy*. The entrance was well illuminated and a police sergeant came to the car and asked for I.D., immediately springing to attention and saluting when he recognized the police commissioner. At that point, he hurriedly waved them through.

The car drove down a well-lit driveway and she could see an enormous manor house in the distance, bathed in lights.

"Why have you brought me here, James?" she asked, as they climbed a short flight of stairs to a pair of enormous, ornate doors.

"You said you were ready for a drink and I knew Alex could not have brought you here!" James explained, winking before opening the door.

Inside, a uniformed policeman snapped smartly to attention as the commissioner passed by leading Emma towards a wide, impeccably polished mahogany staircase with intricately carved roses everywhere but on the handrail. It curved majestically for two stories as an equally decorative chandelier hung regally from its centre.

"Are you up to climbing two stories or would you prefer …?"

"Are you kidding?" she whispered. "I wouldn't miss exercise on this grand a scale. What an amazing work of art, James!"

At the top, they went a short way along a corridor before James opened a door. He motioned for her to enter. Unable to disguise her surprise, she stood for a moment allowing her eyes to survey the large mahogany-panelled room which was obviously a private office. One corner was set up as an office, with neat and quite fashionable, by her standards, office furniture. A large portrait of the Queen hung prominently above a beautiful, but massive fireplace that looked so ancient she pictured it gracing the Grand Hall in some stately castle.

"Allow me to take your coat, my lady," he said, interrupting her assessment of the shiny wood panelling which also covered the ceiling. She put her handbag down on the nearby beige leather sofa and James came over to assist her. He then went over to a door marked *Cloakroom* and disappeared inside.

As she waited, she continued her inspection of the room, noticing a large window to her left. It was actually an immense bay window and inside it was a small table already set with white linen, white china and silver cutlery. James came up beside her and, taking her elbow, steered her towards it. She realized the table was also set with a bottle of red wine chilling in a silver wine bucket, two exquisitely etched wine goblets, and a small vase of enchantingly delicate flowers.

"Even fresh flowers in winter … this looks as if they were expecting someone special," Emma chuckled. "Have I interrupted some previous arrangement?"

"Yes, they were expecting someone special," he replied with a wide grin, pulling out her chair. "It was you, of course, my lady."

She noticed a tea pot on a food trolley and asked James if he would mind if she poured. "By all means," he exclaimed. "I'm ready for a cup." She filled two china cups and handed one to him.

"How in heaven's name did you arrange all of this so quickly?"

"I didn't," James admitted, "Simon did, while you were venting your fury on that poor postal supervisor!"

"But what would have done if I had wanted to go back to the hotel?" she laughed.

"I would have taken you there, but you would have missed a delightful dinner."

"And ruined all your well-laid plans?"

"There were no well-laid plans, my lady; I simply thought this would be a change for you. Would you rather go somewhere else?"

"Certainly not, you have me brimming with anticipation!"

A chef arrived at the table with his great white hat jammed tightly on his head. He was tall, somewhat portly with a red face, and bursting with enthusiastic energy.

"Good evening Commissioner and Lady Traymore, there is no menu tonight. Please tell me your wishes and I will fulfill them, he gushed in a thick brogue, gesticulating with his arms as if in anticipation of having to prepare some gourmet delight for his special guests.

"You did say anything?" Emma murmured with an amused expression as she watched the chef nod vigorously. "Then I would like a hamburger with lettuce, tomatoes, barbeque sauce and chips please!"

James almost choked on his coffee, but fought to control himself as he noticed the smile slowly slip from the chef's face, being replaced by a look of utter rejection. Then, taking a noticeable breath, he turned to James and whispered, "and you, Commissioner MacDonald?"

"Oh, I'll have the same," James spluttered, not able to control his laughter. "Forgive her, Sam, she's missing a popular Canadian meal and it sounds quite delightful to me, for a change that is!"

As they ate, they no longer had any trouble finding common subjects to discuss. When they had finished their second glass of wine, Emma asked him about the function of the academy and he replied by pointing into the darkness when he mentioned the Firearm Training Building. Then, as if remembering some engagement, he glanced at his watch.

"Excuse me, my lady; I had completely forgotten to mention that there is a lecture tonight for the newly recruited detectives. I believe you would find it most enlightening and, if you are game, we could just make it to the lecture room before it starts."

With her agreement, they left immediately and, on the way, they took a quick stop to freshen up and retrieve their coats.

"We may need them in that draughty hall," he explained, hurrying her past several doors until he reached one that was open. Emanating from within was the sound of many male voices. "I trust this will help to quell any homesick pangs you have been experiencing," he whispered. He took her elbow and steered her towards two back-row seats.

It wasn't long before the room was almost full of mainly young men, but more women than she expected. They had filed in very quietly taking no notice of Emma or the commissioner. A bell rang somewhere in the background and a small, bearded man in a tartan cape and a round tartan bonnet swept into the room from a door behind the lectern. He was holding a briefcase and cradled precariously on his other arm lay a pile of dangerously loose papers.

"Ladies and Gentlemen," he began, glowering at his assembled class while he struggled to keep his papers under control. He dropped his briefcase with a crash that sounded like he had lead weights inside of it but was then able to handle his papers successfully.

Emma snickered and the lecturer's eyes immediately locked onto her. Scowling, he snapped, "You find something amusing, young lady?"

James cringed when he saw the flash of light in Emma's eyes. Leaping to his feet too late, she called a resounding, "Yes, sir!" giggling again as she glanced at James.

"Forgive us, Dr. Barton." James' voice rang through the room. Many heads turned but not a sound was heard from the trainees. "Let me introduce Lady Traymore, the new hereditary chief of the Walters' Clan. I'm sure you know who I am, sir. Please continue."

The moment defused, James sat down and took Emma's hand. "Behave yourself or I'll have you arrested!" he whispered.

"Wimp!" was Emma's hissed response, squeezing his hand back.

"We are going to have a practical demonstration of your powers of research and logical deduction," continued Dr. Barton. "A team of four will be selected and their findings will be brought back to class for critique. Does anyone have a suggestion on the subject matter?"

"We could investigate the rumour surrounding the silent monks, sir," a young officer suggested. "It's been on the news every night this week."

"No, we're Scots, young man. We need the subject to be typically Scottish," replied Dr. Barton, obviously dismissing the suggestion.

Emma suddenly stood up, pushing her chair back with a squeak. Ignoring James' pleading eyes, she made her way confidently towards Dr. Barton. James held his breath. Every person in the hall seemed to be doing the same. Dr. Barton glowered at her every step.

"It appears Lady Traymore has something else to share with us!"

Emma stepped up to the lectern beside him, but he was stubbornly holding onto it with both hands. "Well, move over!" she hissed, causing some snickering to run through the class. Dr. Barton let go of the lectern and moved over slightly, but it was obvious to all that he wasn't very happy about it.

"Ladies and Gentlemen, you have heard that I am Lady Traymore; I'm also a Canadian, and a professor of English Literature who lectures at the University of Victoria, on Canada's West Coast." A tiny ripple of applause was heard but she motioned for quiet. "With Dr. Barton's permission, I would like to tell you of a mystery right here on your doorstep. When were the bodies of paupers removed from the abbey lands in Elderslie, and, if they were moved, where did they go? There, you have a Scottish mystery worth solving, don't you agree, Dr. Barton?"

"I certainly do," the lecturer murmured thoughtfully, snatching his bonnet from his head and moving closer, signalling she was excused.

She returned to her seat while Dr. Barton organized his team of investigators. James leaned toward her and whispered, "It's almost 10 o'clock and past my bedtime. Let me take you home." They began to leave and were almost to the door when Dr. Barton called to them.

"Commissioner and Lady Traymore, could you please indulge us for a few moments? Could I suggest, with your permission, my lady, that you revisit us next Friday to hear the results of the panel? If you can come at 5 o'clock, I will take you both for dinner."

"I would be pleased to accept your offer, Dr. Barton," Emma replied, "but the commissioner may not be available." This seemed to satisfy Dr. Barton and his students, as excited chatter again filled the room.

"Why do you want to know about the paupers' graves?" Jim asked.

"Did I say that, James?"

"Not in so many words, my lady, but it's a very interesting subject when one is looking for an old grave." Simon opened the car door.

Light rain mixed with snow made the drive home a bit slower as the radio announced that temperatures were again plummeting. Once in the city, there was a great improvement with almost dry roads. Emma found herself relaxing as she thought of Alex and the day's events.

"We'll have you home in five minutes, you must be tired," James commented. "How is nine o'clock for breakfast, my lady?"

"Perfect. I appreciate what you're doing for me, James. Thank you."

## Chapter 18 – Sunday 3rd – Mabel

Snow fell through the evening and, even as she viewed the city from her hotel window before turning in for the night, there was already a fair covering of white on all but the main streets. Edinburgh's Christmas activities were continuing having been busy all week. As dawn crept over Scotland's royal city, she shuddered at the thought of driving to Stirling to see Alex. By the time she was on her way downstairs, it was almost eight and as she walked into the hotel dining room she suddenly stopped in surprise. Someone was sitting at their table reading the newspaper, just as she would normally have expected Alex to be.

*He couldn't have escaped from the hospital*, she thought, approaching the table slowly.

"Good morning, my lady." James smiled as he folded the newspaper.

"How did you know where I sit?" she asked, frowning, "or that I would come down early."

"I'm a policeman remember, I know how to find out these things."

"You're very sneaky, commissioner," she laughed, as the waitress filled her coffee cup.

Breakfast was almost over when Emma asked what James could tell her about what was happening at the monastery in Yorkshire. He eyed her suspiciously across the table.

"Now why would you be interested in the monastery?"

"It's a Traymore Foundation and I'm concerned for the monks."

"Yes, I'm sure," he said slowly, still watching her.

"So Mr. Policeman, what am I under suspicion for now?"

"I have no proof yet, but my intuition tells me you and Alex had something to do with the mess those monks are in now. It's just that it's very difficult for me to understand why."

"Then shall we go and you can grill me while we travel. I'd like to have lunch with Sir Alex today so I'll be no more than 10 minutes." She got up and walked quickly out to the elevator.

Everything she needed was on the chair near the hall closet so, after putting on her hat and coat, she returned promptly to the foyer. Emma found James waiting just outside the main door.

"Where is the car?" she asked.

"Right there," James replied, grinning as he pointed to a dark blue Land Rover with large, knobby tires and Emma screwed up her face. "I thought we'd take my vehicle today. You'll see a lot more as the seats are higher than in a car."

Emma followed him and, when he opened the door, two steps suddenly unfolded from beneath the door, seeming to leap out at her. She took a step backwards and her heels caught the border of the garden and she sat down rather unladylike into the snow. He tried to grab her but it was too late.

"You dolt, are you trying to kill me?" she shouted, as he helped her up. "I am certainly not riding in that vicious beast!"

The commotion brought Megan, the desk clerk, and a stern-faced, older gentleman out to investigate. They had both seen it all from the window.

"It's all right folks, she's taken a little tumble but landed softly," James explained, hoping Emma wouldn't object.

"Are you sure it was an accident, young man?" accused the older man who now turned to Emma and added, "Would you like me to send for the constabulary, my dear?"

"He is the constabulary," Emma snapped, "and he may owe me a new coat!" Snatching her hat from James, she stormed back inside.

It took almost half an hour for Emma to return wearing a toque with a prominent maple leaf on it, different slacks and a different coat. Making no further objections, she found the high seat a great vantage point, but obviously the vehicle lacked other refinements and was in no way comparable to the car Alex drove. She pointed out the hotel where Alex had taken her for a meal, saying he knew the owners.

"Oh, you don't have to tell me, Alex knows everybody," he laughed. "He should because he and Trevelion Walters scoured the country for the regalia. People say there was no stone left unturned, no clue too small to ignore. But I never heard of them finding anything." James enjoyed driving the Land Rover and they arrived at the hospital on the stroke of noon. He parked and they went inside. He hadn't mentioned the monastery again.

"Sir Alex is in Room 214," the receptionist at the Information Desk informed them. When they arrived at Alex's room, a nurse whom Emma estimated to be in her early-thirties blocked their entry when they knocked at the door.

"No one is allowed in until one thirty," she said, stubbornly holding her ground.

"Are you a hospital employee?" James asked.

"No, sir, I was brought in by Dr. Greare, on the specific instruction of Lady Traymore."

"And your duties?" James gently persisted.

"I'm to attend to the needs and welfare of Sir Alex Wallace, sir."

"Let them in, Mabel!" Alex's voice boomed from inside the room.

"No, sir, this is your lunch time and I'll not have you disturbed by visitors," she called over her shoulder to him.

"Before you go any further, young lady," James smiled tolerantly, "I think we should introduce ourselves. I am the commissioner of police and this is Lady Traymore."

"Very good sir, it's nice to meet you both. I'm Nurse Brown." She looked at James then added sharply, "Sir Alex is resting; please come back at 1:30."

James looked stunned, he had met the immovable object and there appeared no way around it. Emma giggled at his obvious frustration and quickly interceded.

"Nurse Brown, please send a message for Dr. Greare to come," she instructed, using her most patient manner and apparently confusing James by the expression on his face. Even before she went to the phone, they saw the figure of Dr. Greare striding down the hallway towards them.

"Reception told me you were here, my lady," he beamed, glancing over at Nurse Brown. "I thought you might need my help!"

Waving the nurse aside, he led them into the room, where Alex lay with his casted leg raised onto a stack of pillows. Emma went over and hugged him as Dr. Greare checked his pulse, his stethoscope also ready but Alex told him to go away. Unaffected by his patient's anger, the doctor took Emma's arm and led her towards the open doorway.

"Get me a decent cup of coffee, please James," Alex begged. "I've had enough of this dishwater they're trying to poison me with!"

"But, Sir Alex, I assure you the coffee is fresh," Nurse Brown implored, "and ..."

Only able to hear snatches of their animated exchange, Emma sighed then pulled her arm free of the doctor's grasp and turned back to the doorway.

"James," she whispered, "please go and find a bottle of whisky. We can't have Sir Alex doing anything rash!"

Grinning, James winked and left immediately.

"No, no," Dr. Greare argued. "I simply can't allow him to bring whisky into the hospital for Sir Alex. He is on medication."

"Calm yourself, Dr. Greare," Emma's clipped words spoke with authority and remarkably, they seemed to have a slightly calming affect on the doctor. "Is Sir Alex taking any meds that can cause a dangerous reaction with alcohol?" she asked, watching as the doctor hesitated and then shook his head. "Then I will pay for Sir Alex's treatment as a private patient and I make the rules. Can I depend on you to also make this clear to the nurse or you will be hiring another—simple as that!"

Now red-faced and stumbling for words, the last of Dr. Greare's courage quickly wilted. Impressed by the titles of his patient and Lady Traymore, he nodded weakly and called the nurse to come out into the hallway while Emma returned to see Alex, shutting the door behind her.

"You have to get me out of here or I will go crazy," Alex pleaded. "Where did you go yesterday?"

She sat down and related her and James' visit to the police academy for dinner including the lecture they had attended.

"Oh, that sounds very exciting," Alex commented.

"It was actually, I had a little spat with the lecturer!" Alex rolled his eyes but she waved a warning finger at him and continued, "and then they invited me to give the new detectives a challenge for them to solve." Emma could tell that this last remark had gained Alex's absolute attention. "So, I suggested they find out if the bodies in the paupers' graves had ever been moved, and if they had been, where to?"

"Was James there when this was being talked about?" Alex asked.

"Yes, he never left me."

"He's a policeman you know, and a good one," cautioned Alex. "I hope you haven't alerted him to our intentions."

"I don't believe so, however, I did get the feeling it set him thinking about that conversation." Emma paused briefly as if in thought. "James MacDonald is a perfect gentleman, but he will not hesitate to say what is on his mind when he's ready." She didn't want to mention his theory about the monastery.

"What's that I hear?" James interrupted as he burst into the room carrying a whisky bottle. "Is someone taking my name in vain again?"

Emma ordered James to open the bottle as she poured three cups of coffee, adding whisky to two of them. Grinning, James handed the first one to Alex.

"Now, Sir Alex Wallace," said James, standing to his full height and peering down at his friend. "I presume Lady Traymore has been complaining about me, but let me tell you the truth of it." He coughed slightly, pretended to gather his composure, looked over at Emma who was trying hard not to giggle, and frowned. "I have tried very hard to please your lady and I didn't even laugh when she sat down in the snow and got her backside wet!"

Alex almost choked on his coffee, but then he began to laugh, obviously enjoying the picture this story conjured up.

Emma started to object, but gave it up quickly and couldn't help but join in. Suddenly, Dr. Greare was at the doorway with his finger on his lips. When they didn't comply, he waved frantically at them to stop, pointing to his ears and the hallway. Puzzled, they went quiet and he whispered that someone had inadvertently left the hospital intercom open in this area and their laughter was ringing through the hallways. He also told them he had given Nurse Brown new orders.

The transformation of the stubborn, officious Nurse Brown was miraculous. Obviously, Dr. Greare had verified their identities and she was now eager to please. She even offered to add the whisky to her patient's refill of coffee as long as he was reasonable about it.

"I don't suppose you were able to see Duncan Bruce at the postal station," Alex whispered while James talked to the nurse.

"Yes I did, I'll tell you later," she said softly as James came over.

With no other opportunity to talk privately, Emma felt badly that she had to leave Alex wondering. Turning back to wave to him as they left, she knew Alex would be having a bout of cabin fever being trapped in a hospital room with no chance of escape.

"Where to now?" James asked as they returned to the car and he opened her door. "You promised me lunch with Alex, but we were too late. Now I'm famished and it's almost two o'clock, so please feed me!"

"How long will it take to drive to Paisley?"

"About 35 minutes."

"Then do it. I would like to eat at the *Tartan Tea Shop* and listen to the local gossip."

"Are you joking?"

"Of course not!" she snapped before turning to face the window.

James made good time on the motorway and they were almost at the outskirts of Glasgow when he suddenly slowed and drove off the road into a patch of old snow.

"What are you ...?" Emma began, but stopped when James held up his hand and pointed to a flashing red light on the dashboard.

He flipped a switch and a calm male voice came out of the speaker repeating a message over and over again. "We have an emergency, sir." the voice said, beginning to repeat it again until James flipped the switch again and replied, "Give me some details ... standing by."

"A plane crash at the Highland Show Grounds. No further details as yet, sir," the voice advised.

Remaining quiet, Emma felt a cold shudder run down her spine as James pulled back onto the motorway. She could feel the power surge as the Land Rover continued down the M80 turning south at the M73 Junction. Stern-faced, James drove on in silence listening to intermittent messages which alerted him of the situation and that there were fatalities at the crash scene. A marked police car with siren screaming and lights flashing pulled up beside them momentarily before swinging into their lane and proceeding, clearing their approach to the show grounds.

Emma's heart raced as they entered the show grounds and drove over to a large, marked police van in the parking lot. James jumped out and commanded her to "stay here," before slamming the car door. He hurried over to the van and went in through a back door.

Left to her own devices, she sat and watched as uniformed people hurried back and forth, but within 20 minutes the car was growing cold and she was wishing for James to return. Suddenly a young, uniformed, police sergeant opened the driver's door and climbed in, introducing himself as Sgt. Ronald Powell. He addressed her as Lady Traymore and informed her he was going to drive her back to the *Courtyard Inn*. As they started out, he explained that the commissioner had said he would contact her later at the hotel.

"What happened back there?" she asked.

"Oh, it seems a private plane had engine trouble as it made its approach to the airport. It crash-landed onto the grass. They managed to find the only open space but I believe there were fatalities. That information is not for publication, my lady." He turned to her and she nodded.

"I understand sergeant, how dreadful. Local people, I presume?" she asked with a note of sadness.

"No, my lady, they were men coming from outside the country. Oh, here we are," the sergeant murmured as he pulled up to the front door of her hotel. "Can I be of any more assistance tonight, Lady Traymore?"

"Yes, you can," she replied, frowning at the young man in the near darkness. "Would you please help me out of this beast!"

236

Realizing it was almost dinnertime, and she had completely missed lunch, she went to the dining room and ordered an early dinner sent to her room. She would phone and talk to Alex in privacy tonight and James would never be the wiser. News of the plane crash seemed to be the main topic of conversation as people walked by her, but by the time she had ordered, the area was almost empty. Going upstairs, she thought about calling Alex and wondered when James would be available to contact her, she estimated she'd have an hour or two—lots of time to eat and talk to Alex.

Back in her suite, she plugged in the kettle and got ready for dinner, then turned on the TV and made a cup of coffee while she waited for her meal. Suddenly, there was a news flash about the plane crash, but it was only sparse news so she went to find the phone number Alex had written on a card for her. She decided to call him right away.

"Hello, my dear," she whispered when he answered.

"Why are you being so nice to me, my lady? It's completely out of character," he ranted, "unless you're deliberately trying to confuse me!"

"Are you alone?" she asked.

"This is a hospital not a holiday camp, Emma. Yes, I'm alone!"

"Good, now just listen. James took me to see Duncan Bruce at the postal sorting station today and he gave me the addresses of the four blue-stained letters. Two were local mail and one was to England, but the one that interests us was to a PO Box in Edinburgh to the attention of a Mrs. Audrey Spencer. I asked him if they all had postage stamps, but he couldn't remember."

"Who is this Mrs. Spencer?" he asked.

"I don't know, but I'll try to find out."

"You be careful, my lady. James is driving you so it's easy for him to keep his eye on you. He's a crafty devil and nobody's fool. I've known him for many years, so take heed."

"Actually, James got called to an accident this afternoon so he is quite busy for the time being. Did you hear about the small airplane that crashed at the Highland Show Grounds?"

"No, I didn't, what happened?"

"Well, it's apparently been on both radio and TV stations because I heard people talking about it when I was in the dining room. When we left you and were driving to Paisley, James got a message about the crash and we went directly to the show grounds. At the accident scene, he had a young sergeant drive me back to the hotel. That's the last I saw of him, but he sent a message that he would contact me later this evening.

They're not releasing much information yet but my driver said they were men from out of the country."

"You watch the news tonight and bring me some more information tomorrow ... actually why don't you come for supper tomorrow? Give James the night off and call a taxi. I'll order in then we can have a good talk. Now I'm feeling very tired, Emma, but I'm looking forward to seeing you tomorrow, will you come?"

"I'll do my best to lose James and be there at six," she giggled as a knock sounded at the door. "Oh good, my lunch and dinner are here! Good night, Alex."

Quickly replacing the phone, she looked up at the silent TV screen and almost missed the latest news flash about the plane crash as she went to the door. This time the news story featured available video and she watched intently.

The scene looked chaotic with many vehicles and red lights flashing in the dark. She also saw a fire truck before the report ended. Morbid interest forced her to keep the news on for the next report at which time they showed parts of the plane scattered about the area. The announcer said that daylight would confirm the disturbing scene.

At 9:15 p.m. the phone rang and James was on the other end.

"Sorry for deserting you, my lady," he apologized in a very tired voice. "I'll meet you for breakfast at eight, if that's all right?"

"Very good sir, although it's not necessary if you're busy," Emma said softly.

"I'll have the time and I want to see you. I'm on my way home now. Goodnight, my lady."

She said 'goodnight' and, sighing with relief, put the phone down.

## Chapter 19 – Monday 4th – Four Strangers

Waking early after a restless night, she sat at the window and watched the snow as it blew along the streets below her. She shuddered at the thought of going to Stirling in another snow storm. Watching TV as she dressed, she learned two victims of the air crash had died of their injuries. Going down early, she was surprised to find James in his uniform waiting at her table.

"It looks like you're working today," she commented, sitting down and watching him silently nod before taking a sip of his coffee.

"Yes and no," he replied after some seconds had passed. "The crash is in the hands of experts now and our job would normally be finished."

"You're hinting at something, commissioner, as if this crash is out of the ordinary."

"Let's have our breakfast, my lady," he said softly, "then you and I are going to solve a little mystery."

"You have a very unique way of making a date with a lady, commissioner," Emma exclaimed, "but, I must admit, you have my curiosity aroused."

"You'll need your warm woollies on today," James advised as they finished eating, "it's cold and snowy again."

As she walked by Megan's desk on her way upstairs, the clerk waved her over and brought out a parcel from under the desk.

"This was delivered while you were eating, my lady."

"Oh, thank you, Megan. I'm eager to see this. It's my new tartan dress," she confided.

"That's lovely, my lady. I'll look forward to seeing you wear it soon."

Another surprise awaited Emma after she returned downstairs. She went outside to meet James and he was standing by the door of Alex's car.

"Why are we using Alex's car?" she asked suspiciously.

"Because I'm tired of seeing your displeasure and hearing you whine about my vehicles," he replied with as straight a face as he could muster.

As they got on their way, Emma quickly recognized they were heading for police headquarters. Hard-pressed to resist asking questions, she followed him silently past security and up to his office. Moments later, a young constable arrived with a tray containing a jug of coffee, two cups and saucers, and cream and sugar.

"Yesterday," James began, "there was an air crash at the show grounds. You are aware of this. What you are not aware of is that six people, including the pilot and co-pilot, died in the crash. No one survived. There was no fire so we recovered their belongings."

"Why are you telling me this, James?"

"Because you and Alex are mentioned in their papers."

"What papers?" she asked, trying to look shocked rather than merely interested.

As he got up and went over to his desk, she noticed the battered, black briefcase which he now brought back to the table and set it down in front of her. "This briefcase was chained to the wrist of one of the deceased males. This usually indicates that it contains something of great importance," he announced in a very serious tone. He removed a key from his pocket and opened the briefcase, removing a set of papers clipped together with a large paperclip. He looked briefly at the top copy before handing them across the table.

Frowning, Emma accepted them, but her heart was beginning to pound. She flipped through the pages fairly quickly seeing their names near the top of the third. But some of the words and phrases alarmed her, although she didn't know why. It was all very puzzling. She wanted to spend more time reading them but decided to play along.

"Who the hell were these people?"

"That's what I want to know," he replied stoically.

"There must be some identification on the bodies ... passports, driving licences, credit cards or even tattoos?" she replied, frowning.

"Yes, you're actually correct; we did learn their names, ages and addresses." The commissioner allowed himself a frosty chuckle. "But why would both you and Alex's names appear in their documents ... and there's more yet. They had details of your movements in Elderslie and Paisley."

"Hold on a minute." She held up her hand. "James, get me the phone number of the *Tartan Tea Shop* in Paisley."

James went over to his desk and picked up the phone, watching her as he did so.

"Connect me with the *Tartan Tea Shop* in Paisley, sergeant," he told the person on the other end of the line then he put the phone down and carried it over to the table. Almost immediately, it rang. He pressed two buttons then handed it to her. "I've turned the speaker on," he whispered as Moira's voice said 'hello.'

"Hello Moira?" she gushed. "Yes, this is Lady Traymore. I wondered if you had seen Monsignor Sharp over the last two days?"

"Oh no, my lady, nobody has seen him since Friday. Mr. Pooley mentioned this morning that the monsignor had gone to Edinburgh to meet the Pope, but I hardly think that's the truth, my lady!" The girl giggled self-consciously.

"Did you see that American man again?"

"No, my lady."

Thanking her profusely, Emma put down the phone and cocked an eyebrow at the commissioner.

"I think, my lady, that you are trying to connect that nosy monsignor to these people in the air crash. I want to know why because we are definitely missing a link in this case."

Emma took a deep breath. "You could try Mrs. Audrey Spencer on Ester Road; she may be the link you seek, Mr. MacDonald."

Silently, Commissioner MacDonald intensely scrutinized Emma's face and waited for her to elaborate. Realizing no more details were going to be forthcoming, he whispered, "You are particularly well informed, my lady."

"Not really commissioner," she purred, "like you, Sir Alex and I are merely searching for answers."

"Let me give you a few more details," he continued. "We have four gentlemen all travelling together with no apparent connection to each other. After checking their credentials, we find they are totally respectable businessmen, with not a single blemish on any of their characters. Yet, they were all carrying papers implicating you and Sir Alex."

"Implicating us ... in what?" Emma asked fiercely. "You're not making any sense commissioner. Do you know why they were coming here?"

"Intuition tells me they were coming to meet with you and Alex."

"Stop right there, James MacDonald," she snapped. "If you're trying to scare me, it won't work."

"Oh no, my lady, I'm not trying to scare you. I'm trying to warn you to be careful. You've obviously made somebody very nervous and I would like to know why. Are you keeping some important information from us?"

241

Their conversation was stopped abruptly by the ringing phone and James answered. Listening briefly, he grunted a reply and put it down. Returning to his desk, he collected four groups of papers all held together by large paperclips, and lay them out in front of her. "Take a look at these and tell me what you think they are," he said sternly. "I'll be back in a few minutes."

Glad to be released from his probing questions, Emma eagerly began reading the papers, stopping only to replenish her coffee. Finding a pen in her handbag and, acquiring a notepad from the commissioner's desk, she became so engrossed in her task that she lost all sense of time. When a constable brought in a tray containing a plate of biscuits, small cakes and a fresh jug of coffee, then left without a word, she looked at her watch. James had been gone for approximately an hour.

Frowning, she gathered her notes and began the process of analyzing the information, writing several words on a new page of the notepad and then dropping the pen back into her handbag. Replenishing her coffee, she walked over to a large window and gazed at the snow-covered landscape in the distance. Moments later, James returned and came immediately over to her. Picking up her notes, he silently read her conclusions and muttered, "Sorry it took so long. Shall we go have some lunch?"

"Yes, that would be nice. She looked at her watch again and remembered her plans for dinner. "I completely forgot to tell you that I have a date with Alex tonight at the hospital. He's ordering in dinner for six o'clock and suggested I give you the night off! You did a masterful job of taking my mind off my plans, commissioner!"

"Thank you, my lady, sometimes I do my job well," he proclaimed. "Now, come along. We're going to a place where only special people are allowed to eat." Emma took another sip of her coffee and picked up her coat. "You won't need a coat, my lady; we're only going upstairs to the executive dining room."

High-ranking police officers were occupying several tables as the commissioner escorted his guest to a quiet table near a window that looked out across the city to the Firth. Pulling out her chair, he steadied it as she sat down, nodding to some of the other officers before seating himself. The service was good and the meal exceptional; plates had just been cleared when James whispered across the table, "I think you have a visitor, my lady."

"Hello, Lady Traymore," a voice gushed from behind her. It was none other than Professor Barton.

"Hello, Professor Barton," she replied, holding out her hand in an unenthusiastic handshake. She waited for the professor to continue. "I hope we will have some positive results for our meeting on Friday, my lady. You will be coming to my lecture at seven o'clock, won't you?"

"Yes, we will professor," James interrupted, "and you're going to be late for your class today, if you don't make haste, sir."

Blinking, the professor peered down at his watch, mumbling his apologies before hurrying away.

"You certainly got rid of him in a hurry!" she chuckled. "I wanted you on my own; now tell me what you learned from those papers?"

"In my opinion, they were strangers to each other, coming together somehow for a single purpose—deeply religious, but not ministers and definitely associated with the Freemasons." Frowning heavily as she concentrated on remembering the details on the papers, James watched her with rapt intensity. Then, suddenly relaxing, she reached for her drink.

"Is that it?" he asked with a note of disappointment in his voice. Seeing her nod, he added, "Then what made you so excited?"

"James MacDonald!" Emma snapped angrily. "You were watching me on that blasted camera!"

"No, no, I was at a meeting; you heard the phone call."

Glaring at him, Emma's eyes were spitting fire and, as she continued to vent her fury, patrons at nearby tables could hardly avoid noticing. "You miserable, devious, kilted animal," she seethed. "I was helping you and all the time you were spying on me!"

"Keep your voice down," James hissed in a whisper as the colour rose in his face. "Och, ya dun it noo lass!"

Whispers buzzed through the tables as an older gentleman in civilian clothes stood up and approached their table.

"Lady Traymore, I presume," he smirked, causing James to look away. "My name is Ian Allan MacDonald, father of this scallywag on whom you are sharpening your tongue. I would like to compliment you on your excellent choice of words! I'm sure my son will appreciate your opinion. I'll take my leave now to save James any further embarrassment but it has been a pleasure meeting you, my lady! Good day to you, Lady Traymore." He was still chuckling as he walked back to his table and rejoined the two officers with whom he had been dining.

"Och, now you've got my father on your side!" James groaned. "You realize he's going to greatly relish going home tonight and reporting to my mother!"

"I hope she hangs you by your thumbs, outside, on a cold winter's night!" she retorted, smiling broadly.

Miles away at Misty House, the research team was dealing with a situation they had never experienced before. Tom and Charlie had been looking at one of the interment documents from Sir Alex's pouches and Tom had found an unusual entry with some obviously hurriedly written, quite mysterious, notations. Tom had made the quick decision to call matron to come and verify their conclusions. When Ruth arrived, he showed her the original parchment and pointed to a Latin phrase that read, *She will never be lonely* in English. She looked up at him puzzled.

"What is this, Tom?" she asked, noticing the men were both smiling.

"Start reading here, marm," he replied, pointing to the writing immediately above. She began to hurriedly translate, murmuring mainly, then speaking aloud from time to time.

"… *burial in pauper grave … male named Hump … taken from gibbet without permission and laid beneath a heavenly guide.* Oh my, anything else, Tom?" she asked, as she wondered if Lady Traymore could have been right.

"Down here, marm."

Ruth followed his finger again. "*17NW,*" she read. So what are your conclusions, Tom?" Controlling her excitement, Ruth listened carefully to Tom's explanation.

"This indicates to me marm, that there was an unnamed woman and a man named Hump removed after hanging and buried in this monk's grave, but why was a monk in a pauper's grave? Without the monk's biographia box, we might never know! But was the deceased's heavenly guide a monk? We wonder. And the woman with no name … could she possibly be Mary Wallace? Were they in such a hurry they had to bury the third body in the same grave or was that meant to throw us off?" He shook his head and looked at Ruth, confusion on his face.

"I have never heard of a monk being buried with peasants before," she proclaimed. The men couldn't help but notice that Ruth's voice held a definite note of quiet excitement rarely seen in their matron. "But if they wanted to hide Mary's body, what better place than in an already prepared grave for a monk? If found now, in the very least, the monk's biographia box could serve to verify the occupants of the grave."

Tom and Charlie nodded in agreement, their faces portraying a cautious eagerness. Now, the job of identifying the location from the interment documents became the task at hand. 17NW had only one meaning … it had to be Plot 17 in the North West corner of the original consecrated burial ground, but was that the paupers' area or was that important? Difficulties arose while searching the copies of the old maps which Emma and Alex had left with them. Due to the faded areas of the map, they simply could not agree on the exact location of the grave.

Ruth called Alex at his apartment and receiving only his voice mail, she also called Emma. She was politely informed by the hotel that Sir Alex hadn't been seen for days and Lady Traymore had left that morning with the Commissioner of Police.

Fearing the worst and, upset by the news, Ruth called Alfred Holt at the tartan factory and Douglas at the distillery, but neither could shed a glimmer of light on the situation. *Where had Sir Alex gone and why was Lady Traymore with the commissioner?* Wild thoughts flashed through her mind. Almost dreading the result, she phoned the archives to ask John Dunstan if he knew anything.

"There's a rumour that he ran into a police car and has a broken leg. You could try Stirling Hospital," Dunstan told her. "I can neither confirm or deny it, and I have no idea why James MacDonald would have taken Lady Traymore into custody. I suggest you call the police directly."

Thanking him, Ruth sighed and put the receiver down. Gathering her thoughts and, trying to control her imagination, she picked up the phone again and pressed the speed dial for the second time.

"Do you have Sir Alex Wallace registered as a patient?" she asked.

"Yes, we do," a male voice replied, "are you a relative?"

"No, I'm the matron of Misty House and Sir Alex is one of my directors. I've been concerned that I haven't been able to reach him."

"Oh," he murmured somewhat apologetically. "Sir Alex was admitted early Saturday morning with multiple injuries, the result of a car accident."

"Och, is he all right?" she gasped. "Could I speak with him please?"

"Yes marm, I will put you through to his room."

"Hello," a cheery feminine voice said on the other end of the line, "would you like to speak to Sir Alex Wallace?"

"Yes, I would please," Ruth replied.

"Can't you get me out of here?" Alex growled into the phone almost immediately.

"It's Ruth Oxley, Sir Alex," she said gently. "I don't think you were addressing that request to me, were you?"

"Sorry Ruth, I thought you were Lady Traymore," Alex apologized sheepishly. "It's wonderful to hear a familiar voice."

"Oh dear, I'm happy to speak to you as well. Are you all right and is it true Lady Traymore was arrested by the police commissioner? The hospital desk clerk just told me you'd been in a car accident."

Alex roared with laughter. "It's all right, Ruth, my lady hasn't been arrested and I'll survive with a mere broken leg! James wouldn't even dare try to arrest her; she'd tear him to shreds with that wicked tongue of hers! As for me, I'll be fine in a few days."

"I tried to call you both today, but nobody knew where either of you were. I was getting worried because the hotel told me she had gone with the police commissioner in his car."

"Why were you trying to contact us?"

"We believe we have a clue to the whereabouts of Mary Wallace's remains," Ruth whispered excitedly. "Tom found it in one of the interment documents. We have a grave number and a location."

"Who have you told?"

"No one sir, we need you and Lady Traymore to make the decisions."

"Leave it with me now," Alex said gently. "Please don't mention this to anyone else, Ruth. I'll be seeing Lady Traymore later today and one of us will contact you. Goodbye."

Having left the room during the call, Nurse Brown now returned pushing a wheelchair with a pair of crutches balanced on top.

"If you are so determined to leave us, Sir Alex," she began, "I think we had better prepare you. It's not an easy feat walking with crutches and you'll need to get used to them. I know you have the determination, but we don't want you to rush things!"

"Stop prattling woman and let's get on with it," Alex snapped, flinging the cover from his legs. Going red in the face from effort, he tried in vain to move his casted leg.

"Sir Alex, please wait for my help!" she insisted, rushing over to support his leg as he bounced his body towards the edge of the bed. When he lowered it to the floor, he grimaced.

Back at Edinburgh police headquarters, James and Emma were about to leave when he suggested they go find Audrey Spencer on Ester Road. He told her he had asked one of his staff to do a little investigating into the address while they were having lunch.

As he often did, as he drove visitors around, when they passed historical buildings and landmarks, James gave a running commentary similar to Alex's and in no time they were at their destination. Emma frowned at her companion as he pulled off into a parking area where snow had been piled.

"Ester Road is just over there," he murmured, pointing a finger to the other side of the adjoining road. Reaching into the backseat for his briefcase, he opened it and removed his laptop, making room on the console between them. Typing Spencer's name and Ester Road into the search box, her name, address and occupation appeared. The rest of the entry was interesting enough for him to read aloud. "*Proprietor: Private Gentleman's Club?* With a question mark following? How fascinating!" he exclaimed.

Perhaps I should tell you something else," Emma said hesitantly. "It's a thought that came to me while reading those papers today." James looked up at her but let her continue. "They were all Crusaders."

"Crusaders?" he repeated. "What the devil does that mean, my lady?"

"I feel it means that all the ancient knightly orders are combining their efforts to find the lost regalia. All that trouble in Yorkshire with the silent monks and the rumour that the regalia had been found, has probably brought them out of hiding."

"Do you really think that?" James asked, in a doubting tone, closing his laptop and starting the car. "Watch the numbers, my lady, when I cross the street, we'll be on Ester Road."

Traffic was light and he drove slowly, so she could read the street numbers. When Emma cried, "Stop!" James seemed to ignore her and carried on for a short distance before pulling up to the curb. "You passed it back there, you turkey."

Laughing, he replied, "What did you call me?"

"Oh nothing, it's just that we now have to walk back through those old piles of snow and it's snowing again and slippery," she complained.

This was an area of mainly beautiful old stone mansions and they couldn't help but notice that attached to many of the door posts of these once private residences, were shiny, brass name plates engraved with a business name and attempting to add an element of class.

James stared in disbelief as he read the nameplate at Number 81, "K.C. Private Gentleman's Club. My word! Do you think that could stand for Knights and Crusaders?" he whispered. "Stay there, I'll be right back," he said, not waiting for her reply as he hurried back to the car. He got his briefcase and returned. "Now, let's see if we've found a can of worms," he muttered, pushing the doorbell.

They heard the lock click, then a safety chain snapped tight before part of an old man's face with a deep male voice came through the slightly open door. "State your business, this is a private club!"

"Open the door!" James roared. "I'm the Commissioner of Police. Can you read my warrant card?"

The chain rattled as the safety catch was removed and the door closed. Without waiting to see if the door was going to re-open, James gave it a push. The door opened, and stepping inside, they saw a man of about 70 years, dressed in the coat and tails of a butler, backing hurriedly away.

"I want to speak to the manager!" James demanded, as they entered a sumptuously decorated and carpeted foyer.

Glancing around, Emma noted the reception desk and furnishings were from a past era, as was the beautifully embossed wallpaper.

"You are intruding on private property, sir!" said another older, well-dressed gentleman of large stature as he came towards them through a nearby doorway. "Oblige me by removing yourselves immediately!" His face was becoming a blotchy red colour, no doubt due to his laboured breathing. His handlebar mustache twitched as he glowered at the commissioner.

"Shut up!" James barked, holding his police warrant card under the man's nose. Snatching the card, the man stared at it with an expression of disgust, producing some glasses from his pocket. More carefully scrutinizing the warrant, he glowered at James as he handed it back.

"I would like to check your register and your recent bookings," James barked.

"You'll need a search warrant and legal authority to do that, sir. You don't appear to have either, thus I'm going to call our solicitor."

"Do that, but rest assured I do have legal authority as this club is part of an ongoing investigation," James bluffed.

Producing his cell phone, James pressed a button and almost immediately someone answered. "Simon, it's the commissioner, I need two units to 81 Ester Road immediately." The two protagonists locked eyes and James snapped at him again. "Don't you think you should ring that solicitor of yours before they arrive?"

"Damn you!" the old man snorted, going to a cupboard and opening a drawer. He produced two large, gilt-edged ledgers, each identified by a label with gold lettering. He appeared to handle the ledgers with extra care as he placed them in front of the commissioner.

James opened the register at the location marked with a long, thin, bronze bookmark and glanced down the list of recently registered people.

"Make me a list of all the guests who checked in this past week and are still here," he instructed Emma, handing her a notepad and a pen. As he moved his attention to the reservations book, he quickly made some notes on his own pad. He glanced at the Canadian as she handed him her notes, then turned his attention back to the manager who was waiting nervously behind the counter.

"Now Mr. …?" When the man didn't divulge his name, James continued. "Give me two sheets of your letterhead and we will be on our way."

Looking likely to object, the manager, however, did not disappoint, hesitating long enough to hear sirens coming closer until they seemed to stop outside. Within seconds, four burly policemen hurriedly entered the front door.

"You need us, commissioner?" a bearded sergeant bellowed.

"No, sergeant, this man has decided to assist us. You may escort the lady outside."

As she had expected, fresh snow now made walking difficult as they left the stately home. The commissioner directed one of the young constables to escort Emma to the car, handing him the keys before he went to talk to the sergeant. Emma took the arm of the good-looking young man, this time enjoying the walk and thanking the constable profusely. When James appeared, he obviously had things on his mind as he silently negotiated the busy afternoon traffic through Edinburgh.

"So what did you think to that little adventure?" Emma asked as they turned towards Stirling.

"It seems you were right, but now I'm puzzled how you worked it out."

"Sheer genius, my boy," she replied, keeping her thoughts to herself.

"All four of the passengers had reservations to stay at that club. Did you find anything suspicious in the register?"

"Yes, I did actually; Monsignor Sharp was also a guest."

"He was!" James exclaimed. "Were you expecting that?"

"No, I was as surprised as you are, but I got the feeling he had to be meeting someone important."

Darkness had fallen and a clear, star-filled sky to the north was an obvious indication that there would be no more snow tonight although frost was clearly in the air by the time they neared their destination. James suddenly laughed. "It was that phone call to the tea shop in Paisley, wasn't it?"

"Yes," she admitted. "Moira said the monsignor had gone missing and Mitch Pooley had told her that he was going to meet the pope!"

"So it may have been true, in a manner of speaking but I don't believe any of the crash victims was a pope." Rubbing his face, he sighed and pulled into the hospital car park. At that moment, Emma remembered her date with Alex. At a second floor window, Nurse Brown, detailed by Sir Alex to keep a lookout, frowned as she waited for a taxi to arrive.

Dressing as best he could in his own clothes and with a blanket over his legs, Alex sat in his wheelchair waiting patiently for Emma to arrive. He once again examined the table setting he had ordered for his dinner party. Set for two, the small table looked superb, with a lace tablecloth and the catering firm's best china and silverware service. He had used this firm often when entertaining at his apartment and they had outdone themselves tonight. He grinned when he noticed the whisky bottle. When Nurse Brown entered with the news that the commissioner was with Lady Traymore, Alex began giving orders again.

"Call the kitchen and tell the caterers we have an extra guest, and then come help me out of this blasted chair!"

She hurriedly made the phone call and had just set her patient onto his crutches when quick footsteps and Lady Traymore's infectious giggle were heard in the hallway.

"Alex!" Emma beamed when she saw him standing, and rushed over to stop in front of him, a look of despair appearing on her face. "I want to hug you but I don't know if I should!"

"Come here, you wonderful woman, I've been waiting for you all day!" he whispered with a catch in his voice. Emma moved to save his crutches but they clattered to the floor.

"You can stand!" Emma commented jubilantly but then noticed how embarrassed he was as she helped him to get his balance while Nurse Brown picked up the crutches. Emma got out of their way and went over to the table. His frustration was obvious as he handed the crutches to Nurse Brown then awkwardly sat down. He tried to elevate his leg but winced as it dropped to the floor. He regained his composure and beckoned to his guests.

"Come, come join me quickly!" he called, "Dinner will be arriving momentarily. Check on the food, Nurse Brown."

"They're coming, sir, I can smell the fresh coffee," she replied from the doorway. Sure enough two uniformed servers pushing a heated food trolley entered the room. One of them adjusted the table setting while the other poured the coffee. Serving dinner from the trolley, they asked if the guests had everything they needed and then they left. The nurse asked if she could be excused and said she would return in half an hour.

"Take an hour, dear, then come check on us," Emma called after her.

The dinner party was a great success as conversation and laughter flowed easily between the friends. When Emma gave a vivid description of James arguing with the manager at the Gentleman's Club, Alex laughed heartily and wanted every detail. When Nurse Brown returned for the third time, it was almost 8:30 and she insisted it was time for them to leave so her patient could get ready for bed.

Driving back to Edinburgh, the weather was clear and dry now allowing a wonderful view of twinkling lights across the Scottish skies. Conversation crept around to Alex's return home and his inability to drive.

"He'll have some plan in mind," Emma assured James, so he left it alone, busy with his own thoughts about the Ester Road club.

"What made you and Alex suspect Monsignor Sharp was involved?"

"He was always snooping around, watching us, and when Mitch Pooley told us he posted a letter every day, we became very suspicious. The real mystery then became, who was he reporting to?"

"And how did you solve that little problem?"

"That's our secret, Mr. MacDonald."

"It's illegal to steal letters from the sorting station you know," he said, smiling knowingly. He was pretty sure how they had done it but that would all come out in good time.

"We did no such thing, sir!" she declared.

As they pulled into the car park at the *Courtyard Inn*, James suggested a nightcap.

"I will, if you truthfully answer one question for me," she replied.

"Now Emma, when have I ever lied to you, my lady?"

"My, I don't understand how you can do your job so well with such a poor memory! Have you forgotten this morning already ... when you left me alone in your office with all those important papers! I know you were spying on me ...."

"I certainly did not!" he interrupted. "I saw you by accident."

"You're not scoring any points, Mr. MacDonald. Would you know what I meant, if I asked you if you were on the square, commissioner?"

"Yes," James replied hesitantly, "you're asking if I'm a Freemason, and the answer is 'no.'"

"That's why you didn't notice the unusual way a capital 'A' was written on all four sets of those papers you collected from the crash victims. Yes, I will accept that drink now!" she laughed.

Finding the *Hunting Bar* packed to the doors, James led the way around a corner to a carefully hidden room behind a camouflaged door. Emma was delighted, for as they entered, she realized it was a private dining room with only a small number of intimate booths. There were no TVs in sight and subdued music and lighting gave it the desired ambiance, the latter barely allowing a hint to the patrons' identities. A statuesque blonde indicated they should follow her.

Entering a booth, they ordered drinks from a flashlight-carrying waitress. "So, what do you think?" he whispered

"Where the devil have you brought me now, James? This is certainly a private little corner." She looked around, then hesitating, asked, "Do you think Sir Alex has ever been in here?"

Now it was James' turn to chuckle. "We call this the Moon Room for obvious reasons, and I have my doubts about that!" His hand reached across the table to hers, which she quickly slapped ... more sharply than intended. Instant giggles emanated from nearby patrons.

"You were explaining about the Masonic symbols, my lady. How do you know so much about the Masons?"

"I just happen to have read Stephen Knight's book, *The Brotherhood*. A very informative book, you should read it!"

"Actually, I have, some time ago, and I agree completely."

Finishing their drinks, Emma stifled a yawn and, as they left the Moon Room, she tried to ignore the other patrons. He left her outside the lift on her floor after they'd arranged to meet for breakfast at nine.

Exhausted, she got ready for bed and went to stand for a few minutes looking out at her now familiar night scene. Thoughts of Mary again crept into her mind and, as she slipped into bed, she told herself she needed sleep. As she drifted off to sleep involuntary tears wet her pillow.

A startled awakening and a wet pillow helped Emma recall the realistic dream that had just broken her sleep in which Mary Wallace had called her to the graveside and touched her hand.

*You have the answer within your grasp*, Mary had whispered gratefully as a chilling breeze brushed Emma's face but, of course, Emma could not understand.

## Chapter 20 – Tuesday 5<sup>th</sup> – James MacDonald

Shaking at the realism of this new dream, she then stumbled through dressing, made a cup of tea and tried to apply her make-up, but her hands would not stop shaking. Sitting down, she held her hands up to examine them and was acutely aware that the sensation of Mary's cold flesh on her own still persisted. Switching the TV on to the early news, in an attempt to change her focus, did not work; her mind was not yet prepared to release her from this vivid dream experience.

"You didn't sleep well," James commented when she joined him.

"How perceptive of you!" she whispered. "I must look a wreck. I dreamed of Mary Wallace again last night, as I so often do. It was so realistic I woke up in a sweat."

"What time would you like to go to Stirling today?"

"Let's leave it until later," she murmured as the waitress arrived with coffee and a menu, adding a recommendation of the mushroom omelette. Relieved to have that decision taken care of, Emma ordered.

"I think you need a rest today or, at least, a change of pace. Why don't you let me show you my Edinburgh?"

"That would be ideal but I thought that's what you did last night, James," and they both laughed.

"Touché, my lady!"

"All right, let's just wander, it looks quite nice outside, and the stars were profuse last night in case you didn't notice. The views from my windows are absolutely marvellous, especially when it's dark."

"We'd best wrap up warm though if we are out of the car. Although it's sunny, there's a nip in the air."

Christmas was not far away now and shops and businesses were decorated in Christmas colours and lights. As they walked, they window-shopped, admiring the decorations and sometimes going into the stores. She was beginning to realize how much fun James could be when not playing the lawman.

They stopped in front of the National Gallery to admire the architecture, but decided not to go in. A passing taxi driver stopped to suggest to them it was too cold to be walking and, for a minimal charge, he could drive them up to the castle. Intrigued by his brogue and enterprising spirit, Emma quickly agreed, tugging James into the taxi.

"I thought it was illegal to solicit a fare," James admonished the driver once they were seated.

"Oh no, sir," the man assured him with a chuckle, "not if you don't get caught."

"True," James replied, also chuckling, as he withdrew his wallet and removed a £5 note and his business card. Emma watched as he folded them together. When they arrived at the castle entrance and got out of the taxi, James handed it to the driver and they smugly walked away.

"I'll bet you've just made that man's day," Emma laughed. "I'd like to see the look on his face when he reads your card!"

"You have to have fun sometimes," James laughed, "but now I have something to show you. Come and look at this plaque."

Taking her arm, he led her over to the eastern corner of the wall, where a brass plaque had been placed over a small well. Details on the plaque explained that this was the place where more than 300 women had been burned as witches.

"Touch the wall, Emma," he insisted, stepping back a few steps. "Can you feel their vibes? I'm sure some of these women were your ancestors!" Emma turned around and swung her handbag at him, but he yelped and was soon out of reach as they both burst into laughter.

"You, you …!" she searched for the words, making a face at him.

"Stop!" James laughed. "You shouldn't get too excited; remember you're not well today."

"I'm fairly certain I could raise enough energy to strangle you!"

"Okay, let's have a truce for a couple of hours and I'll promise to be nice."

Glancing at her watch, she nodded and suggested he could show her the crown jewels. He took her arm and led her across the drawbridge to stand beneath the statue of a knight in armour.

"This is another of your relatives, Emma," James murmured.

Emma was mesmerized by the larger-than-life figure in stone guarding one side of the entrance on the castle wall above her. Sir William Wallace was every inch a fierce, foreboding figure. When she looked away from the statue, James turned her around and pointed to a second stone warrior at the opposite side of the entrance.

"That one is King Robert I, Scotland's warrior king and I believe he turned out to be very important to the Walters' Family as well."

"Yes, I'm somewhat familiar with Robert the Bruce from Sir Alex's history lessons. I wouldn't want to meet either of them in a dark alley!" They never smiled much in those days, did they?" Taking her camera from her handbag, she handed it to James. "Take a picture of me with King Robert, James." Suddenly, the wind blew her hair about her face and he laughed at her antics.

"There you are, my lady, windblown and all!" He waved her over to Wallace's statue and after taking another photo, hand back her camera. "Maybe they didn't smile because they had little to smile about, my lady. They were very hard times as you no doubt realize by now," he said sympathetically, as if he was remembering them from personal experience. A shiver seemed to bring him back to the present. "Come Emma; let me get you out of this cold wind. It's time to go see the *Scottish Crown Jewels*."

James felt her arm link his and they hurried across Castle Square, their breath floating by as vapour in the freezing air.

"It's too blasted cold to sightsee today, we'll go directly to the vaults where it will be somewhat warmer," he shouted above the wind, pointing to the sign that said *Vaults*.

"I think I would rather wait for summer, James," she protested, shivering as they hurried past signs that announced *Palace*, *War Memorial*, *Great Hall*, *Museum* and *Prison*. Stepping inside, the air was noticeably warmer and Emma audibly caught her breath upon seeing the display signed as the *Honours of Scotland*. James watched her intently. Comprised of the Scottish Regalia and Crown Jewels from the 15th and 16th centuries, the breathtaking simplicity of these old items held Emma spellbound as she thought of all the history these crown, sceptors and jewels had seen over so many centuries. Sculptured in Scottish gold, pearls and precious jewels, the crown exuded an aura of power that sent a shiver down her spine when she realized that the missing regalia was from a time a great deal earlier. Reading most of the signs until she began feeling cold, she finally shivered and then heard James' voice beside her.

"I believe it's lunch time, my lady."

She agreed and allowed herself to be silently led back through the ramparts but she knew now that she must return. James acquired a taxi and they were grateful to be out of the wind. Paying little attention to the direction they were taking, Emma was quite surprised when they pulled up to the curb in George Street.

"It's a surprise," James confessed, as they walked around the corner.

"I'm going to introduce you to Alex's girlfriend," he grinned. "So please behave yourself or Alex will be quite annoyed. We both eat here quite often."

Emma recognized Molly Dugan's tiny café from her and Alex's visit but not wanting to spoil James' surprise, she decided to play along.

Molly's voice called a welcome as they stepped inside the door, asking them to wait a moment while she cleared a table. Beckoning them over, they were seated before she disappeared into the kitchen. Molly quickly returned with two coffees and shocked the commissioner when she greeted Emma with a little curtsey and addressed her as Lady Traymore. They quickly decided on the special.

"I assume Sir Alex already brought you here," he whispered.

"Yes, he has," she whispered back with a rueful smile.

Lunchtime was hectic but they were well looked after by a young waitress. The café had almost cleared out before Molly returned and sat down with a heavy sigh.

"I see you've swapped one scallywag for another!" she laughed. "What did you do with the other one?"

"Oh, he's in hospital with a broken leg. James ran over him with a police car," Emma said nonchalantly, adding a wink. She added quickly, "I believe he was jealous!"

"You did what?" Molly feigned anger, waving a chubby fist at James. "If you've hurt me lad!"

"Hold it, hold it," the commissioner interrupted. "I didn't run over him, Molly, he had an accident with a police car about 1 a.m. on Saturday morning. It was during the snap freeze in Stirling. You, young lady …," he said pointing at Emma, "I thought we had a truce to be nice to each other?"

"We did, but you said a truce for two hours. That was at 11 o'clock, it's now almost three!"

Looking around the tea shop first, James got up and went over to Emma and settled slowly onto one knee, trying to conceal his smile.

"Forgive me, my lady," he begged, "please don't have me beheaded!"

"Glory be!" Molly gasped. "Do something, my lady; if a customer comes in they'll think we've gone totally doo-lally!"

"As you wish, Molly, that sounds much too serious to ignore!" Emma exclaimed. She reached over and picked up the extra dinner knife in front of Molly and, trying to conceal her mirth, turned to the still-kneeling commissioner. She tapped him on each shoulder with the knife and declared, "Rise, Sir Knight, all is forgiven … if you will pay our bill!"

Dutifully, James got up, picked up the bill and helped Emma with her coat. Then, continuing their charade, he asked reverently, "Shall I order a carriage, my lady?"

"I believe we can walk, kind sir, my home is nearby!"

Molly watched in fascination, giggling at their antics, but was relieved when they had gone.

James left her at the hotel saying he would return at 2 p.m and on entering the foyer, Megan called to her.

"There was a package left for you this morning, Lady Traymore. Let me get it." She reappeared quickly with a large flat box and slid it across the counter. Emma picked it up and looked for a return address but there was none, only her name and *Courtyard Inn*.

"Who delivered this?" she asked. "Was it a courier service?"

"I don't believe so, my lady. He was not in uniform. Is everything all right?"

"I wasn't expecting it, that's all," said Emma. "Thank you."

She was in the room and preparing to take a shower when the phone rang. The desk clerk told her the police commissioner's office was on the line.

"Tell him to call back in 15 minutes," she said. "I'm in the shower."

At police headquarters, James MacDonald was informed by a grinning young constable that Lady Traymore was in the shower and wouldn't be available for 15 minutes.

Preoccupied, James nodded, though frowning, as he continued to stare at the open package and its contents now lying on his desk. The box had gone through building security so he knew it was safe but it had him mystified. No note or identification accompanied the package. A blank sheet of paper containing a crudely drawn Gaelic cross, and two items … a protractor and a carpenter's set square. Picking up the phone, he ordered his assistant to connect him with Director Dunstan at the National Archives.

"You have a problem, James," said John, after his friend finished describing the package and its contents. "You've ruffled some feathers, my friend. Are you working on a case that involves the Christian Brotherhood?"

"Not that I'm aware of, but it's possible someone under my jurisdiction is. Are you talking about the Freemasons?"

"Yes and no, I'm talking about copycat groups who refer to themselves as 'Templars.' The lodges have amalgamated over the centuries and only a very few modern groups remain, thank goodness," John explained.

"Is this a warning … to me?" James asked solemnly.

"No, I don't believe it's a warning really. I'd speculate they're making you aware that they are watching."

"Who's watching? There's no identification anywhere on this package."

"Come, James, you know what people do, that adds to the fear factor, my friend. Why don't we meet for dinner so we can talk about it."

"Sorry John, I'm taking Lady Traymore out to Stirling at 5:30, maybe some other time. We'll talk soon."

In her room, Emma was getting dressed when the phone rang and James told her he would be held up for 15 mins. On hanging up, she remembered the parcel on the hall chair. She took it to the kitchen and used a knife to cut through the tape. Almost finished, she felt a strange sensation run down her spine.

*That's odd*, she thought suddenly feeling quite cold so she went to put on her robe. She finished cutting the tape, and then began to open the lid. *I wonder if I should wait for James. No, I may not want him to see this.*

"Freemasons," she whispered when she recognized the Masonic symbols which had been drawn on a sheet of paper. Seeing something else, she lifted the plastic packing and drew out two items, the same that were in the drawing … a protractor and a carpenter's set square. She got her briefcase and put the items and the paper inside and went back to finish getting ready.

Leaving her room, she heard a noisy group of guests waiting at the lift and chose the stairs. Being five minutes late, she checked the bar first. Finding no sign of James, she turned back to the foyer and saw Alex's black car pull up slowly to the door.

Losing no time, James quickly had them on their way to Stirling. Deep in thought, he offered little conversation until Emma spoke.

"Has something happened, James, you're very quiet?"

"Yes, something has," he replied thinking how perceptive she was. "I had a package waiting for me at the office."

"I did as well. Do you think someone is sending us a warning?"

"I presume you got a protractor and a set square?" he asked.

"Yes, the Masonic symbols."

"I called John Dunstan and he says it's a bit deeper than that; he thinks it's the Templars."

Sliding on the icy road as they neared Stirling, brought an end to the discussion and Emma breathed a sigh of relief when they pulled into the hospital's car park.

Alex's angry voice could be heard as they left the lift. Hurrying along the corridor, Emma realized that both Nurse Brown and Dr. Greare were also involved in the argument. Hanging back a little, James allowed Emma to charge into the fray.

"Stop this right now!" Emma hissed looking from the doctor to Alex and noting her bailiff was dressed in pants, shirt and a tie. He was balancing himself on his crutches as he leaned against the wall.

"I will not sign any discharge papers," Dr. Greare argued, keeping well out of range of Sir Alex's swinging crutch.

Nurse Brown had evidence of tears on her face as she pleaded with Sir Alex to calm down.

Trying to keep a straight face, the police commissioner stayed by the door and waited for Lady Traymore to react.

"Sir Alex, sit down!" she scolded him. "If you wave that infernal crutch at me, I'll break your other leg!"

Lady Traymore's reaction caused both Nurse Brown and the doctor to look distinctly uncomfortable. It also stopped them talking and James moved a chair closer to Alex and held it firmly until he sat down.

"Now," Emma said calmly, "will someone please tell me what this is all about ... Nurse Brown?"

"Yes, my lady," the nurse said hesitantly. "Sir Alex wishes to go home with you today and Dr. Greare says he has to stay until tomorrow, as previously arranged."

Nodding thoughtfully, Emma turned to Dr. Greare. "No doubt you have something to say, doctor," she said quietly, "but be aware, sir, that Sir Alex is a private patient. I was not aware he was scheduled to come home tomorrow so I hardly think tonight would be an imposition for you or the hospital. Surely, you can use the bed? Besides, he is getting around very nicely on his own and as a private patient, I see no reason ...."

"I insist he stays!" Dr. Greare interrupted.

"Dr. Greare," Emma's voice snapped her own interruption, "pomposity will get you nowhere with me. Just give me a good reason why you would want to keep Sir Alex another night. I would think you would be happy to see the back of him!" She made a face, trying not to smile.

"It's customary to release a patient earlier in the day," said the doctor.

"I said a good reason, not an excuse, sir," Emma objected. "I require a medical reason or we're taking him now!"

Staring at the floor, Dr. Greare moved slowly towards the door, muttering incoherently. James stood nearby trying to look appropriately serious.

"Am I fired too, my lady?" Nurse Brown whispered, dabbing at a tear.

"Certainly not, please help him get ready and get your things as well nurse, you can go with us. I believe he will still require care for awhile."

"But I live in Stirling, my lady."

"Would you be willing to come to Edinburgh and take care of Sir Alex until his leg heals?"

"Oh yes, my lady, but I will require some time off as looking after my flat from a distance will be somewhat difficult."

"Do you have a family, a pet to feed or your own car?"

"No, my lady, just myself and I don't drive."

"Not to worry then, you can arrange it with Sir Alex as you go. I am grateful that you are able to stay with him and we'll take care of any expense and transportation as needed. We'll take you by your flat when we leave here so you can pick up anything you require and water your plants, if need be. Do you live closeby?"

"Yes, about two kilometres, my lady."

"Excellent! Then it's all settled, we'll leave you to get Sir Alex ready for travelling and we'll wait outside in the corridor. One more thing, Nurse Brown, may we call you by your first name at least when you're not working? I heard Sir Alex call you Mabel."

"Thank you, my lady, certainly," she replied, curtseying slightly.

Alex insisted that he was going to walk out to the car. James took his bag and went to bring the car closer to the door. At Nurse Brown's insistence, however, they used a wheelchair. Under James' watchful eye, Alex was soon settled in the front seat, out of breath, but happy, and with leg room to spare. Minutes later they arrived at Mabel's tidy little row house on the outskirts of the city.

"Have you had dinner yet?" Emma asked Alex as they waited for her.

"No, that row had been going on for awhile before you got there."

"Where would you like to eat?" asked James.

"The *Rogue's Inn* would be a pleasant change," he growled.

James glanced sharply at Emma. "I haven't seen Frank Costello for over a year."

"You know him, too!" she replied, showing only mild surprise. "Then, I would say, it's a perfect choice."

"I agree, James introduced Trevelion and me to Frank many years ago," Alex explained as Mabel returned to the car with a suitcase. James got out and stowed it in the boot.

"Do you take holidays, Mabel?" James asked over his shoulder as they drove out of Stirling.

"Oh no, sir, I don't often get away from Stirling and travel is very dear!"

"You've not always lived in Stirling?" asked Emma.

"Oh yes, my lady, I was born in Stirling. I sometimes go places on the bus but it's been some time now. I prefer to stay home on days off."

Intrigued by this young woman, James continued his gentle interrogation, to the amusement of Alex and Emma. They soon established that Mabel had never been south of the border. "I've been to Edinburgh and Glasgow," she admitted with pride, as James pulled up to the *Rogue's Inn*.

Leaving James to help Alex, Emma took Mabel's arm and led her into the luxurious establishment. Behind them they could hear the men's laughter as they came into the building.

"Shouldn't we help them, my lady?" Mabel asked, turning around to check on them but Emma held onto her arm.

"I think they're managing just fine Mabel and enjoying each other's company! They're very good friends, you know." Emma noticed the young woman's surprise as she looked around at the sumptuous surroundings but she hurried her past the bar area to the restaurant. Noticed immediately as they entered, the genial Texan host showed them to a booth against the wall, which had a view of the whole restaurant and particularly the magnificent crystal chandelier. Mabel was obviously impressed by the splendour of the room.

"What drinks may I get for you ladies?" Frank asked, adding, "Your usual, Lady Traymore?" He didn't notice the men coming up behind him.

"A coffee for you, Mabel?" Emma asked, watching her nod half-heartedly, her eyes flashing about the room as Emma ordered the four coffees.

"Four coffees?" Tex repeated, turning to look behind him as Alex and James arrived. Stepping back in surprise, he watched Alex hop closer.

"What the hell's happened to you, laddie, and who is this rogue you've brought with you!" Holding out his hand, he and James shared a hearty handshake. "Hello James, it's been awhile."

"Frank, meet Alex's nurse, Mabel Brown. We sprung him a bit early and he badly needs your kind of food!" Emma exclaimed. "Oh, and to answer your question, one of James' police cars ran over him early Saturday morning," Emma added with a giggle, suddenly realizing how much pleasure she received by saying those words.

Frank set down the drinks and grinned, recognizing Emma's playful manner. He passed around the menus, explained the evening specials, and then left them to decide.

As dinner progressed, several couples came and went until they were the only ones left and Tex found time to join them, although carefully avoiding the subject of the missing regalia. He was surprised when Emma suddenly asked James if he had his package with him and the conversation quickly changed.

"No," he murmured staring at her with a puzzled expression.

"Mine is in my briefcase in the boot of the car, could you get it for me please," she asked.

Alex waited until James had left and asked, "Has something happened, my lady?"

"Yes, something has," Emma chuckled, "and Frank is just the man to explain its significance." She quickly mentioned the boxes she and James had received, before James returned to the table.

When James returned, he set the briefcase on the floor beside her and then sat down. Removing two items, she put them on the table covering them with the drawing face down. Emma looked around the empty restaurant before turning over the paper and showing it to Alex and then handing it to Frank.

"Now, what do you make of that, Mr. Costello?" she asked.

Alex picked up the two items and Frank watched thoughtfully.

"In my opinion, that's a warning from the Crusaders!" Frank exclaimed. "They're telling you you're being watched."

"Why would the Crusaders be concerned about us?" Emma asked in a puzzled voice, her eyes searching the faces around the table. "I thought they were the good guys of medieval history."

"No, even back in medieval times this was not necessarily true, and now the term is used in a completely different manner. I once had to give evidence against a man who we later learned was a Templar," Frank growled bitterly. "The judge tore me to pieces, threw the case out of court, and literally suggested I should be jailed for even thinking the man was a crook."

"The judge was a Crusader," Alex muttered.

"Tell them about the air crash victims, James," Emma coaxed.

"My lady," Mabel interrupted hesitantly, "I don't understand what this conversation is about and I'm thinking I shouldn't be hearing it. You're making me a bit nervous."

"It's all right, Mabel, there's no need for you to be nervous, we are not giving away any government secrets. If you ever repeat a word of it to anyone, however, we shall have you beheaded!"

Frank, James and Alex watched poor Mabel's reaction to Emma's warning—first of shock and then turning so pale Alex patted her hand.

"Just ignore them," he reassured his nurse. "Please stop frightening the poor girl, my lady. She has enough to contend with from me!"

"Yes, the air crash in Edinburgh," James interrupted looking thoughtful. "It was a chartered aircraft from the Channel Islands, flying from Malta to Edinburgh when something malfunctioned. It crashed onto the exhibition grounds killing all occupants. Naturally, an investigation has begun to find out who they were and to notify the next of kin. Briefcases were found and examined; one of them was even chained to a man's wrist, but now comes the important part of this mystery. Each one of those briefcases carried papers which contained references to our friends here, Sir Alex and Lady Traymore. I am still trying to ascertain why this could be possible and up to now these two," he nodded at both Alex and Emma, "have given me no satisfactory explanation."

"Don't be ridiculous, Mr. MacDonald," Emma snapped, "you're supposed to be the detective. We're waiting for you to inform us."

During the continuing discussion, Frank offered no further opinion and it soon came time for them to leave.

As they drove towards Edinburgh, Mabel suddenly asked, "What hotel am I staying at tonight?"

"You're not staying at a hotel, dear; you were employed to take care of Sir Alex," Emma replied casually, offering no further explanation.

James couldn't suppress a chuckle as he waited for her to elaborate. He tried to see Emma's face in the rearview mirror but it was too dark. Alex knew exactly what she was up to.

"Oh no, you don't," he objected and James began to laugh.

"Oh yes, she is. You have two beautiful guest rooms, Sir Alex, and your apartment needs people. How else can she take care of you?" Emma pointed out. "You'll love it, Mabel!"

Alex tried to turn around in his seat but gave it up and pleaded, "Tell her you won't stay with me, Mabel."

"I can't do that, sir," Mabel objected, smiling in the dark at Emma. "If Lady Traymore says I must, so I must."

"She's not Mother Teresa," Alex snapped back at her. "You don't have to give her blind obedience!"

"Mabel," Emma said calmly, patting her leg. "I will give you written permission to push him off the penthouse balcony if he gives you any trouble!"

"Penthouse … oh my! I mean, no, my lady," Mabel objected. "I shall give Sir Alex every consideration he is entitled to."

"Exactly," Emma laughed, "but when your remedy doesn't work dear, try mine!"

Pulling up to their apartment building, James switched the engine off and briefly collapsed over the steering wheel laughing. Then he got out and opened Mabel's door before going around to assist his friend.

No matter how hard Alex complained, he was ignored and Emma soon had Nurse Brown installed in one of the guest rooms. James, being familiar with the apartment and all its technology, showed her the coffee machine and where all the necessary things as well as the liquor cabinet, etc. It all seemed to confuse the poor girl causing a dreadful expression of helplessness to invade her countenance and Emma intervened.

"Don't look so worried, Mabel, as long as you get the coffee made in the morning, Sir Alex can help you with all the rest and James lives next door in an emergency."

James drove Emma back to the hotel, and as he opened her car door they were surprised to hear a clock booming the midnight hour.

"I shall need a driver tomorrow," Emma commented before leaving him. "Did Sir Alex talk to you about that, James?"

"I thought all you Canadians drove," James replied.

"Of course we do, but you people drive on the wrong side of the road. I think it's better if I let someone else look after it."

"You're afraid!"

"Don't be silly, I'm being practical."

"Tomorrow, my lady, you will be picked up by a sergeant driving instructor and at the end of the day you will be competent to drive on the wrong side of the road! Did I ask if you had a Canadian driving licence?"

"Yes, I have a licence, and I can also hire my own driver."

"I have sworn to my mother that I will look after you. Remember those men in the plane, who can you trust?"

## Chapter 21 – Wednesday 6<sup>th</sup> – Grave Complications

Commissioner MacDonald's parting comment was the one that kept Emma awake, pacing the floor until she hoped sleep would rescue her. James was right—who could she trust? Completely exhausted, she finally went to bed and fell asleep, only to have Mary wake her again. She was pulled out of her dream so quickly she jumped out of bed, believing that Mary was sending her a message that something was wrong. It was sometime before she was able to return to sleep. The sound of the alarm at 7:30 almost gave her a heart attack.

Fortunately, she was totally unaware that out at Misty House things were becoming complicated as Ruth and the men had discovered some confusing information in one of the pouches. It was contained in an interment document that stated clearly it was from Elderslie. It also had the same grave numbers and similar scribbled notations as the earlier one they were hoping was Mary's grave. They wondered if someone had deliberately created a decoy.

Back in Edinburgh, expecting to be eating breakfast alone, Emma was pleasantly surprised when she walked into the dining room and found Alex at their table reading his newspaper.

"Good morning, my lady," he welcomed her, smiling brightly.

"And how did you get here, laddie?"

"I was driven here by your driving instructor on James' instructions! I've given Mabel the day off but told her she could join us here for dinner or return to the apartment. She chose the latter … I think she likes my place! She said she'd see me at home and not to rush on her account.

During breakfast Alex gave her the news. "I had a call this morning from Ruth Oxley, she had called the hospital so was pleased to hear we are coming this morning. They are eager to show us two promising records they've found." He realized he had not had the chance to tell her of Ruth's first frantic phone call, and now made the judgement call not to complicate the situation. "Also," he continued, "after James took you home last night, he came back to see me and told me about his plan to provide you with a driving instructor." Seeing her grimace, he added, "Actually, I think it's a brilliant idea and I told him so, especially because we will want to go to Misty House. He also told me what you thought of his pride and joy."

Emma's head came up sharply. "His pride and joy?"

"His Land Rover!"

"Oh cripes, that's a monster as far as I'm concerned!"

"Well, you won't have to ride in it again. We'll be using our car from now on and, if you pass this road test today, we will be on our own again and that would be splendid, Emma. I hope you consider that makes it worth the effort."

"You're right, Alex, that will be the best part."

"Well no, I think you're wrong. You could also be free of me at that point and go off on your own. We may never see each other again!"

She laughed. "I guess I hadn't thought that far ahead, but I do believe that is still in the distant future! I have no idea how to get anywhere. So, we are going to Misty House now, are we?" she asked.

"We are, so you could go get yourself ready and I'll get Sgt. McLean to help me shuffle into the car. We'll meet you outside."

Grinning, he got to his feet, easily adjusted his crutches and walked slowly over to the cashier's desk, knowing she was watching him. When he finished paying the bill, he realized she had already left him to go upstairs. He took his time going outside where Sgt. McLean was waiting. Having already tested his method for getting in and out of the back seat on the way here for breakfast, Alex knew exactly what to do.

"Take your time sir," the sergeant advised him. "We're lucky this is a large car." Alex managed it quite smoothly and the sergeant complimented him. "There you have it sir, perfectly manoeuvred and with little discomfort."

Emma arrived just in time to see the casted leg disappear and went to investigate. "That's marvellous, Sir Alex, is it very painful?" she asked with concern.

"He managed it all on his own, my lady, and he didn't even grimace! Good morning, I'm Sgt. Roy McLean, your driving instructor for the day. I'm told you've never driven on the left side of the road, my lady?"

The sergeant's statement went unanswered as Emma opened the front door and began to get in but the sergeant acted more quickly.

"No, my lady! You will be doing the driving!" He held the door to prevent her from closing it.

"Later perhaps," she replied sharply, not moving.

"I'm sorry, my lady, but the police commissioner's orders were that you are to do the driving today," the sergeant insisted.

"Are you hard of hearing Sgt. McLean?" Emma locked her eyes on the policeman and tucked her coat around her legs.

"Lady Traymore," Roy McLean's voice snapped, "you are wasting our time and yours. This car is going nowhere unless you are driving it!"

Surprised by the police sergeant's manner, she extracted herself slowly from the car and glowered at him. When he unexpectedly winked, she dropped her eyes and went around to the driver's side. He opened the door and she got behind the wheel.

He delivered a short synopsis on the basic rules of British roads and told her to do a three-point-turn in the car park. When he complimented her on her skill, she had to turn away so he didn't see her smile.

"Sir Alex tells me you wish to go to Misty House today, my lady," the sergeant murmured. "Do you know the way or would you like me to talk you through it?"

"It would be helpful if you were to talk me through it, please," she said quietly. "Do you know Misty House?"

"Yes, my lady, my daughter Janet is a resident there. It's a wonderful place. Ruth Oxley is the closest thing to an angel my family will ever know."

The roads were a bit damp and Emma was very glad to leave Edinburgh and get onto the motorway. Negotiating roundabouts was not her favourite pastime and the ones in Scotland were huge in comparison to home. She was appreciating Sgt. McLean's well-explained instructions and comments as they drove up the M9 watching for the Falkirk exit. The men chatted from time-to-time. All of a sudden, Sgt. McLean's phone vibrated in his pocket.

"Yes, sir, she's doing just fine, as you thought she would, commissioner!" Emma made a face but kept looking forward. "Yes, sir, I will convey your message to them. Goodbye."

"Yes, sergeant?" asked Emma, not giving him a chance to talk.

"The commissioner wants you to meet him at the archives at three o'clock," he said in a serious tone.

"He did mention last night that he was trying to set up a meeting with John Dunstan. Sorry, my lady, I forgot to mention that," Alex apologized.

"All right …," she replied slowly, concentrating deeply as they neared Falkirk and another junction. "I believe I need your assistance now, sergeant. I seem to remember many exits at Falkirk."

The sergeant quickly asked Alex if they would usually take the A883.

"That's a good one for today," Alex confirmed and, within a few minutes, Emma spotted the first A883 sign and soon they were on a quieter country road.

About 15 minutes later, she commented, "It can't be far now," glancing over at the sergeant.

"You're right, slow down when you come to the next stand of big trees and make a sharp left. You'll recognize it then, my lady. You've done an excellent job."

Grateful for little traffic on this narrow road, her memory flooded back. As they drove up to the house, Ruth came to the door, obviously surprised to see Lady Traymore get out of the driver's seat, without a doorman! Her eyes widened still further when Sgt. McLean stepped out of the passenger side and opened the back door for Alex and his casted leg to emerge. Emma was enjoying her independence and waved to Ruth as she went around and watched Alex climb out, cheering him on.

Handing his crutches to the policeman, Alex pulled himself to the edge of the seat and then extricated himself fairly expertly. On the last move, however, he forgot to hold his leg up and it dipped to the ground causing him to groan as he tried to hold it steady. He paused to catch his breath then, pulling himself to a standing position, he took the crutches from Sgt. McLean. He was soon heading towards the door with both of them on either side of him. At that point, he realized Ruth was also watching him with rapt interest.

"My goodness," she gasped as Alex came towards her. Then, looking puzzled, she turned to the sergeant. "Hello Mr. McLean, it's nice to see you. Would you like to see Janet?"

"That would be nice matron, seeing as I am here."

"Of course, in fact your daughter is in her dog class with Jessie right now. You can go watch and have a short visit when she's finished. Sir Alex is in good hands!"

"Thank you, marm, I'm grateful and Janet will be surprised." He left them and went across the drive to the Studio.

Ruth took Alex and Emma into her office, ordered tea and coffee from her secretary and then sat down with a sigh. "Things are just happening too fast for me," she exclaimed. "How are you doing, Sir Alex?"

"I'll be fine in no time, Ruth, especially now that I'm home. It's giving our lady a chance to get used to driving on the opposite side of the road, that's why Sgt. McLean is with us today. I anticipate we will be alone next time you see us!"

Ruth was aware of their attempted tracing of letters posted in Paisley and the assistance that the Misty House technicians had given them, but she was totally unaware of Sir Alex's connection to the Stirling sorting station. She was also aware of the news about the blue dye, but not wanting to think of her friends as being in trouble with the law, she was not going to raise the subject.

Emma told her one of the undivulged bits of information about the plane crash and the mysterious involvement with the Crusaders which added a new element to the investigation. Then Emma asked Ruth about the interment documents her team had discovered. As usual, Ruth had been very efficient, making copies of the two pertinent documents and their translations for her and Alex. She readily admitted that some of entries had initially baffled her and the boys, but they had now worked it out to their satisfaction as the notes indicated. Alex noted that Emma was looking confused and a bit later they discussed it at length. Before they went out to see Tom and Charlie, Ruth asked if they were able to stay for lunch as the children would be delighted. Emma jumped at the opportunity thinking how nice it would be for Sgt. McLean as well.

While Ruth went to alert the kitchen, they went out to the Studio to talk to the boys but found them busy with the children. They noticed their maps were still spread on the tables so that kept them occupied.

They had a delightful lunch being introduced by Ruth and then Emma spoke briefly to the children mentioning how they had watched them train with their dogs on a previous visit. It soon became apparent there was no need at all to feel sorry for these happy and well-adjusted children. It was marvelous what Ruth and the men had accomplished here and she remembered the beginnings of this centre and how far it had come in 700 years.

Ruth said goodbye to them at the door then went quickly back inside as Emma dashed to the car to turn on the heater. The temperature had dropped significantly and a very cold wind urged the men toward the car with Sgt. McLean hurrying to help Alex.

More comfortable with driving now, Emma only needed help to get back to the motorway and simply followed the signs back to Edinburgh. Alex suggested they drop Sgt. McLean back to work before they carried on down Princes Street to the archives. The sergeant agreed she was doing so well he considered her graduated, as long as someone accompanied her until she was more familiar with roundabouts!

"It's been a pleasure working with you today, my lady. Sir Alex will have you driving like a real Scot in no time!" he laughed, as he left them.

She pulled into the archives' car park just before three p.m. and hurried around the car to hold the door for Alex. Beaming with his accomplishment, Alex put his crutches under his arms and moved very smoothly towards the door.

Inside, a well-informed security guard greeted them. "I believe you're expected, my lady, do you need a wheelchair, Sir Alex?"

"Yes, please," Emma replied quickly and Alex offered no objection. When the chair arrived, she loaded Alex's lap with her briefcase and handbag, and they went to the lift.

"Good evening, Sir Alex, Lady Traymore," John Dunstan's private secretary greeted them.

Alex always whispered, "Hello Katie!" in such a way the poor girl blushed every time, but this time Emma was aware of his teasing and poked him first.

They found the police commissioner already sitting at a large round table perusing some papers. The men came to their feet as the wheelchair entered and John made room for Alex at the table.

"I see you've finally got this man of yours under control, my lady!" James quipped, going over to shake their hands.

"Somewhat, sir, but it's affected his hearing," Emma commented.

"His hearing?" James repeated, looking puzzled. "He's deaf?"

"No, just stubborn, he won't listen to me!" The others laughed.

"Do you want to lose that wheelchair for awhile, Sir Alex?" John Dunstan asked, moving some chairs around to make room for either eventuality.

"Ach, I sure would, but I have to admit it's more comfortable than a chair so I better stay put."

John gathered some papers off his desk and took them over to the table leaving a space between him and James so they had lots of room to spread out the papers he had copied for them.

Katie arrived with the tray of coffee and left just as quickly, closing the door behind her.

"I called this meeting because we all seem to be working on the same puzzle but going nowhere," John began. "If each of us has information to share, it seems more sensible to constructively work together."

"That's going on the presumption we all know something different," Emma murmured, looking over at James.

"You may consider John's idea less than perfect," James replied, "but John and I have discussed it at length, especially due to the new developments brought to light by the plane crash. We hope you will both

270

agree to co-operate with us. You're going to need the law on your side and John has all the technical resources and connections that we may all need." He looked from one to the other of them before adding, "My lady, you and Sir Alex will never be able to find the relics without some professional help ... even, if you did somehow, what then? You would have to present them to the nation that Wallace fought so hard to preserve. Isn't that why you are searching for them? We also know you are looking for Mary's body, or some sign of where she was buried. You need us to achieve your goal."

"Trevelion always said he would present the relics to the nation," Alex muttered.

"There's something else, though," Emma said with a sigh. "What if we've broken the law already and you find out about it?"

"Then I shall have you beheaded, my lady!" James laughed. "I know you have broken the law. Good heavens, I probably helped you at the postal sorting station and again at the Gentleman's Club, when I forced the desk clerk to show you his books!"

Sipping on her coffee, Emma's eyes moved from John to James before she spoke again. "If you're so eager to co-operate now gentlemen," she said quietly, "why didn't you offer the same opportunity to Trevelion Walters while he was alive?"

"How do you know we didn't?" the commissioner asked sharply.

"Well, did you?" she snapped, adding menacingly, "Careful Mr. MacDonald, because if you tell me a lie, we shall be leaving." Pursing her lips into a tight line, she waited for his answer.

Annoyed at her challenge, James banged the table and glared at her. "You dare to question my sincerity, Lady Traymore?"

"No one is questioning your sincerity, sir," Emma replied. "Just stop blustering and answer my question!"

"Just tell her the truth, James, so we can get on with this," John pleaded.

"No, we didn't," James finally admitted. "Trevelion was not as aggressive as you!"

Pushing her chair away from the table, Emma came to her feet.

"Please don't leave," John whispered in dismay, and then watched in disbelief as she walked slowly towards the commissioner. Going around behind him, she stopped and placed her hands upon his shoulders and kissed the top of his head.

"I'll bet you were a beautiful baby, sir!" she murmured, and only then did her mouth curl into a tiny smile.

James first blushed and then smiled. John Dunstan attempted, poorly, to stifle a chuckle and Alex roared with laughter. The ice was broken.

The meeting now continued and Director Dunstan produced a file with details of previous attempts to locate the Royal Regalia, handing out copies for each of them to peruse at their leisure. He explained that he had fruitlessly spent too many hours to count trying to find a useful clue or even a hint that someone had unravelled part of the mystery.

"As the history of this period was often not recorded immediately, or was recorded by a prejudiced party, obviously from hearsay, historians have found that few of these 'official' records could be trusted. Therefore," he continued, "any information which surfaced from those early centuries is extremely suspect. Records are scant and always contradictory pertaining to their success or failure. We know of several other attempts to recover the regalia—the last instance on record in 1910 by Sir Charles Brodie. He was convinced it was somewhere on Dorik Island but, again, there was no logical proof."

"And then you came along, my lady," James added with a frown, "a woman determined to solve it all because she was communicating with the dead!"

No one laughed this time and they could have heard a pin drop, but the silence was brief.

"She will fulfill the prophecy, John," Alex proffered. "Lady Traymore has made more progress in three weeks than Trevelion Walters and I made in almost 20 years, the time I was with him!"

"Then please share it with us," John begged and, although his face displayed a certain amount of disbelief, he stared at Alex for a moment before turning to Emma.

"We found the monastery garden shed," Alex began, interrupting John's thoughts. "You didn't know anything about that, did you?"

"You also connected the Crusaders to the mystery and ascertained how they were kept informed," James mused, stopping to let this thought clear the air before he dropped a new one. "What puzzles me is why you gave details of your project to Dr. Barton's students at the academy?"

Alex's senses suddenly became alert. Emma had told him about her and James' visit to the academy and, of her boldly, perhaps too boldly-given, suggestion.

John Dunstan, sitting across from Alex, was obviously also taken aback by James' question and asked, "Whatever do you mean, James?"

"The students needed a project for an assignment and Lady Traymore suggested they investigate if the paupers' graves in the monastery cemetery had been moved and, if they had been moved, who had moved them and where were they moved to?"

"You are still trying to find Mary Wallace's grave, aren't you?"

"Did they find an answer?" Alex asked, turning to the commissioner.

"We don't know," James replied, "but Dr. Barton has invited us back this Friday evening to hear the results of their investigation."

"I would also like to attend, if that is agreeable with you both," Alex said solemnly, looking from one to the other.

Emma listened silently to this conversation, her eyes intensely watching each speaker, her facial expression devoid of emotion.

Alex watched her out of the corner of his eye. *You are masterful and brilliant, my dear Emma. I must remember never to cross you!*

Breaking her own silence at last, Emma commented, "I'm personally inclined to accept your offer, gentlemen, but there are other family members involved. I would beg your indulgence to give me time to contact them and explain the situation."

"I can certainly agree to that," replied the archives director. "We could all meet here on Saturday, shall we say at 10 o'clock?"

James nodded and, with a hint of a smile, murmured, "I shall be looking forward to it."

Wasting no time, Emma pushed her chair away from the table, scooped up the papers that John had given them and slipped them into her briefcase. Putting on her coat and helping Alex with his, she again put her briefcase on Alex's lap before turning to the others.

"Gentlemen, it's been a pleasure; you're a gentleman, John Dunstan, and you, James MacDonald, have slicker moves than a Latin dancer, but even you can be tamed! Until Saturday at ten." There was no emotion in her parting statement and only Alex's voice was heard saying goodbye before the door closed.

After Emma's footsteps had faded away, James sunk into the nearest chair and slammed his hand down on the table.

"Isn't she wonderful!" he gasped through his laughter.

"She's a no-nonsense lady with a sharp mind that is for sure," John declared. "She likes to rattle your cage, and you, my friend, seem to be enjoying it!"

Outside in the car park Emma held the door as Alex carefully manoeuvred himself into the front seat and a member of the security staff returned the wheelchair to the building. She went around and got into the car. There was frost on the windscreen allowing her to set the fan going and gather her thoughts a bit.

"I still don't like the fact you let the cat out of the bag at the academy and John was definitely surprised so James had not told him. We can only hope that the students come up with something of use to us, but in thinking further on this ...," he paused thoughtfully, "this subject has been researched very thoroughly over the centuries. I believe Ruth has the only new information. Let's go get dinner, tomorrow is another day and I have to call the MacDuffs. Actually, why don't I do that right now?" In no time, he had Alfreda on the line. "I'm so glad to find you home, Alfreda. Could my lady and I drop in to see you in the morning? Good ... at 11 o'clock ... goodbye. Done!" The last he said to Emma, putting the phone back into his pocket.

Discussing it before they reached the hotel, it was decided to order dinner from room service. Alex was able to get more comfortable and they spent the evening trying to get all the details of Mary's grave and their timeline organized on paper. Calling it a day at eight o'clock, Emma accompanied him down to the foyer.

"Would you like me to come pick you up for breakfast?" she asked.

"No, that's all right; I'll get a taxi when I'm ready ... nine o'clock?"

"That will be fine, it only takes about half an hour to get to Borthwick House doesn't it?" she asked. He nodded. "I hope you sleep well, Alex."

Tiredness was already showing on his face as he called a taxi—she was surprised he wasn't going to the bar. *He must be tired.* He sat down while he waited and told her she needn't wait with him. She felt the urge to hug him, but thought it too public. Feeling somewhat sorry for him, she was glad of her decision to hire Mabel for home care. As she stood at the lift exchanging waves with him, she had a humorous thought. *Mabel is such a chatterer, she will help to take his mind off his problems for awhile at least!* She waved to him again, giving him a silly smile as the lift door closed. As she returned to her quiet suite she thought how nice it was to be driving again. It surprised her just how quickly she had grown comfortable driving in Scotland, especially in busy Edinburgh. She knew Alex was right, it would be lovely to be independent again and she would also be able to get away by herself. She loved driving and exploring, and with her new car ... *I just need to solve this mystery and gain some much needed free time ... ah, free time, how I have missed it!*

Making a coffee, she sat at the table thinking about the MacDuffs. She looked at the list she had made while they were having dinner ... the family issue and questions which they thought Alfreda might be able to help them. She should talk to Alfreda about some appropriate party clothes for Christmas as well.

She pulled up a map of Scotland on her laptop and worked out her route to Borthwick Hall and then across to Misty House. *That should impress Alex!* And then, on a whim, she typed in *Templars* and chose one of the many links that appeared. It wasn't exactly bedtime reading but it gave her a different perspective than anything else she had read to date. *Their story has been proliferated over the centuries, wrongly or rightly.*

*Not many years after the Wallace family had met their fate, the Templars were virtually wiped out by King Philip of France, so anyone who claims to be a Templar today cannot possibly be what they claim. This does not mean, however, that they can't be dangerous.* She turned off the computer and went to get ready for bed.

She warmed up her cold tea and now found her mind was a muddle of thoughts. She couldn't help thinking there was something else that needed her attention. *What have I forgotten?* All of a sudden, she remembered the papers John Dunstan had sent in that recycled envelope, papers neither she nor Alex had taken the time to read because John had said they were about Paisley. She found them in the drawer with all the other papers they had collected. Reading the headings, she flipped through several double-sided pages until the heading 'Bomb Finds,' stuck to her fingers as if they wanted her attention. *Why has John given us this information? Is it a warning or something else?*

Sipping on her tea, she frowned and continued reading. Twenty-five separate instances of bomb discoveries were listed in detail around the Paisley and Elderslie area. Each was attended by the army's bomb disposal unit. The last one on the list was the metal object Alex had discovered when they were searching for old Joe's shed. It even listed the name of Tom Campbell, the county water engineer who had sent for the army disposal unit while they waited with him. The result of their investigation was in this writeup as well.

Losing all sense of time, she continued to read every single word in the dossier … dates, locations and results, and with each item her mind became clearer. Half an hour passed and then an hour and another hour. An idea was materializing in her tired brain and suddenly it struck her like a bolt of lightning. She banged her hand on the table, almost beginning to cry she was so excited.

"Holy cripes!" she whispered. "John's given us the answer to our digging problem!" She couldn't believe her eyes. "Is this merely coincidental or is he really helping us?" Her brain felt suddenly drained and as she heard the muffled chime of a faraway clock, she realized how long she had been sitting there.

It was 11 o'clock, too late to call Sir Alex, in case she woke him, and besides, she desperately needed her own sleep. She'd tell him tomorrow.

## Chapter 22 – Thursday 7<sup>th</sup> – Special Friends

Waking was difficult but when she saw light creeping around the drapes she realized she hadn't set her alarm and fortunately had not overslept. It was eight o'clock and she sighed with relief. She then remembered her discovery in John's papers and went to put them in her handbag. She couldn't wait to show Alex. They were expected at the MacDuffs at 11 o'clock and she didn't have to hurry. By 8:45 she was ready to go. Grabbing her purse, she took the stairs and could easily see Alex was there ahead of her, as she had suspected he would be. He grinned from behind his lowered newspaper and she murmured a greeting as he beckoned the waitress.

"Do I detect the signs of a disturbed night's sleep, my lady?"

"Didn't sleep a wink," she laughed, making a face, "and you?"

"Slept like a baby and woke to a steaming coffee, hot breakfast, shoes cleaned and shirt and pants pressed to perfection," he retorted. "I could get used to having a servant!"

"Don't you give it another thought, Sir Alex. You'll need the exercise once that cast comes off! Actually, this brings something to my mind that I had forgotten. I think, when this is all finished, we should set a couple days a week to meet for breakfast. You have a wonderful apartment that isn't being used and I need to stop eating large breakfasts and get more exercise … as well as be mindful of my expense account! It's all right, Alex, don't look at me like that. I'm not divorcing you, dearest!" He laughed sheepishly and said she was probably right, and then the waitress arrived.

As they drove to Borthwick House it seemed that Alex was trying to get caught up on all the subjects he had missed while in the hospital. It was easier than she thought to forego a discussion about John's papers and the bombs.

Emma easily found her way out of the city by remembering the map she had checked the night before. The large manor appeared long before they arrived and Alex voiced his surprise. *One mission accomplished,* she thought as she smiled. Stepping into the warmth of the MacDuff's large foyer, warm greetings were extended by their hosts and they entered the warm and cozy sitting room. George took their coats and, in no time, Emma had Alex settled into a chair with a footstool and then she went to briefly stand in front of the crackling log fire.

Drinks were ordered and Alfreda wasted no time in bombarding them with a stream of questions regarding Alex's accident, expressing her shock. Alex added the bit about Emma hiring a private nurse, winking at Alfreda. A serious note entered the conversation when Emma told of the interment documents found at the garden shed site, and how they had kept it a secret from the authorities, namely John Dunstan and the police commissioner.

"Were they in Latin?" Alfreda interrupted excitedly. "I could help with the translation for you."

"I didn't realize you were a Latin scholar, Alfreda," Alex commented. "Ruth Oxley translated them for us but thank you."

Taking up the story again, Emma told her the translation of the interment document which had indicated a woman's body, taken from the gibbet, was buried with a monk.

A smile came on Alfreda's face. "What better place to hide a woman's body!" she murmured. "Who would dream of looking there, especially if that monk was also a Crusader? And the reference to the lady never being lonely indicates she would be a lady of great standing in the community and expect a companion … even to the gates of heaven!"

"I didn't realize that monks were Crusaders until I began reading about the Hospitallers and the Templars," Emma admitted.

"Best soldiers in the world," George offered, proving he was awake.

Noting this, Emma now told them of yesterday's meeting with John and James.

Instantly, Alfreda's expression changed and she hissed angrily. "Don't do it, my lady, those two are much too smart to take a chance with and they will realize you are getting close. They will want to take the credit, if at all possible, and if they think you've found the place, they'll sweep you aside! James MacDonald probably has you under surveillance already. This is a family project and I feel we should keep it that way. I have every faith in you."

"That's what we came for," Alex growled, "but are you absolutely sure Alfreda, what about George? Dunstan could make it very difficult if we start digging and James won't be inclined to help either. We haven't worked that part out yet."

"George … George!" Alfreda shouted. "What do you think?"

George's eyes flicked open and he mumbled, "It's a family matter deary, a family matter." Then, his eyes flickered closed again.

278

The maid came in and left a pot of fresh coffee on a tray near Alfreda. She asked if they would like lunch served in an hour. "I assume you will be staying for lunch, my dears?" Alfreda looked expectantly from Emma to Alex. "Thank you, that would be lovely, Alfreda," Emma replied. Their hostess nodded almost imperceptibly and the maid left. As Alfreda refilled their coffee, Emma raised a subject she had been forgetting for so long.

"I've been meaning to give you a call, Alfreda, but with all this excitement going on the weeks are just flying by. I need to do some dress shopping now that I have decided to stay in Scotland for Christmas and Hogmanay. I thought you could recommend some shops and possibly supply me with your opinion. I never trust a salesperson!"

"How lovely dear, that's wonderful news, my lady, and I am honoured to be asked. Would you like me to take you to some of my favourite shops? You really should get a seamstress, when you find one you like, they can be a lifesaver."

"Actually, Alfreda, this has been on my mind for awhile as Alex had suggested I needed to have a dress for my official portrait. We were in the vicinity of the tartan factory recently and I went to see if Helen was working. She had made me that lovely Walter's tartan dress I wore at Dorik. She was, so I told her what I needed, she showed me a photo and it was ordered. The dress arrived on Monday and it's remarkable. You're absolutely right; it was quick and so easily managed."

This set Alfreda off on a tangent going into raptures over the talents of this lady whom some of her friends also used as a seamstress.

Emma tried not to smile, knowing she had done something right.

"Well then, with that solved, you will still need several dresses for the season's parties. I know a few shops that should still have a fairly decent selection of dresses, but we must do it soon, dear. You have the dress from Dorik and perhaps others, but let's find you something absolutely new and delightful! It would be scandalous for the lovely and single, new Lady Traymore to arrive at each party this season wearing the same dress!" She clapped her hands. "Have you considered that some of Scotland's finest and most eligible bachelors will be attending these parties?" She sat back and studied Emma for a moment. At this point, Alex decided he'd had enough of this woman talk and hopped out to the kitchen.

"You're right, Alfreda. Trevelion left me a note that I should not leave the estate in the same sad position he had. It was plainly on his mind."

"It was, he talked to me about it several times before he went walkabout, poor man! So what about later this week? How is your schedule looking? We could make a day of it, if you have the time, of course, or simply a few hours."

"So far it looks like I will have Friday morning or Saturday afternoon free. Perhaps we should schedule it for Friday and hope for the best."

"Wonderful, that's tentatively settled then," Alfreda exclaimed joyfully. "Now, let me go check on lunch.

Out on the road again, they discussed Alfreda's reaction to Mary being buried with a monk and Emma remembered John's papers.

"We could have made a mistake, you know," she mused. "Mary could be in the monk's section. Alex, can you reach my handbag? It's on the floor in the back. I have something to show you."

He got it and started to hand it to her, but she told him to open it and take out the papers he found.

"Aren't these the papers John gave you in that recycled envelope? I recognize the first page but I didn't get a chance to read any further."

"Read them all now, or skim them at least and tell me the first thought that comes to mind."

There was silence for the next ten minutes with only some short grunts from him as he turned pages, then he looked up. "Bombs, you want us to discover a bomb again? There's a big fine now, you know?"

"Maybe you skimmed them too quickly; the bomb unit seems to have a lot of control, Alex. It becomes a military zone. I'm not sure what that means but if we were to be absolutely sure where Mary's grave is located all we would have to do is to persuade them there's a bomb in the area and they would dig it up. There would be complications I'm sure, but I see this as our only chance to do it on our own. I couldn't believe my eyes when I read this late last night. I wanted to phone you but it was after midnight."

They were nearing Misty House when they noticed new snow on the Highlands but, fortunately, this area had escaped. Ruth met them at the door with a worried frown, shaking Emma's hand as she watched Sir Alex hop inside. As he walked ahead, Ruth softly asked Emma about his well being and he overheard them.

"If you must discuss me, at least let me hear the conversation!" he grumbled. The women giggled and, catching up to him, they continued to talk about him ... in jest.

"Firstly, we need your opinion, Ruth," Emma began as soon as they were seated and tea had been poured. "We have had an offer to join forces with the authorities. John Dunstan and Commissioner James MacDonald want us to pool all our information."

"That could be quite embarrassing, Lady Traymore," the matron commented thoughtfully. "You would have to admit you found the interment documents and kept it a secret."

"I realize that. Alfreda and George MacDuff think that we should continue alone, keeping it within the family."

"I agree. You and Sir Alex are a wonderful team, my lady, but realistically John and James are very powerful men and could make any further investigations very difficult, perhaps impossible. Having said that, I would like to see you solve this mystery and prove the prophecy was right."

"Thank you for your confidence, Ruth. Seeing as my lady apparently has an idea running around in her head, I think we should continue on our own for at least awhile longer. It would be very exciting if all our efforts helped to solve this mystery," Alex added.

"Could we see those two interment documents, Ruth?" Emma asked.

Going to the file cabinet, Ruth pulled out two separate folders and selected two pages of handwritten notes, handing them to Emma, who held them so Alex could also see them. The top part was in point form so they could easily see the similarities. Each had the same name of Martin, plot numbers and the same notation, but the area of location differed. One said Elderslie and the other said Paisley.

"I've thought about these two a lot," Ruth murmured. "It could be they're both genuine. Remember when you found the biographia box under the garden shed but there was no evidence of a body? I remember you asked me if all traces of a body would be gone after so many years and I said 'not often.' If a body had not been buried there, no trace would have been possible."

"You still think that the monk didn't die, don't you?" Emma asked.

"Yes, but everything had been made ready for a monk's body. In war times, his helpers could easily have had to move on, hopefully with him, but they had no chance to retrieve the biographia box. Perhaps the monk died in Paisley."

"My word, that does make sense," Alex agreed thoughtfully. "Tex could have been fooled! Several people may have made notations on the biographia document as it was written in a hurry and possibly begun by the fighting monk who was wounded. Now we have these two documents from the pouches, but how could they have the same name?"

"And the same location number," Emma added, "unless ..."

"Unless," Alex interrupted, "we're looking for a second gravesite!"

Emma sighed, shaking her head in confusion. "Think ... if one of them was badly wounded and they were carrying Mary's body, they wouldn't have the time or energy to dig a second grave. The second document could be the decoy trying to turn us toward Paisley."

"Yes, yes that's it and we've forgotten the key word!" Alex exclaimed. "She isn't buried in a paupers' grave because the interment document said she was buried with a monk, we've been tricked!"

Emma glanced over at the matron, surprised at his outburst.

Ruth sadly shook her head. "We have no proof this is Mary!"

Turning to Alex, Emma's eyes begged him to say something.

"They were monks," he began slowly. "Think about it, they no doubt knew that there would be an open grave in the Brotherhood section. Death was common amongst these fighting monks during times of war. The monastery could have already been prepared for a brother's interment." He sighed, pausing to sip his coffee and let them digest his theory. "We might even be able to prove it, because they may not have had the means or time to seal the biographia box.

"Do we know where the monks were intered, Ruth?" Emma asked.

"I don't, but Tom and Charlie might, they were studying the plans yesterday when I was over there."

Trying to leave Alex in Ruth's office brought a stubborn refusal from the bearded Scot who defiantly set his jaw and hobbled after them. Tom laughed when the matron put the question to him and pointed to several interment documents on his work bench.

"I just finished translating those last night," he grinned. "They're all men of the Brotherhood and, as far as we can ascertain, they're all buried along the eastern end behind the chapel altar. They should be easier to find than the garden shed, Sir Alex!" Tom laughed.

Thanking them all, Emma and Alex went back to the car. A bone-chilling breeze had come up by this time and they were glad to get the heater on.

"Blast it, I want to go and look for these graves but it's too dark to go tracking around in the mud," Emma sighed, pulling out onto the road.

The roads were dry as they drove back to Edinburgh.

"Where would you like to go for dinner?" he asked.

"It's been a most productive day and I feel I should relax but I can't! Do you know of any restaurant near an army camp in this area?"

"What did you say?" he asked in surprise. "Why are you thinking about an army camp?"

"It just popped into my head ... probably because of John's papers. I need an army base or the place where the bomb disposal unit lives."

Alex was alert now. Something *was* going on in her pretty head. *She was taking those papers seriously and he hadn't even read them.* Studying her face, he realized how hard she was thinking.

"All right, that would be Redford Base, my lady. When you turn onto the A8 take the by-pass A720 and watch for the signs to Colinton. We'll eat at Dougal's *Wheat Sheaf Inn*."

Alex's directions were perfect and in under an hour, Emma pulled into their parking area. Music and faint sounds of laughter came from inside as Alex struggled with his crutches on the loose gravel. Holding the door for him, Emma stood for a moment to look around, and a pleasant, older woman came to greet them, calling him by name. Chatting briefly, she directed them to a table, took their drink orders and curtseyed.

"My goodness, what service! An ex-girlfriend of yours, by any chance?" Emma teased, once the waitress had left.

"No, just a very dear friend I haven't seen for awhile, her husband teaches at the Special Units Branch at Redford." Alex's explanation was cut short as the drinks arrived, delivered by the same woman.

"So, you must be the woman in the prophecy, my lady," she began, putting their drinks on the table and curtseying again to Emma. "It's a pleasure to have you visit us. Did you see our Specials Board?"

"Yes, I did thank you. I'd like the poached salmon with a baked potato and all the trimmings," said Emma.

"And you, Sir Alex?"

"Steak just touched by the heat, almost raw when the knife cuts into it," Alex teased, watching Emma's face twist with revulsion.

"You were telling me about that lady's husband." Emma prodded him as they waited for their meal. "Is he a soldier?"

"No, a civilian explosive's expert. He teaches disarming techniques to the bomb disposal unit over at Redford."

"When can we meet him?"

"He'll come join us as soon as we've finished eating."

"Why, did you speak with him?"

Slow to answer, Alex poured a little more whisky into his coffee and hissed, "Sometimes, Emma, you ask too many blasted questions!"

Shocked at his uncharacteristic outburst, Emma sat back and drank her coffee in silence. When they finished, the waitress returned and asked how they had enjoyed the meal as she rearranged the chairs.

"My name is Mara, my lady, and here comes my husband. She pointed to a motorized wheelchair coming towards them. On board was a bearded man who appeared somewhat older than her. His hair was grey and he had a wide grin which Emma knew instantly had melted many hearts in his younger days.

"Lady Traymore, this is my husband, Dougal Graham." Dougal smiled as he shook Emma's hand in a firm but comfortable grasp and then moved in beside Alex. No words of greeting passed between the men but they grasped each other in a powerful embrace of affection that Emma could not dispute. Mara sniffled a little and dabbed at her eyes.

*There's an interesting story going on here*, thought Emma.

Glasses were produced and filled with whisky as Alex, Dougal and Mara drank a silent toast with their eyes intensely focused on each other. Fascinated by their continued demonstration of affection, Emma's inquisitive nature could stand it no longer.

"Will one of you please tell me what's going on?"

"I will, my lady," Mara volunteered. "It was many years ago and these two were unknown to each other. They were both in sports cars travelling home to Edinburgh late one night and no doubt they had both been drinking. Dougal ran off the road and hit a stone wall, the impact sheared both his legs off and if Sir Alex hadn't stopped to help he would have died." Mara paused and dabbed at a tear that escaped onto her cheek. "Sir Alex spent two hours with his thumbs on Dougal's arteries, stopping the blood and keeping him alive until help came. He was a hero and there's nothing we wouldn't do for this man."

"All right, you two, that's enough," Alex objected with embarrassment, "she gets the picture."

"Could you give us a tour of the bomb disposal unit?" Emma asked.

"Why yes, of course, my lady," he replied, looking at her curiously. "If you come to Redford Barracks at ten in the morning, I'll leave word at the gate to escort you to the special unit building," Dougal replied.

Keeping the topic of conversation firmly on the bomb disposal unit, Emma quickly learned of their authority. Overriding county and municipal bylaws, if a situation was deemed dangerous, they could even exclude the police from their area of operation. Dougal admitted he was hardly ever called out to a find and, even then it was only to identify the detonation system. Emma gently probed their training methods, laughing when Dougal explained they could swoop down on an area and seal it off from the public.

"We often make local officials quite perturbed!" he laughed.

Once started, Dougal was hard to stop and, with Emma's enthusiastic encouragement, he told stories of the bomb disposal unit and some of their most laughable exploits. When a farmer near Glasgow found a bomb in his manure heap that was deemed too dangerous to move, the bomb squad blew that poor farmer's rotten manure all over the neighbourhood because the man in charge had forgotten to install bomb suppression blankets over the site. Emma and Alex smiled when Dougal told them of a recent call to Paisley, which turned out to be a false alarm.

As they left the restaurant, Emma remembered her plans with Alfreda and asked Alex to call her and see if the early afternoon would work. He handed her the phone when Alfreda came on and they changed the time to noon. The shopping trip was still on.

The short drive home gave Emma the chance to explain where her mind was going with their exciting discovery. "It's the answer to our digging in the burial grounds. John and James can scream until they go blue in the face, but they can't push the bomb squad around!"

"We have them beat. You've done it again, my lady, and I'm so proud of you." Arriving at his apartment, he took her hand and kissed it before opening the car door, telling her not to get out. She watched him and smiled, keeping her growing emotions in check. As they said goodnight, an unspoken message of hope passed between them. Once Mabel buzzed him in and he got into the elevator, she drove off smiling. *He's becoming very independent.*

Feeling extremely pleased with herself as she pulled into the car park at the *Courtyard Inn*, her elation quickly evaporated upon seeing the monster Land Rover parked in the darkest corner. She knew the police commissioner was inside and probably waiting to pounce on her. There was no way to avoid it. Steeling herself, she marched into the foyer with an air of confidence and met James as he came out of the *Hunting Bar*. He called to her as she tried to go straight to the lift.

"A nightcap, my dear?" The remark brought the desk clerk's head up with a jerk, but Emma stopped and eyed the commissioner suspiciously until he silently mouthed the word, "please."

"Highland Coffee?" he asked, parting the crowd. She smiled.

Glancing around, Emma soon realized it was standing room only and when James returned, they stood in a corner and he asked about Alex. "You know how he is, he's your next door neighbour and I'm sure you talk to Nurse Brown," Emma replied, sipping on her coffee. "What is it you really want to know, Mr. Policeman?"

"Did you go to Elderslie today?"

"No, we went to Misty House to see Ruth Oxley. What happened in Elderslie that you want to blame us for?"

Ignoring her sarcasm, James stoically began to explain. "Sergeant Mackie reported two new bomb scares in Paisley. It seems you've set off a trend with those metal detectors."

"They found two bombs?"

"No, Bill Mackie read the signs and dug out a box of rusty screws from one area and an old pick head from another," James chuckled. "Council has now enacted an edict stating that whoever turns in another bomb false alarm, will be held responsible for the cost of investigation. I thought you should know even though I considered it was a wee bit too amateurish for your style, my lady. I'm merely alerting you."

Thanking him profusely, as she knew he expected, Emma offered to buy him a drink but he declined. Saying goodnight at the lift, she smiled knowing that James had no knowledge of her interest in the bomb squad.

Exhausted when she went to bed, sleep came easily until her recurring dream of Mary woke her with a startled squeal. Fighting her usual inclination to sit up, she concentrated on the vision, trying to stay calm and hoping it would last longer. Mary beckoned her to come closer. Suddenly, in the misty background a stone gatepost appeared. On one of its stones was a crudely carved capital letter 'A.' Emma began to tremble involuntarily, but the image stayed long enough for her to study it before it disappeared. Tears of relief streamed down her face as she stumbled out to the living room, falling to her knees by her briefcase. *Oh, my gosh, she's sent me a clue … she's sent me a clue!* She pulled the briefcase into her arms and sat in the nearest chair, her sweaty clothes pulling at her body. Breathless, she opened the briefcase, found pen and paper and crudely drew the scene she had just viewed. "But where is it?" she whispered. "It has to be in Elderslie, that's what she said earlier."

As her shaking stopped, her breathing returned to normal and she went to get her housecoat and a blanket. Her mind was racing. *This has to be the pertinent clue to find Mary's grave*, she thought. *Was this the reason the dream was recurring … had she earlier missed Mary's most important clue or was Mary giving it to her at just the right time?*

286

## Chapter 23 – Friday 8th – Emma's Plan

When the first sign of dawn crept around the living-room curtains, Emma realized that she had slept the rest of the night in her chair. It was 6:30 a.m. and, too late to go back to bed, she wrapped the blanket around herself and went to turn the heat up and make tea.

Ready to go by 7:30, she got her briefcase and went downstairs. Greeting Megan she made her way to the dining room. Excited enthusiasm bubbled in her brain as she sipped her coffee and studied her drawing of the gatepost.

Suddenly, the voice of Nurse Brown broke into her thoughts and she realized Alex was coming towards her. She slipped the paper into her bag and looked at her watch. It was 8:15.

"Good morning, my lady!" The enthusiastic nurse exclaimed as she helped Alex with his chair, fussing around to make him comfortable.

"You just arrived?" Emma asked.

"Yes," Alex muttered, sleepily.

"Will you join us for coffee, Mabel?" she asked.

"Thank you, my lady!" Mabel blushed. "An Irish Coffee, please."

Making no comment, Emma raised an eyebrow slightly and cast a glance over at Alex. The nurse, who had so adamantly tried to stop Alex from drinking at the hospital, had seemingly become a convert! When she finished her coffee, she left.

Emma was telling him of her latest dream and about to show Alex her drawing as breakfast arrived. He became just as excited as she had and they briefly discussed a trip to Elderslie to search for the gate. Time was getting short before their scheduled tour with Dougal, so they finished eating and briefly ran over their plans for the day. Alex said that James had called him to confirm dinner and would meet them at the academy. Returning to her suite briefly, she also got organized for her lunch and shopping trip with Alfreda.

With only a short drive to Colinton and the Redford Barracks, Emma was grateful traffic was light. Challenged by the duty soldier, they showed their identification and after checking his roster directed them to the Special Units Division at a very large building nearby.

"Welcome, Lady Traymore ... Sir Alex Wallace," the soldier snapped, holding the door open for them. "We have a wheelchair ready for you, sir, and I will notify Mr. Graham that you are here." Their eyes followed his pointing finger to a group of men in serious conversation a short distance away and he went to get the wheelchair. They heard him make a quick call to announce they were here and then he helped Alex sit down before excusing himself. While Alex was busy, Emma had been watching the group of men and soon realized Dougal was there in the centre of the group. He waved them over as the soldier returned with a chair for Emma, explaining that Mr. Graham was about to have a demonstration of how to approach a live, unexploded bomb. Dougal called out instructions and advice to the team as he charged around in his wheelchair. Three-quarters of an hour passed almost unnoticed and soon a bell sounded throughout the building. The men dispersed and Dougal hurried over to greet his friends, sporting a big grin.

"Lunch time for the boys," he told them, "but there's something I want to show you two, follow me."

"Dougal, slow down, lad!" Alex called after him.

Dougal swung his wheelchair around and waited for them.

"If you two teenagers don't quit it," she complained. "I'll need one too! Oh, and Dougal, I'm afraid Sir Alex and I will have to leave for another appointment in half an hour. We regret having to rush you but it couldn't be helped, I'm afraid."

Dougal looked disappointed but said they could always return later for the rest of the tour. He directed them to an outside door and into the next warehouse. It was absolutely filled with odd-looking machinery, which included the usual miniature diggers and tractors of every shape and size. They could tell he really enjoyed explaining the purpose and use of each as if he were the mechanic. One of these was a gigantic crawling tractor which caught Emma's eye as it had large blasting buffers attached to the front, making shivers run up her spine.

Returning to the main building minutes later, they followed him into a large room and they gasped at the huge display of bombs lined up along one wall. Each had a sign describing the bomb, details of its country of origin, type of explosive and detonation system. Never in their wildest imagination could they have envisaged such an array of explosive devices.

"You've studied each one of these, Dougal?" Emma murmured in awe. "Are these all used here in Scotland?"

"No, no, just the ones from Germany were found here, being part of that country's arsenal during WW2."

"Were any of them found in Elderslie or Paisley?"

"Oh yes, it was only a few years ago we found an unexploded 1,000-pound bomb on the edge of Paisley. It was probably meant for the Clydebank Shipyards, but luckily it missed its target!"

"And nobody knew for over 70 years," Emma commented. "It's quite remarkable it hadn't exploded. How in heaven's name do you train for something like that?"

"Very carefully, my lady!" he sighed. "Our training must be conducted in a controlled environment to protect everyone involved. We desperately need some practical experience for the boys, but that is very difficult to come by and, of course, we don't want to encourage it!"

"Those smaller incendiary bombs," Alex said thoughtfully, his brow wrinkled in thought, "if they don't explode, how deep will they penetrate the ground?"

"That depends on the nature of the ground, but not more than thirty feet in soft terrain."

"And how do you determine if there is a bomb?" Alex asked, now appearing to become even more interested.

"Our only option is to send out a field crew. Most times it's nothing, but it's excellent experience for the men."

Patiently, Dougal began describing the procedure … the necessity of police, ambulance and hospitals to be notified; local counties also, due to evacuation areas needing to be defined, and then the exclusion zone sealed off.

"Exclusion zone?" Emma asked. "Who is excluded and who enforces it, the police?"

"No, the military does. Exclusion means everyone, only people with authority from the special unit can go inside the perimeter."

At 20 minutes to noon they were leaving the army base. When they reached the hotel, Emma saw Alfreda just getting out of her car.

"There's Alfreda … are you all right to lock up, Alex? I had better get going. I'll be back by 4:30." Despite not having eaten any lunch, the women decided they would begin their shopping first. When they did stop to eat, they were better able to discuss Emma's style likes and dislikes assisting with Alfreda's next choice of shops.

They had a lovely, although quite rushed afternoon, and Emma soon realized they had a lot more in common than she had first thought. Alfreda had a great sense of humour and turned out to be an exceedingly enjoyable person to have as a companion. By 3:45, Emma had purchased two evening dresses and a long, black slim skirt with two matching tops. She was very happy with their shopping success and now felt quite a bit more eager to attend Christmas parties.

As Alfreda drove her back to the hotel, they chatted continuously. "Has Alex told you, we Scots prefer to migrate to warmer climates for Christmas or, at least, soon after Hogmanay?" Alfreda asked. "The Mediterranean is wonderful you know. Have you been, Emma? It's where all the Scots holiday."

"No, I haven't, but what a delightful thought! We've been so busy; I had forgotten Christmas was getting so close until we attended *Light Night* and now another two weeks has gone by! I believe I must experience Hogmanay this first visit to Scotland! I could stay here forever, I confess I have fallen in love with your country," she laughed.

"It's your country too, Emma. You are already a Scot dear, but George would say you really can't claim to be a *true* Scot until you experience Hogmanay!"

Alex was waiting in the foyer when Alfreda pulled up to the door and Emma ran quickly inside and to the lift, loaded down with parcels, saying she would 'only be five minutes.' When she got to her room, she dumped her parcels on the bed and hurriedly checked her make-up, groaning and grabbing her small make-up bag. She ran a brush through her hair and hurried back to the lift. *I sure hope these students have some good news for us tonight,* she thought, taking the stairs.

They arrived at the gates of the Police Academy minutes before five o'clock and informed the gate officer they were expected by Professor Barton for dinner and his lecture. Checking his list of expected guests, which had a note that Sir Alex was on crutches, the officer showed them parking near the door. Another security officer opened the door to the building, gave them directions to the canteen and paged Professor Barton. Alex grumbled at the long walk and Emma made a mental note to request a wheelchair next time they went out.

"Almost there," she encouraged him.

When they got off the lift, the professor waved at them from the canteen door. Emma introduced Alex and the older man greeted them both warmly. He then hurried them into the canteen where they ordered a meal and found a table. They noticed that Professor Barton kept looking at his watch, which continued throughout the meal. Realizing he intended to eat and run, they carried the conversation knowing they could finish after he left. They were right, for as soon as he finished, he excused himself, mumbling something about his lecture notes. Hurrying away, Emma and Alex began to laugh.

"He's a police lecturer?" Alex asked, shaking his head.

They finished their dinner in a more relaxed atmosphere than it had started, commenting that James must have been held up. As they went to find the lecture hall, Emma ducked into a ladies room to repair her make-up. With five minutes to spare, they joined the crowd of students and were surprised by the number of adults in attendance. Professor Barton had sent a student to watch for them and a young man came to inform them their seats were in the front row and marked as reserved.

"Does he always wear that cape and silly hat?" Alex hissed, "he looks rediculous!"

"Shh, and don't you dare laugh either!"

News had spread through the academy that Lady Traymore would again be attending Professor Barton's evening lecture. Other students, off-duty staff and inquisitive academy workers now quickly filled the lecture room to capacity.

Professor Barton's short stature was barely visible behind the raised lectern as he now called for their attention. The introduction of his two guests was so informative, they were sure James had called to tell him Sir Alex would be attending with Lady Traymore. Then the professor went on far too long before he finally moved onto the subject of the study which Emma had suggested the previous week.

Outlining the problem, he called for participation from the audience which produced a lively debate on how to establish a positive outcome from ancient records and other unlikely sources of information. Calling an end to the debate, he asked for the conclusions of the investigative team and his eyes searched the rows of faces for the designated class spokesman. Rising, Detective Constable George Robertson quickly made his way to the front of the room. He was holding a file folder stuffed with papers. Shaking the constable's hand, Professor Barton quickly vacated the lectern and went to sit next to Emma.

Well used to public speaking, Constable Robertson introduced himself and then addressed Professor Barton, their guests and his classmates before opening his folder.

"Our task sounded so simple when we first encountered Lady Traymore's question. All we had to do was locate and check the appropriate records ... so we thought!"

Suddenly, the door to the lecture room opened with a clunk. Police Commissioner MacDonald had arrived. As he walked to the front of the room, the young constable held his comments and watched as the commissioner nodded to the assembly and Professor Barton then sat down beside Alex.

"As I was saying," said the constable, "it was such a simple question and the monks kept impeccable records, but we found it the most frustrating inquiry. It appears that although they kept records, nobody kept a record of where those records were!" Looking up, he grinned at the expectant faces of the audience and waved a handful of papers from his folder. "These papers contain a list of places where we searched for those records. We found many references to paupers' deaths and burials in three different locations, but not one single mention anywhere of the bodies being moved." He paused while he slid his papers back into their folder, and then, with hands gripping the sides of the lectern, he continued. "Ladies and gentlemen, in conclusion, the committee is forced to admit that Lady Traymore's question must remain unanswered. We are defeated. The dust of time has sealed the answer permanently."

Leaving the lectern, Mr. Robertson bowed to his audience and hurried back to his seat. Thanking the constable and the class for their efforts, the professor then invited Lady Traymore to say a few words.

Standing, she nodded, brushed the wrinkles out of her skirt, adjusted the Wallace broach on her cardigan and walked to the lectern. The smirk that touched the lecturer's face as he moved away had not gone unnoticed by the Canadian.

"Ladies and Gentlemen," she said, smiling at the gathering. "I must admit, you've disappointed me! I was sure your natural, inquisitive instincts would lead you to a more conclusive answer. But when you are taught to follow regular avenues of investigation—duplicate systems that have been in operation for decades, perhaps even centuries, then initiative and the guidance of gut feelings never comes into your calculations. What a shame, when we all realize that it's really the individuals who think for themselves who solve the mysteries of this world ... not the stereotype who follows the rules of a lecturer who doesn't know which side of his head his bonnet is on!"

Muffled laughter ran through the room as Professor Barton touched his head and smiled self-consciously when he felt his famous hat still in place.

Emma finished up by thanking them for allowing her to take part in their class assignment and then she returned to her seat. The room erupted in applause and laughter. She patted Alex's knee and stood up again to put on her coat while Alex also readied himself to leave. They both nodded to the professor before heading to the door. The audience clapped again and Emma looked back and smiled as they left the hall.

"How about a drink in the *Hunting Bar?*" he asked, once the door had closed.

Agreeing to meet him, they found their way to the front door where a security officer let them out. Discussing the students' results once they were in the car, they agreed they were actually quite relieved and glad they didn't have to face either the professor or his students. With James, however, they would have to be truthful and indicate their great disappointment!

"Well, it was a waste of time!" she complained.

"No, it wasn't exactly. It provided you with some goodwill and appeased James. I think we were quite believable, but then I'm biased!"

They were almost at the hotel when Emma asked, "Is something bothering you, Sir Alex?"

"No, my lady, nothing is bothering me at all ... except!" As they drove into the hotel car park, he groaned.

"Well, out with it!" she insisted as she parked. "Cripes, he's here already!" she muttered as her headlights focused on the Land Rover parked in the corner. "Is that what you just noticed?"

"Yes!" he admitted. "That's James' vehicle."

"I know that, but how did he get here before us?"

"Does it matter?" he growled. "It bothers me more, that he was making sure he cornered us tonight before he lost us."

James MacDonald had already secured a table and beckoned them over as they entered the bar. "I ordered," he called, grinning as a waitress arrived with the drinks. Savouring her coffee, Emma sat back and eyed the police commissioner suspiciously, expecting another ulterior motive was behind this last effort to see them tonight.

"So, my lady, you think our detective school teaches archaic methods?" James commented. "That last remark you made about the professor and his bonnet, although humorous, left the poor little man in a state of nervous disorientation."

"Well, I happen to agreed with her," Alex retorted. "Never once did they mention what might have happened or that they assumed something until it was proven. They simply followed a paper trail with no real initiative. The only thing that surprised me was that Lady Traymore let them off so lightly!"

James didn't seem to want to argue with them and when he finished his drink he got up to leave; reminding them they had a meeting at 10 o'clock at Dunstan's office.

So what is our next step, my lady, do we go to Elderslie?" he asked, looking at her curiously.

"I'm thinking on it." She hesitated for so long, he cocked his head at her. "What's wrong, are my thoughts too slow for you tonight?"

"Are you planning to tell me what you have on your mind or is it a secret?"

"Of course I am, I just haven't had a chance between bombs, shopping trips, useless dinners and equally useless meetings! We are going to find Mary's grave tomorrow but we have to work out how to use Dougal's team."

"Is that what all those questions to Dougal were about this morning?"

"Yes, we have to find a way to convince him and the bomb disposal team to dig where we want. They need a bomb, Alex!"

He now realized where she was going with this and he began to explore his memory of friends and relatives, searching for someone they could trust who wouldn't ask too many questions.

"We could give them several bombs!" he began.

Suddenly, Emma whispered, "Jack ... Jack the rebel!"

Alex smiled, and then nodded vigorously. "Exactly! Jack is more familiar with the burial grounds than anyone else except Old Joe. We must go see him in the morning."

"It's too late to call him now but could you do that before we meet in the morning?" she asked. "We need to get an early start and call at Jack's first. We have a busy morning ahead of us and I'd hate for him to go off somewhere and ruin our plans." Emma finished her tea and stood up.

"Sounds good and I'll see you at 8 o'clock. I'm going to go and visit with the lads for a while. Pleasant dreams, Emma."

She was feeling strangely at ease as she hung her new clothes in the wardrobe and then went to sit at the window. *This is a sight I have grown to love so much, but if what I am planning comes off, this visit could soon come to an end!*

## Chapter 24 – Saturday 9<sup>th</sup> – An Old Gatepost

She was surprised to find she had indeed had a restful sleep, when she awakened Saturday morning to the sound of her alarm. She pulled open the drapes in her bedroom, shivering involuntarily, as she watched the trees and, especially a flag, blowing wildly in the predawn light. She dressed warmly and checking her briefcase for any necessary papers, she glanced at the rough drawing she'd made of the gatepost. She felt sure that finding this old gatepost would be crucial to locating Mary's grave.

Happy to be feeling so good, she skipped down the stairs to the foyer, immediately spotting Sir Alex and Mabel at their table.

"Good morning," she murmured taking a seat and accepting a hot coffee from the fast-moving waitress. "Why don't you stay for breakfast, Mabel?"

"Thank you, but no, my lady," the nurse replied with her usual blush, then dropping her voice. "If I don't hear any of your top secret conversations, Mr. MacDonald can't wheedle anything out of me!" Finishing her drink, she left when the waitress came to take their order.

Emma opened her briefcase and took out her drawing, handing it to Alex when he asked to see it. She asked if he had talked to Jack and he told her there was no answer.

"We'll need something metal to set off the detector," Emma continued in a low voice. "Jack will, no doubt, have some bits and pieces that will serve the purpose.

He decided to call Jack again, but there was still no answer. He left a message on the voice mail and they decided to take a chance and go there first.

Breakfast arrived and conversation halted but Alex looked up at her with one of his deep frowns. "You were planning this yesterday and didn't tell me," he said, in an accusatory tone, giving her what she had come to think of as his evil eye.

"Please, eat your breakfast, Alex," she whispered tersely, her mouth full. "We'll discuss this in the car!"

Not being able to be put off quite so easily, he continued to frown and mutter until they were finished. Without a word, he struggled into his coat and went out to the car, leaving Emma to deal with the bill.

"Are you quite finished with your tantrum, my darling?" she teased as she got behind the wheel and started the engine. "I'm not really sure where Jack's pub is. I believe it was off the M8 at Junction 6?"

"It's at Newhouse," he grunted.

Glancing at her silent companion some few minutes later, Emma shook her head slightly and plunged on, laying out her plan. "My last dream of Mary Wallace," she said, "showed a grave and behind it was an old gatepost with the letter 'A' cut into its surface. Firstly, we have to find that gatepost." She stopped talking and concentrated on the junction ahead, negotiating the traffic quite smoothly.

"What if it's been removed?" he asked.

"Old Joe or Sergeant Mackie will remember it."

"Would you really ask the sergeant? I thought we were trying to avoid the police."

"No, you're right, I wouldn't," Emma replied, "but when we find the right area and Jack puts those pieces of metal into the ground, we can call the bomb squad. They'll have the ultimate authority to keep everyone away from the location and they will do the digging. Dougal practically begged us to give his squad some practice!"

"He actually did! I think it's brilliant. How long have you been planning this?"

"Just since yesterday, the idea came to me when we were talking to Dougal."

"Turn off up there at the junction," he ordered.

Recognizing the area now, Emma continued to their destination, driving into the small parking area beside Jack's house. A man using a leaf blower suddenly appeared in her way. Realizing it was Jack and not wanting to startle him, she stopped and got out of the car. When he saw them, he laughed self-consciously and turned off his blower.

"Good morning to you both, this is an unexpected surprise, my lady," he exclaimed, watching as Alex finally got himself extricated from the front seat. "Hello, Sir Alex, I just made some fresh coffee, will you come in?"

"We left a message on your phone, Jack, but decided to take a chance we could find you. We have another little problem we could use your help on and a coffee would go down nicely, thank you," Emma told him.

Inside, they sat at the table while Jack went to wash up. Emma found the cups and Jack returned to pour. Smiling, she watched as the two clansmen made their traditional toast, "To the Rebel of Elderslie."

"Do you need me to do some more digging?" he asked. "Have you found another garden shed?"

"Not quite, Jack," Emma replied softly. "We want to know if you could install four small pieces of metal into the ground for us?"

"Install four pieces of metal into the ground?" Jack repeated shaking his head. "Why the devil would you want to do that?"

"No, Jack," Alex interrupted, "don't ask why, just tell us if you can do it for us."

"Sure I can. I can take the digger and dig a hole anywhere."

"I was thinking of something more like a posthole digger," she added.

"Hold on a minute," Jack replied, his brow wrinkling. "Allen has a post setter that blasts a fence post into the ground, the heads are pointed and screw onto the bottom of a post."

"Can you pull the post back out and leave the head in the ground?" she asked.

"Yes, it's possible, but what's the point of doing that?"

"How long would it take you to put four tips in?" Alex asked.

"If I had everything ready, no more than fifteen or twenty minutes," he replied. "It's tractor-mounted; I could be in and out and nobody the wiser, I have some portable aluminum roadway material that protects the ground and grass from my equipment."

"Now you've got the right idea," Emma complimented him. "How soon can you get the equipment?"

"Any time you want it."

"Just one more question, Jack. Do you know of a gatepost on the monastery land with the letter 'A' chiselled into the front of it?"

Scratching his head, he replied. "Yes, I remember one like that. Allen has it in his builder's yard! We removed it a few years ago. We also took that old wall down. I was told it was the original gate to the consecrated land but it was falling apart ... it's not a letter 'A' you know."

"Then what is it?" she asked, cautiously.

"It's the Freemason sign ... a compass and a set square."

"The sign of our modern Crusaders!" she whispered to Alex. "That's why they were coming to Edinburgh. They knew where that grave was, they had marked it. I'll bet they knew we'd be looking for it and they were coming to protect it!" Then, louder, she added, "Can you show us where that gatepost used to be, Jack?"

"Sure I can, do you want to go right now?"

"We sure do," Alex mumbled, downing the rest of his coffee and standing up.

With Jack in the back seat, Alex now had time to relate the story of his accident to his friend, causing much laughter as Emma silently hashed over her thoughts. Then he told Jack about his hospital stay and ending up with a live-in nurse. "She's a diligent and caring person and she's certainly making my life a lot easier right now."

"Thank goodness for that, we don't want to hear any more complaints," Emma added. "He was worse than a baby in the hospital."

Almost to their destination, Emma followed Jack's instructions and parked the vehicle near the Northwest side of the burial grounds.

"We're walking from here," he announced. "I hope it's not too treacherous for you, Alex."

"I'll just come at my own pace," he assured them.

Walking across hallowed burial ground gave Emma an eerie feeling but she followed Jack along an overgrown path. Looking back, she checked on Alex and despite his groans and quiet cursing he seemed to be doing well until the ground got quite slippery. She now realized how treacherous it could be for him and waited until he caught up. Jack was now a short distance ahead of them and had stopped, staring down at the ground. When they joined him, he pointed to his feet.

"This is where the gatepost sat and the wall ran that way," he raised his arm pointing to the east.

"Why would there be a gatepost in this part of the burial ground?" Emma asked.

"Our thought was there must have been a lane here," Jack explained, "where horse-drawn conveyances could deliver the deceased to the sexton."

"Can you stand right where the gatepost was, Alex?" Emma requested. "You stay here, Jack, until I tell you to move. You're going to put four pieces of metal into the ground about six feet deep and covering an area I'm about to show you. Do you have anything to mark the ground with?"

"No, but it won't take me long to find something," he replied.

"Stay! Right now I want you to stand still," she instructed, actually not sure what she was going to do yet.

Moving a few yards away from the men, she stopped and turned around slowly. She was trying to remember the details of her dream when suddenly the vision became reality. She gasped as her heart began to beat violently, pounding in her throat and chest for only a few seconds until the vision faded. Suddenly feeling dizzy, she stepped towards a large cross and leaned against it.

Not realizing her difficulty, Alex yelled, "Ach, my foot is freezing!" "Can we hurry this up a wee bit?"

Wiping away a tear, Emma closed her eyes briefly as she tried to visualize what she had seen. Opening them, she went to the exact spot she needed and pointed it out for Jack, telling him he could now move. He came toward her picking up some stones at the same time.

"Are you all right?" he asked with concern.

"No, Jack, I'm actually not, but it will pass and we shall carry on regardless. Now …," she said, glancing at her watch, "put down those stones, it's almost noon. I really need those pieces of metal in the ground today."

"Then you'd better get me home, my lady!"

Driving more quickly now, Emma continued to think of instructions along the way but the most important thoughts came just as they pulled into his yard.

"Mark one of the places extra clearly, Jack, so it can be found more easily and, please call Alex as soon as you've finished."

"Will do," he smirked, climbing out of the car.

"You're a good friend, Jack. It's going to be very hard to repay you but we'll think of something!" she laughed.

Jack waved before disappearing into the garage.

Emma noticed the threatening dark clouds and commented to Alex. "I don't like the look of those clouds. I hope Jack is able to get the job done this afternoon."

"He will. I think the rain will be our friend today, my lady, keeping the curious away and obliterating tracks," he declared.

She was a bit surprised that these men were displaying their own interest, even excitement, over this project. Her stomach growled and she realized they had better get some lunch soon.

On the way back to Edinburgh, they talked about the story they were going to give when they called in the bomb report. Finally, when they considered they had it right, Alex wrote it down. Emma told him he should be the one to call it in as he was a Scot and even if he disguised his voice, it wouldn't be so easy to identify him right away. If John or James heard it was a woman with a North American accent, they would immediately know it was her. So, it was mutually decided that he would have to do the dirty work. By the time they approached Edinburgh, wet snow was falling and street lights illuminated people hurrying home under their umbrellas. An almost empty car park at the *Courtyard Inn* suggested the forecast wasn't a pleasant one. She went upstairs briefly and joined him 10 minutes later.

"You look like you have something on your mind," he commented. "What's happened? Are you all right?"

"I'm just wound up; I can't help but feel we're on the brink of a great discovery … that it's all about to happen. The next few days are going to make history! I can feel it in my bones," she whispered, the words tumbling over one another.

"Okay, slow down and relax. We're all alone in this corner so tell me what you're thinking."

Taking a deep breath, she told him how she had felt faint at the cemetery and how she was sure Mary was guiding them.

"You have had signs of this almost since you arrived, so perhaps it is Mary's influence. She has certainly been relentless in your dreams. I can't say I understand it or whether your feelings about Mary are real, but something has definitely changed from the days Trevelion and I did our research."

It was difficult for them to find subjects to talk about during lunch and Alex took his phone out at one point and looked at his calendar. Cursing, he asked her what day it was and she thought Friday.

"No, it's Saturday, and do you know what we were supposed to be doing this morning at 10 a.m.?"

She thought hard for a full minute and then her eyes grew large. "Oh cripes! We forgot our meeting with John and James. This isn't good, we could have at least cancelled. I'm surprised they haven't called you."

"Well, we can't worry about it now. I have a feeling if this thing comes off in the morning, we'll be seeing John anyway. Let's just try forget about it, it's the weekend. We have to focus and Jack's call has to be the only thing on our minds right now. If either of them call or show up we could say you slept in and we went to see friends and just forgot about it."

"Oh thanks, blame me!" she complained and he smiled lamely.

They finished eating and finally, an hour and a half after arriving back at the hotel, Alex's phone rang. Worried now it could be the other men, he looked at the caller ID and smiled before he answered it.

"Jack's done the job and is now going home," he announced, putting his phone away and looking at her solemnly. "He also said it had begun to rain about 10 minutes ago." Alex took the paper out of his jacket pocket. They had already discussed how difficult it was going to be to fool the police once they knew about it. They could only hope the bomb unit got the word first.

"We should get this done," she said hesitantly and in a low voice. "It's almost three o'clock. Go to the phone booth at the corner, Alex. It's sheltered somewhat by trees and, at least, it's not sunny today."

He was taking so long to go, she finally offered to make the call, but he stood up, put his coat on and carrying his hat, left immediately. Almost 15 minutes later, he was back again with a smug look of satisfaction on his face. Without discussing it, Alex waved the waitress over and ordered fresh drinks, but it wasn't long before they decided to go up to Emma's room. They took their drinks with them, so they didn't have to order again. Alone in the lift, Alex admitted to feeling like a teenager hiding his booze. By the time they got to her room, they were giggling and laughing uncontrollably! They found the news boring so they turned on a movie and in an hour they decided to eat again, ordering room service. They were feeling quite comfortable knowing the wheels of discovery were already in motion and knowing that stressful situation was over. After dinner they both began to yawn.

Alex shook his head and tried to stifle another yawn. "Blast it, I don't want to go yet, it's great having your company again, my lady ... and being out of the hospital!"

"You really should learn how to relax at home, Alex. I'm so envious when I think of that lovely apartment you've made. You must get tired out from hopping about on your crutches. I'm relieved you have Nurse Brown to take care of you though. She'll be leaving soon and you'll have your home all to yourself again ... if we're not in jail, that is!" she sighed.

"Then perhaps I should go home and enjoy it, my lady, give you some time to yourself. I'll call a taxi. We don't know what the next few days are going to bring but it should be exciting one way or the other!" He put on his coat and started for the door. "Sleep well, Emma."

"I think I will do that. I'm glad you're home but I'm suddenly exhausted," she admitted. "I can't help thinking about the trouble we're probably going to be in when John or James hear about all this. I'll be down for breakfast at 7:30. I want to be in Elderslie before ten. Good night, Alex."

Readying herself for bed, she took a cup of tea to the window. As she stared out over the rooftops, she realized how very pleased she felt with their accomplishments. When the phone rang, she was surprised to hear his voice.

"You'll never believe what just happened!" Alex said happily.

"The taxi broke down and you're downstairs in the *Hunting Bar!*" she replied, hoping dearly that it wasn't so.

"No, I'm home, but Dougal Graham just called. He invited us to watch the bomb disposal squad in action tomorrow. Paisley's engineering department have called them about a bomb alert at the burial grounds in Elderslie. The unit we watched in practice will be moving out before dawn. Dougal says he doubts it's serious but he sounds delighted that the team will get some practical experience!"

"That didn't take long," she exclaimed. "It's nice of him but rather odd don't you think when they pride themselves so much on security?"

"He said you showed so much interest and asked the most intelligent questions even when you were aware of the danger. He thought you would appreciate this opportunity to watch them in action. Now see if you can sleep with that on your mind!" he teased.

"Yes, thank you very much! Goodnight, Alex!"

Laughing, he put the phone down and glanced across the table at Mabel, who had been very glad to see him home early. Shuffling the deck of cards like a pro, she frowned at her employer.

"You really like Lady Traymore, don't you? You spend so much time together perhaps you should start asking her over for dinner when I'm gone. I bet you haven't told her you love to cook and she loves this apartment, Sir Alex," she said softly, ephasizing the word 'love.' Lady Traymore is a very sweet person."

Alex almost choked on his drink but decided to let it go.

Over at the inn, unaware that Alex had found a chink in his nurse's armour and, that she and Alex were indulging in a nightly card game, Emma's mind was now aflame with possibilities of her own. An opportunity to view the bomb unit in action was more than she had ever expected. Tomorrow would be an interesting day of discovery for certain; she just hoped they'd be discovering something that would help solve their mystery. Her brain was now raging with anticipation and she guessed that sleep would not come easily.

## Chapter 25 – Sunday 10<sup>th</sup> – A New Dig

Persistently ringing, the phone finally woke Emma a little after six the next morning. Forcing her eyes open, she reached out a fumbling hand and finally found the phone. It was Alex telling her he had forgotten to mention they needed to get over to the bomb site by dawn. He would get a taxi over to meet her.

Stumbling out of bed, she staggered to the bathroom. "Damn ridiculous hour," she grumbled splashing cold water on her face. With no time to shower, she made a cup of herbal tea as she got ready. Surprisingly, it lifted the haze that impeded her vision and she was able to apply her make-up. *This is what happens when I follow that man's lead and drink before bedtime. It's all Alex's fault!*

She proceeded to do a few minutes of stretches, groaning until it got easier. Then she finished dressing, cursing under her breath as buttons eluded her fumbling fingers. Finishing her make-up, she was soon ready and hurried down the stairs. She smiled somberly at the desk clerk and proceeded towards the dining room where she met Mabel coming out.

"Good morning, my lady," the nurse whispered. "The master is a little grouchy this morning but he's given me the day off so I can go home. The taxi is waiting for me. I hope it's a lovely day for you both."

She hurried away and Emma was left puzzling over her sudden concern for their day. She'd never said that before. Then she continued on to meet the grouchy master. Breakfast was quiet and quickly eaten with only short attempts at conversation. As they headed out of Edinburgh, she was glad they were going in the opposite direction to the bulk of the morning traffic. At Junction 4, a small convoy of army trucks slowed things down and she was happy to follow along behind them.

"Och aye, they're going to the Elderslie Burial Ground!" Alex predicted with a grin, when all the trucks turned off at the junction.

Nearing Paisley, Alex suggested they stop at the tea shop now that they had caught up to the bomb unit. Emma agreed as a police car flashing its lights, roared past them and appeared to pull in front of the army trucks. At Moira's, she parked quickly and jumped out, saying she would meet him inside. Meanwhile, Alex took his time and followed her inside.

"Top of the morning to you, Sir Alex! You can take any table, I opened a bit early this morning," Moira explained as she passed by with an order and Emma slipped into her chair. "Oh, deary me," she moaned when she delivered their coffee and cream cakes minutes later. "We had such a scare in the night. Soldiers have been here since last evening customers told me. Apparently they think there are four bombs on the old monastery land. Some people have left town until they dig them up and make it safe again. Hillview Road has been evacuated."

"Do you have any idea where their command post is situated, so we can stay out of their way?" asked Alex.

"Oh yes, sir," a customer volunteered. "The army vehicles are parked· on Abbey Road."

"You're not going over there are you, my lady?" Moira whispered, the colour draining from her face.

Emma just smiled. They finished their coffee and left soon after. She drove slowly through the almost deserted streets, until she saw a police car blocking the way into Abbey Road and Constable Falconer came toward them.

"You can't go down there, my lady," he said sternly.

"We have permission, constable. Dougal Graham invited us to observe them today."

"Not possible," he argued, glancing furtively up the road as an army truck lumbered to a halt behind the Traymore car. "You are going to have to move your car, my lady."

Alex slipped out of the car as they talked and hopped towards the army vehicle behind them. Upon seeing him, the police constable's frustration boiled over and he called loudly to Sir Alex.

"Come back, Sir Alex, you're going to get hurt!"

The soldier driver, seeing the man on crutches coming towards him and the constable waving wildly, grinned from his open window.

"Hello, Sir Alex," he called, "are you having some trouble?"

"Is Dougal Graham on site yet?" Alex asked as the constable approached.

"Yes, sir, Mr. Graham is the adviser on site. He's in the command post."

"Then tell him we're here, would you please, and that the police won't let us through!"

Cst. Falconer had to chuckle when he heard Sir Alex's comment. Nevertheless, he touched him on the shoulder and escorted him back to his car. Once he was safely seated, Emma followed the constable's directions and manoeuvred their vehicle over to the shoulder. She held her breath as the military vehicle squeezed past them and the police car, continuing quickly up Abbey Road.

"I told the driver of that truck to notify Dougal that we were here," Alex said breathlessly.

"We can only hope that it works," Emma replied.

Up at the command post, Dougal Graham was staring in disbelief at the object in front of him.

"Well, sergeant," he snapped at the soldier beside him, "do you have some thoughts on this fearsome object?"

"Yes, sir, I do," he replied, springing to attention. "It looks like the tip of a metal fence post, sir."

"You're damned right it does, lad," Dougal exclaimed, frowning. Hearing his name being called, he glanced quickly at the door as an excited young soldier rushed in.

Heavy footsteps sounded on the ramp outside and a loud knock drew Dougal's total attention. Without waiting for permission, a mud-splattered soldier dressed in coveralls stepped inside and saluted Dougal. Remaining at attention, he attempted to speak quietly and calmly but excitement and confusion were twisting his voice.

"They've found some bones, sir!" he announced too loudly and Dougal winced. "Please come quickly, sir, they're erecting a shelter." Beads of sweat appeared on the young man's face and Dougal held up his hand for silence.

"Double the guard and tighten the perimeter security. No one gets near that site without my knowledge!" he ordered fiercely. Then lowering his voice, he added, "You're familiar with our emergency procedure, lieutenant?"

"Yes, sir!" the soldier replied and exited the building rather quickly. At the same time, another soldier entered.

"We have word that Lady Traymore and Sir Alex have arrived, sir!" He handed Dougal a note, saluted and stood stiffly to attention.

A smile crossed Dougal's lips. "Send an escort for them and then make sure there is a pot of coffee available at all times, preferably fresh … as the day goes on. Do you have any questions?"

"No, sir!" The soldier turned sharply and went outside.

Emma, meanwhile, had stepped out of the car and upon hearing the sound of machinery, she began pacing, looking worriedly toward the noise. Suddenly, an army jeep came tearing towards them from the other direction. Grinning, Alex called to Emma. Stopping quickly, the jeep driver jumped out and handed a paper to Cst. Falconer.

"I'm here to escort Sir Alex and Lady Traymore to the command post, sir," he snapped, standing stiffly to attention. "Would you move your car, constable?"

Cst. Falconer read the note then carefully folded it and put it into his notebook. He sauntered over to his police car, got in and slowly backed it out of the way. Allowing the jeep and Lady Traymore's car to proceed, he pulled it back out into the road again. They passed a line of parked army trucks, some familiar from their visit to the army base, as well as two other very unusual-looking vehicles. Alex pointed out a flat-deck truck with a metal hut and a pile of large blasting shields.

"Go straight in," their driver advised upon arrival at the portable unit that served as the Control Centre. "Mr. Graham is expecting you."

Knocking first, and then opening the door, Emma saw Dougal and smiled as he invited them to join him at the table.

"I'm afraid you've missed our exciting bomb discovery," Dougal began. "We've recovered two of them; would you like to see them?"

A knock on the door diverted his attention and he shouted, "Enter!" A young soldier came in with a coffee pot, put it on the table and went to a cupboard. He selected three mugs, sugar and spoons, bringing them to the table.

"Thank you, lieutenant," said Dougal, "do either of you need milk? No, then before you leave, soldier, pass us those two bombs."

"These are the bombs?" Alex muttered, using his limited acting skills, when they were placed on the table. "They're fence post tips!"

"And you thought they were bombs?" Emma challenged with raised eyebrows.

"There was an anonymous tip and we have to be sure, my lady. Our metal detectors found four of them. I honestly don't think there are any bombs in that ground, but we shall have to dig them all out to be sure!" He took a drink of his coffee. "At least the men are getting a training exercise out of this farce."

"How long is that going to take?" asked Alex, noticing that Emma's expression was quickly changing to one of concern. *Is she for real or is she acting*? he wondered, not taking his eyes off her face.

"With our special equipment, not much longer," Dougal reported. "We should be away from here by four o'clock but you're free to leave sooner if you like. It looks as if, once again, we've been caught …."

"You have to stop them ... please stop the machines, Dougal! I need to see what they're doing!" Emma had jumped to her feet in obvious panic confusing everyone. "Excuse me, my lady?" Dougal asked. "You must stop them ... quickly, please! I will explain but you must do it now!" she shook her hands towards the door and her anxiety was growing with each word. Dougal motioned then shouted to one of his men. "Tell the dig to stop the excavation, now!" The soldier jumped up and leapt toward the door. Emma also headed towards the door, slowing only when Dougal's voice stopped her. "My lady, you really don't want to go out there, it could be extremely dangerous."

Alex was squirming helplessly in his chair, expecting Emma to lash out at Dougal but, as she turned around, they suddenly realized the seriousness of her panic as tears flowed down her face. Dougal's expression softened, and he watched her carefully. Wheeling to her side, he gently took her hand and persuaded her to sit down.

"Lady Traymore," he murmured, looking into her eyes once she was seated, "I need you to tell me what you know about this situation. Is it at all dangerous?"

"No, it's not," she gasped, trying to calm down as Alex handed her a handkerchief. "We put that metal in the ground."

"Why on earth ...?" Dougal exclaimed, finally looking across the table at Alex and seeing an expression that told him his friend concurred.

"Dougal, we are truly sorry but it was our only choice," began Alex. "We needed your team to excavate a gravesite without interference."

"Whose grave is this?" Dougal demanded, all gentleness gone from his voice. "There are no graves marked on the survey drawings for that area or we couldn't dig without the necessary permissions." Grim-faced, his eyes demanded an explanation.

Taking a moment to gather her composure, Emma took a deep breath and wiped her eyes again. She had already caught the warning glare in Alex's eyes and now tried to appear calm despite her excitement.

"We believe this is a very important grave that could contain some valuable Scottish relics," she said slowly, choosing her words carefully and keeping her voice as calm as possible. Taking a deep breath, she added, "We must contact John Dunstan immediately."

"Wait a minute, until we're sure what we have here, we're not calling anyone," Dougal said calmly, but at the same time, he pushed a tiny button on his watch and a soldier appeared almost instantly at the door.

Dougal quietly gave him an order, something about an overlander, and the soldier left again. Alex and Emma looked at each other, wondering what was happening. A few minutes later, two smiling soldiers arrived, spoke quietly to Dougal and left quickly, before he again turned his attention back to his guests.

"I have a call button on my watch," he explained, now obviously more relaxed. "My motorized wheelchair is on its way and then we'll all go over to the site." Voices, and a foreign whirring sound, were now heard outside causing Dougal to move closer to the door. The smiling soldiers returned and surprised Emma and Alex by lifting Dougal up and setting him down in a nearby chair. They removed the seat of his wheelchair and took it outside, laughing with Dougal as they did so.

"While I'm getting ready, why don't you go out and have a look at my Moon Machine!" Dougal urged. "You need one too, Sir Alex!"

Curious now, and, surprised with Dougal's change of mood, Alex got up and followed Emma outside. One of the soldiers had set the seat onto a peculiar-looking machine that looked like a mini-tank with rubber tracks. The soldiers went back inside and returned with Dougal sitting upon their interlocked arms. They deposited him onto the seat.

"Quite the Moon Machine isn't it?" Dougal asked as they got him into a shoulder harness. "Are you ready? Follow me!" he announced. He set himself in motion and one of the soldiers jogged alongside.

Emma and Alex followed, but Dougal disappeared about the same time as she spotted a large red tent up ahead. When she looked back to check on Alex, she noted that the other soldier was walking very closely behind him. When she reached the path to the tent, she stopped to wait for them. Emma saw Alex wink at her and he speeded up a bit faster as he got on the paved pathway.

They found Dougal inside the tent which had three sides covered to keep it warmer and a heater had already been installed. They looked down to see a hole dug out of the grass. It was about eight foot square and Emma took note that there were a number of small grave markers in the area but none close to their dig. It appeared the machine had dug down about three feet before receiving the stop order. Dougal pointed to a uniformed army officer taking a video.

At that moment, they saw John Dunstan coming toward them, barely recognizing him in green coveralls.

"Hello, my lady, what brings you here so early this morning?" He looked at her curiously as he waited for an answer.

"Actually, Mr. Graham asked us here as observers."

John Dunstan looked over at Dougal for clarification and he silently nodded. "So, what has happened here, Dougal? I understand emergency services received an unidentified call that there was a bomb in the cemetery, but instead you have discovered some bones?"

Being the first time they had heard about the bones, Emma couldn't contain her surprise, although she quickly realized that John was watching her. Not knowing how much he had been told, she feared she had already given herself away so kept silent and looked over at Dougal.

"Where were the bones found, Mr. Graham?" asked John.

Dougal called one of the soldiers over to answer the question. After that they began to make their plans and John was told what Alex and Emma had admitted doing as part of the bomb ruse.

"I assume you have a good reason for doing this, my lady?"

"You know we do. We have reason to believe that the missing Royal Regalia are in this grave and that is all I can tell you."

John ranted for a minute, and then suddenly changed his mind, sent them away, called for coffee, and he and the others laid out their plans. Two hours later, they were summoned back to the gravesite.

The scene that met them was now considerably different with a somewhat larger hole that appeared to be 4-5 feet deep. The base of the hole was flat and a line had been drawn to outline a grave. Inside the outline was a partial skeleton. Two people wearing green coveralls were on their knees delicately exposing the scant remains of a human skeleton using brushes and other small tools. Dougal came over to see them.

"Are they professional archeologists?" Emma asked with concern. "This could be a very important historical find they're disturbing!"

"This is a team of professional archeologists, my lady. It's all right, we're not amateurs in these matters," Dougal assured her kindly. "As soon as my men discovered the bones this morning, they realized this could be historically significant and contacted John Dunstan, even before you suggested it, I might add! Now they know those bones belonged to a body, a very old body, I'm told. Those remains are what you see. John apparently asked around if anyone knew you or Sir Alex. It was quickly surmised that you were our prime suspects for organizing the bomb alert! This all happened before I was notified because I was with you. You had already explained your knowledge of the events. John and his team arrived soon afterward and you know the rest."

"Does anyone have any information to tell them who is in that grave, Dougal?" Emma's voice quivered with emotion.

"No, my lady, do you?" he asked hesitantly, searching her face.

"Sir Alex and I are hoping you will find the remains of Sir William Wallace's wife, Mary, because if it is her grave, it could also contain the Scottish Royal Regalia missing since the late 13th century!"

"I'm sorry, my lady, but that's quite impossible," Mr. Graham replied. "It has already been established that the skeleton is that of a man, probably a soldier. The team is quite positive about that due to other items which have been found."

"Yes, we realize that. It would be a man … a fighting monk, a Crusader," she replied. "And, beneath him, you will find his biographia box and beneath that you'll find Mary Wallace and possibly another remains. Could I go closer, please?"

Dougal Graham began to shake his head in the negative but then changed his mind, calling over a soldier to escort her. He realized that the importance of this find could be monumental not only for the Wallace and Walters' families but also for the people of Scotland. He could feel the intensity of Lady Traymore's gratitude as she looked back at him and smiled.

Suddenly, two people in the hole stood up and went over to the ladder talking in whispers.

"Dougal, is there somewhere I could sit down?" Alex asked. "These crutches are knocking hell out of my armpits!"

Realizing he had completely forgotten his old friend was there, Dougal beckoned to a nearby soldier to find two chairs, apologizing profusely. He began to say that he had never used crutches, but realized Alex was so intent on watching Emma as he rubbed his legs that he probably hadn't heard him. Time went by rather slowly and Dougal ordered some sandwiches. Two hours later, there was a flurry of activity in the hole.

"The team is coming out!" Emma told Alex.

The three members of the team climbed up the ladder and removed their hard hats. Right away, Emma guessed from her manner that the smaller person was a woman. She was talking to a man as the third person came towards her. It was John. Dressed in muddy coveralls and with a face mask draped loosely around his neck, the archives director was almost impossible to recognize.

"Hello, my lady," was the only thing he said, grasping her arm gently and seeming to give it a slightly reassuring squeeze. Taking her over to where Alex was sitting, the other two people followed them.

"I'll let you introduce your team to our guests, John," said Dougal.

"Thank you, Dougal. Sir Alex Wallace and Lady Traymore, I'd like you to meet Dr. Eric Morse and Dr. Hazel Zicowski who are presently on loan to us from Perth, Australia. They specialize in dating ancient relics and human remains. Dr. Zicowski is also an orthopaedic surgeon, that's a bone specialist in English!" Dr. Zicowski laughed and her headcovering fell aside to expose a mass of blond curls.

Reserved handshakes were exchanged, but not before Emma realized she was looking into the most gentle, and purest blue eyes she had ever seen. She couldn't help but chuckle at the doctor's unusual and most unfeminine outfit of ill-fitting, oversized coveralls. She commented in her usual forthright manner. "Cripes doctor, that's quite an outfit!"

Quick as a flash, the Australian responded, "Yer, but I clean up good, how about you, Lady Traymore!"

Surprised by the banter between the women, the men struggled to contain their laughter until Emma added, "A little more war paint and I'll be just fine!"

"Och aye," Alex commented, "now we've got two sharp-tongued women to deal with!"

Everyone laughed and Dougal suggested they were all in need of some lunch. As they headed out toward the path to the command post, John commented that he and his team were starving. Emma told them Dougal had ordered some sandwiches awhile back. So, John suggested they all go for a meal together.

"Why don't you wait for us inside while we get changed and we'll go over to *The Wallace* in Paisley. It's rather appropriate I thought! This was planned so quickly this morning, we didn't have time to arrange meals but dinner will be catered for everyone here tonight. We were getting cold so they're bringing in more heat and this was a necessary break. Changing is a nuisance but we do hope to finish today.

"Where are you going to change?" Alex asked.

"In our trailer," said John, cocking an eyebrow at the surprised look on Alex's face. "It's the big one on the street just past those trees. We came prepared to stay if necessary!"

John and the two archeologists went on ahead and Emma and Alex went inside the command post and found the coffee pot full again. Sitting opposite Alex at the table, so many thoughts and emotions were going through her mind she didn't know where to start so they got a coffee and talked about the weather.

"I thought John would be angry with us but he almost seems relieved," she whispered to Alex some minutes later.

311

"I agree, it's ironic but we really couldn't have planned this any better," he reflected. We could never have assembled a team like this on our own!"

"Hmm, but I still would have preferred to have found it on our own."

Not long afterwards, footsteps sounded outside and heavy breathing was heard before the door flew open revealing Hazel and John. They almost fell into the command post.

"Hell's bells mates, it feels like a cyclone's getting whipped up out there!" Hazel panted.

"So are we in agreement for *The Wallace?*" John asked. "It's nearby. Dr. Morse is going with Dougal and his group so we're on our own."

Agreeing, they found an overlarge umbrella and, with John holding it for Alex, they headed to Emma's car. The others watched in fascinated amusement as the big Scot got into the front seat.

"That was very slick, Sir Alex!" Hazel praised him.

Emma found *The Wallace* tavern with a bit of help from John and Alex, and they were soon seated in a small side room with a fireplace and dark rafters, on which nestled the most fascinating relics. John ordered Highland Coffee and asked Hazel what she would like to drink.

"What is Highland Coffee?" she asked.

"It's a coffee with an especially tasty Scottish whisky," Emma explained, "but I'll just have mine black, please. Now that I'm driving, it curtails some of my newfound Scottish-style enjoyment of coffee!"

After ordering their meal, the others watched as Hazel tasted her first Highland Coffee and then took a second sip. They teased her as they waited for her opinion.

"De-lic-ious!!" she exclaimed, rolling her eyes in ecstacy. "You're a Canadian aren't you?" she inquired of Emma as the meal arrived. "My parents and I over-nighted in Vancouver a few years ago when we went on an Alaskan cruise."

"I lecture on English Literature at the University of Victoria," Emma replied, "how long are you staying in Scotland?"

"I'm here on contract for one year with the Scottish National Archives and have only arrived. It's my first time in Scotland."

"Do you have any family connection to Scotland?"

"None, with a name like Zicowski you must be joking! Mum is Australian via England and Dad is Polish. What about you?"

"I'm Canadian but my dad was Scottish. I've just inherited a Scottish estate and recently became the first female chief of the Walters Clan!"

"She also inherited a 700-year-old mystery," Alex added, "and a prophecy she's trying to fulfill. That's why we're here today."

"You have something to do with this? What's the prophecy all about?" Hazel asked with obvious interest, as she finished her meal.

"You probably know the story of William Wallace from your school days," Alex told her. "He was the hero of the Battle of Stirling Bridge in 1297, also depicted in the famous Hollywoodized movie *Braveheart!*"

"I've seen *Braveheart* and I am somewhat aware of the Hollywoodisms!" she chuckled. "Please tell me the real story."

For the next ten minutes, the three Scots gave the archeologist a brief historical lesson about the Scots. When they were finished she stared at them wide-eyed.

"You're looking for a king's treasure?" she gasped.

"Historically speaking, yes," John agreed, "and this would be an amazing discovery, but being relics from the 11th century or earlier, there is really no comparison to a royal treasure as we know it today."

"What exactly are we looking for?" asked Hazel.

"The pieces are of old gold ... a ring, a chalice and a coronet," explained Alex. "They could be contained in a sack or a large pouch. We can only guess as to their size and it's rather a pipe dream that they will be found with Mary, if Mary is found, that is. These relics have been missing since before the deaths of either William or Mary and people have been searching Scotland for over 700 years for them."

"Well, that's definitely a treasure in any archeologist's language," exclaimed Hazel. Her demeanor told them her professional inquisitiveness needed to know more, a lot more. As a forensic scientist, she had many questions in her mind and Emma was the object of her undivided attention.

"Were you aware of the mystery before you inherited the estate, my lady? You knew you were next in line for the title, surely? What makes you think you could solve a mystery that old?"

Smiling patiently, Emma held up her hand to stop her questions. "Hold it, doctor, one question at a time, please! I was not aware of the mystery. I didn't know the first thing about Scotland or being in line for anything."

"So, why did you accept the inheritance?"

"That's a silly question," Emma snorted, "what would you do if somebody offered you an estate in Scotland containing several homes, a title, and who knows what else ... would you turn it down!"

"No, of course I wouldn't!" she laughed, her curls bouncing erratically as she moved.

"That's enough," John interrupted, "time to get back. You two can continue this later, when the dig is complete, perhaps next Saturday morning in my office. You no doubt forgot we were supposed to meet this morning, my lady?" He frowned as he watched the Canadian's reaction of surprise. "Perhaps, under the circumstances, we should put that meeting off for a week. I notified the commissioner this morning, giving our excuses, and no, I did not tell him the real reason we were all cancelling!" Emma flicked her eyes up and caught him smiling at her. *Why is he being so agreeable and helpful?*

The bill arrived and John quickly threw his credit card onto the tray.

"Could you answer me one more question, my lady?" Hazel asked, standing up to put her coat on.

Emma also stood up and Alex helped her with her own coat as they waited in anticipation for next Hazel's question.

"When we first met at the site, you appeared to be upset. Was it because of what you hoped to find in the dig?"

"Yes, more or less."

Receiving such a short and indefinable answer, Hazel realized she was probably intruding and decided she had asked enough questions. Going outside, they were all pleased that the rain had stopped and within minutes they were back at the burial grounds. Met by one of the soldiers, he directed Emma to park well inside the security zone.

"Now, I have a question," Emma murmured, before they got out of the car. "You found a body, but did you find any evidence of a coffin?"

"No!" Hazel replied sharply, looking over at John Dunstan. "I presumed he was a pauper and John has not informed me otherwise."

"He was a Crusader monk and below him you'll find the remnants of a wooden box, called a biographia box," Emma began with a sigh. If you're not familiar with these boxes, I know John is. They are buried beneath a monk but this one could be in poor shape. We are hoping that a woman's body, that of my ancestor, Mary Wallace, will be found under the box. I was wondering if we promised to stay out of your way, could you allow us to watch? We are very eager to see if Mary is found here."

When they hesitated, Alex spoke. "It would be warmer in the command post, my lady."

"No, Alex," Emma whispered emotionally, a tear suddenly appearing on her cheek. "I need to be there when they find Mary."

"Oh, you will be, my lady," Hazel gently assured her. "John has explained a little more about this dig than you had divulged, but I have a feeling that some of it is merely his assumption. Now, I can see how much this means to you, Lady Traymore."

"I want you and Alex to return to the command post for comfort and safety's sake," John insisted. "It may be a couple of hours before we know how to proceed, so I'll send someone for you when the time comes unless you would like to leave the area."

"Not on your life, Mr. Dunstan!" she retorted.

John opened his door and they all got out of the car, but by that time he and Hazel were well ahead of them and just entering their trailer.

It was almost four o'clock when a team of electricians arrived to add more floodlights for the night dig. A soldier told them that a cook tent had been erected and they could help themselves to dinner, if they wished to stay on site. He also said the dig would probably continue until midnight and, if necessary, the team would be back on site at eight in the morning.

The soldier left but before Emma or Alex could even move, another soldier came to the door with a tray on which were two heaping plates containing full dinners of fried chicken and two coffees.

Ten minutes later, John and Hazel arrived in their dirty coveralls, looking quite serious. Hazel started the conversation.

"John and I have been discussing our time-frame and it looks like we won't be unearthing anything of interest to you for hours," she said solemnly. "We believe you would be better off going home and getting a good rest for tomorrow's discoveries. John is surprisingly positive that your instincts are going to be proved right and that we'll find female remains in the morning. We'll be here at eight but you can come at nine, no worries!" She grinned then looked over at John and continued. "Tonight will be a slow process and, although we will accomplish a great deal, if we find another remains, we won't have time to do more than an initial work.

"I need to tell you how the police will be involved in this situation, Lady Traymore," John murmured in a serious tone. "When an archeological dig finds a body, the police must be notified. It's the law and can be the only way to keep it out of the newspapers and away from local interference, if the commissioner sees fit that is! Luckily, our commissioner is aware of the effort you and Sir Alex have gone to, to find this site. It was a challenge even for us to try to keep abreast of your moves and we admit you fooled us on this last account.

"We have contacted the commissioner but he is unusually busy at the present time, something about Yorkshire, I believe," he grinned. "Rather than sending someone in his place, he has given us permission to continue. I have not mentioned either you or Sir Alex's involvement just that instead of a bomb, some bones were found and we are investigating.

"Also, now that Dr. Zicowski knows the situation, we have come up with a surprise for you. This is actually a huge concession, never having been allowed in history, to our knowledge. It was unanimously decided that you and Sir Alex may attend the dig tomorrow and, if we do find Mary Wallace, if you wish, you shall be the first to touch her."

Speechless, Emma covered her mouth with her hand to stem the scream of surprise that threatened. She closed her eyes and when she opened them, a flood of tears cascaded down her face. Hazel gave her a hug from behind and James patted her arm, and they all began to laugh.

"I'm sorry," John apologized, "there was no other way to tell you."

Emma shook her head and sighed, trying to gather her composure, then she took a sip of her coffee and looked over at Alex.

"Will you take care of our arrangements for tomorrow, Sir Alex?" she asked emotionally, getting to her feet. "You really must excuse me," she murmured with her head down as she headed toward the toilet.

When she returned, she was relieved to see that John and Hazel had gone but she was feeling better. Alex held her coat. "Are you able to drive, my lady?"

"Of course I am!" she replied, and he knew she was.

She was quite relieved to get home that night. After refusing to allow Alex to help her, she went up on her own. Once inside her suite, she suddenly felt quite weak, leaning against the door for a moment to regain her senses. She went to the hall closet and barely managed to remove her outerwear before she realized that she needed to sit down. She went to open the curtains, but tonight everything felt different. *We were so close. The 700-year-old mystery is actually coming to an end ... or is it? What if it isn't Mary? What if ...!* "Stop it!" she commanded herself aloud. "It *is* going to end tomorrow," she whispered, "and then I have to decide what else I'm going to do with my new life."

For the first time, she really knew she didn't want to leave Scotland, not yet. She could stay months longer, if she wanted, but she had planned to complete her commitments in Victoria. *Oh, for heaven's sake, I mustn't think about this,* she thought. *I really don't have the time or energy. I need some sleep and will just have to put poor Mary's soul to rest before I plan anything more.*

## Chapter 26 – Monday 11<sup>th</sup> – A Flower

Sitting in front of the mirror the next morning, she carefully pinned the Wallace broach to her sweater then slipped the Wallace ring onto her finger. She was nervous for what they may not discover today but certainly ready to face another day at the dig. She had dressed for warmth and, despite her recurring dream, she felt refreshed.

A cheery 'good morning,' from the desk clerk was rewarded with a smile, but then she saw James sitting with Alex at their table. The men simultaneously greeted her but she replied stoically, "Are John and Hazel attending this group breakfast?"

"She's fine," James declared, "barbed wire is back on the menu!"

Caustic banter continued during breakfast and Emma tried to push thoughts of Mary Wallace from her mind. James' cell phone rang as they finished their meal, drawing an instant frown from the police commissioner and he left abruptly without explanation.

The car radio was forecasting 'clear and cool' weather as Emma drove out of the city, welcoming the sunshine by putting on her dark glasses. Conversation centred on their expectations at the dig and what would become of the regalia if it were found.

"Oh, John would take it for sure," Alex growled, "there's no doubt some obscure rule that will make it the property of Scotland! All kidding aside, you do realize it would become part of the Scottish Honours? We won't get to touch it; we're too low on the aristocratic list!"

Arriving in Paisley, Alex suggested they call at the tea shop for a quick drink and to use the toilet. Giggling at his sudden lack of pride, Emma easily found a parking spot and on their way to the tea shop they couldn't help but notice a small noisy crowd had congregated nearby.

"What are those people arguing about?" she asked Moira.

"I don't know, my lady. I think it's something about the army digging up a bomb in the burial grounds."

"They're objecting to having a bomb dug up?" Emma asked.

"Some folks have nothing better to do," Moira called before returning with two steaming coffees. She smiled mischievously. "I have an apple pie just out of the oven, my lady." Seeing the Canadian's enthusiastic nod, she scurried back to the kitchen.

"We must be in heaven," Alex beamed, when Moira placed a piece of apple pie in front of him, "eating fresh-made apple pie on the 11<sup>th</sup> of December in Scotland ... and for breakfast!"

By the time they left the tea shop the curbside crowd had grown to over fifty people, and two police cars with flashing lights were parked nearby. Sergeant Mackie and Constable Lister were in the crowd arguing with some of the participants but Sgt. Mackie noticed them and went to open the barricade, telling them where to park. As they drove up Abbey Road, they noticed an increased presence of army vehicles but few people were in sight. An army sergeant at the checkpoint inspected their IDs and then ran his finger down a list of names on his clipboard, saluting as he let them through. Dougal was the lone occupant at the command post.

"Good morning to you both. You are to stay here with me, Alex. Lady Traymore, you're to go to the archives trailer and wait for Dr. Zicowski. I assume you know your way, my lady?"

She nodded, but she wasn't particularly happy about Alex being left behind and quickly told him so. She knew he could look after himself, however, and put her coat back on.

"I'm glad you've dressed warmly," Dougal commented. "Are you sure you can make it over there by yourself?"

"Dougal, in case you haven't noticed, I seem to be the only fit person amongst us at the present time! I'll find her, don't you worry."

Shutting the door, Dougal noticed Alex was laughing. "You heard?" he asked. "She's a feisty one isn't she? Is she always like this?"

"Only on a good day Dougal, only on a good day!" he laughed.

Today she noticed that the trailer had a small banner on the side that read, 'National Archives.' She went inside and noted that it had a shower, toilet, change room, office space, and a tiny but adequate kitchen. "All you need is a bed and you could live in this thing," she exclaimed as the Australian burst through the door in dirty work gear.

"Oh, we have beds too, they think of everything to keep us working!" she laughed, opening a cupboard door and lowering a bed from the wall. "Now," she said taking off her ball cap and shaking her blond curls loose. I need you to change into boots and coveralls. It's going to get dirty where we're going and we're also going to drop the titles. I'm Hazel and you're Emma and anyone who matters will think you're one of us!"

Pleased with these arrangements, Emma began to unbutton her sweater.

"No, no," Hazel exclaimed, you're fine, the coveralls will cover your clothes and you need to keep warm. It's very cold in the dig."

Luckily they took nearly the same size of shoes and Hazel had an extra pair of boots that fitted Emma.

Standing back and viewing Lady Traymore all dressed for work, Dr. Zicowski murmured, "My word you are quite a sight, my lady!" and burst into laughter.

Seeing the humour in Hazel's statement, Emma laughed as hard as the Australian, recalling how she had criticized the doctor's own appearance yesterday in the exact same manner. Jamming a ball cap on her head, Emma moved towards the door.

Behind her Hazel shouted. "Hey, wait for me, Emma; you don't know where you're going!"

"I would assume the dig is in the same tent as yesterday, Hazel!"

Meanwhile, Alex was about to discover his own unique viewing location. Utilizing an invention made for Dougal, Sir Alex was lifted to the deck of the machine whose job it was to clear dirt out of the dig area with a long boom-like jib. He was shocked to find a comfortable leather chair inside a wire cage which also had a monitoring system which would allow him to keep in touch with both Dougal and the soldier who operated the machine. It was the perfect viewpoint, above everyone, and, without any stress to his leg.

When Emma climbed down the ladder to the gravesite that morning, she was surprised to see the amount of work that had been done the night before as the top part of the first body was now exposed. She soon found out how mesmerizing it was to have a front row seat at an archeological dig. At times it was difficult but still amazing to watch as bone by bone of the skeletal remains of, what she hoped was the monk who had protected Mary's body, was exhumed and the human form took shape. When Dr. Zicowski confirmed it was a male person, she told Emma further tests were necessary to determine other details such as age.

Special containers and packing expertise were now provided by other archives' staff acting under the watchful eye of John Dunstan as he hovered like a too-fussy mother, becoming a nervous wreck. When they were able to dig deeper, they found the remnants of the biographia box and Emma caught her breath when she realized the metal band was missing just as Alex had predicted! It was the first time Hazel had ever seen a relic like this and she was fascinated as Emma described its expected contents.

319

Emma was surprised when the younger members of the archives team took over so John and his team could take a break. Upon their return, the grave was a bit deeper and dirt was being removed by the spoonful. Suddenly, the work stopped as a bone was sighted and John's team took over again. Two hours later, Emma's emotions were almost at a breaking point and she didn't know how much longer her tired legs would hold her. Suddenly, Hazel stood up and made a statement that gave her a chill.

"I'm almost positive it's a woman," she said reverently, looking over at Emma. Quickly recognizing her discomfort, she beckoned to a soldier up top and they send down a chair. "I'll know for sure after we clean up these bones, Emma," she added as Emma gratefully sat down.

Time seemed to stand still now as Emma watched this second skeleton took shape. More flood lights and another heater were added and a rainstorm now beat down on the canvas above with seemingly celestial vengeance, making additional challenges for the army above.

"The gods are objecting," Emma whispered, as from this new location she was even closer and able to watch all three archaeologists at work.

"I wish the gods would do something about this cold," Hazel quipped, "those heaters aren't doing one bloody bit of good down here!"

After another 30 minutes, Dr. Zicowski confirmed positively that this was indeed the remains of a female. She stood up to stretch, taking a drink of hot coffee from a thermos and offering some to Emma. Taking Emma's arm, she pulled her closer, telling her to kneel down. Pointing to a large dirt-encrusted bump on the left side of the body, Hazel explained that this was something unusual and they were going to see what it was. She brushed away the last dust on a small part of what she now believed could be a medieval leather pouch, keeping her thoughts to herself. With Dr. Morse's help, a small section of one quadrant of the bulge was almost exposed and she could see the faint lines of a white, crudely drawn image forming against a background of old cloth or leather. Emma watched breathlessly as first one white point appeared and then another as both Hazel and Dr. Morse worked on the area. She held her breath as each brush stroke revealed more detail until she knew exactly what it was. It was a cross … the same cross she had seen on a Hospitaller's cloak in the book she was reading. She gasped, and, at that moment, John, who was working close to her, looked up and winked. Trying to contain her overwhelming excitement, the work continued until Emma could keep quiet no longer.

"Oh, my gosh, it's the Hospitaller's Maltese Cross!" she said reverently. "This has to be Mary. It just has to be!"

Hearing Emma's excited comment, the team worked even faster with John moving over to assist. Emma stood up and paced as she watched and over the next half hour, voices around them quieted and only a light rain was heard on the canvas. Almost finished, the men stood up and let Hazel complete the detailed work with Emma beside her. By now, everyone else had gathered around the top edge of the excavation knowing something unusually remarkable was happening.

"The pouch was tucked in so tightly to this person's body, it appears to have been unusually well preserved," John explained, speaking softly and, at last, breaking the tension in the air. "You're right, my lady. It is the Maltese Cross!" As he spoke, he lightly touched Emma's back as she knelt below him. "What an amazing find!"

Emma hadn't realized she'd been holding her breath for so long and could have fainted, if John had not touched her. She raised herself to a sitting position, took a deep breath and looked up at John briefly, for she knew this had to be one of the most remarkable archeological finds in Scotland's recent history, a definite thrill for him as well. The pouch, with its plainly visible emblem, presented a remarkable sight lying beside the remains in the dirt … and then John called for his camera.

"May I touch her?" Emma whispered and Hazel nodded. Emma moved closer and suddenly her eyes saw only Mary with her long hair and a happy smile. Emma reached out with trembling fingers to touch her arm and, just as at the *Place of Tears*, an electric shock enveloped her body. This time, however, it was minute in comparison and, as the vision faded, seemingly far away, she heard John announce they were finished for the day.

While the dig was being covered and made secure from the elements, he ordered Hazel and Emma to get changed while he discussed the site's security arrangements with the army.

Alex had watched Emma leave as he was helped down from his perch and now he slowly walked back to the command post to await her arrival. When the two women arrived, wearing street clothes, Dr. Morse and John were with them. Alex immediately began asking her questions. Seeming to ignore him, Emma poured two black coffees, handing one to Hazel before going to sit next to him. She still didn't speak, but instead heaved a heavy sigh and he noticed her ashen-colouring. Waiting patiently for her to speak, he watched her with concern but she seemed to stare blindly off into space.

"Sir Alex," Dr. Zicowski quietly interceded, "we believe we have found Mary Wallace. Lab tests will be performed but we're almost positive. As you can imagine, this is very traumatic for Lady Traymore, so please give her some space to take it all in. John and I will answer all your questions over dinner. Is anyone else coming with us for dinner, Eric? Dinner, Mr. Graham?" she asked as Dougal entered.

"Thank you, but no," Dougal replied, "we have a lot of work to do to secure the site. The rain has created quite a mess for us to clean up."

"Eric and I will go ahead and get a table over at *The Wallace*," John announced. "Hazel are you coming with us? Alex, you two take your time."

Thanking Dougal, the team left quickly.

Emma stayed with Alex, doing as John suggested but she still didn't seem to want to talk so Alex put on his coat and tried to make small talk, telling her where he had sat all afternoon, to no avail. Before going outside, she picked up the umbrella and had to use it. Not a word passed between them until they were almost to the car.

"Forgive me for jumping on you with questions, my lady."

"I touched her, Alex, and saw her broken body." He heard her sharp intake of breath, blowing it out again as she flicked a tear away with her glove. "There was a pouch with the Hospitaller's cross."

"Was it the regalia?"

"We don't know yet, but they think so and I'm sure of it. There's nothing more we can do and John will take everything back to Edinburgh when they finish here tomorrow. Hazel said the pouch was as hard as a rock, like those we found in the garden shed only larger."

They drove to *The Wallace* in silence and she let him off at the door and parked the car. When she returned, he was still waiting. Inside, the others had found tables in a side room which had a cosy fire. Coffee had already been served and Emma took hers to stand by the fire. Alex began to ask questions of the professionals and they answered as best they could.

"Nothing is proven and it will all take time," John reminded him. "There will be a period of intense scientific investigation and many tests will be run. We're afraid you will need to exercise your patience, Sir Alex and Emma as well. I don't want you jumping to conclusions." He watched the eager Scot's mood dissipate.

"Do you expect to find anything else in the dig?" Emma asked tiredly.

"There should be another body."

"Any other remains no doubt belong there," John said solemnly. "I believe we have what we want and I expect we shall be finished here by noon or soon after. In fact, Hazel will be organizing the forensics in

Edinburgh tomorrow and the army will be reconstituting the site. Your vigil here is over, Emma," he whispered. "Now enjoy your Christmas parties."

"Christmas," she repeated, also in a whisper. "You will keep us informed on the forensic results, won't you, John?"

"Of course, my lady, you're an integral part of this investigation, and soon we'll have proof you are the woman of the Wallace prophecy. Let's wait and be sure." He looked at her curiously. "May I ask you a question?" She nodded. "How did you know where Mary was buried?"

"I dreamed it!"

"Come now, surely you're joking?" the director said gently. "You don't expect me to believe that, do you?"

"Stop it, John," Hazel intervened, "Emma has been through enough in the last two days, and besides, it will come out in the hearings. Nothing has been proven yet and this is not an inquiry."

Surprised at Hazel's reaction, but realizing his error, John backed away from a confrontation, first mumbling an apology and then suggesting they had all been working too hard.

Light snow had replaced the rain as they returned to their cars.

"It could be a mess on the roads tonight," Alex muttered.

"I'm a Canadian, Alex; I have driven in snow before, even though I might not like it. So, stop worrying. I think I can handle this slush … it's very mild." When they reached the by-pass, she asked if she could drop him off at home.

"I thought we might have a nightcap," he replied.

"Not tonight, please. I'm mentally and physically shattered."

After leaving Alex at his apartment, she was home in a few minutes and eager to get to her room. She breathed a sigh of relief when she closed the door behind her. Dropping her handbag and coat on the chair, and slipping out of her shoes, she went to plug in the kettle, but the phone began to ring.

"Front desk, Lady Traymore," said a cheery voice on the other end. "We have a message for you from Commissioner MacDonald."

"I'm listening," she replied, her heart skipping a beat.

"No, my lady, it's an envelope, shall I send it up?"

"Yes, please, and would you send a few camomile teabags as well?"

At the archives, John was in a state of aggitation. He was convinced that the body of Mary Wallace had been found and that the pouch would reveal something of great significance to Scottish history. Contrary to Hazel's advice, he wanted to call in the lab staff to start opening the pouch. Angry words were exchanged between them until in desperation Hazel agreed to X-ray it, if he would help her.

Back at the hotel, James' message and her tea had arrived. She looked surprised when asked for her signature. Realizing now that James' message was important, she was most eager to open it. She made her tea then opened her letter, finding a single sheet of paper.

*My dear Lady Traymore*, it began, *or, may I be so bold, to address you as Emma? I understand after talking to John Dunstan that you will not be going to Elderslie in the morning so I would like to invite you to join me at the hotel for breakfast at nine. If this request meets your approval, please confirm to my voice mail.* He ended the note, *Your servant, James MacDonald.*

*So, he probably knows now*, she thought, dialing his number.

Almost afraid to close her eyes as she lay in bed a short time later, her mind was simply unable to release the vision of Mary laying in her grave and she wondered if it ever would. Suddenly, a strange sense of relief flooded through her mind and body like a soft, tropical wave on a white sandy beach and sleep quickly overtook her.

Mary did visit her dream that night but the scene was not the usual graveyard but a lovely forest glade and Mary was picking wild flowers. It was a sunny day and her three happy children were playing nearby. Mary was smiling and waved to them, offering each a freshly-picked flower from the small bouquet in her hand. She held out the last blue flower as if to Emma. Snapping awake, she stared into the darkness. With fumbling hand, she switched on the bedside lamp, sat up and looked around. Then she saw it, on the other pillow lay the blue flower!

"You're saying goodbye, aren't you, Mary?" she whispered, her eyes brimming with tears. "You're finally free! Thank God."

Getting out of bed, she blotted her tears with a tissue, put on her housecoat and went to open the curtains, pacing the room as tears of relief now streamed silently down her face. Not wanting to go back to bed, her thoughts turned to the inquiry that John had said would soon follow. *How on earth will we explain the pouches and will the Scottish authorities ever believe that a dream led me to Mary's grave? Will it really matter?* She told herself she should be happy for Mary and let the pieces fall where they may ... then she went back to bed.

At 8 a.m. she awoke and made coffee. As she got ready to meet James, her eyes kept straying to the flower, now in a glass on the kitchen table. It defied all logic. It simply couldn't happen, but it had, and she knew she could never tell anyone ... no one would believe her anyway!

## Chapter 27 – Tuesday 12<sup>th</sup> – Dr. Hazel Zicowski

Emma wasn't the only one who had experienced a restless night, John and Hazel had worked well into the evening, assessing, discussing and arguing over the x-rayed contents of the pouch found in the grave. The emblem, which was heavily embossed onto the pouch flap was clearly discernable and easily, if not mysteriously, attributed to the Knights Hospitaller.

"Another puzzle to be solved," John commented, still unaware of the importance of the plane crash or the subsequent investigation at the Ester Road location.

X-ray images had proven to be a problem, taxing Dr. Zicowski's tired brain and limited knowledge of the Scottish equipment. Failing was not in the vocabulary of this tenacious young scientist and it drove her on until just before midnight when she solved the problem and the first relatively clear pictures emerged. John was almost speechless when he saw the obvious images of the missing Scottish Royal Regalia.

"There's something else in there," she murmured, pointing to a large, darker mass on the x-ray. "It's not as dense as a metal object … my guess is that it's cloth or parchment."

"Parchment could mean written records," John whispered excitedly, "we need to get it opened."

"I've never seen one of these pouches in such excellent condition before," Hazel admitted. "I don't imagine the person who placed it next to the body would have known how that would have helped us. Do you have anyone on staff who can open this artifact without destroying it?"

"No, but Ruth Oxley at Misty House has two technicians who have had some experience with this sort of relic."

"Who is Ruth Oxley?"

"Oh, don't worry about that now … tomorrow! We're going home!"

At the hotel the next morning, Emma went to meet James a few minutes before nine o'clock. She walked down the stairs and went over to the window to look out at the car park. First noticing the rain in the puddles, she then looked around and saw James' Land Rover. It came as no surprise to find James with Alex and they were in deep conversation.

"Good morning, my lady," James grinned impishly. "I'm glad you accepted my offer."

"What offer?" Alex asked in surprise.

"James sent me a message to meet him for breakfast."

"Och, he knows we always eat breakfast here at nine on a Sunday!"

"Shh, if you could manage to keep quiet for a minute, we might both hear what's on his mind," she said sharply.

James almost chocked on his coffee. Even though well used to their verbal sparring, he now watched a wide grin spread across Alex's face as he replied to her barb.

"Good morning, my lady, I'm so glad you are feeling better!"

"Yes, and I'm very curious what has brought James out this morning." Waving to the waitress, she ordered coffee and an omelette. The men followed her lead.

"I had a call from Sergeant Mackie two days ago regarding the bombs they found in the old monastery land," James began. He showed no emotion when this comment failed to receive any reaction from either of them, so he continued. "He said you were both there observing the bomb unit. What I want to know is, when did either of you two become explosives experts or, better still, tell me what was really going on at the bomb site and why you found it so interesting?"

"Why didn't you ask Sergeant Mackie, James?" Emma asked, her eyes flicking to Alex as she realized James still knew nothing of the dig.

"Because the bomb unit has the authority to keep everybody out of the danger zone and even his men obeyed the rules. He was somewhat surprised when the army authorized your entry. Now, that makes me very suspicious."

"And rightly so," she agreed. "I presumed you would question Sir Alex last night when you arrived home?"

"I tried, but he wouldn't let me in!"

"Oh, I know, he can be stubborn sometimes," she sympathized.

"No, my lady," James objected, "it was actually that woman. I never realized how protective she is, she threw me out, said her master was tired and needed his rest! She is leaving soon isn't she?"

"Nurse Brown," Emma murmured, trying hard to control her amusement. "She's such a sweet young lady and very devoted to the master! He will be lost without her ... and I'll have to learn to play cards!"

Alex apparently couldn't stand their charade any longer and banged his hand on the table, erupting in laughter, which quickly spread. The waitress interrupted soon after with their meals and they silently attacked their food.

Some minutes later, Emma eyed the commissioner haughtily and asked, "Would you like me to tell you how those brave soldiers dug those bombs out and then risked their lives to defuse them?"

"That's another thing that's puzzling, apparently there were no bombs."

"And how do you know that, James?" She was beginning to see some frustration on his face and she had to get him off this subject.

"By law, they have to report all explosive devices to the police, and no such report has been communicated to us."

"You think Alex and I are stealing bombs, colluding with the army?"

"No, not bombs, but there is something very questionable going on and you know I'll get to the bottom of it! Och, I'd be out there myself if I wasn't so busy!" He was now mumbling and looked at his watch. "What were you doing at the bomb site?" he asked again.

"Oh, tell him," Alex retorted, "he won't believe you anyway."

"We were simply observing," she said calmly. "Dougal Graham gave us permission to watch the bomb disposal unit in action. Alex has a cast on his leg, what the devil do you think we could be doing?" She paused for a moment looking across the table at him with her most sympathetic expression. "Have you given any thought to retiring, James?"

The comment brought an instant response from the commissioner. Sighing heavily, he pushed his chair back and stood up, flashing an exasperated glance at them. Striding away, he called, "I've got your breakfast, Alex!"

"He's working too hard," Emma chuckled, "but I don't think he knows anything about the dig!"

"Don't be too sure," Alex growled, "he's no fool, and it could be he wants us to believe he doesn't know what we're doing. Knowing Dunstan as well as he does, he will no doubt contact him now."

At the archives lab, Hazel was conducting her initial investigation on their grave finds … the age of slivers of wood from the damaged biographia box had already been established as close to the date of Mary's execution and her body's disappearance. Carbon dating tests were also underway and a buzz of excitement filled the lab, spreading like wildfire among the participating technicians. John Dunstan strode about the room with agitated energy. His inquisitive nature was almost at a bursting point when Hazel came to him with a pertinent question.

"Do you have a sample of Mary Wallace's DNA?"

J Robert Whittle and Joyce Sandilands

"Not that I am aware of," John admitted reluctantly, "but both Sir Alex and Lady Traymore are purported to be direct decendants."

"We're dealing with the Walters line here, John," Hazel corrected him sharply. "Lady Traymore is the one who carries that boodline. We need a sample from Emma."

"I had better get onto that straight away," John muttered, moving quickly towards the door, his lab smock flying out behind him.

Hurrying along the labyrinth of passages that connected the archives to the laboratory and technical workshops, John was oblivious to the giggles and odd looks he received from passing office staff as he headed for the main lift. "Get me the *Courtyard Inn* on the phone!" he ordered his startled secretary as he stormed into his office.

"Has Lady Traymore left yet?" he snapped into the phone when the receptionist answered.

"Excuse me, sir," she replied. "We don't …."

Interrupting her, John shouted angrily into the phone. "This is of national importance, young lady. Answer my question!"

"N-no, sir, she's in the dining room with Sir Alex Wallace."

"Tell her to contact Dr. John Dunstan at the Scottish National Archives … immediately!"

Startled by the archivist's fierce manner, the receptionist hung up and hurried into the dining room. Approaching Alex and Emma, she delivered the message, and added, "Would you like a phone brought to the table, my lady?" She moved quickly away when Emma nodded.

Making a show of her efficiency, the receptionist arrived at the table with a phone only to be waved away as they used Alex's cell phone. Explaining to his secretary, Alex then handed the phone to Emma.

"You have some good news for me?" she whispered when the archivist answered.

"We need a sample of your DNA."

"Walters' DNA?"

"Yes," John's voice said patiently, "can you come right over?"

Alex was watching her carefully as he listened to the one-sided conversation, but he began to frown when she spoke his name.

"Would you be able to prove Alex was a Wallace?"

"No, we don't have the Wallace DNA on record. How soon can you come, Emma, we're at the archives.

"A sample, that doesn't sound like a blood test."

"Hazel will explain when you get here," he replied impatiently.

"All right, we've just finished breakfast, so we'll come right over." Smiling to herself, Emma set the phone down and glanced at Alex. "Do you want to go with me to see my DNA testing by Hazel?" she asked, seeing him nod. "Good, I just need to go upstairs for my coat and then we can leave."

Relieved that the rain had finally stopped, they arrived at the archives and were surprised when a security guard came to open the car door for them. "If you would wait in the reception area, Lady Traymore, Mr. Dunstan will be down in a moment. I've alerted him that you are here." Moments later, John, still wearing his lab smock and a grin from ear-to-ear, stepped out of the lift pushing a wheelchair. Wasting no time, he got Alex settled and suggested she leave her coat and handbag with him. Then he hurried her along the corridors to the laboratory area. Everyone working in the room was wearing green scrubs and their different-coloured hats were the only key to their identities. John made a beeline for a red-hatted person, in deep concentration at a large microscope.

Emma didn't recognize Hazel until she turned, pulling down her face mask. Grinning, she beckoned Emma to follow her.

"Has he told you?" she asked, unable to hide her excitement. Emma shook her head. "We believe you are right, Emma, and that we have found Mary Wallace! Tests have been made on the wood we recovered and so far it dates to the right time period. Also, a tiny, square nail, no doubt made by a blacksmith, pointed us to the same conclusion. Tests are well underway to find the DNA of the woman's skeleton, but we first need a match. So, are you willing to let me take a sample of your blood, a little piece of skin, a few hairs and a clipping from a fingernail?"

"Wow, you're going to disfigure me for this cause? Oh, I suppose so except …," she looked at her fingernails. "Cripes, I guess I haven't had a manicure for awhile, so sure!"

"Perfect! We'll go for a manicure together when this is over. Follow me into my torture chamber!" Hazel giggled, making a face.

Going into another room, Hazel had her sit in a medical chair which she raised and adjusted to a reclining position before going to make her preparations. Emma watched her intently.

"Are you also a medical doctor, Hazel?"

"Yes, and I'm an orthopedic surgeon too. I worked in Freemantle Hospital for a few years. When marriage didn't seem to be coming my way, I opted for adventure and volunteered for the archival investigative service and, fortunately, love it!"

"And your background is?"

"Farm girl from WA … Western Australia … my dad and brother Ben, farm a large property 200 miles south of Perth, near Albany. If you don't know Australia, that's in the south-western corner of Oz. What is your background, my lady?" she asked softly, removing the needle from Emma's arm.

"Dad was a dockworker in Nanaimo on Canada's west coast; I worked at night and on weekends to put myself through university."

"That was hard, wasn't it?"

"I like to think of it as character building," grinned Emma.

"Married, children?" Hazel asked, readjusting the chair so Emma could stand up.

"No, single and free as a bird!"

Returning to the waiting room together, Alex looked very happy to see them, especially when Hazel said they could go.

"How long will it take to get the results, doctor?" asked Alex.

"We should know by Friday morning."

"You said you were a bone specialist, didn't you, Hazel?" Emma asked, looking at her thoughtfully. Hazel nodded suspiciously. "Would it be possible for you to take a look at Alex's leg? I've been thinking we should get a second opinion before we go back to see Dr. Greare."

"Yes, I can do that for you," Hazel replied. "Give me a few minutes to set it up."

As they waited, John Dunstan came by. "You wouldn't be going to Misty House in the next couple days would you?"

At that point the conversation was interrupted by a staff member pushing a wheelchair, and a request for Alex to accompany her to the x-ray department. After he'd left, they continued their conversation.

"Why? Would you like us to go to Misty House, John?" Emma teased.

"I thought you could take the pouch we found with the body to Tom and Charlie. They're the only people I know of in Scotland who have experience opening them. They've done it for us before."

"Yes, we can definitely do that. We'll go today."

In the x-ray room soon afterwards, Dr. Zicowski frowned as she stared at the x-rays of Alex's leg. "How badly would you like that cast off, Sir Alex?" she asked, but not waiting for an answer, she picked up the phone. A few minutes later, she returned. Going over to the small x-ray projector on the wall, she flipped on the light, slipped in the x-rays of Alex's leg and beckoned Emma over.

"Sir Alex is having his cast removed." Pointing to the x-ray, she continued. "If that leg was broken then it's mended miraculously. Who was the doctor who gave him this diagnosis?"

"It wasn't broken?" Emma asked, obviously shocked.

"Yes, it was, but many years ago ... I would guess he was only a child. What the doctor saw was calcium build up. It's a strange mistake for a skilled professional to make."

"Have you told, Sir Alex?" Emma asked.

"No, I didn't. I thought I'd let you give him the details."

At that moment, John arrived carrying a lab box with handles and passed it to Emma. "Alex is on his way back too."

"That's the pouch?" Hazel asked. "Where are you taking it?"

"Emma's taking it to Misty House for us. They have two technicians who know how to open them," John explained.

"I'd like to go with you and meet them," said Hazel. "All our tests are in progress and you won't miss me for a few hours, John."

"All right, it will give you a chance to see a bit of the country," he said.

"We'd love to take you; we're going straight there now seeing as we don't have to go to the hospital. You'll be surprised; Misty House is a very special place but you realize it will take a week or so for them to open the pouch."

"I'm just grateful there is someone more skilled than our lab to tackle it!" Hazel laughed.

Emma went to the door to look for Alex and saw him walking slowly towards her using his crutches for balance; a green-coated staff member walked beside him. He grinned broadly when he saw her.

As they waited for Dr. Zicowski to get her coat, Alex went into a detailed description of the cast removal, blushing when he told of the soothing leg massage he'd received by the female attendant.

It was just before noon and, before they got on the road, they agreed to go to Toby's for lunch so they could take Hazel to Bannochburn and past Stirling Castle. Roads were clear, the sun was shining brightly and a much happier Scotsman knew he had an attentive audience. On the way to Bannochburn he regaled them with stories of Scottish history. They stopped briefly to take photos of each other at the *Robert the Bruce* statue. Emma found her way to the ale house and a greeting from Toby quickly told Hazel they were again in the company of one of Alex's friends.

When they finished lunch, Toby brought out Alex's favourite dessert which they shared.

"Och, did yee hear aboot the nasty car crash outside on Friday night?" Toby asked. "Fortunately, Dr. Greare was at a Freemason's meeting nearby so the injured got some quick attention."

Alex and Emma's eyes locked momentarily but they allowed the topic to drop. Leaving Alex to pay the bill, the women returned to the car. The drive to Misty House was unusually quiet as Hazel watched the scenery and the others were lost in their own thoughts. When they reached the manor, some of the children were outside with their dogs.

"Those girls are blind," Hazel commented in surprise as they got out of the car.

Ruth had come to the door and now opened it wider for them.

"Yes, they are," Ruth murmured. "Bring your visitor inside, my lady. We'll tell you all about the children and their dogs." Introductions were made and Ruth offered tea but they explained they had just eaten. "Your leg must be better, Sir Alex; I'm relieved."

"Actually, it was never broken," he growled, causing Ruth to cock an eyebrow at him. "We believe," he said glancing over at Emma, "that it was a moment of opportunity that suddenly presented itself and the good doctor used it to sabotage our investigation."

"Oh, come now, Sir Alex, why would Dr. Greare want to do that?" Ruth asked. "He's a well-respected member of the staff at Stirling Hospital."

"He's also an active modern Templar!" Alex added.

Hazel was trying to follow this unfamiliar subject that had entered the conversation, but now she remembered snatches of other comments that had been made at *The Wallace* during that first dinner. The puzzle was beginning to make more sense. *Why would the Templars be so adverse to the Wallace family tracing Mary's grave? Could it be they knew she was buried with the royal regalia in her arms? Their involvement must be unknown to historians and the actual location of the hurried interment had certainly been lost in the annals of time.* The doctor's interest was piqued but she also knew their uppermost concern needed to be centered on the pouch.

"He's right, Ruth," Emma was explaining. "I think they're trapped in a mystery they created and are afraid someone else is going to solve it before they do. Politics and 700 years of keeping a secret, and then I come along. I was more determined to fulfill the ancient prophecy with my snooping and questioning than anyone else had ever dared. But now we have another problem, we'd like Tom and Charlie to open another pouch that we've found." She indicated the box she was carrying.

"They have opened all the other interment pouches now," said Ruth, "but it's going to take years to translate the Latin contents." She sighed. "Come along, we'll go find the men."

She led them quickly across the yard, stopping abruptly once inside to watch a younger group of children walking around the obstacle course with their dogs. One of the dogs suddenly led a little girl away through a door at the side of the building.

"She's going to the toilet; these dogs take care of all their needs!" Ruth chuckled, before leading them over to the workshop area where they found the two men.

Hazel immediately noticed a row of pouches lying on a table. They closely resembled the pouch they had found with Mary Wallace. Beside each pouch were some documents and on the top of each pile was a parchment in a tray. Dr. Zicowski moved closer to the table, leaning forward to get a better view.

"Go ahead, Hazel, before you burst!" Emma laughed.

Hazel shook her head and was presented to the Misty House technicians who were obviously thrilled to meet a modern scientist who studied these old artifacts. They immediately bombarded her with questions. Tom was especially delighted to explain his process of rejuvenating the leather, enabling them to more safely remove the contents. Emma gave Tom the box and he opened it while Charlie went to get the metal detector.

"There's metal in here!" Charlie exclaimed as it buzzed wildly.

"I think you had better give us some more information before we go any further," suggested Tom. The others looked from one to the other and deferred to Hazel.

"We have x-rayed the pouch," she admitted. "It contains a small crown, a drinking vessel and a ring. John Dunstan is sure that it's the missing Scottish Regalia. How soon could you have it open for us?"

"It will take us about a week to treat the leather and open it safely. Do you think there is anything else inside?" Tom asked.

"There could be a parchment as in the other pouches," Emma suggested. "Hazel said the x-ray showed a large, dark mass."

Later, as they prepared to leave, Ruth remembered something.

"Doctor, you were wondering about the children and the dogs. Did you have any more questions?"

"This centre is quite wonderful," exclaimed Hazel. "It boggles my mind and I could spend days here! I will have to return one day and see more. Do you have time to quickly show me a biographia box, Ruth, then I must get back to work."

The women returned to Ruth's office leaving Alex with the technicians. When Ruth opened a cupboard and brought out the biographia box, Hazel couldn't contain her interest. Ruth gave her a fascinating overview of the box and its use in the death and afterlife of a monk. She also showed her copies of a parchment document and photos recovered with contents of other boxes.

"I wonder what we shall find in Mary Wallace's pouch?" Hazel murmured thoughtfully.

"Don't even think about it," Ruth laughed, "whatever is in that pouch will surprise you, and perhaps even present another mystery. Doctor, I would appreciate it if you could keep our secret regarding our work here at Misty House. We do our best to prevent press interference and unnecessary visitors. I'm sure you understand."

"Yes, certainly Ruth, but you must realize that John Dunstan is aware of your work. It was his idea to bring the pouch here."

"Yes, that's true, but he doesn't yet know the extent of our work with the monastery interment records and their translation."

"You have to tell him," Hazel insisted, "they're National historical records."

"We may need another week," Emma said quietly. "One more week and, if your x-ray machine is right, my work here is done and then we'll tell John everything."

"One week won't hurt anything," said Ruth, looking at Hazel.

Hesitating only a moment, Hazel gave her word and shook hands with the matron. "Thank you so much for everything you do here, Ruth. This has been an unusually exciting week. Never in my wildest dreams would I have expected to be taking part in the fulfilling of a prophecy, let alone recovering a long-missing part of Scottish history."

As they returned to the city, the car was noticeably quieter.

"I think we should eat at the Wheat Sheaf," Emma announced as they approached the area of Dougal's hotel. "Hazel might as well learn a little more of the puzzle."

"Sounds good to me," Alex chuckled, knowing the surprise Hazel would have when her incessant questions revealed the close connection he had to the bomb expert.

As they parked in front of the quaint country inn, another successful operation was taking place on the Yorkshire moors. Commissioner MacDonald had acquired a court order that morning enabling them to search the silent monastery. Their conversation had reignited his intrigue with Emma's suspicion that she and Alex had been watched and spied upon when they visited the monastery weeks before. In light of recent events, he had taken quick steps to attain a search warrant.

A team of electrical experts quickly descended on the monastery and discovered a control room, confirming Emma's suspicion. The search had also revealed a hidden library of old documents dating back to the time of the Norman Conquest. Unfamiliar with Latin, James had called in the linguistic department at Edinburgh University, with instructions to search for anything regarding Wallace or the missing regalia. At that very moment, he had a letter in his hand from the Bishop of Glasgow to the Abbot, recording the marriage of William Wallace and Mary Walters in September of 1294.

Unable to read the original letter written in Latin, one of the archivists trained in linguistics had translated it for him. James smiled grimly as he read it silently. *Here at last is the proof that Sir Alex is a legitimate Wallace. I think they will both be pleased.* There were several more documents that referred to Wallace but the one that interested the police commissioner most was a statement from the Knights' Hospitaller. In it they affirmed that they had given Mary Wallace a secret Christian burial, and pledged they would forever guard her resting place.

Scowling at the document, James puzzled over its contents. *Och, no information on where that burial took place! I wonder if the modern day Brotherhood knew? Could that have been the reason those four Crusader lodge members killed in the plane crash, were travelling to Edinburgh?* He already knew for certain about Monsignor Sharp. Slowly, all the pieces of the puzzle were linking together. In a few more days they would have completed their work at the monastery and he would be ready for a showdown with Sir Alex and Lady Traymore, an event for which he had mixed emotions.

As Emma and the others hurried into the warmth of the Wheat Sheaf Inn, they were in a jovial mood. When Dougal rolled up to greet them, he didn't recognize Hazel at first. He took them to a table near the log fire, took their drink order and gave them menus before excusing himself.

"You people are so sneaky! That was Mr. Graham, the bomb expert at the dig but he didn't recognize me in street clothes, did he?" Hazel asked suspiciously, glancing at her companions and grinning.

Neither answered as a waiter appeared with three coffees and menus. He described the specials and they all chose the Salmon. Hazel was impressed by the old inn and its old world charm. When their meal arrived they soon agreed it was the best salmon they'd ever tasted. After dessert a waiter brought fresh coffee and quietly removed the extra chair. Hazel looked over at her companions and giggled when Dougal quietly slid in beside her at the table.

"You looked a little surprised when you arrived, Dr. Zicowski," Dougal laughed. "You had no idea this was my establishment did you?"

"No, I certainly did not and I didn't think you recognized me either," she laughed. "Your friends are very sneaky!"

"Call Mara over here for a moment," Dougal ordered a passing waiter. "I want you to meet my wife. I don't suppose our friends have told you how we became friends. I actually owe my life to Sir Alex but they will tell you that story if you can persuade them!"

"They certainly did not and I will definitely have them tell me very soon!" Hazel replied. "You people are such a delight to have met and I'm very glad I had the opportunity to come to Scotland. So far this job has more than exceeded my expectations!"

Mara arrived as they were preparing to leave, staying just long enough to meet Hazel, hug Alex and curtsey to Emma before being called back to the kitchen. On the way to the car, Hazel requested she be dropped back at the archives.

"I'm sure John will still be at work. This project has him consumed … and me too!" she said with a giggle.

On the way, Emma began to tell her the story of how Dougal and Alex met and in no time they were in town. Hazel thanked them profusely, reminding Emma they were going for a manicure soon! They watched her run into the building.

"Join me for a nightcap," Alex murmured as they drove away.

"Yes, tonight, dear Alex, I will."

A cold wind caused them to move quickly into the hotel foyer, and, as Emma had somehow expected, James was there to greet them.

"Bad night to be out driving," he commented. "I think there's a table empty near the fire." Turning abruptly, he pushed his way through the crowd and called a waiter.

"You were at Paisley today," commented James, immediately after they had sat down.

"No, we went to Misty House," Alex replied.

"And why would it make a difference to you where we were today, Mr. Policeman?" Emma asked flippantly, trying not to sound defensive even though she was nervous of what James was going to ask.

"I've actually been busy trying to make some sense of an accusation you made recently, my lady."

"In my memory, the only thing I've accused anyone of recently is stupidity!" she replied.

"That's where you're wrong, Lady Traymore, and you can't imagine my delight in saying that!" James quipped, smiling broadly. "You accused the silent monks of having a listening system when you visited the monastery."

"I most certainly did, twice actually," she admitted. "You finally took me seriously. Did you ask them if it was true?"

"Something like that."

"And they admitted it?"

"They showed me the control room. Apparently, it wasn't meant to be a secret. It was merely a useful tool due to their inability to speak. They were sorry it upset you."

Alex watched his friend suspiciously, knowing there had to be more to the story than he was admitting. Emma looked pleased, but after one drink, she excused herself and went to her room. When ready for bed, she sat at the window and allowed her mind to return to the first days when she arrived in Scotland. She thought of how much had been going on and how it had all overwhelmed her, although trying not to make it appear obvious. Once the initial shock of it all settled and reality set in she was glad to have the mystery to fill her time and keep her mind active.

Now, as she sat in the darkened room watching the lights of cars go by below she realized her quest to find the Royal Regalia would soon be over. What was she going to do after that? She had told Alfreda she was staying for Christmas and Hogmanay, but then what? She had some travel plans going through her mind, and why not. Perhaps she would even do some writing.

Thoughts of returning to her teaching job after this amazing Scottish adventure were not causing her any excitement at all, although she knew she had to return to conform to the laws. She had not even received an expected email from the University regarding the yearly Faculty Christmas Dinner at the Empress Hotel. *Probably, if the number of emails I'm receiving is any indication, I've not even been missed! I have made more friends in Scotland in five weeks than I have had in years. Is it any wonder I would prefer to stay here!*

## Chapter 28 – Wednesday 13<sup>th</sup> – Return to Dorik

Enjoying the luxury of sleeping in and not having to set her alarm was pure heaven on Wednesday. She'd had a restful sleep and the lack of tormenting dreams was a treat. Daylight was streaming in through the open curtain when she awoke. She got a drink of water and went over to the window, groaning when she saw the white blanket covering the rooftops.

"What is this?" she said aloud. "Alex said Edinburgh didn't get very much snow!" It was almost ten when she ventured downstairs and glanced out at the car park but couldn't see any familiar cars. She headed for the dining room and found Alex reading a newspaper, but he had a pile of them on the table in front of him.

"Good morning, Sir Alex, although that is highly unlikely," she quipped. "Can you use some company?"

"Certainly, my lady, could I coax you to have breakfast with me this lovely morning?"

"You mean you haven't eaten yet?"

"I was lonely so I knew you would arrive sooner or later!"

After they'd ordered, Emma broached a subject that had been on her mind the night before. "Do you realize it's less than two weeks to Christmas?"

"You're not thinking of leaving us are you?"

Before she could answer, James came into the dining room and appeared to be looking for them. "I have some news for you two," he said officiously, sitting down but motioning away the waitress. "The inquiry date has been set for Monday the 18<sup>th</sup> at one o'clock in the boardroom at the police station. You're both required to be there!"

"Required?" Alex hissed. "Are you asking us to be present, James, or is this an official order?"

A wane smile tugged at the police commissioner's mouth as he reached into his breast pocket and drew out two envelopes, handing one to each of them. "There, now it is official, Sir Alex, that's a magistrate's order!"

"And the subject of the inquiry, commissioner?" Emma asked with a look of innocence.

"It's all explained in the order, Lady Traymore! We shall see you both on Monday," James said flippantly, winking at Emma before he left.

Immediately, Alex opened his envelope and read the contents. Throwing it on the table, he whispered, "It's all very vague, they want to know what we know, how and why. James hasn't mention John Dunstan or the archives for awhile. "It's clear they want us to reveal everything." After they had eaten, Alex grinned mischievously, rubbing his hand through his beard. "How would you like to spend a couple of restful days at Dorik, my lady? James can't follow us there and, if that is his intention, he'll get mighty frustrated when he can't reach us easily."

"Oh goodness, Alex, can I deal with that crazy boat ride right now? Although, I suppose it would be relaxing and I should get used to it," she added, making a face.

"We could leave right after breakfast if you like. Remember, it's best to go in daylight! Was there anything particular that you wanted to do today? I just need to go home to get an overnight bag."

"The snow seems to be over so the roads should be clear by now. I had no plans except to relax, so, if we're going we may as well leave as soon as possible. Here are the keys, finish your coffee and go warm up the car. I won't be very long. I have a wardrobe there so I don't need to pack very much."

He took the keys and stood up, picking up the bill.

"I think you've forgotten something, Sir Alex!" she said quietly, watching him walk almost normally towards the cashier. Picking up his walking stick, she caught up to him. "I reckon this is a sign that you're feeling much better, but please use it when you go out to the car," she pleaded, handing it to him. "We don't need any more ice mishaps."

"You're right; I am walking quite well this morning, aren't I?"

In 20 minutes, she returned downstairs and went to join him in the car. He put her suitcase in the boot and she got in behind the wheel. She went upstairs with him while he packed his own bag but Mabel was out for her walk. They drove silently until she had escaped city traffic and then Emma suggested he put on some music.

"Don't be surprised if I fall asleep," he warned her, putting his head back, but then sat up again quickly. "Och, I had better refresh your memory with directions, just in case!" He proceeded to name the exits.

It was turning out to be a lovely winter day with blue sky dotted with light clouds, perfect for where they were going, and she was now looking forward to returning to Dorik. She spotted a road crew working on the A1 but there were no holdups. Hearing a noise, she looked over at Alex and realized he was snoring. Passing the sign to Dunbar, the motorway turned south along the East Lanark coast. Watching for the sign to Coldingham she turned east and saw amazingly flat, dark glimpses of ocean. Alex woke up as they reached the top of the hill overlooking the magnificent, but cold-looking, expanse of the North Sea. Emma's pretty little island was sitting just off the coast.

"Phibbie is coming for us at 1:30 so we have time for a snack, if you like," he told her. "A bit of food might be a good thing, Emma, although the water does look unusually calm."

They finished eating and, soon afterwards, the tavern keeper came to inform them that Abe had arrived. Wasting no time, Emma was eager to get started before her imagination unnerved her, but today the trip was calm and beautiful as if welcoming her home. A bit of snow was already evident as the vehicle made its way over the hill and down through the forest. Traymore House looked wonderful in the distance and the lake, rimmed with snow, sparkled in the sunshine. The staff was very happy to see them after three weeks of too much quiet. Emma went to one of the windows and looked out at the lovely valley and surrounding hills.

"Are you thinking about the *Place of Tears?*" Alex whispered, coming up beside her.

"Actually, this reminds me of home, but yes, I have to go back there."

"We will, but not in the dark, we don't have street lights here yet!"

"I want to ride there like we did last time, Alex. I have such good news to tell Flora."

As they waited for dinner, Emma decided to go to the library to look at the journals and for any other interesting books she might want to borrow. Alex joined her. Noticing the title *The Brotherhood,* she was about to pull the large ledger from the shelf when Alex intervened.

"I wonder what the Hospitallers had to do with the monastery?" she asked, watching as he put the heavy book on the table.

"Oh, I know that answer," Alex growled. "You'll find a document in here where they swear to protect the monastery forever. Rather strange when they were said to be on England's side during the Scottish Wars."

"They didn't do a very good job of it then, did they?"

"You mean when Edward had it destroyed?" She nodded. "Maybe they were hopelessly outnumbered. There could have been a host of reasons. We did find evidence of their existence when we located the grave and the biographia box."

"And Tex did say the monk was probably wounded."

Emma carefully opened the old ledger near the front and turned a few pages. "Oh, you're right, Alex. The pledge to the monastery is right here, but why is it not at the monastery? Why is this book at Dorik?"

"My guess is it came at the same time as Flora, secretly removed from the monastery by the Hospitallers so as not to alert the English of their involvement. This is the secret they've been keeping for 700 years."

"Do you think they knew where Mary was buried?"

"We can't be absolutely sure but they knew this information would be sought after, so they would have hidden it well enough that discovery could take a long time. Someone took careful steps to have the relics buried with Mary. I'd like to think it was the Hospitallers. I hope there will be more evidence in the biographia box or the pouch."

"Who really cares, Alex," Emma exclaimed, "that was 700-years-ago! As long as the regalia has been found and Mary's soul is at peace, I certainly don't."

Sarah came to tell them dinner was served in the small sitting room and Emma closed the ledger. Alex returned it to the shelf and arm-in-arm, they made their way down the hall more relaxed than they had been since her arrival in Scotland. A bottle of white wine was chilling beside a basket of freshly baked bread. The cook himself appeared to serve the meal, describing it as 'Dublin Bay Prawn Tails served in a sea of creamy Marie Emma Sauce.'

Emma was soon swooning over its tasty sweet goodness. "I do like the name choice! Did you pick this for us tonight?" she asked midway through the meal. She watched as a tiny grin grew into a smile. She laughed. "You receive an A+ for achievement in homework, Sir Alex!"

They drank most of the wine, and then Alex made her a camomile tea, beckoning her over to the comfortable chairs.

"Thank you for suggesting this," she said softly. "I think we both need some R&R and I am truly falling in love with this little island. I could happily spend a great deal of time here."

Back in Edinburgh, James MacDonald contacted the archives for help with evaluating the documents which had been discovered at the silent monastery. He and John Dunstan spent the day perusing the document which described in great detail the involvement of the Brotherhood in the disappearance of the royal regalia. Not wanting to totally divulge all he had learned, James did not mention the startling contents of a certain letter written by the Bishop of Glasgow, Robert Wishart, to the Abbott and dated 6th, September 1294.

## Chapter 29 – Thursday 14<sup>th</sup> – A Message to Flora

Dark storm clouds boiled overhead as Alex and Emma mounted horses and set off for the cliffs. Strong gusts of wind tore across the valley as they crossed into the protection of the trees on their way to the *Place of Tears*. Dismounting near the familiar path that went up through the rocks, it was noticeable that the wind was calmer here. As they climbed the path to the cliff top, a shaft of sunlight forced its way through the clouds and beamed directly on the area that had given Emma so much grief that frightening day almost a month ago. She shivered involuntarily, at first, and then shook herself as if to ward off any negative thoughts or feelings.

Today, when she gingerly touched the rock, she felt only the wind, a wind that froze her cheeks. She whispered her news to the elements wondering if Flora was already aware that her mother had been found. Standing with her hand on the wall for support, her eyes on the wild, boiling sea below, Emma whispered a heartfelt goodbye to her long ago cousin, Flora Wallace.

"She's with her family now," she told Alex, fighting off tears as they began their steep, downward trek. Alex grasped her hand as if remembering their last frightening descent of this path.

At the bottom, he stood at attention and silently saluted the craggy lookout, and helped her mount. They noticed dark clouds were gathering out at sea and turned for home.

In Edinburgh, at James MacDonald's office, John Dunstan was arguing with the police commissioner on the merits of charging Sir Alex and Lady Traymore with concealing information on the whereabouts of human remains and a national treasure.

"That's ridiculous," the archive director laughed, "and you could never prove it, James."

"Then I'll charge them with digging in sacred ground without the necessary permission."

"They didn't do the digging, and you can't charge the bomb unit."

"How did they figure out where to dig?" James snapped. "They were the ones who brought the army into this."

"What is it you really want?" John asked. "I think you're frustrated that Lady Traymore bested you and proved the Wallace prophecy."

"Hidden by a woman and recovered by a woman, oh I know the prophecy well, but who would have thought that woman would be a Canadian!" James declared, scowling.

"Are you going to tell Alex you found proof of his birthright at the monastery?"

"I suppose I should, but I would like some answers first. How did you know?"

"I know you better than you think and I know you're not really serious about charging those two with anything. I thought you were Alex's friend."

"Friendship has no place in business, police or otherwise." He paused and looked at John intently. "No, you're right, I won't be charging them, but I need to know how and why the Brotherhood is involved. I'll bet that's something you don't know, John."

"Now, that will be interesting, let's hope they know the answer to that part of the mystery, too!"

While the argument and discussion continued in Edinburgh, a different scenario was taking place on the windy and, soon-to-be rain-swept, Island of Dorik. After riding back to the stables, Emma quietly informed her companion she wanted to ride again in the afternoon. This was probably the last time she would see the island for some months and she was determined to explore every corner, irrespective of the weather.

"Please say you're not serious, my lady; it's very cold," Alex pleaded, handing their coats to a groom. "We'll stay another night or two and perhaps it will warm up a bit. Have you given any consideration to adding an entry to the journal?"

"About the dig, you mean? Yes, I have been thinking about that. I suppose I should do it before the memory fades."

Over the next two days they took the horses exploring two more times. He could tell she was in her element. Her riding skills seemed to have returned and she was now immensely more comfortable with the horse as well as in the saddle. She was especially thrilled to find the underground spring of clear, deliciously cold water bubbling out between rocks at the base of the mountain. It disappeared again after feeding the stream that crossed the valley. Lookout ledges, probably hidden for centuries, were also found, more easily seen through trees now devoid of their leaves. Early Saturday afternoon, red-faced from the wind, she took one last look at the valley from the treeline before Phibbie returned them to the mainland.

As Emma drove toward Edinburgh, they were both immersed in their own thoughts as music droned in the background. "Let's get a coffee, and I can use something to eat," he suggested as they neared Gladsmuir. Stopping at a roadside inn, he ordered coffee and shepherd's pie for them both while she found a table.

"I think I left my walking stick on the island," he muttered as they ate their meal.

"You don't need it any more, your leg is fine," Emma reminded him, "and it's your turn to do the driving."

"But my leg?" he pleaded.

"Bunkum, my lad," she snorted. "You've managed quite well these last two days. I noticed, and besides, it's not your driving leg anyway."

Laughing, Alex realized she was right, and later, when she handed him the car keys, he accepted them willingly. It was almost 4 p.m. when they reached the *Courtyard Inn.*

"Are you going home?" she asked when he pulled up to the door.

"I'll not come in right now, but I'll be back for dinner at 6:30," he informed her, obviously quite content to be driving again. "Dress in one of your tartans, there's a nice pre-Christmas dance here tonight and I thought it sounded like fun. You'll even know a few people." He left so abruptly, she had no time to ask any questions.

Once in her room, she decided to have a relaxing bath, promising herself not to think about graves and regalia for at least an hour. She turned on the TV as she got dressed, studying herself in the mirror as she applied her make-up. She smiled at her rosy cheeks, burned by the wind on Dorik and accentuated by the red in her tartan. Still early, she went over to the kitchen drawer and removed the pile of papers she had collected … copies of biographia boxes, records from the Renfrewshire Land Office, maps and diagrams of the old monastery burial grounds, and many handwritten notes. Totally engrossed, she completely forgot the time until she looked at her watch and jumped to her feet. It was 7 p.m. Getting her shawl, she hurried downstairs.

"Lady Traymore," Megan called urgently as she hurried by the reception desk. "Your guests are in the private banquet room. I'll take you there."

*My guests,* Emma thought, *now what is Alex up to?*

Megan led Emma down a hall she had not seen before and, looking extremely pleased with herself, she opened a door and motioned Emma inside. A rousing cheer ran through the room and Emma spotted Alex, dressed in his Wallace regalia. She realized that something special was happening but there was no sense in asking questions. So, when he came and offered his arm, she accepted it with a puzzled smile and allowed him to escort her to a long table at the front of the room. By now she realized that this large banquet room was full of clapping and smiling people ... all dressed in their tartans. They were now on their feet and their joy was obviously aimed at her. *My guests ... this must be about finding Mary or ....* she noticed the familiar faces at the head table and when Alex pulled out her chair and whispered, 'my lady,' she obediently sat down. Everyone else then took their seats ... except Alex, who tapped his glass to quell the murmur of conversation. Standing tall and obviously proud, he viewed the array of expectant faces sitting at the long head table before speaking slowly and emotionally.

"Tonight, as proud members of the Wallace and Walters' Clans, along with our guests, we are honoured to find ourselves in the presence of a legend. Thus, I believe a toast is very much in order. So, let's raise our glasses in gratitude to Emma, Lady Traymore, for solving our 700-year-old mystery! To Lady Traymore!"

Chairs shuffled backwards as everyone came to their feet, raising their glasses, then cheering, repeating her name. After a few good-natured, shouted comments from various guests, he announced that dinner was going to be served and everyone sat down. It was a wonderful party and Emma was comfortable and completely enjoying herself. Hazel Zicowski had been seated next to her and visitors came up to introduce themselves throughout the dinner period. John Dunstan was seated next to Alex and even James MacDonald was seated at the head table.

When dinner was finished, Alex stood up and made a special announcement. "For those of you who do not yet realize what the 700-year-old mystery was actually all about, allow me to explain, in brief. He went on to tell the story of the missing regalia, who had it and when, and then brought them up to the recent discovery. "We are thrilled to tell all of Scotland that although the Ancient Royal Scottish Regalia was always in Scottish hands, it will now be on display in its rightful place alongside the Honours of Scotland at Edinburgh Castle. Tonight, however, I am most pleased to tell you that we will all be the first to witness this remarkable collection! We'll begin at the head table with Lady Traymore, of course! The two people escorting the regalia into the room are two of the archeologists who unearthed our treasure. I'll ask you to recognize them with a round of applause. This is going to take awhile, so please help yourself to dessert and beverages on the side tables."

He winked at Emma and his hand fell affectionately on her shoulder as the moment of revelation finally arrived. The door opened and two uniformed Scottish Guards came into the room and stood on each side of the door. Another guard pushed a trolley into the room as Dr. John Dunstan and Dr. Hazel Zicowski walked close behind, both smiling broadly as the audience clapped. The trolley stopped in front of Emma and her heart began to race as John and Hazel slowly folded back a royal blue velvet cover, revealing a handsome oak display case with a glass top. Emma stood up and watched as John and the guard picked up the display case and placed it on the table in front of her and Hazel returned to sit beside her, grasping her hand and squeezing it.

As the glass top was opened, Emma stared in awed silence at the sparking gold of the ancient Scottish Royal Regalia lying on its sea of Royal blue velvet. It was an amazing display and one which she had envisioned for the last 30 days. The three relics of gold and jewels had been clean and polished and, although not as brilliant as modern treasure, she was stunned by its magnificence. The Royal Coronet, which except for being used by John Balliol as Edward of England's choice during those terrible years of the Interraregan, was nevertheless grand in its simplicity. More importantly, this coronet had once graced the head of their last true monarch, King Alexander III, until his untimely, accidental death. The Royal Chalice was inscribed with beautiful Latin letters and the wide-banded ring was resting in a small box on its own bed of blue velvet. Suddenly needing to catch her breath, she grasped the edge of the table and Alex helped her sit down. *Be still my heart!* she commanded herself taking Alex's hand, but she couldn't hold back the tears as so many thoughts raced through her head. It was a moment neither she nor Alex would ever forget. Ever watchful, he handed her his handkerchief.

Upon reaching the end of the table, the case was closed, locked and returned to its trolley before continuing on its way around the room. Noisy and excited comments erupted and although disappointed they had to see it through the glass, they were certainly awed.

John Dunstan went to stand behind Emma, holding his hand up for silence. "I speak on behalf of all the people of Scotland who want to thank Lady Traymore for fulfilling the Wallace Prophecy and giving truth to the old legend. It took us 700 years to find her and I suggest we had better keep her!" Polite applause broke out with many 'ayes' and cheers. It was about 10:30 p.m. when people started leaving, coming up to Emma to introduce themselves and thank her personally.

When he had the opportunity, Alex found Alfreda and brought her over to their group. He explained to Emma that it was she who had made all the arrangements for these festivities. "The night before we went to Dorik, I had a call from Ruth at Misty House. She told me the technicians had opened the pouch and verified its contents as the missing regalia. I called John and then the MacDuffs. Alfreda suggested we needed to have a party. I knew I was leaving the arrangements in very capable hands. Thank you, Alfreda!"

Emma held up her glass of wine and emotionally mouthed the words 'thank you' to her Scottish friend and colleague.

The celebration carried on late into the evening with music and dancing. As the guests slowly dwindled away, Emma and Alex sat together and quietly contemplated the evening's events. Alex reached over the table and took her hands in his. "Lady Traymore, you are magnificent!" he whispered emotionally. "I look forward to the new year more eagerly than I have for a long time."

"We did it together, Alex," she replied, feeling a catch in her throat as another tear escaped onto her cheek. "We did it together and I am so very grateful for your help, but I am also so relieved it's over! I've met so many fascinating people and made so many new friends thanks to you. I do hope John and James will continue to be our friends after the inquiry!" Squeezing his fingers, she murmured, "That's the only thing left now."

Alex escorted her to her room and left the hotel immediately, feeling rather chuffed with both himself and the whole evening.

It was almost 1:30 a.m. when she looked out at the castle and realized she would now be viewing the new home of the regalia, giving her a bit of an excited chill. She pulled the curtains and immediately went to bed, knowing that after several nights of peaceful sleep, the subjects of her tormented dreams had now found their peace.

She picked up her book and lay back on her pillow—the sound of a distant emergency vehicle siren sending thoughts of the inquiry coursing through her mind. She knew she would see James again on Monday but this time he would be frowning. He had a part to play and he would play it well as the inquiry stated its case. She was determined to prove herself innocent of any wrong-doing toward the Scottish people—her people.

## Chapter 30 – Monday December 18ᵗʰ, 2006 – The Inquiry

Room service brought her coffee and scrambled eggs which she ate while she sorted through her documents and papers for the last time. Arranging them in order of procurement, she made any necessary notes that would supplement her memory lapses.

At 11:15 the phone rang and Alex's voice asked, "Are you going to get out of bed today, my lady?" This was followed by his usual chuckle.

"I'll be down in five minutes!" She dropped the receiver and giggled.

She skipped down the stairs, smiling a greeting to Megan, before entering the dining room. Alex sat grinning as she walked towards him, his newspaper neatly folded at his elbow.

"Good morning, my lady," he murmured. "I hope you're prepared for our one o'clock appointment."

"More than ready, Sir Alex, I'm eager! I imagine you had breakfast with your nurse, was she sad to leave? I called room service. Shall we call this brunch?"

"I'm glad to see you so chipper today and no, Mabel was not sad. Our cheque for an extra month, and freedom to use my home when I was away, certainly helped. She'd become quite a good card player though, so I may miss her, unless you agree to be my partner and let me win sometimes! The MacDuffs enjoy cards as well."

Over brunch, they steered away from talking about their afternoon appointment and spoke of Christmas traditions, making comparisons of the festive season in each of their countries. She told him about Canadian displays of coloured lights on houses and in yards all over Canada for the month of December, and he told her about an old custom believed to be based on the arrival of the Vikings and re-enacted by many as "first footing." He explained it was a custom which dictated that the first person to cross a home's threshold after midnight on New Year's Eve will determine the homeowner's luck for the New Year. The ideal visitor bears gifts—preferably whisky, coal for the fire, small cakes, or a coin—and should be a man with a dark complexion. Memories of the 8ᵗʰ century, when the presumably fair-haired Vikings invaded Scotland, provided the anxiety that a blond visitor would not be a good omen.

*So many traditions in these old countries*, she thought, wanting to know more, yet realizing she would have plenty of time in the years to come. At 12:40 p.m. Alex drove into the car park at police headquarters and they were quickly shown inside by a sergeant. Another sergeant at the reception desk immediately came to attention and addressed Sir Alex. "You're both expected in Meeting Room Three; I'll take you up."

A lift ride and a long walk along a carpeted hallway took them to a door marked conspicuously with a shining brass '3.' Nervously straightening his tie, the sergeant tapped lightly, opening the door when a muffled voice called 'enter.' He waited then closed the door behind them. She heard the click and took a deep breath.

Emma smiled to herself as she fastened her eyes on the older man sitting at the head of the boardroom table. He silently continued to stare at the papers before him as if she and Alex weren't even there. James came to greet them indicating the cloakroom and toilet before offering to take their coats, but Alex was already helping her.

When Alex returned, James showed them to chairs at the end of the table.

Facing the five members of the inquiry, Emma deliberately inspected their faces. James MacDonald and John Dunstan were known to her, but the sour-faced minister sitting next to the scowling chairman was an unknown entity, until she looked closer and recognized him as the minister she had taken a photo of that day in the hotel dining room. The fifth person was hard to define as he continually rubbed his hand through a thick black beard.

"I think introductions would be in order, sir," John Dunstan addressed his suggestion to the chairman.

"I'll do it," the police commissioner offered, rising to his feet. "You know John Dunstan, Judge Moulder is chairman, on his right is Bishop Watson and on his left, Ken Tourle, our local member of parliament."

"Enough MacDonald," Judge Moulder growled impatiently, "let's get on with this inquiry. Madam, you are charged with desecrating holy ground, withholding secrets of national importance, and misrepresentation of your social stature. How do you plead?"

Staring coldly, Emma got slowly to her feet. Reaching for her briefcase, she swung it onto the table with a resounding crash.

"Judge Moulder," her voice echoed through the room. "If you think to intimidate me by your pompous attitude, you had better get the aspirins ready. I have a legitimate title and you will use it, sir, or you get no co-operation whatsoever from me or my bailiff."

"Madam, this court will operate as I direct it!" the judge shouted angrily.

"May I remind you that this is not a courtroom," James MacDonald stated in a calm voice, looking straight at the judge. "This is an inquiry, sir!"

"And you dare to challenge my authority, Mr. MacDonald."

"No sir, just the method of conducting an inquiry."

Silently digesting the police commissioner's words, Judge Moulder glowered at James MacDonald and hissed, "Perhaps you would like to conduct the questions yourself, Mr. MacDonald."

"Yes, sir, I would like that very much."

Pouting, Judge Moulder wrote something in his notebook and then dramatically slammed it shut, glowering at the tabletop.

Bishop Watson shuffled nervously on his chair, pushing it back slightly before mumbling, "I'm not sure I should stay under the present circumstances."

"Shut up, George!" Judge Moulder snapped at the clergyman. Totally intimidated, Bishop Watson pulled his chair back up to the table lowering his eyes onto his lap.

"It looks like you two will have to ask the questions," Ken Tourle commented. "I'm just an observer."

James nodded and silently invited John Dunstan to begin his questions.

"Lady Traymore, why were you looking for the old gardener's shed in Elderslie?" he asked after checking his notes.

"We had information that some missing burial records were stored in the shed," Emma replied.

"And where did you receive that information, my lady?" John Dunstan asked.

"From Moira Johnson, the owner of the *Tartan Tea Shop* in Paisley," she continued. "Her grandfather was the last sexton at the monastery and as a child she remembered him mentioning some things falling into a new grave that he was digging. He told her he had put them in the shed, but as time went on they were forgotten and he retired."

"But who sent you there?" James interposed.

"Hunger, and the best cream cakes in Scotland," Emma replied, "and that's where we met Monsignor Jason Sharp for the first time."

"And you knew he was spying for the Brotherhood?"

"No, that came later."

"Did you find the lost burial records for the monastery?"

"Yes."

"And where are they now?"

"They are at Misty House, all opened and translated. I have copies with me today."

Frowning, John Dunstan began adding to his notes as the police commissioner took up the questions. "What else did you find at the garden shed site ... Sir Alex?"

"Old, rusty garden tools," Alex smirked, "and a biographia box."

"And a body?" John added.

"No sir, there was no evidence of a body, but the document in the biographia box gave us a clue as to what was going on," Emma stated.

"I thought there was always a body when you found biographia boxes," James frowned.

"It would depend on the circumstances," John replied, "they were fighting monks and maybe they had prepared a gravesite for a wounded companion and were chased away before he died or was buried?"

"They would just leave the box in the grave and move on?" James asked.

"Yes, we don't find it happened very often, but we've found several of these sites around Paisley. When you're in the midst of trouble, often life is beyond your control."

A smile touched James MacDonald's face as he focused his attention on the archives director and continued his questioning. "They were fighting monks you said, were they the forerunners of the Brotherhood?"

"Yes, for the record," John replied, "the Knights of Malta, also known as the Knights Hospitaller and others, were religious fighting monks, as were the Templars. They were, and some still are, secret societies that had secret aims and objectives. They have always been fiercely protective of their members." John's explanation seemed to satisfy the police commissioner for the moment, allowing John to focus his attention back to Alex and Emma.

"Tell us," John continued, "how you came up with the idea of using the bomb disposal unit to circumvent all the regulations for digging in the monastery land? I'd like you to know it was a brilliant manoeuver."

"You can blame Tom Campbell, the Paisley water engineer, for that," Emma laughed, "he warned us we might find a bomb if we kept digging holes around Elderslie."

"Now, my lady," said John, looking intently at Emma, "when the archives representatives arrived at the dig, the bomb unit had excavated the exact location of Mary Wallace's gravesite. I don't believe that was an accident. You and Sir Alex somehow marked out the place, but how did you know where it was?"

"I had a dream, and Mary showed me a landmark."

"Please, my lady, I need a serious answer."

"That's the truth, sir, take it or leave it, I really don't care."

John Dunstan settled back in his chair. "Well, I think you've answered all my questions, Lady Traymore. It's hard to believe you dreamed the answer to a 700-year-old mystery but maybe there was something in the Wallace legend after all."

Judge Moulder and the Bishop had listened quietly, their aloofness obvious, but slowly their interest became apparent as Emma and Alex answered the archivist's questions. Now, they focused their attention on the police commissioner as James produced a notebook and stood up.

Clearing his throat and, with a very serious countenance, he began. "It was you, Lady Traymore, and Sir Alex who started the rumour that the missing regalia was in Yorkshire at the silent monastery, was it not?"

"No, I believe that was a report in Eliza Burn's newspaper column. She asked me where I thought the regalia items were located and I said in Yorkshire. She assumed the rest of her story without checking it."

"Well, it has certainly caused the silent monastery to come into public view," James declared, glancing at John Dunstan who was nodding his head.

"Take note of that, MacDonald, it borders on willful mischief," Judge Moulder growled.

"Yes, sir," James said respectfully, winking at Emma. "How did you find the connection to the Spencer House on Ester Road?"

Alex and Emma glanced at each other and burst out laughing. Alex spluttered, "Do you really want to know, James?"

"Yes, I do, and I know it had something to do with the postal sorting station at Stirling."

"You tell him," Alex smiled at his lady as she composed herself.

"Out of curiosity, we put a tracer on a letter from Monsignor Sharp," Emma began cautiously.

"How and why?"

"I'll answer your second question first," Alex offered. "Monsignor Sharp was always watching us and when Mitch Pooley told us the monsignor had posted a letter to someone every day at a certain post box, we got curious to find out to whom he was reporting."

"Smart thinking," James muttered, "but how did you trace it?"

"Don't tell him!" Emma suddenly interrupted. "We did it, and it led us to the Brotherhood and the house on Ester Road."

"Answer the question, woman," the judge snapped officiously, "or you will be in contempt of this court."

"We are not in court," Emma snapped back at the stern-faced chairman, "and, if you address me in that tone of voice again, I shall come down there and box your ears!" A touch of a smile played around Bishop Watson's lips. He had been listening with rapt attention. Both Dunstan and James dropped their heads to hide their smiles.

It was then that a change came over the stiff-necked judge as he released a rasping chuckle and murmured, "Yes, I believe you would, my lady! Carry on commissioner."

"Just one more question, sir," James continued. "I still don't know why the Templars or the Brotherhood are so interested in the search for the Scottish Royal Regalia. Do you know, Lady Traymore?"

Smiling, Emma took several folders from her briefcase, handing some papers to John Dunstan and a single sheet to James MacDonald.

"Can I see those papers?" the judge asked, eagerly reaching towards John Dunstan, who quickly put them down on the table out of his reach. His face reddening in anger, the judge reached again for the papers and, without changing his expression, James put his copy into the judge's outstretched hand. Watching him closely, Emma noted the judge's changing expression, now coupled with erratic breathing and expulsion of air, as sweat began to form on his brow.

"This is an obvious forgery!" he wheezed.

John Dunstan quickly took the paper from the judge, his experienced eyes flashing over its contents. He slowly raised his head to face James. "There's your problem solved, Commissioner," he announced, frowning. "This paper proves the Brotherhood were trying to keep their *involvement* secret. It states …."

"It's a forgery!" the judge interrupted, shouting and banging on the table. "I will not allow its submission into this inquiry!"

"You're a Templar, aren't you, Judge Moulder?" Emma accused calmly, frowning fiercely as she came to her feet.

Bishop Watson looked terrified as he suddenly pushed his chair back; Ken Tourle banged the table hard with his fist.

"Stop this nonsense!" he commanded. "This is a fact-finding inquiry so let's stick to the facts. Could I please see that paper that's caused all this commotion?"

Sitting next to the politician, John handed him the single page.

No one spoke as Tourle read the document. Finally he raised his head and looked at the judge. "So, what's the problem, judge? Are you ashamed of promising to protect innocent people?"

"It's not that, Mr. Tourle," Emma objected, "the Templars knew that Mary was buried with the royal regalia in her arms, but they didn't know the exact location of the grave. So, they put a spy in Elderslie to keep an eye on the burial grounds, one Monsignor Sharp who reported every day to the Ester Road address."

"There's one more document I would like to present to the archives," James announced, "but first I would like to show it to Sir Alex." Opening his briefcase, he produced a file folder and pushed it down the table to Alex and Emma. Alex picked it up and scanned it.

"You found proof of my birthright!" Alex whispered. "Where was this, James?"

"We found it in the police search of the silent monastery and I thought you would like to know about it."

"Shouldn't we have had a stenographer recording this inquiry?" Ken Tourle asked.

"It's all being recorded, sir," James chuckled. "In case you have forgotten, this police building is monitored."

No charges were laid against either Emma or Alex and, as Christmas festivities took over, they were invited to many grand occasions, throughout Hogmanay and well into the New Year. This gave Emma plenty of excuses not to return to Victoria as she made new friends and became more and more enamoured with the home of her ancestors.

She realized, however, that time was running out for her to make a decision about her future in teaching, especially in Canada. With the Wallace Prophecy now solved and most of the loose ends now dealt with, she had more time to relax and plan the next phase of her life.

As Lady Traymore, she had absolutely no financial worries and very quickly the decision became an easy one. She had never had enough time to do the travelling she had longed for, and so, her planning began. Her first tour of the British Isles would begin in the Highlands of Scotland next summer. She contacted the director of programs at UVic and told him she would not be returning but would be happy to guest lecture if it fit into her schedule. She had also decided to do some volunteer work with children, both in Victoria and Scotland. She was busier and her life happier than she had ever experienced but she also knew she had a void to fill in her life, as per Trev's advice.

Longing to go somewhere warm before returning to Victoria, she visited a travel agency and picked up a selection of brochures with Mediterranean destinations. She also wanted to know more about the Order of Knights Hospitaller of St. John of Jerusalem, Rhodes and Malta, the Order which had apparently guarded the Wallace treasure and Mary's grave for so many centuries until she and Alex were able to take over that responsibility.

Coming to a decision within days, she invited Alex to accompany her as tour guide to the Islands of Rhodes and Malta for a month. She knew he was as eager as she to learn more about these more gentle knights. She wanted to see the islands which had become the last bases for the Order during the 16th century when they took on the Ottoman Empire. It would be a perfect place to start her historical sabbatical of sorts and begin to enjoy her new life.

James drove them to the airport two weeks later and indicated how very much he was looking forward to some exceedingly less-stressful sparring matches when she returned. They shared a long hug before Alex hurried her off inside to check in. Despite knowing she would go on to Canada and not return to Scotland for a few months, tears were difficult to contain as she and Alex walked to their gate.

"Why on earth are you crying, Emma?" he asked with true concern.

"You wouldn't understand, Alex dear. I think I've just realized who I am!" She tried to laugh, at the same time wiping her tears with the perfectly folded, sparkling-white monogrammed handkerchief that Alex handed to her.

"You're wrong!" he grinned. "I understand perfectly, Lady T ... perfectly!"


The End


www.jrobertwhittle.com
www.facebook.com/jrobertwhittleauthor